THE
OF T
THROUGH
SPACE

D0784761

Lionel Shriver's novels include *Sunday Times* bestsellers *Big Brother* and *The Mandibles: A Family, 2029 – 2047*, the *New York Times* bestseller *The Post-Birthday World* and The Orange Prize-winning international bestseller *We Need to Talk About Kevin*. Her journalism has appeared in the *Guardian* and the *New York Times*, the *Wall Street Journal* and many other publications. She lives in London and Brooklyn.

Praise for *The Motion of the Body Through Space*:

'Enjoyably abrasive . . . a compelling read . . . sardonic and elegant'
Evening Standard

'Scabrously funny . . . few authors can be as entertainingly problematic as Shriver'
Guardian

'With laugh-out-loud and sad moments, it's a pinpoint-sharp novel'
Woman & Home

'Darkly funny . . . Shriver is so good at making wry observations about human behaviour and this is particularly witty on the dynamics between couples who have been together a long time'
Good Housekeeping

'Shriver is an exuberant novelist, fertile in ideas, robust in argument and disdainful of economy . . . She writes bold and fearless comedy and delights in slaughtering the sacred cows of the stupid times we live in. Few novelists now raise a laugh. Shriver does so time and again'
ALLAN MASSIE, Scotsman

'A satire on fitness zealotry with a side serving of culture-war intrigue . . . diverting'
Financial Times

'Mischievous Lionel Shriver takes aim at the narcissistic modern cult of exercise. When Serenata's usually sedentary husband, Remington, takes up exercise and engages an attractive personal trainer called Bambi, the couple's lives are turned upside down'
The Times

Also by Lionel Shriver

LIONEL SHRIVER

THE MOTION OF THE BODY THROUGH SPACE

THE BOROUGH PRESS

The Borough Press
An imprint of HarperCollins *Publishers* Ltd
1 London Bridge Street
London SE1 9GF

www.harpercollins.co.uk

HarperCollins *Publishers*
1st Floor, Watermarque Building, Ringsend Road
Dublin 4, Ireland

This paperback edition 2021

1

First published in Great Britain by HarperCollins *Publishers* 2020

A catalogue record for this book is available from the British Library

ISBN: 978-0-00-756081-3

Designed by Fritz Metsch

Printed and bound in the UK by CPI Group (UK) Ltd, Croydon CR0 4YY

MIX
Paper from
responsible sources
FSC™ C007454
www.fsc.org

This book is produced from independently certified FSC™ paper
to ensure responsible forest management.

For more information visit: www.harpercollins.co.uk/green

To Jeff—whose luxurious lassitude
has spared me the plot of this novel.
Added together and divided by two,
we make a perfectly balanced person.

"The glory of suffering might be humankind's biggest, ever-recyclable con trick."

—MELANIE REID, *The World I Fell Out Of*

"Clearly his personal god or *chi* was not made for great things. A man could not rise beyond the destiny of his *chi*. The saying of the elders was not true—that if a man said yea his *chi* also affirmed. Here was a man whose *chi* said nay despite his own affirmation."

—CHINUA ACHEBE, *Things Fall Apart*

ONE

"I've decided to run a marathon."

In a second-rate sitcom, she'd have spewed coffee across her breakfast. Yet Serenata was an understated person, and between sips. "What?" Her tone was a little arch, but polite.

"You heard me." Back to the stove, Remington studied her with a discomfiting level gaze. "I have my eye on the race in Saratoga Springs in April."

She had the sense, rare in her marriage, that she should watch what she said. "This is serious. You're not pulling my leg."

"Do I often make statements of intent, and then pull the rug out: just foolin'? I'm not sure how to take your disbelief as anything but an insult."

"My 'disbelief' might have something to do with the fact that I've never seen you run from here to the living room."

"Why would I run to the living room?"

The literalism had precedent. They called each other out in this nitpicking manner as a matter of course. It was a game. "For the last thirty-two years, you've not once trotted out for a run around the block. And now you tell me with a straight face that you want to run a marathon. You must have assumed I'd be a bit surprised."

"Go ahead, then. Be surprised."

"It doesn't bother you . . ." Serenata continued to feel careful. She didn't care for the carefulness, not one bit. ". . . That your ambition is hopelessly trite?"

"Not in the least," he said affably. "That's the sort of thing that bothers you. Besides, if I decline to run a marathon because so many other people also want to run one, my actions would still be dictated by the multitude."

"What is this, some 'bucket list' notion? You've been listening to your old Beatles records and suddenly realized that *when I'm sixty-four* refers to you? *Bucket list*," she repeated, backing off. "Where did I get that?"

Indeed, incessant citation of the now commonplace idiom was exactly the sort of lemming-like behavior that drove her wild. (That allusion did a grave injustice to lemmings. In the documentary that propagated the mass-suicide myth, the filmmakers had flung the poor creatures over the cliff. Thus the popular but fallacious metaphor for mass conformity was itself an example of mass conformity.) Okay, there was nothing wrong with adopting a new expression. What galled was the way everyone suddenly started referring to their "bucket list" in a breezy, familiar spirit that conveyed they had *always said it*.

Serenata began to push up from her chair, having lost interest in the news from Albany on her tablet. It had only been four months since they'd moved to Hudson, and she wondered how much longer she'd keep up the pretense of a connection with their old hometown by reading the *Times Union* online.

She herself was only sixty, though hers was the first generation to append "only" to such a sobering milestone. Having remained in the same position for half an hour, her knees had stiffened, and extending the right one was tricky. Once it had seized, you had to straighten it *very slowly*. She never knew, either, when one of the knees would do something creepy and unexpected—suddenly go *pong*, seeming to slip slightly out of joint and then pop back in again. This was what old people thought about, and talked about. She wished she could issue a retroactive apology to her late grandparents, whose medical kvetching she'd found so trying as a child. Underestimating the pitiless self-involvement of their nearest and dearest, old folks detailed their ailments because they assumed that anyone who cared about them would necessarily care about their pain. But no one had cared about her grandparents' pain, and now no one would care about the pain of the granddaughter who'd once been so unfeeling. Rough justice.

The segue to a stand was a success. My, what miserable achievements might pass for triumph in a few years' time. Remembering the word *blender*. Taking a sip of water without breaking the glass. "Have you considered the timing of this announcement?" She plugged in the tablet—busywork; the battery was still at 64 percent.

"What about it?"

"It coincides with a certain incapacity. I only stopped running myself in July."

"I knew you'd take this personally. That's why I dreaded telling you. Would you really want me to deny myself something just because it makes you feel wistful?"

"Wistful. You think it makes me feel *wistful*."

"Resentful," Remington revised. "But if I bind myself to a chair for eternity, that won't help your knees in the slightest."

"Yes, that's all very rational."

"You say that as if it's a criticism."

"So in your view, it's 'irrational' to take your wife's feelings into consideration."

"When making a sacrifice won't make her feel any better—yes."

"You've been thinking about this for a while?"

"A few weeks."

"In your mind, does this uncharacteristic blossoming of an interest in fitness have anything to do with what happened at the DOT?"

"Only in the sense that *what happened* at the DOT has provided me a great deal of unanticipated leisure time." Even this brush against the subject made Remington twitchy. He chewed at his cheek in that way he had, and his tone went icy and sour, with a few drops of bitterness, like a cocktail.

Serenata disdained women who broadcast their emotions by banging about the kitchen, though it took a ridiculous degree of concentration to keep from unloading the dishwasher. "If you're looking to fill your dance card, don't forget the main reason we moved here. It's already been too long since you last visited your father, and his house is a riot of repair jobs."

"I'm not spending the rest of my life under my father's sink. Is this your version of talking me out of a marathon? You can do better."

"No, I want you to do whatever you want. Obviously."

"Not so obviously."

The dishwasher had proved irresistible. Serenata hated herself.

"You ran for such a long time—"

"Forty-seven years." Her tone was clipped. "Running, and a great deal else."

"So—maybe you could give me some pointers." Remington's suggestion was halting. He did not want any pointers.

"Remember to tie your shoes. There's no more to it."

"Look . . . I'm sorry you've had to give up something you loved."

Serenata straightened, and put down a bowl. "I did not *love* running. Here's a pointer for you: no one does. They pretend to, but they're lying. The only good part is *having run*. In the moment, it's dull, and hard as in effortful but not as in difficult to master. It's repetitive. It doesn't open the floodgates of revelation, as I'm sure you've been led to expect. I'm probably grateful for an excuse to quit.

Maybe that's what I can't forgive myself. Though at least I've finally escaped the great mass of morons chugging alongside who all think they're so fucking special."

"Morons like me."

"Morons like you."

"You can't hold me in contempt for doing what you did for, I quote, *forty-seven years.*"

"Oh, yeah?" she said with a tight smile before pivoting toward the staircase. "Watch me."

Remington Alabaster was a narrow, vertical man who seemed to have maintained his figure without a struggle. His limbs were born shapely. With slender ankles, firm calves, neat knees, and thighs that didn't jiggle, given a quick shave those legs would have looked smashing on a woman. He had beautiful feet—also narrow, with high arches and elongated toes. Whenever Serenata massaged the insteps, they were dry. His hairless pectorals were delectably subtle, and should they ever bulge grossly from a sustained obsession with bench-pressing, she'd count the transformation a loss. True, in the last couple of years he'd developed a slight swell above the belt, whose mention she avoided. That was the unspoken contract, standard between couples, she would wager: unless he brought it up, such vacillations in his bodily person were his business. Which was why, though tempted, she hadn't asked him squarely this morning whether freaking out about what had to be a weight gain of less than five pounds was what this marathon lark was all about.

The harmless bulge aside, Remington was aging well. His facial features had always been expressive. The mask of impassivity he'd worn the last few years of his employment was protective, a contrivance for which a certain Lucinda Okonkwo was wholly to blame. Once he hit his sixties, the coloration of those features ashed over somewhat; it was this homogenizing of hue that made Caucasian faces look vaguer, flatter, and somehow less extant as their age advanced, like curtains whose once bold print had bleached in the sun. Yet in her mind's eye, Serenata routinely interposed the more decisive lines of his younger visage over the hoarier, more tentative present, sharpening the eyes and flushing the cheeks as if applying mental makeup.

She could see him. She could see him at a range of ages with a single glance, and could even, if unwillingly, glimpse in that still vital face the frail elder he'd grow into. Perceiving this man in full, what he was, had been, and would be, was her job. It was an important job, more so as he aged, because to others he would soon be just some old geezer. He was not just some old geezer. At twenty-seven, she'd fallen in love with a handsome civil engineer, and he was still here. It was the subject of some puzzlement: other people were themselves getting older by the day, themselves watching these mysterious transformations not all of which were their fault, and knew themselves to have once been younger. Yet the young and old alike perceived others in their surround as stationary constants, like parking signs. If you were fifty, then fifty was all you were, all you ever had been, and all you ever would be. Perhaps the exercise of informed imagination was simply too exhausting.

It was also her job to look upon her husband with kindness. To both see and not see. To screw up her eyes and blur the eruptions of uninvited skin conditions into a smooth surface—an *Alabaster* surface. To issue a blanket pardon for every blobbing mole, every deepening crag of erosion. To be the sole person in the entire world who did not regard the slight thickening under his jaw as a character flaw. The sole person who did not construe from the sparseness of the hair at his temples that he didn't matter. In trade, Remington would forgive the crenulations atop her elbows and the sharp line beside her nose when she slept too hard on her right side—a harsh indentation that could last until mid-afternoon and would soon be scored there all the time. Were he to have registered, as he could not help but have done, that his wife's physical form was no longer identical to the one he wed, Remington alone would not regard this as a sign that she had done something wrong, perhaps even morally wrong, and he would not hold her accountable for being a disappointment. That was also part of the contract. It was a good deal.

Yet Remington had no need to draw drastically on the bottomless reserves of his wife's forgiveness for not having been dipped in preservative plastic when they met, like an ID card. He looked pretty damned good for sixty-four. How he'd remained so slim, vigorous, and nicely proportioned without any appreciable exercise was anyone's guess. Oh, he walked places, and didn't complain about taking the stairs if an elevator was out of order. But he'd never even experimented with one of those "seven minutes to a better body" routines, much less joined a gym. During lunch, he ate lunch.

More exercise would improve his circulation, build vascular resilience, and forestall cognitive decline. She should welcome the turned leaf. She should ply him with protein bars and proudly track his increasing mileage on a pad in the foyer.

The whole supportiveness shtick might actually have been doable had he introduced his resolution with suitable chagrin: "I realize I'll never manage to cover *nearly* the distances you have. Still, I wonder if maybe it would be good for my heart to go out for a modest, you know, two-mile jog, say, two or three times a week." But no. He had to run a *marathon*. For the rest of the day, then, Serenata indulged the pretense of intense professionalism the better to avoid her husband. She only went back downstairs to make tea once she heard him go out. It wasn't nice, it wasn't "rational," but this specific subset of human experience belonged to her, and his timing was cruel.

Presumably, she herself began by copying someone else—though that's not how it felt at the time. Both her sedentary parents were on the heavy side, and, in the way of these things, they grew heavier. Their idea of exertion was pushing a manual lawn mower, to be replaced by a power mower as soon as possible. That wasn't to criticize. Americans in the 1960s of her childhood were big on "labor-saving devices." A sign of modernity, the reduction of personal energy output was highly prized.

A marketing analyst for Johnson & Johnson, her father had been relocated every two years or so. Born in Santa Ana, California, Serenata never knew the town before the family shifted to Jacksonville, Florida—and then they were off to West Chester, Pennsylvania; Omaha, Nebraska; Roanoke, Virginia; Monument, Colorado; Cincinnati, Ohio, and finally to the company headquarters in New Brunswick, New Jersey. As a consequence, she had no regional affiliations, and was one of those rare creatures whose sole geographical identifier was the big, baggy country itself. She was "an American," with no qualifier or hyphenation—since calling herself a "Greek-American," having grown up supping nary a bowl of avgolemono soup, would have struck her as desperate.

Being yanked from one school to the next as a girl had made her leery of forming attachments. She'd only inculcated the concept of friendship in adulthood, and then with difficulty—tending to mislay companions out of sheer absentmindedness, like gloves dropped in the street. For Serenata, friendship was a discipline. She was too content by herself, and had sometimes wondered if not getting lonely was a shortcoming.

Her mother had responded to ceaseless transplantation by fastening onto multiple church and volunteer groups the moment the family arrived in a new town, like an octopus on speed. The constant convenings of these memberships left an only child to her own devices, an arrangement that suited Serenata altogether. Once old enough to fix her own Fluffernutter sandwiches, she occupied her unsupervised after-school hours building strength and stamina.

She would lie palms down on the lawn and count the number of seconds—*one one-thousand, two one-thousand*—she could keep her straightened legs raised a foot above the ground (discouragingly few, but only to begin with). She was gripping a low-hanging tree branch and struggling to get her chin above the wood well before she learned that the exercise was called a *pull-up*. She invented her own calisthenics. To complete what she dubbed a "broken leg," you hopped on one foot the circumference of the yard with the opposite leg thrust forward in a goose step, then repeated the circuit hopping backward. "Rolly-pollies" entailed lying on the grass, gripping your knees to the chest, and rocking on your back *one-two-three!* to throw your legs straight behind your head; later she added a shoulder stand at the end. As an adult, she would recall with wan incredulity that when she strung her creations together to stage her own backyard Olympics, it never occurred to her to invite the neighborhood children to join in.

Many of her contortions were silly, but repeated enough times they still wore her out. Pleasantly so, though even these fanciful routines—of which she kept an exacting secret record in crimped printing in a bound blank book stashed under her mattress—were not exactly fun. It was interesting to discover that it was possible to not especially want to do them and to do them anyway.

During the "physical education" of her school days, the meager athletic demands placed on girls were one of the few constants across Jacksonville, West Chester, Omaha, Roanoke, Monument, Cincinnati, and New Brunswick. The half-hour recess in primary school usually sponsored kickball—and if you managed to get up before your teammates lost the inning, you might run an entire *ten yards* to first base. Dodgeball was even more absurd: jumping one foot this way, one foot that. In middle schools' formal gym classes, twenty of the forty-five minutes were consumed with changing in and out of gym clothes. The instructor would direct the girls in unison to do *ten* jumping jacks, do *five* squat thrusts, and run in place for *thirty seconds.* Given this limp gesturing toward strength training, it hadn't really been fair to subject these same girls to a formal fitness assessment in eighth grade—during which, after Serenata sailed past the one hundred mark in the sit-ups test, the gym teacher intervened and insisted in a shrill panic that she stop. For the following decades, of course, she'd be doing sit-ups in sets of five hundred. They weren't really efficient, abdominally, but she had a soft spot for the classics.

To correct any misimpressions: Serenata Terpsichore—which rhymed with *hickory,* though she grew inured to teachers stressing the first syllable and pronouncing the last as a tiresome task—had no designs on professional athletics. She didn't want to earn a place on a national volleyball team. She didn't want to become a ballerina. She didn't aspire to take part in weight-lifting contests, or to attract an Adidas sponsorship. She'd never come near to breaking any records, and hadn't tried. After all, the setting of records was all about placing your achievements in relation to the achievements of other people. She might have engaged in rigorous, self-contrived conniptions on a daily basis from childhood, but that had *nothing to do with anyone else.* Push-ups were private.

She'd never identified in an elaborate way with a particular sport. She ran, she cycled, she swam; she was not *a runner* or *a swimmer* or *a cyclist,* designations that would have allowed these mere forms of locomotion to place a claim on her. She was not, as they say, a *team player,* either. Her ideal running route was deserted. She gloried in the serenity of an empty swimming pool. Throughout her fifty-two years of biking for primary transportation, a single other cyclist in sight despoiled her solitude and ruined her mood.

Given that Serenata would have thrived on a desert island in the company of fish, it was disconcerting to have so frequently been co-opted by, as Remington had said, the *multitude.* Sooner or later, any quirk, any curious habit or obsession, was eventually colonized by a throng.

Impulsively, when she was sixteen, she'd slipped into a shadowy establishment in downtown Cincinnati to have a tiny tattoo inscribed on the tender inside face of her right wrist. The design she requested was snatched, literally, from the air: a bumblebee in flight. With no other customers, the artisan took his time. He captured the diaphanous wings, the inquiring antennae, the delicate legs poised for landing. The image had nothing to do with her. Yet in crafting character from scratch, one reached for what lay to hand; we were all found artworks. Thus the arbitrary soon converted to the signal. The bumblebee became her emblem, doodled endlessly across the canvas covers of her three-ring binders.

Tattoos in the 1970s were largely confined to longshoremen, sailors, prison inmates, and biker gangs. For wayward children of the middle class, what were not yet called "tats" were a defilement. That winter, she concealed the inking from her parents with long sleeves. That spring, she switched her watch to her right wrist, with the face flipped down. She lived in constant fear of exposure, though secrecy also freighted the image with mighty powers. In retrospect, it would have been nobler to have declared the "mutilation" voluntarily and taken the consequences, but that was an adult perspective. Young people, for whom time moved so sedulously that every moment could seem an eternity of reprieve, put a great deal of store in delay.

Inevitably, one morning she overslept her alarm. Come to rouse the sleepyhead, her mother discovered the naked wrist thrown upright on a pillow. Once the teenager confessed that the image wasn't felt-tip, her mother cried.

The point: Serenata would have been the sole student in her high school to brave a tattoo. Nowadays? Over a third of the eighteen-to-thirty-five demographic sported at least one, and the total acreage of American skin aswirl with hobbits, barbed wire, or barcodes, eyes, tigers, or tribals, and scorpions, skulls, or superheroes, was the size of Pennsylvania. Serenata's adventure into the underworld had inverted from intrepid to trite.

In her twenties, frustrated that traditional ponytail ties snagged the strands of her thick black hair, Serenata set about stitching several tubes of colorful fabric, through which she threaded sturdy elastic. After tying the ends of the elastic together, she sewed the cloth tubes into gathered circles. The resultant binders kept the hair from her face without grabbing, while adding a flash of pizzazz to her crown. Some peers found the handicrafts kooky, but more than one coworker asked where to get one. Yet by the 1990s, most of her female compatriots owned a set of twenty-five in a rainbow of hues. She hacked her hair to just under her ears and tossed what were apparently called "scrunchies" in the wastebasket.

It would have been circa 1980, too, that she made one of her effortful bids for friendship, inviting a handful of coworkers at Lord & Taylor's customer service to dinner. For the previous couple of years she had dabbled in Japanese cuisine, an enthusiasm rescued from a dead-end date who'd taken her to a hole-in-the-wall counter that served his countrymen's expats. She had loved the smoothness, the coolness, the subtly. Later back home, she experimented with vinegared rice, green powdered horseradish, and a sharp knife. Eager to share her discoveries, she laid out multiple platters for her guests, aiming for what a later era would call the wow factor.

They were horrified. None of the girls could bear the prospect of raw fish.

Yet nowadays it was not unusual to find three different sushi bars along a single block of a midsize town in Iowa. The dreariest undergrad had a preference for fresh or saltwater eel. It wasn't as if Serenata could take the slightest credit for the centuries-old traditions of a storied island nation in the East. Nevertheless, what was once an idiosyncrasy had been crowd funded.

The watch, which obscured her sin of self-defacement? It had made for an effective disguise because it had once been her father's. Serenata had been wearing oversize men's watches ever since. Lo, come the 2010s, every other woman in the country was wearing massive, masculine-style watches as well. Favorite books that made little or no splash on release—*A Home at the End of the World* or *The City of Your Final Destination*—invariably got turned into movies, and suddenly these private totems belonged to everybody. She'd no sooner revive the nearly lost art of quilting, stitching swatches of worn-out corduroys and old towels while watching *Breaking Bad* before anyone had ever heard of it, than quilting bees would sweep the country as a nationwide fad. If Serenata Terpsichore ever seized upon the music of an obscure band that only played pass-the-hat clubs and wedding gigs, that veritably guaranteed that these same nobodies would hit the top forty by the following year. If she happened to pick up the habit of wearing incredibly warm, soft sheepskin boots hitherto confined to the small Australian and California surfer sets, the better to weather an Albany winter, you could be damned sure that Oprah Winfrey would make the same discovery. Ugg.

The same thing must have happened to plenty of others as well. There were only so many things to wear, to love, to do. And there were too many people. So sooner or later whatever you claimed for yourself would be adopted by several million of your closest friends.

At which point you either abandoned your own enthusiasms or submitted numbly to the appearance of slavish conformity. For the most part, Serenata had opted for the latter. Still, the experience was repeatedly one of being occupied, as if a horde of strangers had camped out on her lawn.

Which, steadily yet at an accelerating pace for the last twenty years, was what had been happening to fitness in any form. She could almost hear them, rumbling the inside of her skull like an oncoming migration of wildebeest, the dust catching in her nostrils, the beat of their hooves pounding from the horizon. This time the multitudes could be spotted not merely aping her tastes in music or fiction in the quiet isolation of their homes, but in aggregate, pounding in droves over the hills and dales of public parks, splashing in phalanxes across all six lanes of her regular pool, clamoring with crazed, head-down pumping in swarms of cyclists, every one of them feverishly desperate to overtake the bike ahead, only to come to a stop at the next light—where the pack would twitch, poised to get a jump on the others like hyenas straining toward a fresh kill. This time the incursion into her territory wasn't metaphorical but could be measured in square feet. Now her beloved husband had joined the mindless look-alikes of the swollen herd.

TWO

Though the right knee rebuked her when it bore the load, Serenata refused to take the stairs one at a time, like a toddler. Hobbling down for tea the following afternoon, she found Remington in the living room. While she was still unaccustomed to his being home weekdays, it wasn't fair to resent the presence of your husband when it was his house, too. Early retirement hadn't been his idea, or, precisely, his fault.

Yet his getup was annoying by any measure: leggings, silky green shorts with undershorts of bright purple, and a shiny green shirt with purple netting for aeration—a set, its price tag dangling at the back of the neck. His wrist gleamed with a new sports watch. On a younger man the red bandanna around his forehead might have seemed rakish, but on Remington at sixty-four it looked like a costuming choice that cinemagoers were to read at a glance: *this guy is a nut*. In case the bandanna wasn't enough, add the air-traffic-control orange shoes, with trim of *more purple*.

He only bent to clutch an ankle with both hands when she walked in. He'd been waiting for her.

So, fine, she watched. He held the ankle, raised his arms overhead, and dived for the opposite leg. As he teetered on one foot while tugging a knee to his chest, she left for her Earl Grey. On her return, he was bracing both hands against a wall and elongating a calf muscle. The whole ritual screamed of the internet.

"My dear," she said. "There's some evidence that stretching does a bit of good, but only *after* you've run. All it accomplishes beforehand is to put off the unpleasant."

"You're going to be a real bitch about this, aren't you?"

"Probably," she said lightly, and swept back upstairs. When the front door slammed, she ventured onto the second-story side porch to peer over the rail. After poking at the complicated watch for minutes, the intrepid began his inaugural run—trudging out the gate and down Union Street. She could have passed him at a stroll.

The impulse was wicked, but she checked the time. The door slammed again twelve minutes later. His shower would last longer. Is this how she'd get through this ordeal? With condescension? It was only October. It was going to be a long winter.

"How was your run?" she forced herself to inquire during a laconic dinner.

"Invigorating!" he declared. "I'm starting to see why you went at it, those forty-seven years."

Uh-huh. Wait till it gets cold, and sleets, and blows a gale in your face. Wait till your intestines start to transit, with seven more miles to go, and you huddle in a cramped scuttle, praying you'll make it before they explode all over your shiny green shorts. See how invigorated you get then. "And where did you get to?"

"I turned around at Highway Nine."

Half a mile from their front door. Yet he was bursting with accomplishment. She looked at him with fascination. He was impossible to embarrass.

And why ever would she wish to embarrass him? Precisely what inflamed her about this stupid joiner impulse of his to *run a marathon* was the way such a mean-spirited desire had already arisen in her head, after her husband's sole athletic achievement constituted running—if you could call it that—again, you see, this contaminating contempt—a single mile. She was not a combative harridan, nor had she been for their thirty-two years together. To the contrary, it was in the nature of wary isolates to give themselves completely and without stint once the formidable barriers they routinely erected before all and sundry had been breached. Most people regarded Serenata as standoffish, and she was fine with that; being seen as a woman who kept others at bay helped keep them at bay. But she was not aloof with Remington Alabaster, as of halfway through their first date. Largely keeping to yourself did not mean you lacked a normal human need for companionship. It did mean you tended to put eggs in one basket. Remington was her basket. She could not afford to resent the basket—to want to embarrass the basket, or to hope that when the basket set his sights on what had become a rather mundane status marker the basket would fail.

She owed him for the fact that what might otherwise have become an arid solitude was instead round, full, and rich. She'd relished being his sole confidante when the situation at the DOT went south; it was too dangerous for him to talk to anyone at work. She missed the camaraderie of shared indignation. Throughout the whole debacle, he'd have been unwavering in his confidence that she was staunchly in his corner. They'd had their differences, especially about the children, who had both, frankly, turned out a little strange. Nevertheless, the measure of a marriage was military: a good one was an *alliance*.

Furthermore, when they met she was floundering. She owed him for her career.

As a child, after a family vacation on Cape Hatteras, she'd declared her reigning ambition to become a lighthouse keeper—thrust on the prow of a spit, raised high with a view of an expanse that could make you feel either very small or very big, depending on your mood, with regal control of a great beacon. She would live in a small round room decorated with driftwood, heating up cans of soup on a hot plate, reading (well, she was only eight) *Pippi Longstocking* under a swinging bare bulb, and watching (ditto) reruns of *I Dream of Jeannie* on one of those miniature black-and-white televisions they had at the hotel on the Outer Banks. Later during the usual equine phase for girls, she imagined growing up to be a national park warden who toured vast public woodlands alone on horseback. Still later, inspired by a newspaper's unusual job listing, she became enthralled by the idea of caretaking an estate on a tropical island owned by a very rich man, who'd only visit with an array of celebrity guests in his private jet once a year. The rest of the time she'd have a mansion to herself—with dinner seatings for a hundred, a chandeliered ballroom, a private menagerie, a golf course, and tennis courts, all without the bother of making a fortune and thus having to build a boring old business first. In the latter fantasy, it never occurred to her that infinite access to a golf course and tennis courts was of limited value with no one else to play with.

By her teens, the backyard frolicking of her childhood having given way to a covert if demanding fitness regime, Serenata entertained jobs that might put exertion to practical employ. She pictured herself as the only woman on a construction crew, pounding spikes, wielding big flats of Sheetrock, and manipulating heavy jackhammers—thus amazing her male coworkers, who would scoff at the upstart girlie at first, but would come to revere her and defend her honor in bars. Or she might become a great asset to a team of moving men (who would scoff, come to revere her, and defend her honor in bars . . .). She contemplated tree surgery. Alas, hard physical labor was apparently low-skilled and low-waged, and her middle-class parents dismissed all these backbreaking prospects as preposterous.

For years, the only child had amused her parents by performing original radio plays. She recorded all the parts on a portable cassette player, punctuating the dramas with sound effects—door slams, floor tromping, crumpling paper for fire. At once, her girlhood's reigning ambition to pursue a solitary occupation seemed to display a gut self-knowledge. What fit the bill, then, was to become a writer.

Oh, her parents didn't regard this aspiration as any more practical than becoming a construction worker. They expected she'd just get married. But at least a literary bent would argue for a college education, which would raise the quality and earning power of her suitors. So with their blessing she enrolled at Hunter, within shouting distance of New Brunswick, emerging like most liberal arts graduates as roundly unemployable.

Serenata's twenties were aimless and hand-to-mouth. She couldn't afford her own apartment, so (anathema) had to share digs with other girls whose twenties were aimless and hand-to-mouth. The menial jobs she procured hardly required a college degree. She tried to make time for "her work" without saying the pretentious expression aloud. Mortifyingly, every other peer she encountered in New York City also described themselves as writers, who were also making time for "their work."

It was manning the phones at Lord & Taylor's Customer Service that turned her tide. A young man called about needing to return a gift of a tasteless tie. He described the gaudy item in comical detail. He enticed her to explain what a customer should do both with and without a receipt, when surely he had the receipt or he didn't. It dawned dimly on the store's representative that he was keeping her on the line. Finally he implored her to repeat after him, "Please watch the closing doors."

"What?"

"Just say it. As a favor. *Please watch the closing doors.*"

Well, it wasn't as if he'd asked her to repeat "Please can I suck your dick." She complied.

"Perfect," he said.

"I'm not sure how one would say that badly."

"Most people would say that badly," he countered—and proceeded to explain that he was a civil servant with the city's Department of Transportation. He'd been tasked with finding a new announcer for recorded public transit advisories, and begged her to try out for the job. She was leery, of course. As a precaution, she looked up the NYC Department of Transportation in the phone book, and the address he'd provided matched.

In the end, it was decided higher up that New Yorkers weren't quite ready for female authority, and she didn't get the job. As Remington shared with her later, one of the other men on the team had declared after replaying her audition tape that no male passenger listening to that sultry voice would ever hear the content of the announcements; he'd be fantasizing about fucking the loudspeaker.

Yet before the disappointing determination was made, she did agree to a dinner date—albeit only after Remington's second invitation. She was obliged to turn down the spontaneous one on the heels of her audition because the bike trip between her East Village apartment and the DOT office downtown was officially too short to "count," and it wouldn't do to dine out when she hadn't yet *exercised*. They agreed to meet at Café Fiorello on Broadway, a high-end Italian trattoria that longtime New York residents would generally consign to tourists. Despite the upscale venue, Serenata, as ever, insisted on cycling.

From a distance in the restaurant's entryway, Remington had apparently watched her standard Cinderella transformation beside an alternate-side parking sign. She toed off a ratty sneaker, balanced on the other foot, and shimmied from one leg of her jeans—ensuring that the skirt fluttering over them continued to cover her person in a seemly fashion. It was still nippy in March, and ivory panty hose had doubled as insulation. From a pannier, she withdrew a pair of killer heels in red patent leather. Steadying herself on one high heel by holding the bike seat, she repeated the striptease with the opposite leg and stuffed her rolled jeans into the pannier. After giving the skirt a straightening tug, she applied a hasty touch-up of lipstick; the ride itself would provide the blush. She removed her helmet, shook out the thick black hair, and bound it with a homemade fabric binder not yet called a *scrunchie*. By then Remington had tucked back into the restaurant, enabling her to check her filthy jacket and the greasy saddlebags, their erstwhile hi-viz yellow now the queasy, sullen color of a spoiled olive.

Over a lobster pasta, her date responded to her hopes to become a writer with a neutrality that must have disguised an inner eye roll. After all, she was rolling her eyes at herself. "I'm afraid the aspiration has started to seem self-indulgent. And everyone I run into in this town wants to be a writer, too."

"If it's what you really want to do, it doesn't matter that it's a cliché."

"But I wonder if it is what I want to do. I do thrive on isolation. But I don't yearn to reveal myself. I want frantically to keep other people out of my business. I prefer to keep my secrets. Whenever I try my hand at fiction, I write about characters who have nothing to do with me."

"Ha! Maybe you do have a future in literature."

"No, there's another problem. This isn't going to sound good."

"Now you've intrigued me." He leaned back, leaving his fork in the fettuccini.

"You know how people on the news are always starving, or dying in an earthquake? I'm starting to realize that I don't care about them."

"Natural disasters are often far away. The victims seem abstract. Maybe it's easier to feel for folks closer to home."

"Suffering people don't seem abstract. On television, they look real as sin. As for the people closer to home—I don't care about them, either."

Remington chuckled. "That's either refreshing or appalling."

"I'd opt for appalling."

"If you don't care about other people, what does that make me?"

"Possibly," she said cautiously, "an exception. I make a few. But my default setting is obliviousness. That's a lousy qualification for a writer, isn't it? Besides. I'm not sure I've got the voice to stand out."

"On the contrary," he said, "you do have the *voice*. I'd gladly listen to you read the entire federal tax code."

She enhanced the silky tone in her throat with a rough edge: "*Really?*" Remington admitted later that the adverb gave him an erection.

They moved on. Merely to be courteous, she asked why he'd ended up at the DOT. His response was unexpectedly impassioned.

"It may sound mechanical, but transport is massively emotional! There's no other aspect of urban life that arouses such strong feelings. On some streets, if you take out a lane of traffic to build a bike lane, you'll start a riot. Miscalibrate a pedestrian light to last a whole two minutes, and you can hear drivers pounding on the steering wheel with their windows shut. Buses that don't come for an hour when it's five below . . . Subways stuck indefinitely under the East River with no explanation on the loudspeaker . . . Terrifyingly designed freeway entrance ramps, where vision of oncoming traffic is occluded by a blind curve . . . Confusing signage that sends you plummeting south on the New Jersey Turnpike for twenty miles with no exit when you want to go north, and you were already running late . . . You may not give a hoot about other people, but transport? Everybody cares about transport."

"Maybe so. I think my bicycle is a horse. A beloved horse."

He confessed to having watched her sidewalk burlesque. "So what if we went somewhere together?"

"I'd meet you there on my bike."

"Even if I offered to pick you up?"

"I'd decline. Politely."

"I question the 'politely,' when refusal would be obstinate and rude."

"Insisting I alter a lifelong practice just to suit you or convention would also be rude."

Like most rigid people, Serenata didn't care whether inflexibility was an especially entrancing quality. You never coaxed the deeply obdurate into a more ingratiating give-and-take. You got with the program.

At the disarming civil engineer's urging, Serenata did indeed audition for a voice-over job at an advertising firm, and was hired on the spot. Similar work came in with sufficient regularity that she was able to quit Lord & Taylor. She gained a reputation. In time, she would extend to audiobooks, and nowadays much of her work was infomercials and video games. If she cared little about other people, she did care about excellence, and was forever delighted to discover new timbres, or to extend her upper and lower registers to convey cranky children and grousing old men. It was one of the pleasures of human speech to be unconstrained by a limited number of notes in a scale, and she relished the infinite incremental tonalities in a glissando of disappointment.

Having moved so often as a kid had left her diction exotically nonspecific and usefully fluid. All variations in the pronunciation of *aunt*, *syrup*, or *pecan* were to her ear equally correct and equally arbitrary. She readily picked up accents because she wasn't attached to her own—and even sly lingual detectives failed to pin the origins of her argot. As she explained to Remington, "I'm from nowhere. Sometimes people mis-hear my first name and write it 'Sarah Nada': Sarah Nothing."

Yet their courtship was curiously chaste. Her guarded quality had tempted earlier suitors to try to overrun the ramparts—with fatal consequences. Perhaps Remington was thus cannily counter-ing her withholding by withholding in return, but she began to worry that he kept his hands to himself because he just didn't find her attractive. "I know you fell for my voice," she noted at last. "But when the voice showed up in the flesh—were the three dimensions a turnoff?"

"You police your borders," he said. "I've been waiting to be issued a visa."

So she kissed him—taking his hand and placing it firmly on an inside thigh, with the formality of stamping his passport. These many years later, the question was: If she'd first been captivated by Remington Alabaster's respect for her fierce sense of territory, why was he now invading it at the age of sixty-four?

"That's it for the upstairs bathroom," the young woman announced, tugging her rubber gloves from the wrist so that they came off disas-trously inside out.

Serenata nodded at the gloves lying moist and smelly on the kitchen island. "You did it again."

"Oh, bastard!"

"I'm not paying you by the hour to work those fingers one-by-one back through the other way." Her tone, however, was teasing.

"Okay, off the clock." With a glance at her wrist, Tomasina March—Tommy for short—began the arduous business of poking the inverted forefinger of the first glove and edging it down through the sticky yellow tube by the quarter inch.

Although her parents had hired a cleaner, before the move to Hudson Serenata had spurned domestic help. Oh, she didn't suffer from liberal discomfort with servants. She simply didn't want strangers—*other people*—in her house. Yet reaching sixty had put her over the hill in a panoramic sense. She had crested, and could see from here the decline that spread before her. She could choose to spend a measurable proportion of this surprisingly short and potentially precipitous decay scrubbing the soap buildup around the shower drain, or she could pay someone else to do it. No-brainer.

Besides, though she'd usually have been put off by the proximity of one more exercise fanatic, something about the nineteen-year-old next-door doing hundreds of squat thrusts in her busted-furniture-strewn backyard on the day they moved in had reminded Serenata of her own childhood's "broken legs" and "rolly-pollies." Glad for the pocket money (Serenata paid $10/hour—appallingly, in upstate New York a generous wage), Tommy was a stalky girl, long-limbed and awkward, thin but shapeless. Her honey hair was fine and lank. Her face was open and guileless. Its unwritten quality brought back in a rush how truly awful it was to have this whole stupid life looming before you, a life you never asked for in the first place, and to have not an inkling what to do with it. At Tommy's age, most kids with half a wit would be visited by a sick feeling that by the time they finally cobbled together a plan it would prove too late, because there was something they should have done—*at nineteen*—to put the stratagem into action. It was a wonder that people grew nostalgic for youth. The wistfulness was pure amnesia.

"So where's Remington?" Tommy asked.

"Out for a *run*, believe it or not. Which means we have a whole six more minutes to talk about him behind his back."

"I didn't know he was into running."

"He wasn't. Not until two weeks ago. Now he wants to run a marathon."

"Well, good for him."

"*Is* it good for him?"

"Sure." Tommy was concentrating on the glove. She still hadn't rescued its forefinger. "Everybody wants to run a marathon, so what could be wrong with it?"

"That fact that everybody wants to. I know he's at loose ends, but I wish he'd latched on to something more original."

"There's not that much to do. Whatever you think of, somebody else's done it already. Being original is a lost cause."

"I'm being mean," Serenata said, not referring to Remington— but of course, she was being mean about him, too. "Those gloves—I should just buy you a new pair. Though you'd make quicker work of them if you stopped pacing."

Tommy continued to lunge back and forth across the kitchen while victoriously inverting the forefinger. "Can't. Only at twelve thousand, and it's already four o'clock."

"Twelve thousand what?"

"Steps." She gestured to the plastic band on her left hand. "I got a Fitbit. A knockoff, but same difference. Also, if I stop, this thing won't count your first thirty steps for some dumb reason. In the instructions, it says, 'in case you just shaking hands,' as if anybody shakes hands thirty freaking times. Those instructions are all written by Chinese people who obviously don't know anything about American customs. Not that I mean there's anything wrong with Chinese people," she added anxiously. "Is that what you're supposed to call them? 'Chinese people'? It sounds kind of insulting. Anyway, those lost thirty steps, over and over—they really add up."

"And this matters why? That back-and-forth of yours is putting me into a trance."

"Well, you post your steps. Every day. Online. Just about everybody clocks up, like, twenty K or more, and Marley Wilson, this total cunt from senior year, regularly posts *thirty*."

"How many miles is that?"

"Just under fifteen," Tommy said promptly.

"Unless she's really hoofing it, walking that mileage could take five hours a day. Does she do anything else?"

"Whatever else she does isn't the point."

"Why do you care how many steps other people take?"

"You don't get it. But you should. The main reason it bugs you that Remington's started running is you stopped."

"I didn't say it bugged me."

"Didn't have to. He's beating you. Even if he's only gone six minutes, he's beating you."

"I still exercise by other means."

"Not for long. You went on that whole rant last week about how impossible it is to do anything aerobic that doesn't involve your knees. You can't even swim, when they get too puffy."

It was ridiculous to feel wounded when Tommy was only quoting Serenata back to herself.

"If it makes you feel any better," Tommy added, waving a fully outside-out rubber glove in triumph, "most people who do marathons totally give up running pretty soon afterward. Like those World's Biggest Losers who go right back to being fat. They check that box on the bucket list, and then move on."

"Did you know the term 'bucket list' only goes back about ten years? I looked it up. A screenwriter wrote a list of things he wanted to do before he 'kicked the bucket.' So he called it 'The Bucket List.' Since at the very top was getting a screenplay produced, he wrote a movie with the same title. It must have done okay, because the term went viral."

"Ten years ago, I was nine. Far as I'm concerned, we've said that forever."

"That expression 'going viral' itself *went viral* only a few years earlier. I wonder if there's a name for that—something that is what it describes."

"You care more about the names of stuff than I do."

"It's called being educated. You should try it sometime."

"Why? I told you, I want to be a voice-over artist, too. I can already read pretty good. Now I just have to get better at *once more, with feeling*, like you said."

This peculiarly age-discrepant friendship had first taken off after the girl discovered that Serenata Terpsichore had recorded the audiobook of one of her favorite young adult novels. Tommy had never known anyone whose name had appeared on an Amazon download, so the credit made her next-door neighbor a superstar.

"I think what grates about these abruptly ubiquitous expressions—"

Tommy wasn't going to ask.

"Meaning, suddenly everyone says it," Serenata added. "It's just, people throwing around fashionable lingo think they're so hip and imaginative. But you can't be hip and imaginative. You can be unhip and imaginative, or hip and conformist."

"For a lady who doesn't care about what other people think, and what other people do, you sure talk a lot about what other people think, and what other people do."

"That's because other people are constantly *crowding me*."

"Do I crowd you?" Tommy asked shyly, actually coming to a stop.

Serenata pulled herself up—it was a Bad Knee Day—and put an arm around the girl. "Certainly not! It's you and I against the world. Now that you've paused, the next thirty steps are a write-off. So let's have tea."

Tommy slid gratefully into a chair. "Did you know that within fifteen minutes of sitting down, your whole body, like, changes and everything? Your heart and stuff."

"Yes, I've read that. But I can't stand up twelve hours a day anymore. It hurts."

"Hey, I didn't mean to make you feel bad, before. About the running and stuff. 'Cause anyway, for an old person—you still look pretty hot."

"Thanks—I think. Strawberry-mango okay?" Serenata lit the burner under the kettle. "But being halfway well put together won't last. Exercise has been my secret. A secret that's out, I gather."

"Not that out. Most people look terrible. Like my mother."

"You said she has diabetes." With bad timing, Serenata put out a plate of almond cookies. "Cut her some slack."

Tommy March was not unloved, but under-loved, which was worse—just as full-tilt fasting had a strengthening absolutism, whereas a never-ending diet made you peevish and weak. Her father had cut and run long ago, and her mother rarely left the house. Presumably they were on public assistance. So even in a town with depressed property values—this vast brown clapboard had been a steal at $235K, with two baths, three porches, and six bedrooms, two of which they still hadn't put to any use—naturally Tommy's mother was still renting. She'd never encouraged her daughter to go to college. Which was a shame, because the girl had plenty of drive, but her urge to self-improvement was unmoored. She pinballed from fad to fad with little awareness of the larger social forces that worked the flippers. When she declared herself a vegan (before realizing two weeks in that she couldn't live without pizza), she imagined that the idea just came to her out of the blue.

Typically for the time, then, Tommy was skittish about sugar. As if stealing the confection behind her own back, her hand darted at a cookie like a lizard's tongue and snatched the snack to her lap. "You're still being, like, all grumpy-out-of-it-old-lady about social media, right?"

"I have better things to do. In the real world."

"Social media is the real world. It's way more real than this one. It's only 'cause you shut yourself out of it that you don't know that."

"I prefer to use you as my spy. I used Remington the same way for years. He went out into the American workplace and reported back. As for what he found there . . . A layer of insulation seems prudent."

"I just think you should know . . . Well, on these YA platforms . . ." Tommy had stopped looking Serenata in the eye. "It's got kinda not so great, for white readers of audiobooks to use accents. Especially of POCs."

"People of color!" Serenata said. "Bet you thought I didn't know that. Remington always thought it was hilarious that at work if he'd ever said 'colored people' instead, he'd have been fired. But then, he was fired anyway. So much for hoop jumping, if you're not in pro basketball."

"Look, I don't make the rules."

"But you do make the rules. Remington says that it's everyone slavishly obeying these capriciously concocted taboos that gives them teeth. He says rules that are roundly ignored are 'just suggestions.'"

"You're not listening! The point is, your name came up. And not in a nice way."

"So what's wrong with doing accents again? I'm not following this."

"It's—problematic."

"And what does that mean?"

"It means everything. It's a great big giant word for absolutely everything that's super bad. See, now they're all saying that white readers pretending to talk like marginalized communities is 'mimicry,' and also it's like, cultural appropriation."

"It depresses the hell out of me that you can rattle off 'marginalized communities' and 'cultural appropriation,' whatever that is, when you don't know the word *ubiquitous*."

"I do now! It means everybody does it."

"No. Omnipresent, everywhere. Now, why does my name come up?"

"Honest? Your accents, on the audiobooks. I think it's because you're so good at them. Like, you have a reputation. So when these guys reach for an example, it's your name they think of."

"Let me get this straight," Serenata said. "I'm now supposed to deliver the dialogue of a coke dealer in Crown Heights as if he's a professor of medieval literature at Oxford. 'Yo, bro, dat bitch ain't no better than a ho, true dat.'" She'd given the line an aristocratic English snootery, and Tommy laughed.

"*Please* let's not tell Remington about this," Serenata said. "Promise me. I'm deadly serious. He'd freak."

"Shouldn't tell Remington what?" Himself closed the side door behind him. It was November, and he'd made the usual mistake of bundling up to excess, when the biggest problem of running in cold weather was getting hot. Underneath all that winter sports gear he'd be drenched, and his face was red. The ruddy complexion was further enhanced by a glow of a more interior sort. Good grief, she prayed that she herself had never returned from some dumpy old run exuding this degree of self-congratulation.

THREE

"Right, I've bled and treadmilled and wired up for you, and got the all clear," Remington announced just inside the door. The checkup had not been his idea, and he was humoring her. "Doctor Eden located a minor cardiac irregularity, but he assured me it's common, and nothing to worry about."

"What irregularity?" He'd not have wanted to mention any negative findings at all, but luckily for Serenata her husband was a stickler for the truth.

"I don't remember what it's called." He had chosen not to remember, to prevent her from googling for alarmism. "The point is, I'm fine. Eden sees no reason I can't run a marathon, so long as I up the distance gradually and stick to the program."

"What program?"

"I'm following an online schedule." His tone was officious.

"You couldn't figure out how to run a little bit farther every week by *yourself*?" she said to his back as he returned to the car.

"It's not that simple," he said, lugging two sagging bags from the backseat. "You have to set goals, do longer runs, and shorter ones in between. Vary the pace. There's a science to it. You've never run a marathon yourself—"

"So now we're pulling rank."

"I don't understand this disdain you have for any undertaking that involves anyone else." He clanked the bags beside the dining table. "Why does my consulting the considerable literature on this subject seem to you a sign of weakness? Your declared hostility to the rest of the human race is what's weak. It puts you at an evolutionary disadvantage. Humble yourself, and you can learn from other people's mistakes."

"What's all this?"

"Free weights. I need to work on my core."

Serenata battled a wave of mental nausea. "What's wrong with the word *torso*? And I have free weights. You could have borrowed mine."

"Your attitude from the get-go has hardly been share and share alike. It's better for me to have my own equipment. I thought I'd use one of those empty bedrooms for my home gym."

"You mean you'll commandeer a bedroom," she said.

"Haven't you *commandeered* one for your own gyrations?"

"You also have your study. Though I'm not sure what it's for."

"You can't possibly be goading me for being unemployed. Tell me that's not what you meant."

"No. Or maybe, but that was unkind. I disliked that word *gyrations*. I was getting a dig in back. Sorry."

"A bigger dig. I retract 'gyrations.' Workouts. I'll call them whatever you like."

"Oh, go ahead then, take one of the extra bedrooms. This is a large house, and we're hardly the European powers carving up the Middle East after World War One."

She took Remington's face in her hands and kissed his forehead, to bless their restored truce. It was past six thirty p.m., and in Serenataland, dinner had to be earned.

She slipped upstairs and changed into grubby shorts and a tattered T, anxious whether that "cardiac irregularity" was truly nothing to fret about; doctor-patient confidentiality precluded getting the real lowdown. Although she trusted that her husband wouldn't lie about that "all clear," he was so invested in running this Saratoga Springs event that he could have trivialized an anomaly that was cause for concern.

Of more immediate concern was the snippy tenor of their interchanges since October, which displayed little of the dry, *Thin Man* repartee polished early in their marriage. The past two-plus months had been punctuated by the cheap potshots of empty nesters who without the children underfoot had nothing in common, although years ago their own return to just the two of them had come as a relief. It rankled that she got no credit for restraint. As of earlier this December, after all the training, scores of hours online, and nearly two thousand bucks in gear (she'd kept track), he'd worked up to a respectable five-mile run. But his pace, if anything, had grown even slower! Having completed that landmark distance last Saturday in well over an hour, he had to be clocking a thirteen-minute mile. He didn't faintly appreciate the self-control required to keep from making fun of him.

As ever, this segment of the day inspired nothing like eagerness, and if it weren't getting so late she'd have found herself seized with a sudden determination to fold the laundry. She was always amused by sluggards who explained, you see, they "just didn't enjoy exercise." Granted, some sports were diverting enough to distract from the effort they demanded, but straight-up exercise was odious, and a sane person approached it with dread. This evening was scheduled for a raft of "gyrations" focused solely on her legs, which her orthopedist had stressed *could not be too strong*, a declaration that this patient took as a dare. Of her variety pack of masochisms, the legs routine was streets ahead of the rest in sheer tedium.

She kept the radiator valve closed, so it was freezing in here— leaving exertion as the only route to warming up. As for the TV, it was large, loud, smart, and replete with hundreds of cable channels, as well as Netflix, Hulu, and Amazon Prime. As emergency backup, the hard drive was bursting with recorded films and box sets. With no television, she'd have skipped this whole ninety-minute folderol of holds and lunges and raises and pulls, and shot herself in the head.

Yet the range of optimal on-screen fare was narrow. It shouldn't be too serious, because she couldn't spare the energy to be moved. It shouldn't be too funny, because she couldn't spare the energy to laugh. Subtitles were out. Documentaries were okay, so long as they weren't too arty. What you wanted was *good crap*. Unfortunately, she'd finished the last season of *Crazy Ex-Girlfriend*, which had hit the sweet spot.

Opting lazily for network news, she looped a nylon strap around an ankle and closed the door on its anchor. Tugging through the four stations of the hip-tightening raises—stretching the black rubber TheraBand by pulling the straightened leg (theoretically straightened; suffering "loss of extension," the right one was permanently crooked) forward, to the right, backward, and from the left, twenty times each direction—she considered what proportion of her life so far had been devoted to this sort of monotony. Ninety minutes of a sixteen-hour waking day was . . . It was impossible to make mathematical calculations while tracking repetitions (*one, two, three, four . . .*). Suffice it to say that the percentage was high: a source of pride, or horror? Drawing a last breath, would she echo Jackie Kennedy's apocryphal deathbed keen, "Why on earth did I do all those sit-ups?" Serenata had already spent a massive whack of her discretionary time on this earth deliberately boring herself to death. (Left leg, second set.) *One, two, three, four . . .* She'd also spent a staggering amount of her short finite life *counting*. Like a kindergartner.

In the pharmaceutical ads on-screen, square-faced older men with full heads of salt-and-pepper hair joined comely wives in bright leggings and matching jackets, a colorist's gray streak at the women's hairline a sole gesture toward the geriatric. Despite the debilitations of whatever ailment the actors were aping, in every single advertisement the sufferers were running along a riverside, cycling country roads, or hiking woodsy trails. They were always laughing, which made you wonder what about this ceaseless bustle was so hilarious.

Oldsters in drug commercials used to stare sweetly out the window at the setting sun while pinching china teacups. Something had happened, and Serenata had made a study of it. The transformation had been gradual at first, insidious even, and then, in its perfect universality, abrupt.

The change had been most striking in relation to women, who throughout her girlhood might have yearned to be slender, but regarded discernable muscles on the female form as unsightly, unseemly, and butch. Her own enthusiasm for well-defined biceps was peculiar if not suspect for the time, and in short sleeves she'd more than once been catcalled as a "dyke."

Fast-forward to the present. Models marketing even classically feminine products like fragrances wore running bras. Silhouettes in magazines were still photoshopped to a narrowness that wouldn't allow for kidneys, but the ripples like windblown sand across bare midriffs were new. On the sides of buses, women's blown-up shoulders were cut, their thighs chiseled. On billboards, even lovelies languishing in nightwear slipped calves from the slits of their negligees that were full and taut. With so much money on the line, advertising held a well-researched mirror to the modern ideal, and in the commercial representation of today's daily life, beguiling young ladies were consistently pictured kayaking, mountain climbing, swimming laps, taking spinning classes, overdoing it on rowing machines, and pummeling punching bags. Keen awareness that

Serenata of all people should have found her sex's contemporary aspiration to strength culturally auspicious and altogether marvelous made the frenzied female hard bodies bannered across the marketing landscape only the more grating.

Placing her right foot on the seat of a wooden chair, she pushed the left foot off the floor, stood on the right foot, and brought the left knee chest-high. A hundred on the right, a hundred on the left, exhaling on every rise. The hard part was keeping your balance.

Mind, she regarded this ninety-minute tune-up as no nobler than a tune-up for a car. Conscientious motorists maintained their automobiles, but didn't expect a medal for changing the oil. She, too, was trying to be the responsible custodian of a mechanism. This was a devotion, but not in a sacred sense. She was devoted to the upkeep of the vehicle out of sheer self-interest: it got her from place to place.

Pulling the Velcro taut on the two ten-pound ankle weights, Serenata was reminded by a sharp twinge that were she ever to have considered a daily athletic ordeal as exhibiting moral properties—as raising her high on a ladder of enlightenment or hoisting her to a superior position in the social hierarchy—these ritual efforts at redemption had backfired. She was being punished. Dr. Churchwell's diagnosis had been insultingly prosaic, grandmotherly, and out-to-pasture: osteoarthritis, in both knees, in all three sectors bone-on-bone. Absent a familial history of the disease, he'd pronounced dismissively that the condition had clearly resulted from "overuse." The expectation that, if not virtue, then at least good practice would necessarily be rewarded was naive, but that didn't alter the ferocity of the feeling—that *it wasn't fair.*

At dinner, Remington had an agenda.

"It hasn't escaped me," he began, "that you experience my discovery of endurance sport as something being taken away from you. So

I would like us to examine what I can only call your sense of *ownership* of physical fitness."

"I suppose I do own it," she said coolly.

"You invented it?"

"I invented it for myself."

"So the Greeks who ran the original twenty-six point two miles from the town of Marathon to Athens—they sent a time traveler to steal the idea from you."

"That would be unlikely. Since, as you observed so pointedly earlier this evening, I've never run a marathon, have I? Though I have run sixteen, seventeen miles in one go—that time I got lost in Australia, and had to keep going until I located civilization again—so I could probably have managed another ten, if I were determined to."

"You've always said that if you ever ran a marathon you'd do it by yourself."

"That's right."

"Except that now you never will."

"Well, this isn't exactly Make Serenata Feel Better Day, is it?"

"The only way you'd ever have gotten around to running twenty-six point two miles on any given day is by participating in a group event, the way everyone else does it."

"I find large numbers of people doing the same thing in one place a little repulsive."

"No, you find it a lot repulsive. But for normal people, the company of many others engaged in a common pursuit is uplifting."

"I'm incapable of losing myself in a crowd. I have no desire to melt into some giant pulsating amoeba."

"Does it ever occur to you that maybe you're missing out on something?"

Serenata considered. "No."

"You feel *above* people capable of collective experience."

"Yes, I suppose I do. Church services, football games, and even rock concerts leave me cold. Maybe that seems a pity, but I'd also remain unmoved by swastika-waving rallies for National Socialism."

"As far as I know, you aren't a member of anything. Not a professional organization, not a political party; I can't even remember your joining a private library. So at least you're consistent, though the purity of your lack of communal ties is a little chilling. But I want to get back to this *ownership* business."

"All right," she said tolerantly.

"Think about it: all the sports people play, and have done for generations. You're so proud of doing 'push-ups,' but long ago someone else coined the term. The record books are strewn with achievements beyond your ken: the first woman to swim the English Channel. The bicycle you rode to Café Fiorello, and have insisted on riding to restaurants ever since: you didn't *invent* the bicycle—"

"Ownership is a sensation. I can feel I own something without being given formal title to it."

"But 'owning' physical fitness isn't just irrational. It's mentally ill. Furthermore, for you and me right now, your lunatic patrolling of this territory is highly problematic."

"Oh, don't use that word. According to Tommy, *problematic* is now a label for the trespasses of white people who are unfathomably evil."

"Meaning, white people, period. The unfathomably evil part goes without saying."

For a moment, they were on the same side.

"You understand much better than you're pretending," she said. "Obviously, plenty of people before me have run around, and jumped up and down, and biked places—though nowhere *near* the number who've discovered the bicycle now, nowhere *near*. Obviously, there's such a thing as the professional athlete, too—which isn't what we're talking about. Suddenly you turn on the TV, and all the characters are in the gym. For the last several years, the *one* topic *guaranteed* to shoot to the top of the Most Popular list on the *New York Times* website is anything whatsoever to do with *exercise*. About the only articles capable of nudging a recommendation of interval training out of first place are the ones touting the health-giving properties of red wine. Meanwhile, magazines are crammed with profiles of icons who run fifty miles a day. Or seventy-five, or a hundred. Marathons—sweetie, marathons are old hat. You're supposed to run a plain old marathon before breakfast."

"That's not very helpful."

"I'm not trying to be helpful. I'm trying to explain how I feel. And I'm observing that your turning to exercise for absolution, or a purpose in life, has been imposed on you from the outside. It's a contagion, like herpes. You've always been more suggestible than I am."

"If according to you the whole country is suddenly consumed with fitness, how come Americans keep getting fatter?"

"Because this tsunami of a social tide isn't a matter of results. It has to do with what people aspire to. Nobody cares anymore about getting to Italy before they die, or reading *Moby-Dick*. Goodness, I don't even think they all want to write a novel themselves anymore. It's all about seizing on some extreme athletic event, after which presumably they'll sit on the right hand of God the Father."

"*I* think the rising popularity of endurance sports bothers you because you're being beaten at your own game. A lot more ordinary amateurs are pushing their limits beyond what you ever have, isn't that right?"

"Do I feel like my comparatively minor league *gyrations* are being shown up? Yeah. I probably do."

"In which case, if I complete that marathon in April, a distance you've assumed for years that you could handle—and I tend to agree, though you've never tested yourself, so now we'll never know—your own husband will show you up."

"Is that your intention?"

"No it isn't, and correcting that misimpression is one reason I wanted to have this conversation."

"So far, it's been closer to an interrogation."

"I also think you resent the fact that fitness has become more exalted at the same time that you're growing—somewhat prematurely at sixty—increasingly infirm."

"Well, congratulations, Sherlock."

"I meant that sympathetically."

"It didn't sound sympathetic. But if you are trying to beat me at my own game, even if you claim you're not—triumphing over a cripple seems like cheating."

"To the contrary, if you had the cartilage for it, I might have proposed that we run the race this spring together."

"Liar," she said. "You want credit for that cozy idea, but you can only suggest it because you know it's impossible."

"Who knows what's going to be possible, after you finally bite the bullet and get knee replacements."

"Do you realize what they *do*? I forced myself to look it up. They actually *saw off* the ends of your bones. In videos on YouTube, the doctors and nurses all put on, like, welding masks, to keep off all the blood spatter. One guy who refused general anesthesia described online how his whole body vibrated and he could hear the earsplitting rasp of the blade, as if he weren't in a hospital but on a construction site. They remove the patella and replace your kneecap with a piece of plastic. They'll throw my knees in the wastebasket. And pound metal knobs into my tibias and thighbones, *bam, bam, bam,* the way you sink a wedge in a log to split firewood."

"Knee replacements have become much more commonplace—"

"Just because you do something often doesn't preclude it being a big deal. These operations don't always go according to plan, either, because no major surgery does. I could end up with chronic pain, chronic inflammation, or catastrophic infection."

Remington sighed. "I'm so sorry you may have to go through this."

"Yes. Yes, I know you are." She took his hand. "But if it goes wrong, that operation could ruin my life."

"Isn't that an exaggeration?"

"No," she said readily. "I would have to become someone else. We'd both suffer a bereavement. So if Churchwell is right, you have eighteen months at the outside of being assured the company of the woman you married."

"You'd still be the woman I married with stumps at the end of your thighs."

"Oh, how I wish that were true. Unfortunately, emotions like bitterness and acrimony spread like potato blight. Already when I read about those superheroes running ultramarathons all day long, I think: *just you wait.* You'll end up on a gurney in the shadow of a surgical saw in no time, you fucking idiots. The vision fills me with glee."

"You do have a spiteful side."

"*Side?* I don't think it's just a side." Behind closed doors, one of the joys of their marriage was mutual permission to be horrid.

They rose to collect the dishes, whose remaining tidbits had long before congealed. "You know, this recent fetishizing of fitness has a particular *texture* to it," Serenata said. "You described athleticism as having become 'exalted.' That's an apt word. But I've never seen exercise as exalted. It's biological housework, like vacuuming the living room rug. These days, to wear yourself out is to attain a state of holiness. All these newbies seem to think that they're making the leap from man to god. This . . . sanctimony, this . . . self-importance. It's started to contaminate the flavor of my own workouts, like that metallic taste in my mouth when I was pregnant. So I worry that, well . . . I don't want that anointed, pseudo-Nazi narcissism to infect you, too."

"You're afraid I'm going to become an asshole," Remington surmised. "But, my darling wife, and I say this as affectionately as one can: you're the asshole."

"Well! I'm not sure one can say that affectionately, darling husband."

"Regular, vigorous exercise helps to maintain a healthy weight. It can put type two diabetes into remission, reduces the likelihood of cancer, and may even help diseases like Parkinson's. It improves your sleep. It promotes longevity and mental acuity, and it's often more effective than medication for treating depression—"

"So *you're* one of the readers driving all those articles to the Number One slot."

"Not to mention," he continued, "that you might find a husband's better toned body more attractive. But your reaction to your compatriots becoming more active is despair. You want to hog all the benefits of your lifelong habits to yourself. When you do something, it's a wise, considered discipline, and when everyone else does the same thing, it's a disgusting fad. So: you're the asshole."

Serenata laughed. "Fine, I'm an asshole. Except it doesn't matter how I feel. I can sit there stewing in silent rage that all these other cyclists are suddenly glomming around me at intersections. Not a single one of them will forgo the healthful benefits of cycling and throw the contraption back in the cellar—all because they picked up strange, terrifying waves of hostility emanating from a crazed-looking older woman gripping her handlebars with white knuckles. Emotions, like opinions, are entertainment. If I celebrated this athletic revolution instead, would a single extra American pick up a barbell? No. And I'm not the rah-rah type. So it amuses me to be resentful instead."

"But it does matter," Remington said with sudden seriousness, placing a dishwatery hand on her cheek, "how you feel about me."

In January, Serenata acted on the theory that it was especially after the holidays when old people got lonely. Relatives could be tempted to use having been doting at Christmas as an excuse to skate for a while.

Surveying the streets on the short walk over, she speculated what it was about Hudson that conveyed the impression that the town wasn't exactly flourishing. All the chain-link fences weren't rusted, but some of them were. On a given block, only one building might be boarded, but that created an economic and aesthetic ambiance in considerable contrast to a block on which none of the buildings was boarded. Several businesses along Warren Street were perky and new—often given to wince-inducing wordplay, like Flower Kraut, or Mane Street Hair Styles—but their aura of optimism seemed of the delusional sort. Most instilled a powerful inkling that they weren't going to make it. Church windows were masked with protective sheets of plexiglass, making the stained glass look black, as well as a little hostile, as if ill-behaved local youth with poor prospects might throw rocks. More than one church having been deconsecrated and repurposed planted the suspicion that the congregations of those that remained were on the elderly side and dwindling.

The small town of six thousand people or so was holding up better than most in the region. If you kept abreast of which perky cafés were still open, you could sit down to a decent cappuccino. There were properly up-market restaurants for a passable meal. The train station was on the Hudson Line, which ran directly to the city on a picturesque journey along the river; thus the town benefitted from a range of weekenders and wealthy New Yorkers with summer houses and their visitors, who might linger for a drink or a poke around the antique stores before escaping to scenic verandas in the Berkshires. Nevertheless, as a place to remain rather than pass through, Hudson had a beleaguered feel, as did anywhere whose underlying economy was too dependent on a hospital.

Remington had grown up here. The tendency with small home-towns was to either revile them and flee, or romanticize them—having fled. Her husband had made the mistake of doing both. Confiningly provincial only became charmingly provincial from a distance. Even in his teens, he'd leaped at any excuse to streak south to civilization. When they'd needed to leave Albany if only for its associations, Hudson had beckoned as a safe, comfortingly famil-iar bolt-hole for the licking of wounds. Perhaps it was predictable in retrospect that Remington was already going stir-crazy. Having sampled the gamut of her country's geography, Serenata never much cared where she was; she was her own location. But anyone ending up precisely where he started couldn't help but fear that in the in-terim he had gone nowhere. She wished her husband were able to infer that the same experience of stasis and even of doom was bound to issue from running a marathon, once his heart rate settled and his exorbitant sneakers had lost their noxious smell. Lo, there you were, where you'd begun, and nothing had changed.

"Please don't get up!" Serenata shouted through the front door. "You know I've got a key. I only ring the bell to give you fair warning."

The remonstration was wasted. Griff Alabaster had still not re-linquished the protocols of hospitality—not that he'd ever been that polite, but he didn't want to be treated like an invalid. By the time she entered from the foyer, he'd struggled to a stand, and was ne-gotiating the obstacle course of his cluttered living room. Refusing the indignity of a walker, her father-in-law planted his cane before him and pulled. Wavering with the instability of the high seas, he traversed the floorboards as if poling a boat.

"Just you today, sugar?"

"Yes, I'm afraid you're stuck with *just me*," she said with a smile, removing the shepherd's pie from her tote. She wondered if he didn't prefer it when she visited alone. He'd long been sweet on her, embarrassingly so. His wife, Margaret, had been industrious but unassuming. She'd only been to secretarial school (she'd picked up her younger son's distinguished-sounding Christian name from the typewriter company); before the industry in Hudson collapsed, she abetted the family's meager income by cleaning fish. When the dowdy, compulsively self-deprecating woman was still alive, her trim, arty daughter-in-law had made Margaret jealous.

"I swear, I saw that boy more often when you folks lived in Albany," Griff said, "'stead of six blocks east."

"Well, you know how seriously he's preparing for that marathon in April!" she said, trying to convey chirpy enthusiasm as she carried the casserole to the kitchen. She'd paid Tommy to clean the place a couple of days before, and the counters were filthy again.

This whole house wasn't exactly messy, but it never changed, except in that steady, inexorable way that you didn't notice when witnessing the decay day by day. The faded floral curtains were often drawn during the daytime to skip the bother of opening and closing them again. Cheap reproductions of Old Masters in homemade wooden frames had light-bleached, until the oils looked like watercolors. It would never have occurred to Griff to buy new throw pillows, much less new furniture, but all the paddings had flattened and exuded cough-inducing dust if you plumped them up. The heavy leather coat he'd worn to work in cold weather was still on its hook in the catchall utility room off the kitchen, but the garment had stiffened into a kind of mounted hunting trophy. The living room walls were darkened by years of an open fire; the kitchen was mottled with stains in corners that Tommy found hard to reach. Though the trinkets littering every available surface weren't likely to Griff's taste—china figurines of milkmaids—they'd been chosen by his late wife, and perhaps more importantly had always occupied a precise location, where they would therefore remain for eternity. Griff gave Tommy no end of grief if while dusting she returned the empty milk-glass candy dish two inches from its appointed perch.

Serenata's father-in-law couldn't bear the notion of *a* home as opposed to his own, but maintaining the viability of his independence was in Remington's and her interest as well. A nursing facility would necessitate selling this house, whose proceeds would evaporate from monthly fees. Her own parents had died in debt, like good Americans. Griff's expiring in situ was their only chance at a modest inheritance—which, what with Remington's punitively reduced pension, the unreliability of her freelance work, a real estate downturn that had shrunk the equity in the Albany house, and a steady drain from two grown children who never seemed to quite get their adult acts together, they might need.

"In my day," her father-in-law called, "you got paid to tucker yourself out!"

"Exhaustion has become an industry," she said, back from the kitchen. "Just think! These days, you could *allow* people to carry all that lumber you lugged around, and hoist your steel beams for you, and you could charge them for the privilege. Just don't call it a 'building site,' but a 'sports center.' Oh, and we'd have to come up with a snappy name—so instead of Pilates, or CrossFit, you could call your regimen . . . *Erection.*"

Griff emitted a wheezy laugh as he sank into his saggy brown recliner. "You have a mind like a cesspit, kiddo."

"I think *Erection* is inspired. You could trademark the term—just change the *C* to a *K*—and start a franchise. Your membership, being gluttons for exercise, could dig foundations, and frame buildings, and hand-plow access roads with miserable little shovels—all the while paying a stiff monthly fee. You'd make a fortune. The income from selling off the actual structures they built would be incidental chump change."

"Folks used to look down on a body for working with his hands," Griff said as she settled in the wing chair once reserved for his wife. "Earning your crust by breaking your back not only landed you in an early grave, but got no respect. Including from my sons, I'm sorry to say."

"You're hardly landing in an early grave, Griff, at eighty-eight. Still, I don't think manual labor gets any more respect now than it ever did. Maybe that's why 'Erektion' would never work: lately you only get credit for running yourself ragged to the point of collapse if by doing so you accomplish absolutely nothing."

"You're one to talk."

"I *am* one to talk. And I have the knees to prove it."

"Never forget your nipping upstairs to put on them skimpy red shorts, first time you crossed this threshold," he reminisced (again). "Rushed out the door without a word, leaving poor Remy to explain—with the chicken steaming on the table. Margaret was livid." His wife hadn't been the only one who was livid—Griff had lit into quite a tirade when the new girlfriend returned from her ten-mile run—but over the years the anecdote had softened.

Much like Griff himself. His forearms broad and scarred, Remington's father had been a burly man prone to rages. A drinker (who still put away more stout than his doctors advised), he'd doled out a fair share of corporal punishment as a father, and by the time they met, the man still wielded a brutal frankness like the retired tool belt with which he'd beaten his sons. She'd found him intimidating. The ease with which they could speak now was hard won.

But then, his figure had grown far less imposing. After forty-some years of physical toil, ill health had forced him to retire; his joints were gravel, and he was suffering from chronic back pain. In the last decade, Griff had shrunk like a parade float with a slow leak—an impression only heightened by his insistence on wearing his old forest-green Hudson Valley Construction work clothes, which dwarfed him now. His default expression of belligerence had over the years been replaced by one of wariness—the same emotion, inverted. It was not in his interest to alienate his caretakers, and to a degree his more amiable latter-day bearing was calculated.

She missed being afraid of him. Griffith Alabaster had been a formidable man, and though he'd never gone to college—the minimal importance of which was only apparent to those who had—he was smart. Even now, he had his lapses, but was nowhere near senile.

"What bee's got under Remy's bonnet? Years of urban planning and mass transit and traffic flow, and suddenly all I hear about is *jogging*. That silly business at the DOT must have something to do with it."

"Oh, it's in the mix. He needs distraction. As hobbies go, running is probably better than taxidermy, or becoming a drunk. Though come to think of it, taxidermy might interest me more. Foxes poised with bared teeth in the basement? I'd be enchanted."

"Only thing worse than working," Griff declared, "is not working."

"But he's not going to get another job at sixty-four. And Remington could be looking at another thirty years. I hate to think of those three decades as time to kill."

"Tell me about it," Griff said.

"He's taken an indignant line. But on some level, he's ashamed. No one wants to leave a job of such long standing with his tail between his legs. I'm sure he feels self-conscious about how it turned out, and worries he's let me down. Let you down, too."

"Truth be told, I was relieved to learn that boy *has* a temper to lose."

"He didn't used to be like this, you know. So imperturbable, so steady-state."

Indeed, Remington's most taxing professional achievement was learning to keep his mouth shut. But self-control was one of those virulent capacities that, ironically, was hard to control. The last few years in Albany, he'd grown laconic even at home, as if to speak his mind would encourage bad habits. When he did talk, he cloaked all his remarks in a disguising mildness, so that listening from the next room you could never tell if he was noting the loss of a sock in the last load of laundry or saying goodbye before blowing his brains out.

"He acted like a man for five seconds, and paid the price," Griff said. "I turn on the TV lately, and there's all these men got their willies chopped off, 'cause they *feel like* girls. I don't doubt it. They act like girls. Real men've got rare as hen's teeth."

"Mm," Serenata said noncommittally. "Possibly some men don't always feel up to being the responsible one, the expert, the authority. The one who has to be strong and confident. Always the protector, never the protected. That's a tall order. Women nowadays get to choose. We squeal and make the men kill the water bug in the kitchen, and then when anyone questions our courage in the face of threat, we can get on our high horse and act insulted. Pretty good deal, when you think about it. We can be world-beaters, and run whole companies, and then claim to be traumatized by a hand on our knee when helplessness is politically useful. Men aren't really given that option. And they're continually set up to look like disappointments. Because masculinity as an ideal is pretty ridiculous.

Then if they do improbably succeed in being fierce, and fearless, and emotionally impassive no matter what horrors befall them—pillars of might and right and agency, slaying the dragons every which way, well—that's only to be expected, isn't it? Lose-lose. Maybe it's no wonder that so many of them want to wear a dress."

"Remy wants to wear a dress?"

"Not last I checked my closet."

"But he finds being a man a terrible cross to bear."

"No, I think he's worn the weight of his sex quite lightly. But he does find the current climate of damned if you do, damned if you don't, unfair. Go soft, and you're a sissy. Keep holding up the side for the team, and you're not only a bully, but a relic."

"I put in a long day's work supporting my family, and I didn't see that as a choice. I didn't feel sorry for myself, either."

"Neither does Remington. Underneath all that calm and placidity, he's homicidal. And he'd like to kill someone in particular."

"But he ain't murdering anybody. He's jogging for twenty miles. What's that prove?"

"Twenty-six *point two* miles," she corrected. "Oh, and you must have noticed that he's dropped a couple of pounds."

"Big whoop." Griff had dropped fifty by accident. "I'd think better of his figure if he slimmed down by bringing me in some firewood. Down to sticks last week, till Tommy stopped by."

"She must've leaped at the job."

"How'd you know?"

"More *steps*," Serenata said enigmatically. "But now that you mention it . . ."

She brought in two wheelbarrow loads from the back, mindful to remember kindling as well. Stacking the logs by the fireplace, she asked diffidently, "Should you still be having open fires? With flying sparks . . . What if you fall asleep?"

"I built more fires than you fixed hot dinners. Only decent thing about winter. I pull that mesh curtain round. I'm old, not a dummy."

"Would you like me to build you one? It's getting dark."

"Wish you wouldn't. Have my own way of laying the logs, and you'd pile 'em different—"

"And you'd bite my head off."

"I don't got that much to do. Nice point in the day, laying the night's fire. Guess I enjoy it."

She focused on her hands as she spanked off the grime. "You know, given that Remington was never very athletic . . . Might you ever consider venturing some appreciative comment, like, I don't know, 'You've really surprised me, my boy!' or 'Good show, kid!' or even—"

"No, and I don't plan to." He'd cut her off with a forcefulness that took her aback. "You're a mother, so you should know this yourself. It's a right pain in the rear to have children always expecting you to pat them on the head for whatever they've a notion you ought to admire. You always got to bear in mind if you say the wrong thing— and ask Remy, I guess I said the wrong thing plenty—they'll end up bawling in the corner and you'll be sorry. So when they're small, you indulge them. You magnet their crummy drawings to the fridge. But once they're grown, they can't expect to be treated like adults, and at the same time expect the empty compliments you chucked them when they were kids. Remy got to live with my real opinions, and suck it up. I was right impressed when that boy drew a line in the sand at the DOT. That respect's freely given. But at my age, I should be past the point where just 'cause I'm his father I got to play pretend in case I hurt his feelings. No grown man over sixty should still be holding out for his daddy's damned approval. Tell me, lamb chop, that you don't also find this whole marathon malarkey tiresome as all get-out."

She took a breath, and chose her words with care. "If it's important to my husband, then I wish him the best. But as an answer to what to do with the next tranche of his life, I do find endurance sport a little . . . *thin*." She was about to add more, and pulled up short.

"It's *vain*," Griff announced.

"The race at least gives him a goal." This qualified as a brave stab at sticking up for her husband, surely. "I'll speak for myself, but one's sixties do seem difficult. I guess all ages are difficult. And maybe being your age is even harder. But for Remington and me, there's just not that much to look forward to."

"Anticipation's overrated. For years I was *looking forward* to the days I'd get to sleep in. I been at liberty to sleep till noon since 1994, and still get up at five."

"But our generation is likely to live into our nineties, if not past a hundred. Facing all those decades of decline—well, the future seems sort of horrible. Some days I walk around in a state of apprehension, start to finish—wondering what disease is lurking around the corner, and fretting about what I'm supposed to be doing with the tiny amount of time left before it hits. Remington might be going through a variation on the same thing."

"He reckons he can stop the clock."

"If not turn it backward. But leaving him to his delusions doesn't cost us much."

"A lie always costs something."

"Well, we've only got three more months to go." Serenata rose and fetched her coat. "Oh, I almost forgot." She rustled through her bag. "I brought you a set of CDs. Though you'll need to upgrade your technology soon, because this format is being phased out. It's my most recent audiobook. A thriller, but you never seem too picky."

"Can't follow what's happening most of the time, but you know I'll finish it." Griff had never been much of a reader, but most of his friends were dead. He enjoyed listening to her recordings for company, and to bask in the sound of her voice.

"People make a to-do about how unnatural it is to lose a child," she reflected as he insisted on seeing her to the door. "But it must feel almost as unnatural to watch your own kids *get old*."

"Oh, to me, you and Remy still look like new lovebirds, fresh as peaches."

She raised a forefinger. "You watch that! *A lie always costs something.*"

On the stoop, she leaned down a bit so that he could kiss her goodbye on the cheek. "Um—one last thing," she added. "In April, Valeria and her family are piling into their van, and then we'll drive up and watch the marathon in Saratoga Springs together. If you'd like to come, too . . ."

"Why in God's name would I want to travel all the way upstate to watch a bunch of fools jog past with numbers on their shirts and clutching little bottles of water?"

"Because one of the fools is your son. I'm sure your coming to applaud him at the finish line would mean a lot to him." There. She'd done her duty.

FOUR

She should have been able to predict it. He was a serious, methodical person, and not long ago accustomed to shouldering significant responsibility for the physical functionality of a medium-sized American capital. She couldn't even call the gravity with which he attacked the project disproportionate, when thanks to having responsibility for the physical functionality of a medium-sized American capital yanked out from under him, this ever-loving marathon was the biggest thing in his life.

Still, she'd been surprised by his slavish adherence to an online schedule that some ignorant chump could have just made up. Previous to that sadly seminal evening in July when her knees swelled big as grapefruits, she'd usually slipped off for her regular ten miles with so little ceremony that Remington wouldn't even have noticed she was gone by her return. The trot alongside Normans Kill was a routine to be wedged into her day, after a recording session, scheduled with an eye to the weather, and the solitude it provided was primarily precious for the opportunity to think about other things (like, if she'd been a very different kind of mother, would matters with Valeria have turned out otherwise?). For her husband since October, whatever run or strength-building arose on the chart *was* his day, into which distractions like grocery shopping and visiting his father were required to fit—and strangely enough, so terribly often there wasn't time. To her amazement, when she asked him once what he thought about when hitting the pavement, he'd responded without hesitation, "Well, running, of course."

"But what's there to think about running?" she asked, genuinely baffled.

"Pace, foot strike, breathing," he said impatiently. The condescension now worked both ways.

Naturally, there were smoothies. Self-deservingly large portions of meat. Cases of high-end sparkling water spiked with electrolytes. And the supplements! Rapidly multiplying hard plastic bottles crowded the toaster from the counter to the top of the microwave. Upstairs, he had gathered a collection of liniments. After showering, he smoothed oily concoctions into his muscles to such excess that the sheets on his side of the bed turned a shade darker. He'd taken to wearing five-pound ankle weights around the house, his thudding tread vibrating the worn, uneven floorboards and amplifying the creaks. Extra poundage swung each foot forward in a pendulum lunge, *pa-foom, pa-foom,* imparting an emphatic character even to a trip to the refrigerator.

She could have warned him that running outdoors during a New York State winter was sometimes unpleasant, and at first she'd hoped that he might come to appreciate the array of disagreeable conditions his wife had endured for decades with so little complaint. But Remington's focus on his personal beatification was sufficiently fierce that her own vicissitudes of times past never entered his head. When he returned once that January and closed the door behind him, he pressed his palms to the wood as if to prevent some fiend from following him inside.

"*Wind,*" he announced after a dramatic pause. Apparently the motions of the atmosphere were her husband's personal discovery. If so, the genie would go back in the bottle: he ordered a treadmill.

Not just any treadmill. This was a brushed-steel, state-of-the-art monstrosity with surround sound and a thirty-two-inch touch screen that virtual-realitied your progress over pastured hill and dale, replete with bleating sheep. Or you could choose a display of conifer fronds brushing on either side as you snaked its woodsy mountain trails; she'd not be surprised if it also exuded a resinous scent of pine needles, with a biting singe of forest fires drifting from the distance. With another poke at the menu, you could switch to a watery horizon as you padded the lapping waters of a beach at sunset. During the coastal program, breakers rolled and crashed in the background, while in the audio foreground a bare foot slapped and splashed every time your shoe landed; for all she knew, it smacked your cheeks with a bracing breeze and stung your mouth with salt.

She hated it. The thing was enormous and loud. The thumping sound was far worse than the ankle weights, and vibrated the whole house. When Remington opted for music over sound effects, he tended to prefer either bombastic symphonic selections or dated disco playlists of a trashy sort he'd not even listened to in the 1980s. The acquisition racked up yet another substantial expense, for Remington had fallen prey to the very American impulse to lavish money on what could not be bought.

The worst was the long runs, which at least he executed outside. The night before, he'd go to bed primly at nine, which necessitated dinner at five. Breakfast would be ecclesiastical, a starchy white napkin laid out like altar linen. Lost in priestly reverie, Remington would take each bite of his eggs gravely, chewing for a long time. He drank his orange juice in reverent sips, like communion wine. He spent forty-five minutes in the bathroom. After donning his vestments, he tugged each lace of the orange shoes from the bottom up, tested the tightness with a pensive pace, pulled the bow, and adjusted the tension again. His wife's dismissal of the rite had inspired him to elaborate stretches of half an hour or more. When he finally headed for the door, he departed with such solemnity that you'd have thought they'd never see each other again. "Wish me luck," he'd command mournfully, tucking a strand of hair behind her ear.

"Good luck," she'd say obediently—whatever that meant.

Finally, with two weeks to go, Remington tackled the truly demanding distance of twenty miles. He was gone for *five and a half hours*—during which it crossed his wife's mind that perhaps this whole training regime was a charade, and he was really up the road at their local coffee shop, doing crosswords over refills of decaf. In truth, she was dumbfounded that her husband could run that far, at any pace—since twenty miles was a fair distance even to walk.

When he returned that afternoon, he spread himself on the living room's Oriental carpet, arms extended, long legs straight and crossed at the ankle, head dropped sorrowfully to the side, maintaining this pose of horizontal crucifixion for a solid hour.

Oh, she'd have willingly pampered him on days like this, if he weren't already pampering himself. His glorification of these great feats of locomotion drove her to a blitheness that read as callous. Their contrary perspectives on his grand project were opening up a fissure between them that at their age shouldn't have been possible. This sense of separation hadn't visited since their divisions over what to do about Deacon during his shattering adolescence. (Remington's solutions were ever more authoritarian, while Serenata thought coming down hard on the boy only backfired; Remington would accuse her of proposing to do nothing, and then she'd admit, yeah, probably: impasse.) Long happily married with a complacence that was underrated, she'd forgotten what it was like to not know what was going on in his mind and to be a little paranoid that if she did she wouldn't like it.

There was no disguising it, at least from herself: she couldn't wait for this race to be over.

"I worry there's something wrong with me, to be dreading the arrival of my own daughter." The fact that all the preparations for their guests—making up beds, designing menus, laying in groceries—were now Serenata's problem made her only more cross.

"The sorry truth is," Remington said, "she probably dreads coming to our Godless household, too."

One week of his training remained. Closing on the marathon itself, the program slackened, the better to preserve energy for the big day. Today's distance had been his wife's squalid old standard of ten miles. Thus Remington was actually upright, albeit draped over two chairs at the dining table, hands dripping from his wrists in entitled fatigue. Early in his involuntary retirement he'd offered to take over the cooking. Since October, he'd dropped the kitchen duty cold, and Serenata was back at the stove.

"Valeria claims she doesn't proselytize," she said, stirring a roux. "But she does, and relentlessly. By pushing all that why-don't-you-give-yourself-over-to-Jesus crap, she forces us to reject her. Over and over."

"Which confirms her version of events," he said. "Cold, meanie parents; loving, long-suffering child. But you can't be nostalgic for the days she made herself scarce."

"Not days. Years. And disappearing altogether is a great deal worse than 'making yourself scarce.' She has a lot of gall to refer to our 'abuse.' A child going completely AWOL, from the age of twenty-five to twenty-nine, without so much as a postcard—now, that's abuse."

"Don't get worked up all over again. Not with their arriving tomorrow."

"Oh, I guess I shouldn't stir up old grievances. After all. That's Valeria's department." Actually, Serenata was shamelessly using their difficult daughter to excite a sense of camaraderie. They'd both felt mistreated, they'd both been flummoxed by whatever it was the girl held against them, and they'd both despaired of her membership in the Shining Path Ministry, whose founders were surely ignorant of the fact that they'd named their church after a Peruvian terrorist organization. United in dismay was still united, and she didn't even feel bad about brazenly deploying Valeria's thoughtless history to generate solidarity. Heartache should be good for something.

"She's made such a song and dance about 'forgiving' us—" Remington said.

"Me. It's sweet of you to include yourself, but we both know that her problem is with me."

"It's just, the forgiveness needs to work both ways."

"I have no desire to be forgiven. I didn't do anything. That girl lays forgiveness as a bear trap. Thank her for her clemency? *Gotcha*. Guilty as charged."

"Maybe you've asked for it. All that guff about how you 'don't care about other people'—"

"But I don't."

"It's a pose, and it's a lie. You're often very tender. Look at the way you take care of my father. Look at the way Tommy adores you. You've even been pretty nice to me," he added with a touch too much effort, then qualified, "most of the time. And you were a much more doting mother than you remember. But Valeria, since it dovetails with the story she tells herself—"

"The *narrative* she tells herself," Serenata corrected. *Narrative* had replaced *story*, as *core* had replaced *torso*, as the coyly understated *troubling* in an otherwise febrile political landscape had replaced *cat-*

astrophically fucking horrible. These substitutions were strict. Equally strict, as with the abrupt ubiquity of *bucket list*, was the moratorium on acknowledging that you had ever said anything else.

"Of course—the *narrative*. She gladly takes your description of yourself as a cold, solipsistic misanthrope at face value. So you should stop playing to that silly self-caricature." Despite his theatrical weariness, Remington had roused himself to plant a kiss on her nape at the stove. "Time to face the awful truth: Serenata Terpsichore is a nice person."

She was not a nice person, and had no desire to be one. Her unalloyed hostility to his 26.2-mile holy grail certainly wasn't nice. True, on the surface she'd stopped fighting his vainglorious training. But she was only looking forward to his crossing the finish line as a stepping-stone to the day after that, when they could go back to being a team. She could even brownie-bake that gentle bulge back into his waistline, because they were getting old, and one of the only good things about getting old was mutual permission to be imperfect.

The plan was for Valeria and the two oldest grandchildren to drive over from Rhode Island to visit for a few days, and then on Friday they'd all head up to Saratoga Springs. (Fortunately, Valeria's witless husband, Brian, was staying behind with their younger kids; he was a prim, judgmental man whose reaction to social discomfort was to sit in the corner sanctimoniously paging the New Testament.) The marathon was on Sunday, but Remington wanted to arrive two nights before to "settle" and check out the course. An extra overnight for their whole party would cost hundreds of dollars, another day's worth of eating out hundreds more. But the once-in-a-lifetime occasion would leave many years thereafter to economize. Maybe they could sell the newfangled treadmill. Though if she didn't miss her guess, the American market for secondhand treadmills—and

StairMasters, and elliptical trainers, and rowing machines—was flooded.

Valeria had been a fearful child, somewhat overweight, as she was still, which generated some tension with her rail-thin mother. It was of little importance to Serenata whether her daughter was a bit chubby, though she wasn't about to lay on forty pounds just to make the girl feel better—which it wouldn't. At thirty-one, Valeria had a pretty face, round and dimpled, and regular coloring had revived the golden curls of preschool. Mother and daughter bore some resemblance to each other, but you had to look closely. Perhaps detecting the genetic relationship was visually impaired by their weak resemblance in other respects.

Hauled to yet another city with dreamlike frequency, from an early age Serenata was a self-contained unit, like a portable washing machine on castors whose hoses tuck neatly into the undercarriage. By her teens, she had already become a loner by choice—whereas Valeria's difficulty making friends as a girl had been (or so her mother came to grasp only much later) a source of torment. Serenata had always been a good student, if a particular sort. American public schools simply weren't very demanding, and clearing their preposterously low bars had been effortless; only by college did she develop any idea of what was meant by the expression "studying." Although pedagogical standards for the next generation did nothing but sink further, Valeria had struggled. She was loath to make it known when she didn't understand something, and readily fell behind. But she was quiet, not a troublemaker, thus the kind of educational casualty whom teachers could overlook.

As a girl, Serenata was grateful to her parents for their light touch. If anything, she wished they'd allowed her even longer sessions by herself in her room, where she would experiment with sound effects for her radio plays and try to break her record time for maintaining a headstand. So when raising her own daughter, she tried to be the kind of mother she'd have wanted herself.

Which was a mistake. In the interim, parenting fashion had become hands-on. No one released children into the wild anymore "to play." Parents were expected to get even more upset than their offspring that Marigold Battersby had spurned their kid in Saturday playgroup. So rather than having her mother regard her figure as her own business, perhaps Valeria would have preferred weigh-ins and targets and charts. Treated to a vengeful four-year vanishing act to contemplate her sins, Serenata had finally concluded that what, to her, was freedom, to Valeria was sheer neglect.

It was Valeria's younger brother who grabbed the lion's share of parental attention, for all the wrong reasons. Deacon would have *liked* to be ignored, the better to get up to no good. Contemporary developmental psychology asserted that lying in children was a sign of intelligence, in which case Deacon was a genius. In contrast to his sister's weak sense of self, Deacon knew who he was, all right; he was simply hell-bent on disguising that nature from everyone else. He stole—and once he was caught, it would turn out that he had swiped objects for which he'd have no earthly use: a girl's compact, a CD by a band he disdained, or a teddy bear he was too old for. He preferred the purloining of articles important to people he knew to impersonal shoplifting—which culprits imagined, however errantly, to be victimless—because material covetousness had nothing to do with it. He stole to steal. He liked the sensation. In adolescence he moved on to vandalism, more damage for its own sake. Yet meanwhile he exhibited a glossy politeness that teachers and administrators amazingly bought wholesale. Unable to snow Serenata, he delivered his *and how are you today, Mother dear?* with a tongue-in-cheek sneer. And she learned early on that you did not leave *Deacon* unattended in a room or yard, or you'd pay the price; worse, someone else might. Not that it ended up mattering, but she had watched him fiercely. When one of your children was obedient, subdued, and unassuming, while the other was repeatedly sent to the principal's, expelled, and later arrested, the agent of mayhem would suck up all your time. It was said that life wasn't fair; well, neither were families.

Valeria and Deacon had nothing in common, and as children they weren't close. Upending the conventional birth-order dynamic, their daughter had long seemed afraid of her little brother. Whenever she'd plied him with presents as a girl, these gestures came across as appeasement. More peculiarly, Deacon didn't appear to have much in common with either parent. Oh, he inherited Remington's lanky good looks, but none of the contemplativeness or self-control. And she didn't recognize herself in the boy, either. Where she was solitary, Deacon was secretive, and there was a big difference. Where she was uninterested in the abundance of other people, Deacon seemed to wish humanity at large actively ill, and that was an even bigger difference. By and large, it was genetically baffling how these two people had emerged from such seemingly unrelated parents, and Serenata would never have credited such a family as possible before perplexedly waking up in one.

As for their daughter's recent born-again Christianity, she could solve it like a math problem, but not with any gut comprehension. These now-we-gather-at-the-river movements came with ready-made social sets, and their members weren't choosy. You didn't have to be smart, lively, likable, attractive, or funny; you merely had to "accept Jesus as your Savior." Presumably this cheap fealty was a modest price of admission for a girl who'd felt so ostracized in her school days. Left too much to her own devices, or so it turned out, Valeria had always seemed wobbly. She was given to sudden fancies—salsa dancing, Hello Kitty—which she would rapidly drop, and she always caught an enthusiasm from someone else, like the flu. Later she ducked going to college, if only because she had no idea what she might major in, and by nineteen—oh, how lovely it would be if one's children were to come up with truly novel turns of the wheel, which entertained and astonished—got pregnant instead. As a follow-up to the first mistake, she made the same mistake three years later. People were always harping on parental responsibility; too little was made of parental impotence. You could give your children opportunity, but you could not give them form—which meant that you could not give them what most children craved above all else. Were it possible to purchase for a daughter passion, intention, direction, and specificity—or whatever you called being-somebody-in-particular-ness—Serenata would have rushed off to the Identity Store before Valeria turned ten.

Thus the evangelicals offered what a mother could not: a mold for Valeria's Jell-O. Overnight, lo, a shaky young woman had firm guiding principles and practical rules to live by. Best of all for someone who'd underperformed as a student, had never found a career calling, and had always felt more than a little hard done by, the Jesus brigade bestowed on the convert an arch superiority to all the other benighted heathens who hadn't seen the light—like her parents.

That said, Serenata didn't understand the attraction at all, not really. Signing up to be told what to do, what to think, what to say? What a waste of adulthood.

Exactly what triggered the filial absenteeism was never clear. Some six years ago, she and Remington had been parents in good standing, or so they imagined, when it occurred to them that they hadn't heard from Valeria for a couple of months. A call to her cell established that the number had been recycled, connecting to one Lee Fong, who sounded friendly, but did not speak English. Serenata tried the last landline number they had for her in Buffalo, where their daughter had been part-timing at a nail salon. Out of service. Emails bounced back NO SUCH USER. A newsy postal note to Buffalo boomeranged to their mailbox, and the scrawled "Return to Sender" didn't resemble their daughter's loopy handwriting. The assumption that Valeria would contact them in due course at least to apprise them of her new whereabouts proved mistaken. More months went by. They were on the cusp of reporting her missing when Deacon allowed on yet another visit asking for money that he had heard from her, and that she didn't wish to be found, or not by her parents. He said airily that his sister seemed to have "a bone to pick," and declined to elaborate. He enjoyed the power of the go-between a bit too much. They didn't press him unduly for her contact details. At least Valeria was alive.

Cutting off communication without explanation and whisking away their only two grandchildren struck Serenata as cruel and, if she didn't say so herself, unchristian. But as punishment, the stratagem was savvy. Valeria's disappearance exacted a subtle daily toll even when they weren't thinking about her desertion per se, and before she resurfaced the parental boycott had threatened to be indefinite. Savvier still was devising punishment for an unnamed crime, which cast a Kafkaesque suspicion over the whole of the girl's upbringing. No one had branded the child with a hot iron. So what had they done that was so terrible? Aside from that ambiguous impression of having been insufficiently hovering, Serenata still had no idea. Yet she had put together this much: Valeria wanted them to have done something terrible, and powerfully enough that by now she could well have reverse-engineered her entire familial history.

On a seemingly arbitrary date about two years ago, their daughter called her parents in Albany. Serenata picked up the phone, and though she'd every reason to be angry, the feeling was akin to those arcade games when a treasure teetered on the tip of a hook. She remembered moving superstitiously with no sudden jerks. A stiffness hinting at rehearsal, Valeria explained that she had been in therapy and had found Jesus. After consultation with her doctors and extensive prayer for divine guidance, she had decided to forgive her parents for everything they had done to her. She was strong enough now. Adhering to the tenets of her faith, she planned to turn the other cheek, and to embrace a largeness of heart only made possible by direct communion with Our Lord, because moving on from the past was now in the interest of her "recovery." Valeria could have been speaking Urdu for all the sense this made to her mother, but Serenata was patient and let her talk. It must have been twenty minutes before Valeria mentioned in passing that oh, by the way, she had also married and borne two more children.

Serenata hadn't shared the observation about how curious it was that couples with the largest families were so frequently the very people least capable of supporting them, and she continued to keep the thought to herself—even when the girl got pregnant again eight months later. Ever since Valeria restored herself to them, visits had been permeated by the same poisonous caution that had seized Serenata when Remington announced he was running this dratted marathon. She and her husband seemed to be on probation. Given the provisional texture of renewed relations, she hadn't pushed Valeria to spell out what on earth her parents were meant to have done wrong.

Given these fragile circumstances, when their daughter expressed such startling enthusiasm for the trip to Saratoga Springs, Serenata had encouraged her to come and cheer her father on. Yet Valeria's presence was bound to put further pressure on her mother to be unimpeachably well behaved. Artifice, performance, dissociation, a forced gesturing toward the cardboard cutouts of Wife, Mother, and

Grandmother: the whole package was why she'd had reservations about having a family in the first place.

That Monday, Valeria's minivan pulled to the curb at that awkward time of day, about four p.m., which was too late for an excursion or even lunch, but too early to start on dinner. It left only time to *visit*, not a skill at which Serenata excelled with the most companionable of guests, much less with a churchy child who had a chip on her shoulder. Scuttling down the yard to meet them, she had no idea how they'd get through the next few hours, much less the next week's worth of all that *visiting*. These days politics were out. Inquiries about how the eldest was taking to seventh grade were pointless, since Valeria's children were homeschooled. Once they ran through the weather and the second-to-youngest's psoriasis problem, all that would remain were subjects that would get them into trouble.

She stood back and waved as Valeria took her time messing with seat belts, shouting orders to the children, and unbuckling her baby from the booster in back. Serenata hadn't realized that her daughter was bringing the youngest of her brood, too.

But then, why would she leave behind such effective self-protection? Valeria hefted the seven-month-old onto her substantial hip in the spirit of buckling on a holster and six-shooter. You couldn't criticize a mother with a baby, you couldn't say anything disagreeable around a mother with a baby, and you couldn't ask a mother with a baby any uncomfortable, prying, or challenging questions—for the Madonna beside the Dodge Grand Caravan radiated wholesomeness, sanctity, and self-sacrifice, placing the possessor of the baby above reproach.

Everybody should have one.

"Hey, Mama," Valeria said, avoiding eye contact as her mother, confused about the cheek-or-lips protocol, settled for a poorly landed peck near the girl's left ear. Before her four-year game of hide-and-seek, her parents had been "Mom" and "Dad." The reconciliation onward they'd morphed mysteriously into "Mama" and "Papa," like the rock band. Whatever lay behind the rechristening, it felt as if Valeria had forgotten their names.

"Hey, Gramma." The twelve-year-old flicked her grandmother an anxious glance, hands folded piously over her crotch. From either a private ritual or nervous tic, she repeatedly rose onto the balls of her feet, then brought her heels to ground. It was balmy for springtime in upstate New York, but she looked cold.

"Hi, there, Nancee," Serenata said. "Hi, Logan. It's so nice to see you again!" Nancee was a victim of a nomenclatural fad that celebrated an inability to spell as a manifestation of originality. "So, sweetie, did you have a good trip?"

"Oh, sure." Valeria began fussing out diaper bags, totes, and crackling sacks of road food. Three nearly back-to-back pregnancies had taken their toll; she looked closer to forty-five than thirty-one. "We sang the whole way. Show Gramma how we pass the time, Nancee. Sing Gramma 'Jesus Loves Me.' That's one of your favorites!"

Staring straight ahead, Nancee launched into a tuneless, double-quick rendition absent an ounce of fondness. ". . . LittleonestoHimbelong, theyareweakbutHeisstrong . . ."

To her grandmother's horror, Nancee churned through all five verses, including the refrains—rising on her toes in time to a monotonous, pseudo-Soviet Christian ditty whose melodic line had always seemed slightly menacing in its sheer idiocy, and whose lyrics taught children not only to be indoctrinated automatons, but also to have no self-respect. At least the grisly performance gave Serenata a good look at the girl. Even more so than last time, she looked malnourished. Her coloring was ashen. Her shoulders were narrow and sharp. Her arms and legs were sticks, and at the neck of her clinging polyester muscle-T her breastplate striated like the grille of a Cadillac

Coup DeVille. Just like her mother, who hadn't a sporty bone in her body, the girl was clad in below-the-knee nylon leggings logoed with a Nike swoosh, an open zip-up pastel sweatshirt, and souped-up running shoes—in sum, "athleisure wear," which seemed something of an oxymoron. Her body language was fretful—all Valeria's children had developed a darting hypervigilance—but her eyes shone with a steeliness that Serenata recognized.

By contrast, at nine her brother was soft, with his mother's fleshiness. Logan alone didn't look en route to the gym. He wore shapeless jeans and a corduroy jacket—one of the only coats that Serenata had seen on a child in years that didn't look like you'd conquer Everest in it. Given that modern American kids wore nothing but athletic shoes, he must have looked hard for those leather loafers. Buried in his phone, the boy hunched with a truculence of which she could only approve. One of the inscrutable aspects of these born-again families was why the children so rarely told the parents to shove their Jesus Christ Our Lord and Savior right up the ass.

Remington loped down to help with the luggage as Nancee wrapped up her last *the Bible tells me so-o-o*.

"Papa!" Valeria exclaimed with gusto. "My gracious, you look so strong and slim! I'd hardly know you on the street! Saints be praised, you must have trained like the dickens!"

"Oh, just followed an online program," he said modestly.

"I'm so proud of you! I'm just—so impressed! The kind of inner strength you must have to summon, I can't imagine! I hope you don't take this wrong, Papa, but Lord have mercy, I had no idea you had it in you!"

Clearly, Valeria had not always talked like this. Perky evangelical positivism jumped up her speech with implied exclamation marks and lifted the ends of her sentences with wonder. She had to have been aware that programmatic jubilation drove her parents up the wall.

By the time they schlepped the chattel into the house, coats, shoes, plastic bags, and packs of disposable diapers cluttered every surface, and Serenata wondered why she and Tommy had bothered to tidy up. Valeria made a great show of authority in hectoring the kids to take their luggage upstairs and wash their hands and put their empty glasses in the dishwasher and be sure to thank Gramma for the apple juice and Logan, would you please sit up straight with your shoulders back, now that's better. Don't you dare play with that darned phone when you're a guest in someone else's home, it's impolite. The ceaseless instructions established her total dominion over a fiefdom of three, the stay-at-home parent's standard compensation for commanding so little elsewhere.

"So, Mama, how's the knees?" Valeria asked offhandedly, settling at the dining table with the baby.

"Better some days than others."

"Papa said you had to quit running. Isn't that a shame."

"I can still do high-knees running in place on a swatch of carpet."

"But that's not the same. Not real *running*, is it?"

"No, not exactly."

"I guess you're best off being philosophical. Like, you're starting a whole new chapter—the last chapter. And you kind of brought it on yourself, in a way."

"You mean I deserve it?"

"I mean that God gives us what we need."

"I thought that was Mick Jagger."

Valeria glared. "When you get old, you have to draw on the biblical concept of *grace*. You have to bow out and make room for more energetic people to take your place, right?"

"You're quite the expert on the elderly, for thirty-one."

"Maybe you should think of becoming, you know, *impaired* as an opportunity. To become a better person. You might find out that not being all perfect anymore makes you more sympathetic with other people's foibles, too. My pastor says that when we require forgiveness ourselves, we're more inclined to be forgiving of others."

"Sweetie, I think you should save your forgiveness for someone who really needs it. The best treatment for osteoarthritis isn't clemency, but joint replacement."

"You never ran a marathon, did you? Seems like I'd remember that."

"No, but honestly, my darling?" She patted her daughter's hand. "I don't find never having run twenty-six point two miles at one go especially devastating." Serenata excused herself to look up the router password for Logan in the upstairs study, grateful to escape. Wasn't it children who were supposed to squirm at family get-togethers, to beg to be allowed to go play? As she rounded from the ground-floor hall, Nancee was descending the staircase, only to reach the bottom, pivot, and run back up. "Did you forget something?" her grandmother solicited. Nancee froze on the top landing. "Not really."

To her husband's disgruntlement, Serenata had put their grandson in Remington's workout room, which had a foldout futon; Marathon Man was supposed to be taking it easy in the lead-up to Sunday's race anyway. But hunting the boy down to give him the password, she discovered Logan sitting on the floor in the underfurnished spare room she'd given to Nancee.

"You like this room better? Not that I care."

"Nancee wanted the one with the weights and stuff," he said, entering the password. "Of course."

"Your sister doesn't look as if she lifts a lot of weights."

"Well, she does. And whatever. Toe touches. You name it. Her and Cynthia, the girl next-door, they have this contest, with lists and everything. I think it's dopey. I don't even know how she keeps track of who's winning, 'cause she can't add for beans."

"The fitness shtick—it's not your thing."

"It's boring. You do all this stuff, and after—you haven't earned any money, or learned anything you didn't know before. I don't understand what she gets out of it."

"You'd rather read, or watch TV or something?"

"We're not allowed to watch TV," he said glumly.

"You can't watch TV, but your mom will let you go *online*?"

He finally looked up, taking her measure. "She thinks my phone has parental controls."

"Don't worry. I won't tell."

"It's a cinch to crack. Sometimes it's lucky when people think you're stupid."

"Our secret. I won't tell your mom how smart you are, either."

"Thanks."

Heading heavily back to the *visiting*—damn, it was still only five fifteen—she encountered Nancee again, trotting to the bottom of the stairs, pivoting, and powering back up. Spotting her grandmother on the upper landing, she froze again midflight, as if caught at something naughty.

"You're running stairs," Serenata determined. The girl nodded reluctantly. "I used to run stairs. I *invented* running stairs. When I was in college, my dorm was on the twelfth floor. I never took the elevator. Going back and forth to classes, sometimes I'd run those flights ten times a day. Like climbing the Empire State Building. Later in my twenties, I'd use the emergency exit in my apartment building when it was snowing or something. I worked up to two hundred flights at a time."

"Two hundred?" Nancee repeated with a skeptical squint. Perhaps stair running wasn't very grandmotherly. More likely, even an un-derfed twelve-year-old detested anyone else trumping her personal best.

Downstairs, Remington had joined Valeria at the table—an unfortunate place to convene, because it created an expectation that anytime now they'd be having dinner, which they wouldn't be. There was little enough to look forward to anyway, since Valeria wouldn't *allow* her parents to drink wine in her children's presence—and it was a testament to the delicacy of their relations that her parents let their daughter order them around in their own home. Later everyone would be grateful that they hadn't used up the dither of dinner too early in the evening, thereby leaving a vast desert of *visiting* before bedtime.

"We're a little curious how he makes a living," Remington was saying.

"It floors me, how naive you and Mama can be about Deacon," Valeria said.

"Oh?" Remington said. "I think Deacon has knocked the naivete right out of us."

"Let's put it this way." She checked over her shoulder for kids within earshot, and lowered her voice. "With so many opioid addicts in this country, somebody must be selling them the stuff."

"That's what you presume he does, or what he's told you he does?" Serenata asked, resuming her seat.

"It's obvious," Valeria said. "But I don't expect you to believe me."

"I didn't say I didn't believe you," Serenata said. "It hardly strains credulity, after all."

"No, it doesn't. Because Deacon is damaged. Just like I'm damaged."

Serenata flicked a warning glance at her husband: *don't take the bait.*

"My question is why he's still coming to us for handouts, then," Remington told his wife dryly. "If he has the job Valeria claims— reputedly well remunerated but landing one in a surprisingly low tax bracket."

"I suppose he'd be considered a participant in the 'gig economy,'"

Serenata said. "Unpredictable hours, a notoriously erratic revenue stream, and no health insurance. And we have to consider his high capitalization costs."

"You think what Deacon's up to is *funny*?" Valeria exclaimed. "He's in league with Satan!"

As Valeria drew herself up in offense, shielding the baby, it dawned on Serenata that the urbane back-and-forth that endeared the girl's parents to each other was a prime source of their daughter's antipathy. All this time, she and Remington imagined that their dinner table repartee had charmed their children. Now, *that* was naive.

"I don't find it funny," Serenata said. "But Deacon's default setting is contempt. Selling soul-destroying drugs is just the sort of work that would appeal to someone with disdain for his own customers. I have a horrible feeling he's good at it."

"I've poured out my heart to him on the phone, trying to convince him that God loves all sinners, but only if they repent. He's living in darkness. So are you and Papa. If you'd only humble yourselves before the Lord, and open your hearts, and stop being so smarty-pants, you could know the same boundless joy that I do."

Serenata had learned numbly to ignore the Bible thumping like the dull thud of a drum track leaking through the floorboards from someone else's apartment. If what their daughter was exuding was boundless joy, she'd take despondency, thank you.

"You know, I thought I'd mention," Serenata said, changing course, "though I don't mean to interfere—"

"You just mean to interfere," Valeria said.

"No, but. Don't you worry that Nancee is a little thin?"

"Oh, she's just a picky eater. And she's a real Energizer Bunny. Can't sit still." Valeria bounced the baby on her knee, though the infant didn't seem to be enjoying it. The aggressive nurturing felt pointed: *this* is what good mothering looks like, *Mama*.

"Have you tried protein shakes?" Remington said. "They come in flavors kids would like—strawberry, chocolate, banana."

"Nancee wouldn't come near that. Not if it's marketed for weight gain."

Valeria's responses were inconsistent. But Serenata wasn't going to press the issue. "Jacob is quite a handful, with four other kids to keep track of," she observed politely of the baby. "Do you and Brian imagine that you'll stop at five?"

Valeria examined her mother's face, perhaps for signs of criticism, though Serenata had asked the question as neutrally as she knew how. "If God sees fit to bless us with more precious new lives, the least we can do is welcome His little ones into the world. The size of our family isn't in our hands."

A few packets of contraceptive pills in those hands might do wonders for her daughter's sense of agency, but Serenata held her tongue.

"Isn't it getting a little . . . difficult?" Remington said. "I mean financially."

"Don't you worry, the Lord will provide. He always has."

All five kids were on Medicaid. Brian's parents were "helping," and had bought the Dodge Grand Caravan. Remington had slipped them substantial checks on the previous three visits, claiming jocularly that she'd "missed a lot of Christmases and birthdays" during her *family vacation*. Privately, Serenata had wondered whether what really tipped the scales when their daughter decided to resume contact wasn't so much prayer or therapy as money. So far the Lord had provided precious little.

"You mentioned Brian has been getting some work . . . ?" Remington said.

"He's got a part-time shift at Wal-Mart, but he can't take on any more hours because he needs time for his studies."

"Oh!" Remington said. "I hadn't realized Brian had gone back to school. That's good news! What kind of degree?"

"I mean Bible studies, of course. And then there's our mission. Spreading the gospel. I haven't been able to so much, 'cause of the kids, of course, but also due to my own emotional journey. Which has been super time-consuming and super hard work. Both my therapist and my pastor say I should consider self-healing my full-time job. But that means Brian has to ring twice as many doorbells to pull our weight for the church."

Serenata and Remington locked eyes: our son-in-law is the guy on the porch from whom we hide in the kitchen, careful not to turn on a light or run the coffee grinder.

"So! Papa!" Valeria said, shifting gears. "You've got to tell me about all this training! I'm so excited about Sunday I could bust! You have to explain how you've worked yourself up to the point where you can run a whole *marathon*. You may not realize it, but I bet you're drawing strength from a higher power. Learn to channel that power, like plugging an extension cord into the sky, and it could be like having motors on your shoes! I swear you look ten years younger! Like, how did you start out?"

Remington enthusiastically detailed the progression of distances, the bursts of speed training, the working on his *core*. Serenata sneaked a peak at her watch.

"Sorry," she said quietly, standing. "Lest this conversation wear me out first, I've got to get a little exercise myself."

Valeria's expression curdled. "Typical. Right when we're all getting hungry, and my kids are running on fumes. After a long drive with bad traffic. But never mind, we'll all wait while you hop around. I've already spent enough of my childhood starving and bored to death, waiting for you to finish *exercising*, so what's another two hours."

For once, there was no procrastination, and no dread. Serenata had never been happier to do five hundred sit-ups, and would gladly have done a thousand more.

Getting ready for bed that night, she asked, "So what's on the docket tomorrow?" She'd vowed to act more interested during his last week of training.

Naturally Remington didn't misinterpret the question as regarding what on earth they were going to do with Valeria and the grandkids all day. But his answer—"Forty minutes easy, with four one-minute speed intervals"—was distracted.

"You hail from a pretty prosperous family," he began a minute later as he undressed. "Your father earned the corporate stripes of a successful American man of his generation. Your mother did volunteer work, but that was standard for the 1960s, too. On your own steam, you established yourself, after a mis-start or two, as a recognized voice-over artist, with steady work, producing quality recordings you should be proud of. My father may have hit us, but he was old-school, parents did that back then, and he was always a solid guy who kept up his end of things. Never having taken a dime from the state is a badge of nobility for him, as he must have regaled you more than once; Social Security being his money, he says it doesn't count. Plenty of the buildings he constructed are still standing. My mother typed invoices, and later cleaned fish, coming home reeking every night just to afford clothes for her kids that were clean and new. I was the first in my family to go to college, and bootstrapped myself a full class up, with a career in civil service that should qualify as distinguished, however it ended.

"But our children"—he paused before stepping out of his boxers—"are white trash."

FIVE

They'd planned to drive up to Saratoga Springs late that Friday morning, but the children were fussy eaters. After the preparation and cleanup of multiple breakfasts, Valeria announced it was time for lunch.

Though Serenata had worried how on earth they'd fill the previous three days, this domestic entropy had been the norm every time they committed to an outing—a trip to the Museum of Firefighting (which she imagined Logan would like; he didn't), a boat trip on the Hudson (they missed the last departure), or a tour of the Dr. Oliver Bronson House, with its famous elliptical staircase (restrictive viewing hours required getting out the door at an appointed time: forget it); sadly, the most enjoyable leisure activity in the area, a wine-tasting tour, was out of the question for a devout teetotaler, and even Remington now barely drank. Whenever the baby was changed and fed and bathed, the children were dressed for the weather, and the household's intestines and bladders had been evacuated, it was time to fuel and hydrate once more, the better to shit and pee again. This awful life surely characterized Valeria's days in her own home: frantic with a semblance of activity while running in place—the only kind of running Serenata herself could do now, in intervals, on carpet, bouncing on the balls of her feet, so she was all too familiar with the experience of applying so much onward effort only for the scenery to never change. The one benefit of the visit so far was greater sympathy for her daughter. With still two more of these engines of stasis who sucked the oxygen from their mother like extraction fans, the young woman could hardly be expected to make much progress even on her "super hard" and "super time-consuming" *self-healing*.

Naturally, when Remington had left for the shorter, easier runs prescribed for his final week's training, he attracted nothing but exuberant *Go get 'em, champ!*, while his wife exercised upstairs in secret with the door closed, lest she trigger another burst of Valeria's lifelong resentment. Serenata had foolishly imagined that while the family was here she might also devote a few hours to the Logitech infomercial. Yet folks who didn't work—a cohort, dismayingly, that now included Remington—often found the notion of doing anything other than eat, clean, and shop completely foreign. The one time she'd tried to excuse herself to her studio, she might as well have announced that she was waltzing off for a pedicure. To Valeria, her mother's work was a vanity.

She'd had the same problem writ large when Jacob's birth coincided with recording a tetralogy of fantasy books last August. Typically for the genre, the novels were enormous. The Manhattan studio was booked, the six-week job paid well, and she'd made the commitment before learning that another "precious new life" was on the way. When Serenata explained that she simply could not spend those weeks in Rhode Island relieving the new mother of caring for her *four* other children, Valeria blew up. "Work," whatever that was, didn't count as a viable excuse, especially for the self-employed, who could presumably wedge this frivolous elective activity between loading the dishwasher and brushing their teeth. She accused her mother of being selfish. So on top of recording days long enough that by their end she was losing her voice, Serenata was consigned to feeling like a Bad Grandmother on the dark train rides home—returning, since the Good Grandfather played pinch hitter, to an empty house.

They didn't pile into Valeria's minivan until mid-afternoon, so what should have been a ninety-minute trip was bogged down by Friday commuter and weekender traffic on I-87. A longer drive wouldn't have mattered if it weren't for the consequently more extended torture of Bible songs—"This Little Light of Mine," "He's Got the Whole World in His Hands," and worst of all, "I've Got the Joy, Joy, Joy, Joy Down in My Heart," which the kids sang three times. Touched to have been invited, Tommy was just entering into the spirit of the occasion, but her humming along felt like betrayal. For the relentless *joy, joy, joy, joy*s pounded Serenata's head like a sledgehammer. Surely it was perverse to use the redundancy of your incredible happiness as a bludgeon. Did anyone actually *like* these songs? She'd yet to discern whether Nancee and Logan had been genuinely indoctrinated or were doing a fiendishly well-crafted imitation of having been indoctrinated. She had the same problem parsing vox pops from North Korea.

Saratoga Springs was a wealthy town, lush with mature hardwoods and looming with stately, big-porched nineteenth-century homes, built when the affluent flocked to its spas for the waters. Still heavily dependent on tourism—she and Remington had sometimes celebrated anniversaries here—the town had accrued hefty cultural credentials, with an arts center that housed the New York City Ballet in the summer, theaters, a college prestigious enough that neither of their children would have been admitted had either improbably wanted to apply, and a writers' colony whose implicit pretension made Serenata grateful to have changed careers in her twenties. Broadway, its main drag, was aptly named, with up-market chains housed in sedate red brick. Of course, for most people the place was synonymous with its storied horseracing track. Nancee craned through her open window toward the stables, petulant that the track wouldn't open until July. "Where are the *horses?*"

Lavishing still more limited resources on a normal human activity that in the olden days was free, Serenata had eschewed the budget motels on the edge of town, which might have risked the appearance of an under-ardent attitude, instead booking three rooms at the Saratoga Hilton on Broadway. A private plus: it had a fitness suite.

The lobby was a sea of sportswear. The majority of contestants wouldn't arrive until tomorrow, so this was just the beginning.

As Serenata waited to check in while the others circled for a place to park, the woman behind her in the unexpectedly long line asked, "You do have reservations, right?" Affirmative. "Because they've increased the number of runners admitted this year to five thousand. I think it's cynical—more admission fees, and of course the town is greedy for all the extra tourists. Since so many entrants show up with a whole entourage, the pressure on hotel rooms is intense. Oh, I'm sorry," she apologized. "I'm just assuming—you are one of the marathoners, aren't you?"

"No," Serenata said.

"Well, gosh—I hope you take it as a compliment, then—it's just, you look like one. I mean, like a real runner. Not one of the plodders."

Serenata was both flattered and depressed. "Plodders?" she asked blankly.

The woman lowered her voice. "The dregs at the back. Also known as the run-walk crowd. Emphasis on walk. The charity and novelty acts are bad enough. But nowadays, all these"—she lowered her voice further—"fat, out-of-shape bucket-list box-tickers take seven or eight hours to finish, and still claim afterward they've 'run a marathon.' We're talking, like, a *twenty-minute* mile. Holy crap, in Honolulu, which has no time limit whatsoever, the plodders take a break for lunch. They cheapen what completing this distance means. Sorry, that's just me. I guess my outlook isn't very democratic. Maybe there's a thin line between being in the *elite* and being an *elitist.*"

Indeed, the woman had a look that had grown recognizable. Clad in Lycra and an unzipped fleece, she was stringy and weathered with cropped hair. She had a small cave under the center of her rib cage, where even trim postmenopausal women usually gathered flesh. Much like Nancee, she couldn't stand still, lifting one Adidas and then the other, shaking each leg out. At least fifty-five, she doubtless imagined that she didn't look anywhere near that old, though her bony, sinuous frame advertised every year. Alas, you couldn't think such a thing about another woman at Serenata's age without its boomeranging back in your face. Serenata didn't imagine she looked sixty, either.

"I'm surprised this race has grown so big," Serenata said, pushing herself to be sociable. "This is a minor event. Nothing like New York or Boston."

"It used to be if you wanted to pull in tourists you'd found a literary festival. Now every dot on the map sponsors a marathon. Draws much bigger crowds. Whatever limit Saratoga puts on registration, they'll still be turning contestants away. The lesser races are popular with the wannabes, because they don't require a qualifying time."

"You do a lot of these?" The interest was feigned.

"Best thing about marathons popping up everywhere is I can pretty much go from race to race year-round. I hit the Florida, Arizona, and California ones over the winter. I always enter the lottery for London, but no luck so far. The odds are against you. Only forty thousand are allowed in, and two hundred fifty thousand apply."

"Seriously?" Serenata said. "A *quarter of a million people* apply to run the London marathon."

"Goes up every year," the woman said glumly.

Serenata nodded at reception. "Doesn't your circuit get expensive?"

"You sound like my kids. But I'm not about to lie in bed with cats, just so they can get an inheritance. They seem to forget it's still my money. When I was first talking myself into this, I realized that *I'd* forgotten it was my money. What else is early retirement good for? I'm not into bingo."

"But what about injuries?"

Her smile was tight and grim. "How long have you got? Hey, you're up."

Once the others arrived and got settled, Serenata slipped off to the fitness suite before dinner, but the place was mobbed. There were lines for all the machines, with a scrawled waiting list taped to every stationary bicycle. The scene was repulsive. Resigning herself to a few calisthenics in front of CNN, she took the stairs back up to their room, and even on the staircase, commonly deserted in hotels save for the odd cleaner, she had to thread between guests hurtling themselves up and down.

Serenata had outdone herself in the service of appearing to outdo herself. Dinner reservations tomorrow night were considerably early, that Remington might have no trouble hitting the hay by eight thirty, the better to arrive at the race in advance of a seven thirty a.m. starting gun. Their mattress was bigger than some hotel swimming pools, so she shouldn't wake him creeping into bed later that evening. Tomorrow was a rest day, and he planned to drive Valeria's minivan around the course that morning to familiarize himself with any "challenging topography" before the roads were closed to traffic. For the afternoon, she'd booked him into the Roosevelt Spa for a mineral bath and massage.

While Remington was being worked over, she'd also treat Valeria to a Detoxifying Algae Wrap and Arctic Berry Illuminating Facial at the same facility (the anti-cellulite option seemed impolitic). The spa treatments alone would come to over $700, though at least the fact that Serenata secretly considered all these pawings and unguents a load of hooey meant she wouldn't further inflate the bill by steeping in seaweed herself. The real present to Valeria was volunteering to take care of the children while the young woman was being what passed for pampered for three solid hours. Were Valeria anything like her mother, she'd find the hands of strangers prodding all over her body not just a little strange but invasive. But she wouldn't dare to say so. Women were programmed to regard facials, massages, and soaks as the acme of indulgence, and Valeria hadn't the originality to trust her disappointment.

Prudently well in advance, given that apparently up to *five thousand* other parties could be prowling downtown for a festive venue, for the end of the Big Day she'd made reservations for a blowout at 15 Church, where she and Remington had dined for their thirtieth wedding anniversary; should her husband's performance on Sunday prove ignominious, she could always cancel. The restaurant was pricey, and Buttermilk Crispy Oysters with ponzu and foie gras butter was bound to be wasted on the kids. But the trappings of jubilance routinely stood in for jubilance itself. Rare was the bash that better than gestured toward celebration, a sensation so taxing to inhabit in the present that most honorific occasions only truly happened after the fact, when the laureate gazed fondly at photographs. On the other hand, Serenata might be feeling jovial at that. This clubby bunkum would be over, and she and her husband could go home in every sense.

Yet for all her loyal wifery, Remington announced quietly while getting ready for bed on Friday night, "You're not fooling anyone, you know." He declined to explain, because he didn't have to.

While Remington was driving a course that would take an hour even in a car, Serenata had a late, leisurely breakfast in the hotel dining room with Tommy, whom she'd put in a double with Nancee. The two seemed to have something in common—which proved the problem.

"Crunches," Tommy despaired over toast. "Raises, planks, and lifts. Plus a lot of goofy twirling and leaping things I think she made up. It's like sharing a room with Hurricane Sandy. I said I was heading out after dinner last night to rack up some steps, but I really hit the halls just to get away from her."

"Isn't 'racking up some steps' on the same continuum? What's the difference?"

"You know how it works. Anyone who does less exercise than you is pathetic, and anyone who does more than you is a nut."

"So Nancee's a nut."

"She's an exercise bulimic."

"Have you caught her throwing up?" Serenata asked sharply.

"I mean she pukes energy."

"She looks ill to me."

"She doesn't eat enough to build any muscle. So all the jumping up and down doesn't accomplish anything."

"And what does all your Fitbitting accomplish?"

"Watch it. You're the one who claims everyone's *copying* you. What did being a fitness fanatic for fifty years 'accomplish'?"

Serenata added a contemplative smear of butter to a miniature cranberry muffin. "When I was younger, I was testing myself. Setting goals and exceeding them. The trouble is, you can't keep beating yourself indefinitely."

"Like Fitbit," Tommy said. "Once you've ever done thirty thousand steps in a day, any less steps—"

"*Fewer*," Serenata said.

Tommy glared. "Any *fewer* seems kind of sad."

"Personal bests are a tyranny. Run ten miles, and tomorrow you have to run eleven, or the ten even faster. The problem may apply to more than just athletics."

"Obviously the answer is to stay really shit at everything."

Serenata laughed. "Maybe. But trying to surpass yourself, you'll always approach a limit. Of what your body is capable of, but also of how much you care."

"Yeah, I'm running into that with the Fitbit, too," Tommy said. "I mean, it's just a game, in case you thought I actually take it seriously. I want to beat Marley Wilson. But I'm starting to, like, slightly not give a shit, 'cause of what you said. The limit thing. And once you start coming up against the limit, it stops being interesting."

"And that's assuming it ever was."

"You know, I still don't totally understand why you don't want Remington to run. It seems kind of mean."

"I don't really care if he runs by himself. It's this mass goat fuck I can't stand."

"Shut *up*," Tommy whispered, gesturing at the other diners. "You're being *inappropriate*. Pissing on marathons, and not being 'supportive' of anyone who wants to run one—I can't hardly think of anything more uncool. It's like, almost worse than being a racist or something."

"Thanks for the tip."

"You've no idea what it's like online right now. People post how much weight they're pressing, how many squats they do, how low their heart rate is. There's all these Instagram glam shots of girls with six-packs all greased up and tensed in running bras. The standards keep going up, too, what counts as really 'fit.' What seemed awesome last year now gets dissed as totally lame. It's one thing to get so you can't beat yourself anymore, like you said. But it's way worse to get beaten by everyone else."

"A lot of those online posts must be exaggerated."

"Maybe. But some of these guys really do spend all day, every day, in the gym. All I've got is our backyard. You and Griff will have to get a whole lot filthier if I'm going to spring for a hundred twenty-five dollars a month at BruteBody year-round."

"Is that really the best use of your savings?"

"Without those machines, I can't keep up. Last year, my friend Anastasia celebrated her eighteenth birthday at BruteBody. The 'party' was a bunch of unbelievably hard and complicated boot-camp routines to techno-rap. They all kept an eye out for anyone who couldn't keep up so they could razz you later. There wasn't even any cake. The main event was a contest: who could skip rope the longest without messing up. I did okay, but I didn't win. *You*, though," Tommy charged. "*You* feel superior to everybody."

"I do not! I want to have nothing to do with most people. That doesn't mean I feel superior to them."

"Liar. It's obvious, just in the way you stand. All tall and straight and a little pulled back, and then when people are around you don't like, you don't talk very much, and I can tell what you're thinking."

"Do you think I feel superior to you?"

"Well . . . I don't like it when you correct my grammar and stuff."

"I'm only trying to help you. Do you want me to stop?"

Tommy folded her arms and thought about it. "Nah. I mean, it's irritating, but at least you care. Nobody else listens to me. When you go all schoolteacher, I know you're paying attention."

Pious yogurts on all sides drove Serenata to fetch a second muffin.

"You know, over time," she said on return, examining the baked good critically, "the reasons I exercise have changed. At your age, sure, I wanted to be attractive—and strong, not just thin. But for years now . . . That daily routine has been mostly about maintaining a sense of *order*. Order and control. I do it because I've always done it. I'm completely convinced that if I ever stop exercising, everything else in my life will fall apart. Instantaneously. And disastrously."

"What, like you'd become an alcoholic heroin addict—on welfare, who smokes?"

"And shoplifts. And steals from charity piggybanks at checkout."

"Maybe you should try quitting, then," Tommy said with a grin. "Sounds like you'd finally have some fun."

They dined that evening at the barbaric hour of five thirty. Valeria made such a fuss over her father's order for his "last supper"—"carb loading" being out of fashion—that her mother finally interrupted, "Sweetie—he's not about to be executed."

When she returned to the room after a mutinous nightcap—at the teetotal dinner, the confining rectitudes of Jesus and fitness freakery had overlapped—Remington was abed but restive. She recognized his frequent glances at the clock from the latter days at the DOT, when he worried about getting to work on time, but also about what would happen when he got there. Only when she smoothed against his back, kissed his neck, and wrapped an arm around his chest did he quiet. They'd always been a good fit. Although the cleaner lines of his leaner frame the last few months were pleasing to the eye, he'd been wiry to begin with, and his naked body at rest felt comfortingly unchanged. An alarm set for five a.m. seemed extreme, but this one time, she thought, dropping off, she wouldn't mind getting up with him out of solidarity.

Wrong.

With psychic violence, the alarm rang during her deepest slumber. Until this moment, the weekend had exhibited the indolence of a getaway, so why was she stumbling for the bathroom light switch when it was pitch-dark? What shocked her fully awake was a burst of rage. This whole undertaking was stupid. She'd been pretending for months that it wasn't stupid, and now that she had to keep pretending just one more day she wasn't going to make it. Her pose of taking this circus seriously, or at least of tolerating it until her husband's groupster infatuation went the way of the Hula-Hoop, had fatally, as they said in the marathon biz, hit a wall.

While Remington stuck moleskin to the parts of his feet that chafed, she found Tommy already stalking the hallway, dressed and ready to roll. Not to be outdone, Nancee was close on her heels, hopping behind her on one foot.

"Twenty-two hundred steps!" Tommy said, raising the hand with the aqua strap. "Now, that's what I call getting a jump on the day." Bright-eyed and bushy-tailed, the young woman seemed not the least irked by the savagery of the hour.

Yet despite all their daughter's previous gung ho go-Papa, in the room down the hall Valeria responded neither to a decorous tap-tap nor, at first, to full-tilt pounding on the door. Slit-eyed and tousled, she finally appeared in a waffled hotel robe. "Jesus, Mom, it's the fucking middle of the night!" She forgot that she never took the Lord's name in vain. She forgot that she now said "Mama." She forgot that she didn't curse. If Valeria got up at the crack of dawn more often, they might get on.

Serenata borrowed the minivan keys and promised to drive back later to pick up the slugabeds. Given Remington's pace, his daughter and grandkids wouldn't miss his crossing the finish line if they slept in till eleven and ordered the eggs Benedict.

Other parties were gnawing energy bars in the lobby; the hotel dining room was closed. Kitted out in the green and purple nylon in which he had initiated this six-month fool's errand, Remington was swinging his personalized goodie bag: bananas, energy gels the colors of plastic toys, Red Bull, and something called "chews." But Serenata wanted *coffee*, thank you, and all the cafés down Broadway would be closed, too.

"You could be a *little* more cheerful," Remington said on their way to the van.

"At this time of day? I'd settle for civil if I were you."

The grounds of the Performing Arts Center in Spa Park were humming when they arrived at six. Peppy staff wore hot-pink T-shirts proclaiming SARATOGA SPRINGS GIVES YOU A RUN FOR YOUR MONEY! Remington reverently pinned his black-and-white race number, 3,788, to his shirt, and snapped on the chipped ankle bracelet that would record his time to the hundredth of a second when (and if) he finished. The spectators and contestants rapidly thickened.

Serenata reviled crowds. Furthermore, the world record for this distance was about two hours, and this event had a cutoff of eight hours. There was no earthly reason to begin the race at seven thirty a.m. They could have released the first group of men, eighteen to twenty-four, at noon, in which case she'd be well rested and fortified by cranberry muffins.

The up-and-at-'em start time was all for show. For humanity divided into mutually hostile camps: bounders out of bed and burners of the midnight oil. The distinction went way beyond schedule. The late nighter was synonymous with mischief, imagination, rebellion, transgression, anarchy, and excess, not to mention drugs, alcohol, and sex. The early riser evoked traditional Protestant values like obedience, industry, discipline, and thrift, but also, in this gladness to greet the day, a militant, even fascistic determination to look on the bright side. In short, rise-and-shiners were revolting, and being flapped by so many birds getting the worm felt like getting trapped in an Alfred Hitchcock remake. These bouncy, boisterous, bubbly people loved their seven thirty start, which shouted earnestness and asceticism, and any attempt to move the time to noon for next year would trigger a riot.

Mercifully, as the sky lightened refreshment stands were opening, so Serenata bought the two girls doughnuts and herself coffee. It was weak and tasted like dirt, but coffee in the morning was as much idea as beverage—an idea of normalcy and entitlement—so the cardboard cup settled her mood from fuming to surly. When a younger booster jostled the coffee onto Serenata's shirt, instead of apologizing the woman shot her a smile of manic benevolence. "Isn't this *exciting*?"

"Why," Serenata said flatly. "Why is this exciting."

"Wow, you've really got to work on your attitude," she huffed, and flounced off.

As Serenata threaded with Remington toward the flag under which his age group was gathering, a distinctive subsection of the over-the-hill contestants began to exert a queasy fascination. All men in their seventies and eighties, they were lean to the point of desiccation, with limbs like beef jerky. They went shirtless, despite the morning's chill. In April, they were tanned. Their eyes burned with mission. They did stretches with the self-conscious air of feeling observed. Their watches were flashy: erstwhile professionals or CEOs, then, climbing yet another ladder in retirement. She caught snippets of their conversation, which were all of a piece: "Under five, if there's a God"; "Break the nine-minute mile, I'll sleep sound tonight"; "Finished four twenty-two eighteen in New York, but that race has become such a free-for-all . . ." The wizened immortals cut only side-glances at each other, in that reluctance to quite take in the full person that marks the highly competitive. Should he really catch the bug, was this a snapshot of Remington's future? Because the geriatric elite had one more trait in common: as company, they'd be unbearable.

Several hundred young men had now assembled behind the starting line. After a welcome speech from a town functionary, the gun went off at seven thirty precisely. The spectators roared, screaming and waving placards (WE BELIEVE IN LEONARD!). The men surged forward in a mass, filling the roadway from the Arts Center to its edges like corpuscles in a vein. If she didn't find the spectacle uplifting, she had to concede, however sullenly, that at least these eager-beaver entrants weren't hurting anybody.

More to the point, Remington wasn't hurting anybody, including her. He'd worked hard for this, and in the context of a rough couple of years. This event mattered to him, and it wasn't her business to decide for him what should and shouldn't matter. Although he sure knew how to pick his spots, it wasn't his fault that she'd ruined her knees. So when at 8:40 men sixty to sixty-four were summoned on the loudspeaker, she placed a hand on each cheek and looked him in the eye. The little wryness in her delivery would certify the sentiment was sincere: "Go get 'em, champ!"

This wasn't mere going through the motions of "supportiveness," and to show he knew the difference he embraced her for longer than he could afford, because the age-group starting times were strict. Good grief. When had she last been tender? He must have been starving.

Scanning for her charges, Serenata spotted Tommy dragging Nancee harshly by the wrist. "She keeps trying to join the pack," Tommy said when they met up. "Then the other spectators think it's so *cute*. I've told her and told her, she's only here to watch."

"Look at all those moldy oldies!" Nancee whined. "If they can make it, I could, too, no problem!"

"You have to pay an entry fee," Serenata said. "And be over eighteen."

"That's not fair! I'm way faster than them fuddy-duddies. Let me go, and I'll show you!"

"Nancee, sweetheart. I'm sure you're one of the fastest in your neighborhood—"

"Not only fast! I can run a really, really long time! A lot longer than *you*."

At this point, the girl's claim was horribly true.

When Serenata drove the girls back to the hotel just after ten, Valeria, Logan, and the baby were breakfasting in the dining room.

"See, Mama," Valeria said, "you can download this app, enter Papa's registration number, and follow exactly where he is in the race!"

The course on the app cut a long straight diagonal on Ballston Avenue, whose scenery over eleven miles Remington had described as "abusively monotonous." The return journey described two peaks—up Goode Street, right on Charlton, left onto Middleline, and right on Geyser for the final four miles back to Spa Park: a shocking length of public roadway to close to traffic for a self-regarding middle-class pastime.

"Oh, wow!" Valeria said. "They've just declared the winner!"

"Who gives a crap," Logan muttered.

"Golly," Valeria said. "Our number three-seven-eight-eight has twenty miles to go. Good news, actually. We've plenty of time to visit the house of the Lord, kiddoes."

The reaction of the two older children was impassive. They didn't squirm, or kick the table in frustration, or even glower. Fascinating.

"Papa is running for the glory of God, whether he realizes it or not," she regaled her mother. "This is the perfect day for you to raise your face to the light. Why don't you join us? You never know what might happen."

"I have a pretty good idea," Serenata said. "But after the service, you could use the app to find intersections where you can cheer your father on. He'd like that."

"Won't you want to cheer by the roadside, too?"

"I think I'll save my enthusiasm for the finish line."

"What enthusiasm?" Valeria said sourly.

"What about you?" Serenata asked Tommy, once the family had bustled off to some happy-clappy revivalist hootenanny. "Want to plant yourself along the course and yell 'Go, Remy, baby!'?"

"Honest?" Tommy said. "Standing around watching other people exercise. Not my idea of a good time."

"Let's see . . ." Serenata tapped the calculator. "Even if he keeps averaging a twelve-minute mile, Remington won't finish for another four hours. Since my husband is sacrificing himself for our sins, I don't see why we shouldn't enjoy ourselves."

Surely she was intent on a rigorous workout, too, to prove she was still a contender? Au contraire. From a funny little belligerence arose an ease, a lightness, a liberation. She'd fit in calisthenics in front of *Frasier* the two days previous, and couldn't remember the last time she'd taken an exercise day off. Today? She'd take a day off.

For her very awareness that Remington was at that moment thudding down Ballston—straining to slow his breathing, using the runner in front to maintain a pace with which he wasn't quite comfortable, and panicking that the first right turn was still nowhere in sight—inspired his wife to extend across her chair, arms draped languidly to either side. She'd rarely so inhabited a state of repose. Why, she felt like a movie star. Everything seemed so terribly pleasant.

On Sundays, brunch lasted till one p.m. So many hotel guests were running or watching the race that the bountiful buffet was barely touched. Serenata floated to the long white table and assembled an alluring plate: brioche with a loll of smoked salmon. A wedge of honeydew topped with three fresh raspberries. A perfectly fried piece of bacon—not flabby, but with a droop to it. A miniature lemon tart with a garnish of fresh mint. She and Tommy ordered more coffee, which was fresh and strong and hot and didn't taste like dirt. Every tidbit was delectable. They went back for seconds.

In the main, Serenata hewed to a sartorial formula: dark leggings or black jeans, scoop-necked tops in muted solids, black ankle boots, and a timeless leather jacket; Remington said she dressed like one of those thriller heroines who were experts at kickboxing. So she seldom shopped for clothes. Yet today the quotidian diversion presented itself as positively heady. Leading Tommy down Broadway, she assumed a long idle saunter that made simply walking feel as sumptuous and silky as that smoked salmon. The air on her cheeks was bracing, yet not so cold that she tightened against the chill. At the hoary old age of sixty-one, she passed a fellow arranging a sidewalk table of horseracing souvenirs and turned his head. The knees were taking one of their capricious timeouts from torture. Fingertips resting lightly on the navy leggings, she followed the undulation of her thigh muscles. Funny, she'd spent so much of her life working her body, pushing it, punishing it, but far too little just hanging out in it.

Tommy looked at her companion askance. "Why do you look so happy? I thought the marathon would put you in a bad mood. But you seem almost drunk."

"Turn it off."

"What?"

"The Fitbit. Turn it off."

Consternated, Tommy came to a halt. "Why?"

"Do as I say. Then we're headed for that boutique, and we'll find you some killer gear." She wouldn't proceed until the aqua wristband went *bee-beep*.

At first anxious about accepting her neighbor's largesse, Tommy soon plunged into the spirit of their spree. Together they found her a lined, sleeveless dress in white cotton; the draping at the dropped waist smoothed over the gawkiness of the girl's frame. Serenata located a soft, flannelly floor-length garment in light blue denim with long sleeves and pearled snaps—the ideal weight for the midday breeze, and a stunning accompaniment for the dress. Short, blond leather boots completed the look. For herself, she found a long black rayon wrap with trench-coat styling and the same slither she looked for in shirts. "Lord," she declared to the mirror. "All I need is a revolver."

Instead, she bought a cocky black fedora. Tommy was more suited to a sun hat in straw with a thin ribbon that uncannily matched the denim. Blues, Serenata informed her charge with authority, were prone to clash.

There was lunch. Suffice it to say that the arugula salad with shaved Parmesan and a side of tomato bruschetta improved on Remington's *chews*.

"What I want to know is . . ." The new outfit imparting a fresh sophistication, Tommy wielded her slender breadstick like a cigarette holder. "Are you faking?"

"Faking not being jealous and miserable? What do you think?"

Tommy poked the breadstick in the olive caponata as if extinguishing an ash. "If it's an act, it's darned well done."

"I don't see why I'd be jealous of my husband huffing the streets of Saratoga when we're having such a charming time. How's the intrepid doing, anyway?"

"Huh," Tommy said, checking her phone. "He's slowed down. He still has ten, eleven more miles to go. Don't take this wrong, but his time kind of sucks."

Serenata stretched. "Why don't we go back to the hotel for a swim?"

"That seems like backsliding. More exercise. You're taking the day off."

"I don't want to exercise. I just want to be in water."

Once they met back up at the deserted indoor pool, Serenata descended its steps slowly, taking time to acclimatize. Ordinarily, she'd immediately start swimming laps. Why, in her adulthood, she couldn't recall *ever* gliding serenely into water for the sake of the sensation alone. Floating on her back with her eyes closed. Slipping below the surface, touching the drain, and dolphining to air. Parting the water with a few expansive breaststrokes not to meet a stringent private requirement, but to feel the pressure against her cupped hands, the ripple across her neck.

Yet Tommy lingered at the shallow end. For pity's sake, no one had ever taught her to swim. For their last twenty minutes, Serenata supported the girl's torso in place so she could practice breathing for the crawl. Should the usual edict to complete a mile or two have prevailed, she'd never have made time for the lesson.

After a long hot shower upstairs, she hastily toweled her hair, slid into the flowing rayon trench coat, and bunched the damp hair under the fedora. She and Tommy would be the only spectators at the finish line who weren't clad in sympathetic athletic apparel. At 3:20 p.m., she reconnoitered with Tommy in the lobby and called Valeria.

"You're cutting it awful close," her daughter snarled.

"Not especially. According to Tommy's app, Remington won't approach the finish line until after four. I thought you might pick us up, and we can watch together. Have you been able to cheer him on at various points?"

"It's been a little trying, to be honest. Constantly finding a place to park. Changing and feeding Jacob in the backseat. And then Nancee keeps *walking* alongside Papa at the same speed, and I'm afraid she's been demoralizing. Also, at our last vantage point, there was some woman . . ." Valeria trailed off.

"We'll be at the back entrance, by the parking lot."

When the harried young woman pulled up in the minivan, she shot a malignant glance at her mother, who looked svelte, stylish, and refreshed: the very picture of what three hours of spa treatments the day before had failed to do for Valeria. Logan announced grumpily from the back, "This is the boring-est day ever. When I grow up, I'm never gonna stand around clapping just 'cause a bunch a people went *jogging*. My hands hurt. When anybody claps for *me*, it's gonna be 'cause I actually did something."

"Grampa is totally slow," Nancee said. "I coulda run that course three times by now. It's embarrassing. Tons of the other oldies finished hours ago."

"Now, honey," Valeria said. "Remember 'The Tortoise and the Hare.'"

"But 'slow and steady' *doesn't* win the race," Nancee said. "Some other guy won it, and Grampa's practically last. Besides, that story is dumb. Everybody knows the rabbit is way faster, and no one really wants to be the crummy turtle."

They'd no trouble parking at the Arts Center. Most runners and their retinues had cleared off by early afternoon. The crowd was so sparse that their party could stand right by the finish line. The grounds were littered with confetti, burst balloons, and discarded noisemakers. Committed to every finisher's enjoying a salute, a small, dedicated group of staff in pink T-shirts was positioned beside the banner. Whenever a laggard approached, this volunteer cheering section punched the air screaming, "Way to go!" or "Only a few more feet, man!" or "Earned your brewskie tonight, bro!" The limited selection of encouragements was regularly recycled. Each time another marathoner crossed the line, running 26.2 miles seemed a little less amazing.

At this tail end of the field, many participants were running for charity in costumes. Amid the commercial Batman and Underdog outfits tottered homemade creations: a papier-mâché Eiffel Tower, a possum, a human calculator, and a giant slice of cheese. Between them wove the power walkers, chins high, elbows out.

At 4:10 p.m. Remington was advancing on the home stretch. A time of about 7:25 translated into an average mile of 19:30—which was appalling. Serenata mulled over what to say to buck him up, and to ensure he'd accept his role as guest of honor tonight at 15 Church. She'd hate to cancel the reservation. After six months of training, he deserved better than a room-service ham sandwich.

If she wished for his sake that his time were a little better, she was genuinely astonished that he was completing the course at any speed. Nevertheless, she relished the prospect of the months ahead, during which he'd grow gradually less touchy about the whole fandango, until they could laugh and roll around on the bed and remember this weird period of their marriage, and at last he'd ruefully admit that, as for endurance sport, well, okay, right—he wasn't very good at it.

"There he is!" Valeria cried, spotting the wilted purple and green kit. "Go, Papa! You can do it! Jesus loves you, whether you know it or not! Glory be! You show 'em! Go for it! You're almost home! Go, go, go! Yay! Yay, Papa! Rah, rah, rah!"

Her daughter carried the gene that Serenata lacked. Perhaps it skipped a generation: this mystifying capacity for getting swept up in the fervor of crowds. For once resisting the urge to disparage the girl as "a joiner," instead she found Valeria's rare display of filial loyalty rather sweet.

Not wishing to be ungracious, Serenata brought her hands together *pat-pat-pat* whenever another "plodder" completed the course. Yet as Remington began his last hundred yards, her bellowing of bolstering slogans would have seemed fake. So she dropped her hands and settled on a smile. It was a warm smile, a private smile—a smile of truce, of quiet apology for having been a bit of a dick, and women could be dicks; a smile of welcome and congratulation and restoration of whatever in the last six months had been put out of whack. It was the smile of a wife.

Yet Remington's expression was neither haggard nor infused with desperate gratitude that the ordeal was almost over. He looked *rapt*. Rather than scan the straggle of spectators for his spouse, he gazed to the left, nodded, spoke quietly, and chuckled. Even when she shouted, "Remington!" he didn't turn toward her voice.

Stung, Serenata dropped the smile. That competitor alongside was not overtaking as she'd first imagined, but conversing in conspiratorial tones with her husband. The fact that Remington's running mate was matching his tortoise-like pace was odd, because this woman was a hare. Perhaps in her late thirties, she had the kind of figure used to sell gym memberships—the kind of figure that no one had really, that would have appeared in advertisements for CrossFit only after having been doctored. Banded with fine intersecting lines, her body recalled the diagrams of human musculature in anatomy textbooks. She looked flayed.

The shoulders were broad and cut. Her forearms were veined. Bandaged by a lavender sports bra, her breasts were tight and high. Her stomach was flat, and shadowed by the telltale ripple of a crunch fanatic. The shorts were skimpy enough that if she didn't shave her bikini line everyone would have noticed. Narrow knees and ankles punctuated dense thighs and full calves. Dancing at Remington's side on the balls of her feet, she made running three miles per hour appear balletic. Her cropped sandy hair gleamed with fashionable gray highlights, and its smart styling looked salon-fresh. Maybe her neck was a tad thick, and on the short side. Still, face it: she was *pretty*.

Serenata returned to pallid clapping. As Remington and his new little friend crossed the finish line, the two high-fived. Clutching him in a bear hug, the anatomy illustration rocked from shoe to shoe. Here Serenata had worried he'd be gutted by his poor show-ing. Instead he acted elated. He embraced Valeria, then Tommy. He accepted his grandson's lackluster handshake. He lifted Nancee overhead. He kissed the baby. It was humiliating to have to stand in a receiving line at all, much less last.

"Congratulations," she said formally, and pecked his cheek.

"Thanks," he said airily. "Serenata, this is Bambi Buffer. I don't think I'd have made the last five miles without her."

"Bambi" biffed his shoulder. "Oh, sure you would have." Her voice was throaty, deep with a rough edge, and Remington's weak-ness was aural; Serenata should know. "I keep telling you, man, you got the stuff!" If she spared the wife so much as a nod, it was the sort you gave to ancillary characters who simply weren't going to feature.

There was no question about keeping the restaurant reservation. They all piled into Valeria's minivan—including "Bambi," who was staying in the same hotel, and whom Remington had invited to join them for dinner.

With little ado upstairs, Remington showered and set an alarm.

"You're not saying much," Serenata noted. All her earlier grace and élan had fled.

"It's not a day for talk," he said on the bed with his eyes closed.

It was sure a "day for talk" with that "Bambi" woman.

He slept like a corpse until seven fifteen, awaking invigorated. He dressed in a dark suit and crisp white shirt with an open collar. She couldn't remember ever before having rued the fact that her hus-band was still, at nearly sixty-five, an attractive man.

When a large party is getting seated for a meal, one enjoys a brief window in which to position one's self next to the people one actually wishes to talk to, and Serenata missed it. She landed without design on a corner, a chair removed from Remington. The chair had Bambi in it.

In a clinging cherry-red sheath whose high neck disguised her only aesthetic shortcoming, the gate-crasher knew how to wear her body. Because that's what she was wearing, her body. The dress was an afterthought. If anything, it was wearing her.

"I'm surprised you were pulling up the rear today," Serenata said, trying furiously to avoid overt reference to the woman's physique.

"Oh, that was my second time around," Bambi said, perusing the appetizers. "I often do an extra lap, to spur on any newbies who seem to be struggling."

Now a marathon was a "lap." "That's altruistic."

"Mm, not totally. Hey, Rem. You been here before. How do you rate the oysters?"

Their guest ordered heavily—more than one first course and multiple sides. The contemporary female being famously fearful of food, hunger was seductive in a woman; if nothing else, the appetite hinted at other kinds. Bambi's eyes proved the equal of her stomach, too. She inhaled every dish set before her, and single-handedly ravaged the breadbasket. Table manners weren't her forte. She ate like a fucking animal.

"Tried to tell you, dude," she held forth to Remington while stripping frogs' legs. "Your big mistake was training for that race by yourself. I've seen it a million-bazillion times: harness the energy of other athletes believing in you, and rooting for you, and helping to bring out your best self, your true self, your *über* self—the God inside every damn one of us—and performance improves by, I ain't kidding, a hundred percent." Bambi's folksy pronunciation— "*hunerd* percent"— didn't seem to hail from a regional dialect, for which Serenata had an ear. Rootlessly eclectic, the vernacular conveyed a generically down-home, tell-it-like-it-is toughness.

"I really respond to that idea of everybody having a little kernel of God in them somewhere," Valeria said. "That speck of the divine is what links us up with God Himself—like a sim card connecting with a satellite."

"If people thrive athletically in social contexts," Serenata said, "don't you just mean they respond to competition?"

"That's a poisonously negative way of putting it," Bambi said. "I'm talking about the giganto power of the many over the pissy power of the one. Rem, you gotta try one a these. I'll trade you for a scallop."

"I didn't think about it at the time, that I was training on my own." Remington piled pancetta and truffle shavings onto the gifted sea scallop. "I may have been unwittingly influenced by Serenata. My wife doesn't believe in group participation, do you, my dear? Marathons, for example," he cited mischievously, "disgust her."

"Your loss, honey." Bambi forked the plump scallop in one bite. "See, Rem, you've shut yourself off from the *community* of other athletes, and that's put you at a disadvantage. Place yourself in the middle of the whole movement, and you can feed off an awesome force, like, a whole collective consciousness. 'Sides which, like I told you after we eased you past that wall you hit, in the end this isn't about the body. Has nothing to do with the body. I could take any guy's body on earth and turn it into Michelangelo's *David*, long as inside he has the *stuff*, man."

"What about people in wheelchairs?" Logan said.

"Watch the Paralympics someday, kid, and you'll see it's all about heart. It's about truth. About becoming what you were fated to be, about being reborn in a state of perfection. About the will to greatness."

"The will to power?" Serenata said. "I think Nietzsche got there already."

Bambi ignored her. "Hey, figure we can nab another couple bottles of this cab-sav?" she proposed, nodding at the empty that listed for seventy-six dollars. "I'm running dry."

"I didn't think fitness freaks were drinkers," Serenata commented to Tommy at her right.

"Work hard, play hard!" Bambi said. "You guys who hung out on the sidelines can pick-pick and sippy-sippy, but us athletes got us some serious refueling to do."

Serenata had ordered the first bottle at the risk of Valeria's disapproval. Should the evening turn into a booze-up, the grandparents were bound to be chastised as immoral influences. But Bambi was such a force of nature that when a replacement bottle arrived, Valeria poured herself half a glass.

Meanwhile, Tommy looked miserable. The outfit from the afternoon's shopping had subtly rearranged itself—the denim wrap had dropped down one shoulder; the dress was wrenched askew—so as to look like everything else she wore, in which she looked drowned and forlorn. The source of Tommy's dejection was surely Bambi, who personified all those online paragons eternally upping their games whenever Tommy was close to catching up. By contrast, swooning from across the table and uncharacteristically shy, Nancee was in love.

"I should never have turned off my Fitbit," Tommy mumbled, fiddling with the band. "Now I'll never make my steps today."

"So, *Bambi*, what do you do?" Serenata inquired.

"Personal trainer," the woman said through her food.

Serenata said, deadpan, "What a shock."

"You?" she asked tersely.

"I'm a voice-over artist. Audio—"

"Whoa, too passive for me. All that sitting."

"Actually, recording video games is surprisingly physical—"

"It's unorthodox"—she'd turned back to Remington—"but I don't recommend much resting up after a marathon. Sure, take tomorrow off. But then get right back in the saddle. You gotta master the body, teach it who's boss."

Holding her emotional breath, Serenata had succeeded in making it through Remington's infernal marathon. In kind, to enter the glorious rest of her life in which she'd never again lay eyes on this insufferable cunt, she only had to make it through this meal. Merely being conversational, she inquired, "So where do you live?"

"Well, that's what made Rem and me decide we were destined to come in as a team. Since whadda ya know—we both live in Hudson!"

Officially, the point at which the couple returned to their hotel room marked the beginning of restored normal life that Serenata had been anticipating since October.

"So!" she said, closing the door on a great deal more than the hallway. "The marathon. After all that training. Was it worth it?"

"Sure," Remington said coolly, removing his jacket. "It was interesting."

"Funny. *Interesting* was exactly what I thought it wasn't."

"You were just watching. Only at the end, I might add. You make a lousy spectator."

She tossed the fedora on a chair in disgust. "I can't believe her name is actually *Bambi Buffer.*"

"It's obviously a work handle." Remington had been on a high all night. Only alone with his wife did he seem exhausted. "Like a stage name."

"Which is worse. She can't even blame her parents."

"Her encouragement was a great help to me at the end of that race. So I was sure you wouldn't mind that I asked her to join us."

"Why should I mind? Just because she's a fucking idiot?"

"That's unworthy of you. I can't recall her saying anything especially dumb."

"All that *find the God in yourself*? I call that dumb."

"Know what she told me on the way back to the van? 'Your wife is pretty dark.'"

"And getting darker. You used to like it." Serenata attempted to control herself. This wasn't the night for a spat.

"Anyway, you're going to have to get used to Bambi. I'm hiring her."

Serenata turned sharply from her toiletry kit. "To do what? The race is over."

"Because on one point, you were right."

"This I have to hear."

"You said from the start that finishing a marathon isn't a claim to fame anymore, but a cliché. Even Bambi agrees that completing that distance has become old hat."

"Well, it's still an achievement—"

"*Triathlons*," he said. "*Triathlons* are where it's at."

SIX

"Have you noticed, in these arts programs," Remington noted in midsummer as they were tidying the lunch dishes with NPR in the background, "how often you hear, 'You wouldn't be able to say that now'? And they're usually talking about a film or a stand-up routine that's only three or four years old. *You wouldn't be able to say that now.* Soon you won't even be able to say what it is that you're not allowed to say. We'll become convinced that to express anything at all is extremely risky, and the species will go mute."

"Don't forget, there's a certain contingent that doesn't seem to feel stifled in the slightest."

"Yes, and they're not helping. The implication is that to say anything is to speak abominations."

"Why are you limping?"

"It's nothing. A hamstring."

"A hamstring is a great deal of something, in my experience. It can take months to heal."

"Bambi says you have to power through injuries. You can't allow them to defeat you."

Serenata could never get used to her husband's saying that woman's loopy handle with a straight face. "In a battle with the body, the body wins every time."

"Only if you let it. Bambi recommends imagining yourself back on the veldt, pursued by a lion. Would you stop, and elevate your leg on the limb of an acacia, and rub hippo grease into your poor sore little hamstring, and tell the lion to come hunting you in three months' time when you can really give chase, if not three thousand years later, after the invention of ibuprofen?"

"I should 'power through' two knees without cartilage, then. I should go back to distance running, despite the crepitus, and the bone bulging out of the right one, and the pains shooting up my thighs, because giving into the agony is a display of weakness?"

"You're picking a fight. I might add, another one."

True, but he hadn't answered her question.

"You know, I'm a little tired of being told how 'privileged' I am," he said a minute later, alluding to the NPR interview with an activist playwright. "How as a member of the 'straight white patriarchy' I have all the power. I'm supposedly so omnipotent, but I live in fear, less like a man than a mouse. I check everything I plan to say three times before I allow it out. At least when I'm training I keep my mouth shut. I might fall on my face, but I won't be arrested."

"That sounds a little paranoid."

"It is not. I was informed in no uncertain terms that she might have pressed charges. *Criminal* charges. For threats of bodily harm."

"My dear," Serenata said with foreboding. "Let's not get into that again."

"We already criminalize emotions. 'Hate crime.' You get an additionally long sentence for how you *feel*. I'm confident that most Americans now believe that *being* a racist is against the law. Not doing racist things, or saying racist things, but the state of being racist should get you thrown in jail."

"In that case, the whole population belongs behind bars."

"We're well on our way to criminalizing anger, too. If you express so much as impatience at airport security, you will literally be arrested. Or all those students. If you shout at them, they don't feel 'safe.' Anger is too frightening. It has to be managed away, in special courses that teach you how to get in touch with your inner pussy. Anger is now regarded as a form of assault. It's too masculine an emotion for Wuss World, where masculinity is also a form of assault. So we contain all male fury, within lead walls like toxic waste. It doesn't surprise me in the slightest that a man my age would suddenly with no warning smash the window of his hotel room and strafe a country music festival."

It started a few years ago: Remington's adoption of a robotic monotone, especially when delivering what might otherwise qualify as a rant. The absence of inflection was more chilling than rage. He made no eye contact. He spoke to the sink.

"You know, when you're running, swimming, and cycling, I don't believe you think about running, swimming, and cycling," Serenata said. "I think you think about Lucinda Okonkwo."

"I think about *not* thinking about Lucinda Okonkwo. It takes vigilance. But you seem to imply that concentrating on going from one place to another is empty in some way. If that's the case, then life is empty. Life comes down to nothing more than the motion of the body through space."

The assertion seemed a mantra of sorts. "So if I remain perfectly still, I'm dead."

"It's impossible to remain perfectly still, which should tell you something about the nature of being alive. Why do you think I chose to work for the Department of *Transportation?* Traversing distance. That's all there is to do. It's no different for us than for a fly, buzzing around the room, jiggering across a windowpane, and then it dies."

"For you, then, a triathlon is just jiggering across a windowpane."

"Yes."

"Your friend *Bambi* seems to promote a more exalted version of the project."

"It's to her professional advantage to frame the endeavor in more attractive terms."

Determining the precise nature of the "project" was Serenata's project. She was privately compiling a list of her husband's objectives. (1) To kill time—to systematically massacre the barren months that lay before him, like a modern-day great white hunter. (2) To embrace silence, and so to embrace a passive defiance. Breathless on a track, plunged into the pool at the Y, head to the wind in a velodrome, he couldn't talk, which afforded a narrow refuge. If not impossible, it was harder to burn heretics for what they didn't say. (3) Not to repress anger so much as to become chronically too exhausted to give rise to it. (4) To become a man again, but with a frenzied futility that contained the noxious qualities of his sex within the safe circumference of the hamster wheel.

The appointment of Lucinda Okonkwo as his immediate superior had obviously come as a blow. At fifty-nine, Remington Alabaster had blithely assumed that he'd rise to head of the department, as he might have much earlier if his colleague Gary Neusbaum hadn't run out the clock on retirement. Salary was at issue, of course, but more, pride. Lucinda Okonkwo was twenty-seven.

Remington described her as insecure, and she may have felt that way for good reason. At college, she hadn't majored in transportation, civil engineering, or even urban planning, but gender studies, and she had no graduate degree. Naturally the City Council never said so per se, but Lucinda's exhibiting the "intersectionality" of a seven-exit traffic circle must have made the new hire irresistible.

"She's black," Remington told his wife the night after he'd learned the news. "I mean, African-American—"

"Drop it," Serenata said. "You're among friends. Besides, I don't think that term earns you a gold star anymore."

"No, but Lucinda is *African* African-American, which confers extra points. She's second-generation Nigerian, which means she nominally gets credit for being an immigrant, too. She's a she—"

"Careful, even pronouns can get you into trouble. Try, 'She's a *they.*'"

"Or a *zee*," he said. "But on the diversity section of her application, she apparently answered all the questions about gender and sexuality 'Prefer not to say.' Which terrified the HR people at City Hall. You can't protect yourself against discrimination suits when you don't even know what you're discriminating against."

"What's left? Don't tell me. She's in a wheelchair. Can you say wheelchair? Do you have to say 'wheelchariot'? I have a hard time keeping up."

"She's not *differently abled*, no. The problem is otherwise, and please don't take this wrong. She's extremely attractive. Meaning, she's a sexual harassment case waiting to happen. If it's ever her word against mine? With one look at that figure in an era when we're supposed to 'believe women' no matter what kind of crackpots they might be, anyone will assume that I couldn't control myself."

"But from your description, she has no qualifications for the job. You said her only previous position was working at a shelter for victims of domestic violence."

"You mentioned gold stars? That's a gold star. When I applied for my first post in the Albany DOT, I'd been working for the New York City DOT: boring and obvious. I'd never have snagged the job today."

Indeed, to describe Lucinda Okonkwo as having been promoted to her level of incompetence, via the "Peter Principle" popular in Serenata's adolescence, wouldn't have been strictly accurate. Skipping altogether the multiple stair steps of proficiency that classically preceded the final stage of ineptitude at which, according to the theory, managers indefinitely stagnated, Lucinda had been *airlifted* to her level of incompetence. Thus to be fair, the fact that she had no idea what she was doing was not her fault.

A rational man, Remington didn't hold Lucinda accountable for a Council mistake. Cultivating a demurral that couldn't have come easily in relation to a woman less than half his age, he claimed to have approached his new superior in a spirit of collegiality. But youth and inexperience made Lucinda understandably defensive, and defense often expressed itself as aggression. So intent on proving who was boss, she mustn't have entirely believed that she was already the boss.

Serenata met Lucinda more than once. She had full breasts, powerful hips, and high cheekbones. Her bearing was statuesque. In middle age she might possibly run to fat, but in the full bloom of young adulthood her mass was magnificently distributed and made her only the more formidable. She'd a habit of looking unwaveringly straight at you, as if sighting through crosshairs; even Serenata had broken eye contact first. Born and privately educated in the States, Lucinda spoke with an American accent whose degree of Black English inflection fluctuated (with whites, she went street; with black employees, she could sound aristocratic). Everyone in the department was afraid of her.

Remington had also met her parents, when they drove up from the city to see where their daughter worked. He described them as lavishly courteous and warm. They both spoke English with a musical African lilt. The mother was slender and also quite beautiful, in a colorful blouse with echoes of her homeland, but a slim Western skirt. The handsome father's charcoal suit was classily tailored. Yet despite a junior professional standing in relation to their daughter, Remington was several years older than Lucinda's parents, so the couple accorded him the deference their culture demanded toward elders. Unusually for their nationality, Lucinda was an only child, and perhaps they'd spoiled her. But in any event, Remington's problem with Lucinda was not that she was Nigerian. The problem was that Lucinda was American. All too.

Lucinda Okonkwo was well educated, in a particular vein. In due course, Remington had altogether too much cause to research her campus activism in back editions of the *Columbia Spectator*. Serenata had sometimes wondered what happened to university firebrands—who spent their undergraduate years brandishing placards, campaigning to de-colonize the curriculum, and getting professors sacked for screening ostensibly "alt-right" YouTube videos—once these tempest-in-a-teacup hotheads graduated into the larger world of actual bad weather. Well. Now she knew.

At first, Remington was unfazed by his new superior's initiatives—the gender-neutral restrooms, or the requirement to introduce yourself including your "preferred pronoun." Announcing "I'm Remington Alabaster, and I'm a he" was no skin off his nose; he was able to find it comical; and public employees were accustomed to statements of the obvious. Sexual harassment and racial awareness workshops were opportunities to catch up on his expenses. Oddly, as second-in-command of the Department of Transportation, he reserved his zeal for issues of transportation. So long as Lucinda kept to social justice, Remington could get on with his job.

He and Gary Neusbaum had already transferred ownership of Albany's streetlights from a private utility to the city, with the aim of lowering both carbon emissions and metropolitan lighting bills by switching to more contemporary illumination. Increasingly popular with urban bureaucrats across the country, light-emitting diodes consumed a fraction of the energy that yellow-tinted sodium lamps drew, and lasted up to three times longer. Yet a range of subsidiary matters remained to be resolved: whether the new LED streetlights would be shielded on top, thus preventing upward glare that disturbed wildlife; whether the units would be shielded on the sides, to prevent light invasion from piercing residential windows; whether the city would invest in a decorative, retro post and housing to suit Albany's original architecture, or purchase a starker yet more economical product; and most of all, what Kelvin rating to opt for.

Much of Remington's work was arithmetic: obtaining accurate cars-per-day figures on a side street that residents had petitioned to have closed to through traffic or quantifying the low ridership on a bus route with an eye to reducing scheduling frequency. But the research on LED streetlights that Remington had just begun when Lucinda took over soon became the source of a passion one associates not with math but with art.

Inflamed by revelation, he had dragged Serenata from the door on her return home from a late recording session, intent on showing her a series of photographs on the family tablet. All the shots captured the same roadside scene, but each was illuminated by LED streetlights with different Kelvin ratings: 2.3, 2.7, 3, 3.5, 4, or 5.

"Look, I admit the two point three is a little dingy," he'd said. "But the two point seven is perfectly pleasant. You could picnic under that light. You could kiss your girlfriend under that light, or even propose marriage. It's an LED, but it's human light. It still has warmth, a hint of the golden. It still shines with benevolence, with kindness. If you were one of those people in that photograph, and someone emailed you the pic, you wouldn't be likely to anguish, 'Oh, no, where did all those mottles on my face come from?' You might think instead, 'Hey, I look pretty good in that red shirt, don't I?'

"But now . . . Look at Kelvin ratings four and five. You could slit your wrists under that light. Better yet, murder somebody else. Why not, when that figure on the left already looks like a cadaver? That's the kind of light in which people confess to being terrorists under torture. It's the gruesome glare in which you'd shoot those movies, you know, about kidnapped women kept starving and pregnant and chained in the basement. When I first read about the hoopla in some communities over *streetlights*, for pity's sake, I thought, come on, people, get a life. But now I get it. High-Kelvin LEDs are mercilessly destroying the touch and feel of urban nightlife all over the country. Honestly, blue-spectrum LEDs are a form of emotional vandalism. They're not only about how things look. They're about how people feel. Like—terrible."

"I have to agree," Serenata said, swiping between the shots. "The atmospheric difference between these lightings is extraordinary."

"Lower Kelvin diodes are *slightly* more expensive, and *slightly* less energy efficient. But the massive trade-off in ambience more than compensates for the sacrifice."

The methodical Remington Alabaster commonly thought in terms of interlocking systems. He'd always enjoyed the puzzle-solving of controlling traffic flow, but the pleasure was quiet, like a watchmaker's—a private satisfaction that a mechanism ticked along. But his devotion to the gentle, enfolding glow of low-Kelvin diodes, and his ferocious opposition to the brutal, ghoulish blue spectrum to which too many municipalities were subjecting their residents—often in the face of virulent local opposition—was the first instance in which he'd taken on a professional cause with crusading fervor. For once, his central concern wasn't functionality or finance but aesthetics. He believed vehemently that blue light was ugly, and was therefore profoundly damaging to the daily lives of millions of Americans, a discrete subsection of whom he could personally rescue from its suicidal blare. He further believed that the aesthetic bled not only to the psychological but to the existential. Under the cold, prying, pseudo-Soviet beam of high-Kelvin interrogation, all of life itself seemed bleak.

The months of Remington's streetlamp research saw a late blossoming of their marriage. The distance narrowed between their work worlds. Serenata dwelt in a universe of tones—nuance, mood, suggestion, pauses that said more than words—and her husband's new dedication to color in a visual sense ineffably connected with her own dedication to color in a vocal one. He had hitherto left most decisions about household decor to his wife, so she was pleased to discover that he had an appreciation for beauty after all, one that also translated into a revived appreciation for his wife. They had more sex. When he finally delivered his thick report, they were both a little bereft.

Lucinda Okonkwo responded with stonewalling silence. When after months of no uptake on his recommendations he asked whether she'd found time to survey his findings, she said something like, "You wouldn't be telling me how to do my job, would you?" No, no, certainly not; it's just that he was *terribly interested* in her opinion. "I got stacks of way more pressing problems to deal with. You wouldn't be asking me to *privilege* your report, would you—which took you a weirdly long time to compile, truth be told—just because a white department lifer got a bug up about freaking streetlights?" Obviously, Remington backed off.

Alas, it was around this time that Lucinda ran short of ideas for how to upend the awful inequities of modern-day Albany, right the grotesque historical wrongs of her shameful country, and save the planet. She'd already commissioned a report on the department's gender pay gap. She'd already declared the office a no-go zone for single-use plastic—which meant that employees shoveled in their lunches out of doors before chucking their deli containers in the public trash can on the corner. She'd already introduced a climate-change points system, which rewarded employees for biking or walking to work and staying home on vacations; winners would earn a bottle of no-alcohol chardonnay. In a highway meridian park, she'd already ordered the exhumation of a plaque that celebrated a local nineteenth-century philanthropist, now that archived letters documented his belief that homosexuality was depraved. Because the city's byways were cluttered with the names of "too many dead white male presidents," she'd already changed Buchanan Street to Robert Mugabe Terrace and Roosevelt Street to Jacob Zuma Way. Alas, little territory remained over which to exercise her decision-making powers other than Albany's actual transportation system.

Making a costly gesture toward a low-carbon future, she commanded the construction of elaborate bike lanes on both sides of Highway 20/Madison Avenue, which might have been all very well and good—except that she did no study in advance of the modest demand. Designed with wide concrete barriers between bicycles and traffic, the lanes took nine months to construct, backing up traffic for half a mile during rush hours. Once opened, the bike lanes continued to create a crippling pinch point for cars. Yet the paths extended a mere two hundred yards, after which cyclists rejoined the main roadway at a perilous juncture. In practice, then, savvy two-wheelers shunned the lanes altogether. Remington believed that intrusive, merely symbolic projects of this nature made motorists revile cyclists even more than they had already, and neither party needed any encouragement to despise the other.

In the interest of traffic calming, Lucinda commissioned raised platforms for dozens of downtown intersections. Each ramped elevation comprised thousands of small, fiddly cubes of granite. Yet the slopes proved far too gentle to slow drivers in the slightest. Worse, she spent most of the project's budget on classy materials, and cut corners on labor. Carelessly grouted, the cobbles began to rattle when vehicles traversed them after only a few days. Within three months of the project's completion, the stones were sinking, lying at cockeyed angles, and fracturing into shards.

Lucinda's messing with one-way systems was a catastrophe for the Dunn Memorial Bridge. The untried, innovative material she selected for repaving began to decay the first time a UPS van drove down a re-surfaced road, picking up gooey chunks of gravelly terra-cotta tarmac with its tires. Her free bus passes for recent immigrants, the under-privileged, and other "vulnerable" groups was widely abused, and left a massive hole in the budget.

Three years after Remington delivered his streetlight findings, Lucinda announced in a departmental meeting, casually, amid a range of other business, that the conversion was going ahead. After-ward, Remington stopped by her office. That evening, he recounted their conversation to Serenata as best as he could:

"So—you got around to looking at my report, then?" Not invited to sit down, Remington remained standing.

"Skimmed it," Lucinda said. "Thing was thick enough to use for some toddler's booster chair. Too many trees, Alabaster. Time's short. I need forest."

"I thought it was important to be thorough. This is a long-term investment—"

"*Too* thorough amount to a kind of sloppy. I can't spend all day reading booster chairs."

"It's just, that report raised a number of issues that need to be re-solved before the conversion goes ahead. For example, R&M makes a faux-gaslight, nineteenth-century-style post and fixture that, while a little pricey, might be worth the historical touch around the capitol—"

"Albany taxpayers don't want fancy-pants street furniture. This is a modern American city, not a Sherlock Holmes movie set. If you and your wife are partial to antiques, I could steer you toward a shop on Learned Street. But not on the department's dime."

She'd not been nearly as concerned with taxpayer value for money when commissioning those crumbling raised platforms.

"More substantively," Remington said, "there's the shielding question. The nonprofit Dark-Sky has documented disturbance to nocturnal wildlife from vertical light escape; I included their report in my appendix. As for lateral escape, other municipalities have met widespread popular uproar over the invasive penetration of powerful LED streetlights into people's homes—"

"Let 'em get curtains. There's your 'shielding.' Streetlights supposed to be bright. That's what they're for. So you can see. Is that all, Alabaster? Seem to me you're making this way more complicated than it need to be."

"No, that's not all. The biggest issue is obviously Kelvin rating. I concede there's room for debate over the middle range—"

"Mister, I'm a busy woman."

"But I'd lobby for as low a rating as possible. Considerable data substantiates that blue-spectrum light interferes with the production of melatonin, and disrupts sleep rhythms—"

"This isn't more of you worrying about the raccoons, is it?"

"Human sleep rhythms. It's the same sleep disruption caused by looking at smart phones and computer screens before bed. As a woman, I'd think you'd especially respond to the gathering evidence that prolonged exposure to blue-spectrum illumination may significantly increase the incidence of breast cancer—"

"You buttering up to me, figuring I'll go weak at the knees and do whatever you say so long as you go on about *breast cancer*? That's some manipulative shit. It's a kind of misogyny, wanna know the truth. Sexist condescension."

"I apologize. I shouldn't have made assumptions."

"No, you should not." The response was typical. Whenever you gave ground, she took it.

"You see, blue light exposure also substantially raises the incidence of prostate cancer."

"Oh, so now it's a *man's* problem, it matters."

Remington confessed that at this point he'd been stymied. "Then there's the intangible but," he resumed unsteadily, "I would argue, not incidental matter of the appearance of this city at night—when we want residents to feel enthusiastic about eating out and going to clubs, which stimulates the economy. And we want our citizens to be happy, don't we? To feel good."

"Now you're losing me for true, Alabaster. Happy citizens aren't in the DOT's remit, or I'd of ordered fifty crates of diazepam 'stead of a full container load of LED streetlights from Guangzhou."

"What?"

"I been trying to tell you, friend, but you just had to go on about all your hokey gaslights and breast cancer and *shielding.* I already place the order. It's warehoused and ready to be installed. And I didn't get the goods from Amazon. It's not like I can print out a return label and carry a box to the post office. We're talking done deal."

"Well, what kind did you order?"

"Standard, off-the-shelf, cheap as I could get. That's my job. The department's in overspend. The savings is a double-whammy, too. The electric bill for streetlights about to go through the floor."

"And what Kelvin rating did you choose?"

Lucinda met her subordinate's eyes defiantly. "*Five.*"

Serenata wasn't obliged to fill in the blanks of her husband's employment tribunal. Owing to a mistrust that proved justified, he turned on the recording function on his phone.

As described secondhand by the Albany city employee Remington Alabaster, hauled up on disciplinary charges for threatening behavior and racially and sexually aggravated assault, the other principals were:

CURTIS PEPPER: White male, somewhat shy of forty years old. Suit with interesting blue sheen, jacket short in the sleeves; untucked V-neck green T-shirt. Dark leather shoes, *no socks.* Ostensibly the chairman of the Human Resources Diversity and Equality Committee, but tends to lose control in the wake of his more forceful female associate.

BRANDON ABRAHAM: Black male, over fifty. Loosely fitting, unassuming gray suit with carelessly wound tie—but still, a tie. A few unimportant pounds overweight. Amenable expression, with difficulty meeting the defendant's eyes. Looks tired. Often steals glances at his watch.

TRINITY CHASE: White female, mid-thirties. Short, jagged hair, bleached white, which makes her look older. Not bad looking but squarely built; defies her sex's reputation for softness. Wearing disconcerting mismatch of clothing that seems to pass for trendy: long-sleeved velour turtleneck in bright cornflower blue, plaid track bottoms whose turquoise clashes with velour top, and untied platform tennis shoes. Tasteful nose piercing. Fiercely upright posture compromised by slight predatory lean toward the accused. Fiery but officious. Takes copious notes.

CURTIS: Now, before we get going, I'd just like to acknowledge to this committee that I'm a little embarrassed to have been designated the chairman—*chair,* sorry—because I'm painfully aware of representing the white patriarchy. At least I identify as bi, so I have some sensitivity to the issues confronted by marginalized communities, by dint of my sharing the LGBTQIA space. Still, as far as I'm concerned we're all three on the same level here. If anything, as a privileged white male I have way less right to speak, and I'm humbled by your comparatively more extreme encounters with imbalances of social power. Now. Remington—I can call you Remington?

REMINGTON: Given the indignity of this whole tribunal, being called by my first name is the least of my problems.

TRINITY: It's not a "tribunal," Mr. Alabaster. It's an informal hearing in which we'd like to hear your side of the story. I'm troubled that your attitude seems so adversarial. We're only interested in the truth.

CURTIS: You're aware that, uh . . . [*flapping of paper*] replacing high-pressure sodium street lighting with light-emitting diode technology could significantly reduce Albany's carbon footprint, thus mitigating climate change. You're also aware that, you know . . . despite high initial capital costs, conversion is also in the city's long-term economic interest.

REMINGTON: In that you're reading from the preface of *my own report*, I am obviously aware of these matters.

CURTIS: But according to Lucinda Okonkwo, who testified to this committee last week, you became resistant to the very project that she'd entrusted you with.

REMINGTON: Gary Neusbaum entrusted me with it, actually. But my so-called "resistance" to LEDs in general is a mischaracterization.

TRINITY: According to Ms. Okonkwo, your approach to the conversion was "obstructionist," your dealings with your superior on this issue were "oppositional," and your concern with the minutiae of implementation grew "unhealthily obsessive."

BRANDON: Like, Lucinda seems to think you saw a bunch of problems where she couldn't see how there were any. So you like, got on the wrong side of each other. I've seen how that can happen. It almost always gets worse and worse. Instead of talking out differences of opinion rationally, everything gets all personal. So nobody wants to back down, because any compromise would seem like surrender. That's how cases like this end up before this committee.

REMINGTON: But I didn't initially approach this conversion as a contest of wills, Mr. Abraham. I simply identified a range of issues that had given rise to protest, sometimes highly organized and vociferous protest, in other cities. I realized that all these objections could be headed off by choosing the right housing and fixture.

CURTIS: But according to Ms. Okonkwo, the products you recommended were too pricey. And much less energy efficient. Which would defeat the purpose of the conversion in the first place: to save both money and the environment.

REMINGTON: They were *slightly* more expensive, and *slightly* less efficient, which I documented in detail in my appendix. Amortized over the lifetime of the units, the *incrementally* higher cost and *minor* reduction in energy savings would be more than offset by a range of beneficial trade-offs.

TRINITY: According to Ms. Okonkwo, all you cared about was that the new lights were "pretty."

REMINGTON: That's a trivializing way of putting it. But yes, I did think the city should take into consideration the powerful aesthetic impact of public illumination. Blue-spectrum light has been strongly associated with depression—

TRINITY: Don't you think that *mood lighting* is an awfully middle-class, even elitist concern? Do the poor and marginalized communities of this city care first and foremost about appearances?

BRANDON: Hey, just because you're broke doesn't mean you have no feelings about what shit looks like.

TRINITY: Still, I said *first and foremost*—aren't the poor and marginalized more likely to care about the cost-effective use of their tax dollars?

REMINGTON: "The poor and marginalized" contribute very few tax dollars. Since for the lower income we're largely spending other people's money, I don't imagine they care about our economizing in the slightest.

"You shouldn't have said that," Serenata pointed out, pausing the recording at the horrified silence.

"But it's true," Remington said.

"That's why you shouldn't have said it."

CURTIS: You're not exactly doing yourself any favors here, Remington.

BRANDON: Come on, Curtis. Statistically, the guy's got a point.

TRINITY: We're not talking about statistics, Brandon. We're talking about attitude. Furthermore, the vulnerable communities for which you exhibit such contempt, Mr. Alabaster, are especially concerned with safety. So the street lighting Ms. Okonkwo preferred—

REMINGTON: Purchased. Flat out, with no consultation.

TRINITY: The lighting that she *purchased* is rated as extremely popular in high-crime neighborhoods, because their brightness makes residents feel safe.

REMINGTON: They *feel* safer—

TRINITY: You don't care about how vulnerable people feel?

REMINGTON: They are not, in fact, any safer—or any less *vulnerable*. As I documented in Appendix D, high-Kelvin-rated diodes have no correlation with a reduction of the real crime rate.

BRANDON: Can we just say you two disagreed, and get on with it?

CURTIS: So Remington—when you learned that Ms. Okonkwo—your superior, who after all was only obliged to consider your findings, but didn't necessarily have to take your advice—

REMINGTON: I believe Ms. Okonkwo only consulted the document that I delivered to her *three years ago* in order to do the exact opposite of what I recommended. At every point during her tenure, her decisions have been purely reactive. I may even have performed a useful service. Only her strict adherence to an oppositional formula—doing whatever I thought she shouldn't, and refusing to do whatever I thought she should—has rescued her management of our department from perfect chaos.

TRINITY: You seem to have a hostility problem, Mr. Alabaster.

REMINGTON: I do indeed, Ms. Chase. Ably observed.

BRANDON: [*muttering*] That Lucinda can be prickly.

Serenata stopped the recording again. "I'm just curious. That Curtis guy made a big deal about calling you 'Remington' and even asked your permission, and then this Trinity person keeps calling you 'Mr. Alabaster.' What's with that?"

"Huh. I didn't notice that at the time," Remington said. "But listening to it now? I think, conveniently, either choice is an insult. 'Remington' is presumptuously chummy, as if we're all friends here, which under the circumstances impugns my intelligence. 'Mr. Alabaster' is depersonalizing and artificially formal, now that in practice pretty much nobody in work situations uses titles and surnames. 'Mr. Alabaster' makes me sound older and fustier, but also accords the proceedings a judicially exalted texture at odds with the obvious:

the whole hearing is absurd. Interestingly, all those citations of 'Ms. Okonkwo,' by contrast, accord my so-called superior a reverence and respect that confers righteousness on the white members of the committee."

"Nicely parsed." Serenata tapped PLAY.

REMINGTON: If you want another example of this *reactive* principle of hers, take the restaging of traffic lights all over town—which I vehemently opposed. The entire network is now deliberately out of phase. You stop at one red light, only to stop at the next. And the next. Taxi drivers are livid.

BRANDON: Son of a bitch. Are you telling me that's on purpose? I swear, sitting at every intersection on Clinton Avenue adds ten minutes to my commute.

REMINGTON: All to "discourage car use."

CURTIS: Well, doesn't it?

REMINGTON: What it does is send idling through the roof, and all this stop-start driving exacerbates air pollution.

TRINITY: Unless the cars aren't there at all.

REMINGTON: Excuse me?

TRINITY: Unless Ms. Okonkwo is right, and motorists get so frustrated that they use other forms of transport.

REMINGTON: I've been in this department for over thirty years, and take it from me: frustrated drivers lean on their horns in the short term. In the long term, they vote out whole City Council administrations and replace them with elected officials who put the traffic-light phasing back the way it was.

CURTIS: Look, Remington, can we return to our central agenda, please? When Ms. Okonkwo told you about this LED purchasing order, what did you do?

REMINGTON: I slammed my hand on her desk.

CURTIS: And why did you do that?

REMINGTON: Because I lost my temper.

CURTIS: And would you say that you "slammed" the desk very hard?

REMINGTON: That is what the word *slammed* was meant to convey, yes.

CURTIS: And would you say that the sound your hand made was extremely loud?

REMINGTON: It was fairly loud.

CURTIS: And how did Ms. Okonkwo react?

REMINGTON: I think she was startled. *I* was startled. I very rarely lose my temper.

TRINITY: If you had it to do over again, Mr. Alabaster, would you have kept yourself under control?

REMINGTON: [*pause*] I'm not sure.

TRINITY: The consequences of this inappropriate behavior could be grave, Mr. Alabaster. And you're *not sure* that you wish you could take it back?

REMINGTON: It was a relief. I wouldn't make a habit of it. But expressing my feelings from the gut . . . As I said, it was a relief. And the gesture made my opinion of her capricious decision far clearer to Ms. Okonkwo than anything I might have said.

BRANDON: Any chance we could resolve this with a simple apology? Because it seems like this incident is getting blown up all out of proportion. So Alabaster here lost his rag. Would you be okay with telling Lucinda you're sorry, man?

REMINGTON: I'm not apologetic about my strenuous opposition to nearly all her policies. But on reflection, I suppose I am sorry

that I gave into my anger, however briefly. Because in doing
so I gave that young woman exactly what she wanted.

TRINITY: Due process-wise, I'm afraid we're well beyond making
this all go away with a mere apology. Especially an insultingly
insincere apology like that one.

CURTIS: According to Ms. Okonkwo, your dealings with her from
the very beginning of her employment were "weirdly careful."
Your exchanges were, she said, conspicuously "by the book."
She says you were "pulled back, all inside himself, like he's
looking at me from way far away." You seemed "more like
some guy from England than a regular American." Does that
description ring true to you?

REMINGTON: I have been careful. I wouldn't say "weirdly" so.

TRINITY: But why would you need to be careful?

REMINGTON: [*pause*] I sensed Ms. Okonkwo was on the lookout.

TRINITY: On the lookout for what?

REMINGTON: Just . . . on the lookout. I felt that whatever I did and
said was being scrutinized. I sensed I should watch my step.

"You shouldn't have gone there," Serenata said.

"They took me there. And it didn't matter where we *went*," Remington said impatiently. "In a kangaroo court, the kangaroo can hop
all around the edges of the cage, or even play dead. It doesn't matter.
The kangaroo's fate is sealed."

CURTIS: So that would explain why Ms. Okonkwo described you
as "wary" and "guarded" and "reticent" and tending to "speak
only when spoken to."

REMINGTON: I tried to be cordial. I did sometimes make small
talk about her family. But can you explain the purpose of this
line of questioning, please?

CURTIS: Well, when people seem to be putting a whole lot of effort into controlling themselves, you can't help but wonder what all they're controlling.

TRINITY: Right. We can't help but wonder what exactly it was that you were so determined to keep from getting out. What disturbing things you might have done and said if you hadn't felt "scrutinized."

REMINGTON: Let me get this straight. You've hauled me before this committee because I *lost* control for two seconds. And now I am being raked over the coals because the rest of the time I *exercised* control?

CURTIS: Do you consider yourself a racist, Remington?

REMINGTON: No. Although I have yet to witness anyone declaiming about how they're not a racist without sounding like one.

CURTIS: And do you consider yourself a misogynist?

REMINGTON: I can't imagine how I could possibly be a "misogynist" and still have married a woman who's far smarter and more talented than I am.

"Flatterer," Serenata said. "You knew I'd be listening to this."

BRANDON: You should meet *my* wife, man. That woman makes me look like a genius. Folks think, if he's married to a lady that sharp, that guy must really have something going on.

CURTIS: And, Remington, do you have a problem with immigrants?

REMINGTON: Ms. Okonkwo was born in this country, and last I read that makes her an American and not an "immigrant." You can't have it both ways.

TRINITY: But is there any chance that some of the thoughts you've been so determined to stifle because you've felt "scrutinized" . . . Given all the post-9/11 anxieties about terrorism, well . . . When you look deep into yourself, might some of these dangerous thoughts you've suppressed qualify as Islamophobic?

REMINGTON: I fail to see the pertinence of your question.

TRINITY: I'm afraid it's all too pertinent. Since 2001, anti-Muslim hate crimes in this country have multiplied by several times. In this climate, you honestly believe your own attitudes haven't been influenced by the abuse, and the tarring with a single jihadist brush, that's all over social media and the internet—

REMINGTON: Ms. Chase, Lucinda Okonkwo and her whole family are Christians.

"Ha!" Serenata paused the recording at the discomfited silence. "They just assumed she was Muslim."

"It was another box their diversity hire was supposed to check," Remington said. "I'm sure they were grievously disappointed. About half of Nigeria is Christian, so their assumptions about Lucinda were supremely ignorant—although every time I flustered them, the worse I knew it would go for me."

REMINGTON: Listen, may I please speak freely?

CURTIS: I hope you *have* been speaking freely, Remington.

REMINGTON: Lucinda Okonkwo is belligerent, high-handed, and unqualified. She's also lazy. I don't think she's unintelligent, which makes her especially culpable.

TRINITY: And you don't think you're a racist.

REMINGTON: Her autocratic ordering of new streetlights for this entire city was typical—after no small-scale trial, no consultation with either the public or her own colleagues, and no consideration of my report, aside from the flip-through that would guarantee she selected the perfect opposite of the products that I recommended. I would submit that she resents my long tenure in this department, my consequent experience in matters about which she is poorly informed, and my academic credentials in this field—

TRINITY: Isn't the truth of the matter that *you* resent Ms. Okonkwo being given the job of department head four years ago, and not yourself?

BRANDON: She's got you there, bud. You had the seniority big-time. I'd have been resentful, in your position.

REMINGTON: Of course I resented it. But I'd never have held on to a sense of grievance if the new department head was skillful and dealt with his—or her—employees in a spirit of cooperation. I got on brilliantly with Gary Neusbaum for decades.

TRINITY: How surprising. Another aging straight white male.

REMINGTON: My point is, I dislike my immediate superior, I concede that, I do—but not because I'm racist, or sexist, or anti-immigrant. Not because I'm a whatever-ophobe. I dislike her *personally*. As an individual. Is that possible anymore? Is it legal to harbor animosity toward a specific person who just *happens* to belong to a "marginalized community"?

TRINITY: Prejudice often runs very deep, and thrives on an unconscious level. I don't know how you could possibly tell the difference between this so-called personal dislike and your own bigotry.

REMINGTON: So the answer is no. No, you cannot personally dislike anyone anymore.

TRINITY: The answer is that your so-called personal dislike is going to look suspicious to this committee.

CURTIS: I'm afraid we're going to have to focus here on the central charge of violent assault by a subordinate in the workplace.

REMINGTON: But I didn't touch her. How can you call that "violence"?

CURTIS: Your actions, as described, were violent.

REMINGTON: [*crackling, from disruption of mic*] According to the internet dictionary at the top of my Google search, *violence* means "behavior involving physical force intended to hurt, damage, or kill someone or something." I didn't even hurt her desk.

CURTIS: Well, that's the dictionary definition.

REMINGTON: I think I *said* it was the dictionary definition. And what other definition is there? I don't want to go all *Alice in Wonderland* on you, but words have to mean something in particular or there's no point in using language to communicate.

TRINITY: Your superior felt threatened. She feared for her physical well-being, and even feared for her life—

REMINGTON: You cannot be serious.

TRINITY: Threatening members of staff is grounds for dismissal.

REMINGTON: Just because she *felt* threatened doesn't mean she *was* threatened.

TRINITY: I'm afraid it means exactly that. You can't argue with what people feel.

REMINGTON: But just because she *told* you she felt threatened doesn't mean that she actually felt that way.

TRINITY: How else are we to learn how she felt other than by having her tell us? We can't do a Vulcan mind-meld. Feeling threatened was her lived experience.

REMINGTON: Excuse me, but what exactly is the difference between "lived experience" and "experience"?

BRANDON: Can we stay on the subject? This thing is running kind of late.

REMINGTON: Sorry, Mr. Abraham, but I think that is on the subject. That is, you people are following a script whose terms you didn't originate. Lockstep identikit vocabulary suggests a subscription to a rigid orthodoxy that is distorting the nature of this case.

TRINITY: Our frame of reference is progressive contemporary mores, and you seem to be clinging to the past, when you and other people like you always retained the upper hand. Well, times have changed.

REMINGTON: What has not changed—what has always been the case with human beings—is that "feelings" are no more factually sacrosanct than any other form of testimony. So you *can* "argue with what people feel." Because people lie about what they feel. They exaggerate what they feel. They describe what they feel poorly, sometimes out of sheer verbal inadequacy. They mistake one feeling for another. They often have *no idea* what they feel. They will sometimes mischaracterize their emotions with an eye to an ulterior motive—such as to slander a man who does indeed "threaten" them, but only with his comparative professional competence.

TRINITY: Are you saying that Ms. Okonkwo lied to us?

REMINGTON: I imagine she's been accurate about what happened. I doubt her veracity in regard to the texture of our encounter. I don't believe I frightened her. To the contrary, after having been trying to goad me to anger for years, I think she felt supremely satisfied.

TRINITY: She tells us she was frightened. How else are we to know how she felt?

REMINGTON: [*weakly*] But people lie about what they feel . . .

"Tell me this doesn't go round and round all day," Serenata said.

BRANDON: You know how I feel? I feel worn-out. I feel like we're getting nowhere, and we're going to be here till midnight.

REMINGTON: My apologies, Mr. Abraham, but what about how I feel? For example, I *feel* persecuted. Doesn't that mean, ipso facto, that I *am* being persecuted?

TRINITY: Mr. Alabaster, you're privileged. You hold all the cards in a stacked deck. You're an older straight white male who has attacked a young female-identifying person of color—

REMINGTON: Just as a point of information, whatever happened to "African-American"?

TRINITY: *Person of color* is HR's preferred term of art. *POC* is also acceptable.

REMINGTON: Don't you find this eternal merry-go-round of racial terminology a little humiliating? Surely there's an element here of making whitey dance.

[*guffaw*]

"Who laughed?" Serenata asked.

"Brandon," Remington said. "In fact, Brandon was the only one who *ever* laughed."

TRINITY: There's no need to be offensive, thank you.

REMINGTON: Honestly, Mr. Abraham. When you're around other *persons of color*, just you and the brothers, do you call each other *persons of color*? Or for that matter, even *African-American*?

BRANDON: What we say, just us, well—I can't repeat it here.

REMINGTON: See? This churn of euphemisms is solely for the crackers, and for interfacing with crackers. But do you notice how the word for *white* never changes? Even though it's broad-brush and genetically kitchen-sink. My whole life, *white* has simply sat there. Short, unhyphenated, inglorious, lowercase.

TRINITY: What of it? You're feeling neglected? You want some special new word? A capital letter? Why don't we uppercase White Nationalism, then? It's certainly on the rise. Would that make you happy?

REMINGTON: I simply meant—if we keep having to re-launder labels in order to rinse off the stigma that immediately re-attaches to the latest "term of art," the linguistic redress of racial prejudice obviously doesn't work.

BRANDON: I'm totally cool with "black" myself, if that helps. Can we get back on track here? My wife's waiting dinner.

REMINGTON: Fine, I agree, and I'm really sorry about the digressions, Mr. Abraham. But because this label appears to entirely invalidate *my* feelings, and also seems to translate into my having no rights whatsoever, can we look at this "privileged" business—?

TRINITY: Straight white men have had nothing *but* rights, so if it swings slightly the other way—

REMINGTON: [*plowing on*] Lucinda Okonkwo was privately educated at Horace Mann prep school. She went to Columbia and would have had to pay full tuition, because—well, I've asked her about her background, and she's quite proud of the fact that her father made a killing in the oil industry back home. In Lagos, the Okonkwos are upper crust—which she went out of her way to emphasize to me, in a spirit I can only characterize as one of *entitlement*. Her family now lives in an area of Manhattan that I could never afford, much less could my parents have afforded. I grew up in a cramped, grungy house off the beaten track in dumpy Hudson, New York. I was the first in my family to go to college. My father was a construction worker, and my mother cleaned fish. Who's really "privileged"?

TRINITY: Ms. Okonkwo has been subject to racial and gender-based discrimination of a sort you couldn't possibly imagine.

REMINGTON: But *you* can.

TRINITY: I've made it my life's work to try to imagine it, though I always defer to lived experience. Whatever her family's economic position, Ms. Okonkwo would have grown up subject to the discrimination—

REMINGTON: You don't call this show trial discrimination? We wouldn't be here if Lucinda had slammed a hand on *my* desk.

TRINITY: *Please.* She was subject to discrimination born of America's greatest crime against humanity, the mass enslavement of her people. In comparison to which your mother cleaning a few fish, Mr. Alabaster, is neither here nor there.

REMINGTON: Sorry to be niggling—can we use that word anymore, *niggling*? But Ms. Okonkwo's parentage is Nigerian. A full twelve percent of the slaves—

TRINITY: We prefer "enslaved people." They were not, in their essence—

REMINGTON: Twelve percent of the *enslaved people* exported to the United States were captured and sold *by Nigerians*. It was a joint effort. Now that we visit the sins of the fathers upon the sons—and daughters—that makes Lucinda one of the oppressors.

BRANDON: [*quietly*] You know they think they're better than us, don't you?

TRINITY: That was a breathtaking example of blaming the victim, Mr. Alabaster.

REMINGTON: You're aware that Ms. Okonkwo sued her last employer—I should say her last and *only* other employer—for racial bias?

TRINITY: That merely supports my point. Ms. Okonkwo would have been systematically—

REMINGTON: It demonstrates a pattern.

TRINITY: Two examples don't make a pattern.

REMINGTON: They do if you've hired such a young, inexperienced employee that two examples are all you've got. She sued a nonprofit, too, with meager resources, which settled out of court, and was subsequently obliged to fold.

CURTIS: I'd like to get back to the charges under consideration: threatening a member of staff, violent, potentially criminal assault, insubordination, intimidation—

REMINGTON: *Intimidation?* That's a stretch. In wrestling, that woman would get three-to-one odds against a weed like me.

TRINITY: So: not only are you a white supremacist—

REMINGTON: [*laughs*] Now it's *white supremacist?* Hyperbole is the red flag of a weak argument.

TRINITY: —And not only are you a misogynist, but you're a xenophobe who blames POCs for their own enslavement.

REMINGTON: While we're throwing around trendy pejoratives? I don't much like the word, but let's talk about *ageism*, then. This whole proceeding is designed to oust a dinosaur whose management seniority makes his salary burdensomely high for the city, isn't that right? Even better, if you fire me before I retire, you reduce my pension to peanuts. I should remind you that unfair dismissal of inconveniently older employees is illegal. The next hearing at which we meet, you folks could be the ones in the hot seat.

TRINITY: So being accused of a hate crime isn't enough for you? You're threatening this committee, too.

REMINGTON: [*raising his voice*] *Hate crime?* Is this the point at which Number One promises to send me to a Siberian re-education camp instead of having me executed, if only I confess—?

CURTIS: [*loud rap*] We really have to return to the core allegations, here!

[*elongated pause*]

REMINGTON: [*dryly*] I'd like it lodged in the record that Mr. Curtis Pepper just slammed his hand on the table.

[*pause*]

REMINGTON: I'm *terrified*.

[*paper shuffling*]

TRINITY: [*quietly*] Curtis, I think we've heard all we need to, don't you? Mr. Alabaster, you're excused.

[*stacking of files on table, scraping of chair legs, fading rap of shoes*]

BRANDON: [*under breath*] Hey, man. Sorry about all that. It seems like this whole thing got out of control. But they got their ducks in a row before I came on board. Don't think I don't know it, too: I'm just here to make the committee look good.

REMINGTON: [*also under breath*] Don't worry, I knew my goose was cooked before I walked in here.

BRANDON: That woman—she's a piece of work, she is.

REMINGTON: Trinity?

BRANDON: Her, too. But I mean *Lucinda*.

"That closing irony," Serenata said. "Will it help you?"

"It'll make things worse," Remington said. "I made them feel embarrassed, no one likes to feel embarrassed, so the level of hostility will only ramp up."

"If they do end up firing you—"

"I expect the letter to hit the franking machine by noon tomorrow."

"When it will be dark, presumably." Remington looked blank. "Arthur Koestler. You are in a funk. You don't even get your own allusions."

"I should never have alluded to Stalinism. The comparison was historically obscene. Fighting hyperbole with more hyperbole just lands you in the mud with the idiots."

"I thought you kept a grip pretty well, until the end. But by way of perfect payback, you could post this recording on YouTube. There's a constituency—if not necessarily the constituency you want—that would spread this like wildfire. And not to your HR department's advantage. Especially with the table thumping, you could make them a laughingstock."

Remington was old-school, and considered the ploy déclassé. Nevertheless, replaying choice segments became a dinner-party staple in the proceeding weeks, and the few close friends who rallied around found the inquisition hilarious. But the loss of Remington's salary wasn't funny, the drastic reduction of his pension wasn't funny, and the ignominy that attached to the range of prejudices of which he was accused wasn't funny, either—for in the febrile climate of the time, the only evidence required to certify you as a racist was that someone had called you one. More than one secondary friend and colleague withdrew from their acquaintance.

The couple stayed in Albany just long enough for the first tranche of Lucinda's top-Kelvin-rated streetlights to be installed. Her decision to convert the sodium lamps to LEDs first in her former subordinate's neighborhood of Pine Hills may have been no coincidence. The new fixture screamed through their bay windows, insinuating through every crack to score the carpet like a *Star Wars* light saber even after Serenata hung blackout curtains. It pierced the window over the front door, slapping a blaring square of blue-white on the opposing wall like an eviction notice. It seared through their bedroom's narrow wooden blinds and left parallel streaks on the bedspread, as if some predator had raked it with claws. Once the streetlights blazed into a whole second daytime after sunset, their leafy street looked like a prison yard, and skulking in and out of the house they felt watched. The area's inquisitional nocturnal character naturally recalled the HR grilling, and they put the house on the market after a few months. The brave march of technological advancement may have knocked a few thousand off the closing price, because nighttime viewings were so depressing. Return to Remington's hometown of Hudson was financially sensible and considerate of his failing father, but it wasn't where they'd imagined they'd retire—if they'd ever imagined retiring at all, which, like most permanently young people, they hadn't.

Thus in the wake of his dismissal, Serenata's husband felt insulted, humiliated, and unmanned. He felt punished all out of proportion to his "crime," and unappreciated for over thirty years of dedicated service to the city of Albany. He was footloose. Having expected to spend up to ten more years applying a lifetime's expertise to his calling, he was disappointed. He felt ashamed of himself, and doubly ashamed of himself for feeling ashamed of himself. He craved self-respect, but was now ousted from the very arena in which he had always earned it. Early retirement made him feel old. As Serenata had tried to explain to his father, he had too little to look forward to, and had no idea how to navigate the decades that might or might not lie before him in the absence of tangible goals. Walking it back, his indoctrination was inevitable. He couldn't have made a more perfect target for MettleMan.

SEVEN

"You do realize that organized endurance sport is an industry," Serenata idly observed while making dinner later that summer.

"Soft drinks are an industry," Remington said. "We still buy Poland Spring soda water."

"Your spiritual aspirations are being taken advantage of."

"Poland Spring takes advantage of our thirst. Why shouldn't MettleMan capitalize on my other thirsts? Someone might as well."

"Because the money they make off your psychic dehydration is money we can't easily spare."

"Our children are grave disappointments, which relieves us of any obligation to provide them an inheritance. We're old. There is no future. That makes me feel free."

"It makes you feel panicked. Besides. We could live thirty more years."

"Look at my father," he said. "I don't want to."

"That's easy to say."

"That's right," he agreed. "It's very, very easy to say."

"Am I to infer that you intend this undertaking to be a form of suicide?" she asked lightly. "Because I'd count that as abandonment."

The better to one-up a competing franchise, MettleMan boosted the distances of its epic triathlon an increment over previously established standards: not a 2.4- but a 2.6-mile swim; not a 112- but a 116-mile cycle; not a 26.2- but a 26.4-mile run—one feat after the other, with nothing but a frantic change into suitable clothing between events. (Even the original distances seemed perversely specific. What was wrong with swimming *two* miles or cycling *one hundred?*) Making the ordeal closer to a quadrathlon, the cherry on this sundae of insanity was a single chin-up on the finish line—a modest enough exploit you would think, yet a final exertion rumored as the great bridge too far for any number of contestants, especially women, who would sometimes collapse under the bar in tears now that no MC would call out on the loudspeakers, "You are . . . MettleMan!", and they'd not get their fluorescent-orange trophy mug.

Serenata had never been wowed by marathoners, even if confidence that she could have conquered that distance in her heyday was undermined by never having conquered it in practice. For years, a two-mile swim had been routine. Ditto cycling a century, which she'd exceeded countless times in her twenties, when to visit a friend in Woodstock she'd saddle up and hit the George Washington Bridge pedestrian walkway, if only to save money on bus fare.

Yet after a two-mile swim, she always lay flat on the deck for twenty minutes, perfectly inert, every muscle spent. Even after a plain old ten-mile run, she'd often faded off with Remington that evening, eyelids heavy over the main course. As for cycling over a hundred miles, it had always filled her with an hysterical obsession with dinner. Once when she'd clocked the requisite distance after a late start toward Amherst, only to find herself in a rare commercial desert in Connecticut—no restaurants, fast-food outlets, or mini-marts—she'd sullenly set up camp in a roadside wood, gnawing the stale half onion roll and the remains of her peanut butter from lunch with a fury that would have driven a sizable generator.

One by one, then, each feat seemed achievable. All three without

pause seemed both flagrantly impossible and mentally ill. Tommy
was right: people who exercised less than you were pathetic; people
who exercised more than you were nuts. Doubtful that even at her
strongest she'd have been up to a MettleMan, she couldn't trust her
contempt for it. In the face of her husband's deranged aspiration, she
was horrified, intimidated, and completely outclassed. Ergo, she had
to keep her mouth shut.

According to Bambi—and Remington's whole catechism was
now *according to Bambi*—one trained for a "full Mettle" a minimum
of nine months. The client for whom the trainer successfully trawled
in Saratoga Springs in April would never have gotten up to speed
in time for the annual northeastern MettleMan in Lake Placid two
months later. So Remington had set his sights on June of the following year.

That was a long time to keep your mouth shut.

Little matter, since the clamor that descended on their household
when Remington returned from training with the rest of his tri club—
that's right, there was such a thing as a *tri club*, and enough fitness
fanatics even in tiny Hudson, New York, to fill out the membership—
she rarely got a word in edgewise.

Remington was the more gregarious spouse, long accustomed to
the society of the workplace, without which he felt cut off. Joining the
Hudson Tri Club restored that sense of shared mission. As the oldest by twenty-five years, he gave the younger athletes hope for their
futures while never threatening to overtake them on a bike. Paying
his dues with casual self-deprecation, he took gladly to his role as
token geezer, and in short order became something of a mascot. Like
the rest of the club, he joined BruteBody, to which Remington often
repaired for hours, presumably clanking through strength-building
sets, but also shooting the breeze and chugging energy drinks with
his newfound soul mates.

Serenata did not, strictly speaking, hate them, or she didn't hate them all. But she did hate them as an aggregate, and as an invading army. They'd taken to calling her "Sera," which however you spelled it sounded like "Sarah," and that was not her name. Even the cheerful, improbably overweight Cherry DeVries, who really *was* a housewife, treated her like The Wife. Whenever the crew descended, histrionically tired, Serenata was expected to hang jackets, fetch drinks, and knock up impromptu suppers. True, she might have retreated upstairs. But Remington was living more and more of his life away from her. Mutely distributing rounds of G&Ts like some barmaid was worth the abasement to spy.

For who led this ragtag band of second-string superheroes? Who set the distance and sport for the day and charted the course? Who was their inspiration, their savior, and their taskmaster, both feared and revered, if not idolized?

"Are you sure she knows what she's doing?" Serenata finally asked her husband, when his pounding onward on that sore hamstring had not—surprise—allowed it to heal.

"Obviously. Look at her."

"Yes, I've noticed you doing that rather a lot. Just checking her qualifications?"

"You and I are physically faithful, but we're allowed to window-shop. And these days, it's a relief to find one woman who enjoys being looked at—"

"And how," Serenata muttered.

"The 'male gaze' is supposedly an insult. But Bambi would only be insulted if men looked away. Her body's her calling card. It's also her creation, her artwork."

"I don't see *art*. I see maniacal self-involvement. I see spending hours and hours in the gym, every day, and rarely doing much else."

"That's her job."

"It's a dopy job."

"Nothing stops you from joining BruteBody and developing your forearm flexors, if hers make you that jealous."

"I have a real career. I've put some effort into not falling completely apart, but it's a sideline. I try to maintain a sense of proportion."

Or so she claimed. Yet Serenata had grown convinced that this cultivation of the body to the exclusion of all else had somehow sprouted from her own original sin. Was she not always asserting, however tongue-in-cheek, that the rest of the world was "copying her"? So her ten-mile teeming along the river had tracked the seeds of fitness fundamentalism into the house. She couldn't discourage her husband without sounding like a hypocrite. She'd created a monster.

"My trainer believes in me."

"You buy her belief in you. Stop paying that $1,200 monthly retainer, and just see how long her faith in your prowess lasts."

Although Serenata was pretty good at divining what made people tick, Bambi Buffer's motives remained elusive. Obviously the woman wanted the money. Few amateurs in this mildly depressed small town would be able to afford a retainer that size. Why, their household couldn't afford it, either. But even a well-paid trainer wasn't obliged to drop by a client's house five times a week, to prop her feet on an opposite chair and smooth a palm along the hard hillocks of her quadriceps, or to reward his occasional quip with a deep-throated laugh incommensurate with the modest joke. In her doting there seemed, if not an element of the maternal, at least one of possession. Remington had become *her creature*.

Crushingly, too: ever since the spontaneous lesson on marathon day, Serenata had been teaching Tommy March to swim at the Y. Like most adults who never mastered this crucial survival skill as kids, Tommy had freaked out the moment she couldn't touch the bottom of the pool. Easing the girl past that primitive terror had been psychologically interesting, since giving into panic invited exactly what you were afraid of, and the experience of near drowning reinforced the fear. The key turned out to be the soothing lower tones of Serenata's voice, which could induce a state close to hypnosis. Thus by July, the stalky girl had blossomed into an aquatic natural. Her instructor's reward? In August, Tommy joined the tri club.

Remington's long absences allowed Serenata plenty of solitude for catching up on voice-over work. But it was one thing to be left alone, another to feel left out. Rather than get lost in a script, she'd check the computer clock too often. Unsettled, she'd stop the recording to drift downstairs and fail to remember what she'd come down for.

When it was time to exercise, the ritual dread had grown more intense. It was bad enough that running no longer got her out of the house. It was bad enough that biking was blighted by bevies of zealous "fellow" cyclists. It was bad enough, too, that the pool at the Y was forever churning with members of the tri club, whose self-importance could put her off her laps the way a waft from a restaurant toilet could put you off your meal. But now the home calisthenics she'd substituted for all that *motion of the body through space* would not only be tedious; they also felt measly. Compared to the *tri club*'s, her workouts were a joke. This dwarfing was so disagreeable that she was sometimes tempted to skip exercise altogether. But she refused to let these maniacs control her.

Thus on a bright late Saturday afternoon in early September, Serenata duly undertook her high-intensity interval training, trying to put out of mind that at the same time Remington's tri club was feverishly cycling seventy miles cross-country. She took care to stay on the cushioning double layer of fluffy bath mats, to raise her knees all the way to her waist, to maintain a ramped-up pace whose rhythm clashed with the recurring intro soundtrack of back-to-back *Big Bang Theory*, to quell her irritation when the bath mats constantly separated, and to determinedly ignore the building inflammation in her right knee. With fifteen repetitions of a thousand steps, and one hundred cool-down paces between each set, her high-knees running in place lasted one hour and fifty-eight minutes—and still felt paltry.

When she had four sets to go, voices sounded at the side door. As the rabble downstairs grew louder, she upped the tempo, rushing to join the party. Funny how a crowd you wanted no part of could still make you feel excluded.

Entering the roomy, rustic kitchen at last, Serenata found the tri club all in Lycra—which did Cherry DeVries no favors. She wasn't obese, but looser fitting sportswear would have been kinder, and she'd bought aspirational shorts a size too small. By contrast, Tommy's secondhand gear was overlarge and fatigued, and she kept pulling her waistband up and tugging gathered fabric down her thighs. Universally unbecoming, cycling shorts having ever come into fashion was inscrutable.

Mind, the style was *almost* universally unbecoming. On Bambi Buffer, the sleek shorts in sunny yellow conformed to her sharp hip bones, across which a yardstick could have balanced without touching flesh in between. They showed off her ass as hard and high. Each buttock shadowed when she took a step and the glutes contracted. A sleeveless V-neck, her tight powder-blue vest zipped up the front, pressing breasts the better part pectoral muscle into a semblance of cleavage. She'd burnished a smashing summer tan. Sun had lightened her tawny hair, its close boyish cut recently trimmed.

"I can't tell you what a relief it is to no longer be the only woman in this club," Cherry confided to Tommy. "That ride has set my you-know-where just raging. Yeast infection. The guys wouldn't understand."

"Hey, whadda ya mean, you've been the 'only woman'?" Bambi said, pulling a bottle of red wine from the rack. Another sat empty on the counter.

"You don't count, Bam-Bam. Whatever you are, plain old 'woman' ain't it." Lanky, about forty, and the club's sole MettleMan veteran other than their Dear Leader, Sloan Wallace had two identical double-*M* tattoos on his right bicep: four peaks of adjacent orange, like a child's drawing of a mountain range. If you didn't recognize the signage, you weren't an initiate but a slob.

"Think about getting a wider seat, Cherry," Bambi said, popping the cork.

"Or let me take a look at the height and tilt." Chet Mason was the club's technocrat. "The bones of your ass should hit the back of the seat. You may be sitting too far forward on the tongue—"

"Whoa, baby!" cried Hank Timmerman, the sleazebag. "Sounds like some happy ride!"

Remington pecked his wife's cheek distractedly. "Hey, we have any snacks? Everybody's starving."

These convocations now frequent, Serenata had begrudgingly laid in crackling bags of solidified palm oil. The crunchy crap would be just the beginning.

Bambi nodded at Serenata's ratty cotton shorts. "Had your own little home workout?" She was prone to address The Wife at a perpendicular, throwing the odd lazy looping side-glance, as if underhanding a softball.

"Yeah, you know, one of those Jane Fonda videos," Serenata said. "I know she's pushing eighty, but I still can't keep up with her. And I find getting sweaty kind of icky."

"Sweat's the Chanel of tri, honey," Bambi said coolly, taking an inattentive gulp from a juice glass. She'd managed to locate their last bottle of pricey Napa syrah.

"Bam-Bam gets extra Kettle chips," Sloan said, "after all that doubling back to check on Rem. Rest of us did seventy; add the babysitting, I bet Bam put in one-forty."

"You do realize I'm riding the brake," Remington said genially. "Just so Bambi gets a proper workout."

"You really shouldn't feed the beast," Sloan said. "Bam's being a glutton for punishment is still greed of a kind."

"You should consider replacing that clunker, Rem," Chet recommended. "Titanium tri bikes are so fucking frictionless that the biggest problem is falling asleep."

In contrast to Serenata's battered warhorse, circa 1991, Remington's $1,300 "clunker" was only five months old.

"Rem says you've biked a bit yourself?" Bambi asked as their hostess fetched Sloan another beer.

"Here and there." Vulgar submission of an athletic CV was out of the question.

"At your age, Sera, you might consider an e-bike," Bambi suggested. "I recommend plug-in models to older clients all the time. Keeps them on the road, even with, you know—bum joints."

"Yes, I've considered one of those," Serenata said brightly. "But it seems more cost efficient to go straight to the mobility scooter."

She retreated to the women by the stove.

"You don't have to make supper for this crowd every time," Cherry said. "We could always order takeout."

"Oh, pasta's no big deal," Serenata said, pulling out their largest pot. Having tried the takeout option, she knew the drill: getting everyone's orders straight was exhausting, and she and Remington would get stuck with the bill.

"What do you want me to chop?" Tommy offered, jumping up.

"Aren't you tired?"

"Some," she allowed, then lowered her voice. "Fucking Sloan is always showing off in the lead, and I just . . . Twenty-five *m-p-h*, steady? And twenty uphill? I can't keep it up. Then I fall back, and feel like a girl."

"Don't tell anyone, but you are a girl," Serenata whispered. "If you're going to participate in a mixed athletic club, cut yourself some slack."

"But aren't *you* tired?" Tommy solicited as Serenata filled the pot with water. "I heard you upstairs when we got here. HIT is a killer."

"Yes, but unlike some people I think that's my business. Here. Parsley."

As the three women did what women almost always ended up doing, the men defaulted to a stock sport: razzing their absent member Ethan Crick for having begged off the afternoon's cycle training at the last minute.

"So what was Crick's excuse this time?" Hank said.

"Stubbed his toe," Sloan supposed. "Swelled up something awful, and wouldn't fit in his bike shoe."

"He's been shaving his legs to decrease his wind resistance," Remington said, "and now he has ingrown hairs."

"He did fwee cwunches wivout AC," Hank lisped, "and cowapsed fwum heat stwoke."

"Oh, it was a ton more creative than that. You know Ethan," Bambi said. "Something about how this particular back muscle knots, so that whenever he turns his head a paralyzing pain shoots up his neck. That bozo never just has a headache."

"But I know what he means," Serenata said, stemming cherry tomatoes. "From hunching for hours over the handlebars, a shoulder muscle cramps and pinches a nerve. The pain goes straight up the back of your neck, and it feels like a bee sting."

"Funny," Bambi said reluctantly. "That's what Ethan said. 'Like a bee sting.'"

Serenata should have stayed out of it, but this hacking on Ethan Crick had become an ugly club dependency, because it made them feel hardier by comparison. She was relieved that Remington had escaped being the club's punching bag. Nevertheless, this mild-mannered ophthalmologist was the only member of the tri club who resisted Bambi's defiant approach to injury. He'd no desire to wreck his body in the process of perfecting it. Yet Ethan's proclivity for moderation might indeed have ill-suited him to MettleMan, whose website claimed that moderation was for chumps.

"Weekend after weekend," Sloan said, "Crick is getting just the practice he needs. He's a DNF in training."

"What's a DNF?" Serenata asked.

They recited in unison with melodramatic horror, "*Did Not Finish.*"

"I've heard more than one MettleMan DNF has actually offed himself," Sloan said. "Talk about double loser."

Bambi clapped Remington's shoulder. "Mind you, now! Not one of my clients has ever DNF'ed. You finish, or I don't let you start. Sloan's right. I seen folks' spirits crushed for life—*for life*—by staggering to that chin-up bar after midnight."

"That's when the race always cuts off?" Serenata asked.

"Like Cinderella," Bambi said. "*Bong-bong-bong*, riches to rags."

"I think quitters should be branded," Chet said. "Sizzle it right on the ass with a hot iron: '*D-N-F.*' Which also stands for 'Disgraced Numb-nuts Fuck-up.'"

In his mid-twenties and perpetually gung-ho, with puppy-dog eyes and floppy brown hair, Chet was a local kid who'd gone to some community college, studying one of those broad, bland subjects like media studies that left you in much the same place as before you enrolled. He was now a barista at a Hudson internet café, and still living at home. A gym junkie, he'd developed a bunchy, constricted physique that wasn't altogether fetching. Lately he'd latched on to the idea of becoming a triathlon pro. He certainly seemed to have the chops. Still, with these events now attracting participants in the tens if not hundreds of thousands, no big commercial sports company was likely to shell out gear, expenses, and a stipend for a male triathlete who was barely five-foot-eight.

Sloan Wallace was the one who looked the part. Leggy, lean, and languorous, he must have been at least six-three. But Serenata couldn't imagine Sloan going up against an intimidating elite for Nike sponsorship. He was a small-pond competitor, who after ditching the scramble of Wall Street had moved up to Hudson to start a second life renovating classic cars. He appeared to be good at it and eked out a living preying on the adolescent ambitions of retirees with capital. In a one-horse town like this, he attracted the awe of younger provincials, who all thought re-chroming the grille of a 1957 Pontiac Bonneville was the coolest job ever. Sloan had cachet in these parts, and his suave, syrupy bearing made him a magnet for women. Naturally he was divorced—he was the sort of man always looking to trade up—and in the world of endurance sport, his brazen braggadocio was an asset.

"So are your kids really into your tri thing?" Tommy asked Cherry over broccoli. "Or are they all like, 'Where's my dinner?'"

"Oh, the kids are super supportive," Cherry said. "When I come back from training, they bring me pillows and herbal tea."

"What about your husband?"

Cherry paused the paring knife over a floret. "I guess Sarge is another story."

"Why's he down on the idea?"

"He thinks it's ridiculous, to be honest. Not triathlons, but the idea of my doing one. He thinks I'm only trying to lose weight. He thinks I don't have a chance in heck of finishing, so I'm only setting myself up for a fall. Then I'll comfort eat and only get fatter."

"*Are* you trying to lose weight?"

"Well, sure. But that's not the only reason I'm doing this. We got married pretty young—even if we didn't think we were young, you know how that is, or you will in a few years. I tended a grocery store till after high school, but I've never had a real job, because I got pregnant right away—which is fine, of course, I love Deedee to bits. But I want something, you know, to be proud of. I'm proud of all three of my children, but they're not my personal accomplishments. They're people, and they're their own accomplishments. Sarge has the antiques shop, and though it's been through some tough times, he can still say he's made a go of a business. I want to be able to say I've done something, too."

"Are you hoping to, like—show Sarge?" Tommy asked. "That he's underestimated you?"

"Better believe it! Though I'm worried that if I ever do become a triathlete, well—that it'll just make him mad."

"Is he mad already?"

"Yeah. He's pretty mad. He thinks I'm out-guying him—if that's a word."

"If it isn't, it should be," Remington chimed in, while searching out another bottle of red. "The women are *manning up*, and the boys all want to wear dresses."

"They can have 'em!" Cherry said. "I'd rather have breathable spandex."

Serenata had once supposed that during training surely Cherry DeVries kept Remington company at the back. He said no—Cherry maintained a position solidly in the middle of the pack. The assumption that a heavy woman would lag exhibited a certain prejudice, but mass had to have been a disadvantage—exaggerating her drag in water, increasing the pull of gravity on a bike, and forcing her to propel more weight on a run. If she kept up with Tommy, Cherry was the more impressive athlete.

Serenata threw herself into parboiling the broccoli and dissolving anchovies in hot olive oil, all the while telling herself that no one had forced her to make this meal, and nothing was more unbearable than people who freely elected to do something and then turned around and resented the imposition. But after the interval training, the right knee was yowling. The worst possible activity for these joints wasn't walking or running but *standing*—also known as *cooking*. Fetching snacks, refilling drinks, and initiating supper for eight, she'd been on her feet for three hours. Slicing olives, she rested all her weight on the left leg. Unused, the right knee stiffened, and crossing the room to salt the pasta water she had to haul the bum leg straight. As Bambi stretched out at the dining table and crossed her legs prettily at her slender ankles—she'd had the presence to bring flattering ballet flats to change into—Serenata noted that her own knees had puffed up again. The swelling had spread to her lower thighs, creating an unpleasantly tubular effect. Since childhood, her legs had been her finest feature. In the end, she lurched to a drawer for a longer apron, not to protect her shabby sports clothes from anchovy grease but to conceal her *finest feature* from the tri club's critical gaze, including the appraising eye of her husband.

"You're limping," Tommy whispered.

"In that I'm the one doing the limping," Serenata snapped, "why do you think I need to be *informed* of that?"

Tommy looked as if she might cry. She was only twenty years old. Surrounded by prospective antagonists, you didn't take out your frustrations on your only ally.

Serenata quickly laid a hand on Tommy's arm. "I'm sorry. Thank you for noticing. You're the only one who does."

"Have you scheduled the surgery yet?" Tommy asked sternly.

"No." Serenata turned back to the olives. She should never have bought the kind with pits.

"Why not?"

"I'm managing."

"You're not managing. They're only getting worse. You keep exercising on them every day, and then afterward you can hardly walk."

"I don't want to get knee replacements. People say online you'd better get both done at once, because when you find out how awful it is, you'll never do the other one."

"It's not like you can wait till you're in the mood. You'll never be in the mood. At some point you won't be able to exercise at all, and then you'll be sorry."

"I'm already sorry. I've seen pictures of the scars. They're hideous."

"Scars? Who cares. You're getting old. You're being a little princess."

"I won't be lectured by a whippersnapper."

"The *whippersnapper's* riding you 'cause nobody else is, far as I can see. Why doesn't Remington notice you limping? Why doesn't Remington mash a phone in your hand and make you fix a date?"

"Because Remington doesn't care about anything to do with *me* anymore." The words were out before Serenata could stop them. She'd barely rescued herself from announcing more starkly still, *Because Remington doesn't care about me anymore.*

"But he's your husband." Tommy sounded bewildered.

Serenata smiled tightly. "We are specializing in statements of the obvious tonight. I just meant, he's not thinking about my problems right now. If you're ever in a long-term marriage, you'll find out: spouses drift. It doesn't mean they're cheating or anything. Their attention wanders. And then it comes back."

Tommy looked skeptical. Serenata didn't find this version of events persuasive herself. Rattled, she dumped three pounds of rotelli in the pot, though the water hadn't quite come to a rolling boil—much like the unease in her marriage.

This time when they settled down to dinner, Serenata placed her wineglass firmly next to Remington's usual chair at the end of the long, planked table. That didn't prevent you-know-who from taking the chair at his other elbow, but at least she'd not be exiled at the opposite end with Hank, who'd been hitting the G&Ts and was getting wasted.

"Check out the commuters chugging around town," Bambi said after the pasta had been demolished, touching Remington's slender wrist. "They most always go *choom-choom-choom*—pressing heavy on the downstroke, then letting up on the upstroke. But what you want is a smooth, steady application of force. Remember to pull up on the cleat. You don't want variable surges of power."

It was a wonder that the average schoolchild mastered riding a bike at six, given that operating the mechanism was so terribly complicated.

Serenata had remained quiet throughout the meal, while Chet got excited about brands of wet suits, Cherry confided her embarrassing incontinence on long runs, and Bambi chided Hank to stop teeming ahead and then blowing out too early. Passivity was as enervating as the conversation, so at last Serenata put a hand in.

"I wonder," she said carefully, "if a lot of older people are able to take part in endurance sports because they weren't especially active when they were young."

Bambi looked up sharply. "How do you figure that? Sitting on your butt being the best preparation for getting off it."

"I talked to some elderly marathoners in Saratoga Springs," Serenata said. "Every single one discovered exercise in their fifties or even sixties, like Remington."

"That's not surprising," Bambi said. "It's an era thing. This is a movement, sweeping across the country, and pretty soon we're gonna see a whole super race—"

"Social trends are part of it. But maybe what makes it possible to demand so much from an aging body is that you haven't already worn it out."

"Exercise don't wear you out, honey. It builds you up."

"Only up to a point," Serenata said. "The body is a mechanism, with moving parts that degrade from use. Some of those parts break down, like the parts of a car if you drive it too far."

"The body's an organism, not a machine," Bambi said. "It thrives from being stressed. The more you ask, the more you get. Maybe you never asked enough."

"Oh, Serenata's asked plenty," Remington intervened. His defense was touching, but Bambi ignored it.

"There are limits," Serenata said.

"That has to be the most suck-dick motto I ever heard. How about, *Fuck limits*. Limits are all in your head. See, this is what I was warning you about, Rem."

"Negative thinking," Remington said.

"All this, *oh, he's gonna wear out like a car*. It's fear-based. But I guess that's the kind of mind-set you get when you make a living from talk."

"That's me," Serenata said. "Blah-blah-blah."

"My wife is an accomplished voice-over artist." Remington pressed his trainer's arm with a forefinger. "I told you to watch that."

"Bambi's right about limits, though," Cherry said. "At first, I didn't think I could run to the end of the block. But I've been plumb dumbfounded what it turns out I can do! You have to keep telling yourself not to be a little baby."

"But sometimes that 'little baby,'" Serenata said, "might be aware that you're damaging yourself, that you're overdoing it."

Tommy grinned. "Bambi doesn't believe there's such a thing as overdoing it."

"But the vogue for extreme sports is pretty recent," Serenata said. "Is there any research on what happens to people who keep at it year after year? For decades?"

"Planning to find out!" Chet said down the table. "By Rem's age, I'll be tri-ing to the moon!"

"Either that or you'll be wheeled around on a gurney with a tube down your throat," Serenata said sweetly. "That's the question."

"I learned a hip word from Rem the other day," Bambi said. "You know your hub's pretty smart?"

"After thirty-three years, I might have noticed that."

"*Catastrophizing*," Bambi pronounced with relish. "That's what you're doing, and it's corrupting my client. *Catastrophize*, and you can wreck all my hard work."

"I thought it was Remington's hard work."

"Joint effort, hon. This crew builds muscle as a team. And know what the most important muscle is? Not the glutes, not the quads, but the mind. Familiar with that expression 'muscle-head'? Supposed to be an insult. It ain't. Your mind *is* a muscle, and your hub's brain, with a little help from his friends, is getting big and hard."

"With a certain ass in the saddle out front," Hank said, "it's not only his brain getting big and hard."

"When I was in high school," Serenata said, turning a blind eye to the juvenile trash talk, "the jocks were considered the morons. Now that the educated class has discovered athletics, suddenly sport requires vast cognitive powers."

"You can overthink tri, no question," Bambi said. "But smarts is still an advantage. Rem here has met his distance, every single time. He's a little slower than the rest of us—"

"You're overgenerous," Remington said. "I'm a lot slower."

"But this guy, he's never once set out to finish a certain number of miles and stopped short. You *are* aware of that?"

"Sure," Serenata said casually. In truth, she was not aware of this.

Bambi clapped Remington's shoulder again; it was a habit. "You got the determination. I can coach technique, I can design you a sked, but the *ferocity* got to be there from the start."

"Some forms of determination are dangerous," Serenata said.

With a guffaw, Bambi poured herself another glass of red, then topped up Remington's to the rim. Should Serenata want a refresher, too, she'd have to open another bottle. "You are a trip and a half, sunshine. I got half a mind to print that on our club T-shirts: SOME FORMS OF DETERMINATION ARE DANGEROUS."

Serenata clarified, "I'm not happy about that hamstring."

"You and Crick," Bambi said. "Worrywarts in a pod."

At the other end of the table, Chet was talking up his future as a tri pro to Sloan. "Once you start pulling in the sponsors, they give you all this free stuff! Running shoes, bike shorts, swimming goggles, you name it! And especially if you land a title or two, some of these deals include a serious whack of cash. So I've got my eye on one of your muscle cars. Kind of appropriate, right? Like that 1964 GTO."

"I shouldn't be telling you this," Sloan said tolerantly; no way did that man believe Chet would ever make pro. "But mechanically, that GTO is shit. You'd be way better off with the '67."

"Chet," Serenata said, "do you have any backup ambition? A plan B? Because even if you do go pro, it must be hard to maintain peak performance at such a grueling sport for more than a few years."

Bambi slammed the table hard enough that at the DOT she'd have been fired. "Sweetie pie, you generate more clouds of doom than a fog machine in the movies. It must be so dismal in your head, I don't know how you get out of bed."

"Plan Bs are for suckers," Chet said. "A backup would be planning for failure."

"Yeah, you're not supposed to let those thoughts into your mind,"

Tommy agreed. "Like that MettleMan bumper sticker I put on my bedstead: DOUBT NOT."

"Has a biblical ring to it," Serenata said. "Like Moses."

"If that's your idea of ridicule," Bambi said, "you're gonna have to make more of an effort. Tri is a belief system, all right. But the belief is in yourself."

"But if *all* you believe in is yourself," Serenata said, "isn't that on the slight side? It sounds awfully like egotism. If nothing else, it sounds lonely."

"Look around you," Bambi said. "We're among plenty of friends. You're the one sounds lonely."

Serenata pulled up short. She did feel lonely.

"Tri's been my salvation, man." Hank had passed through the raucous phase of inebriation, and had progressed to the maudlin one. Cherry having extricated herself from his arm around her by at least pretending to need the bathroom, he'd now draped himself over Chet.

If Cherry was unfeasibly heavy for endurance sport, Hank was unfeasibly gaunt. His jagged black locks always looked unwashed. His stick-thin limbs were covered in straggles of disagreeable dark hair. He was still pale in early September. His expressions ranged from leering to desperate. Perhaps twenty-eight, he'd been imprisoned for possession at least once.

"When I was inside, the only thing kept me sane was the weights room," Hank went on. "I promised myself this time when I got out I'd keep it up, right? I wouldn't make bad decisions. I'd realize I had an illness, right? And the illness is inside me, but I'm not actually the illness, right? So first thing on release I joined BruteBody on one of them one-month free trials. They kept telling me in the joint that I had to believe it was possible to change, or I could be a danger to myself. Sure enough, it wasn't much more than a week of going to the gym every day when I start to spot the warning signs. Racing thoughts. Intrusive thoughts. Basically, I just couldn't stop thinking about scag. I knew I was right on the edge of scoring. And that's when Bambi rescued me, man. Instead of copping a bag, I find myself out on this run with her, man. And I look back now and think it's funny, since I bet it wasn't longer than five miles or even less, but it seemed like *forever*, man. Like it just about killed me. But now I can go twelve, even fifteen, no problem, right? I got something to live for. I'm not addicted to scag, I'm addicted to going out there and fucking killing myself, man, on the road and in the pool. It's a totally different high, a clean high. So I got to thank you guys, right? I'm gonna tri, tri, tri, tri, over and over again, man."

Serenata had heard this testimonial before. The tuneful *tri, tri, tri, tri* recalled Nancee's *"joy, joy, joy, joy* down in my heart!" on the trip to Saratoga Springs.

Tommy joined Cherry in volunteering to help clean up.

"For ten bucks an hour?" Serenata's wisecrack came out doleful.

"Nah," Tommy said. "For you? Seven-fifty."

The removal of dishes cleared space for Bambi and Remington to arm wrestle. Even after all that red wine, Bambi would have little trouble winning the day, though she kept her opponent's arm straight up for long enough to ensure that the older man saved face. Besides, the pressure he applied brought out the dazzling definition of her bicep.

Serenata watched unresponsively with her chair pulled back from the table, though she felt a great deal farther away than that. On the occasions she and Remington had asked people to dinner in times past, the biggest problem had been entering into a rapid, playful back-and-forth that excluded their guests, because the couple never managed to invite anyone they wanted to talk to more than to each other. Equally alienating for visitors who just wanted to move on to

the cheese course, they would wrestle for too long over a point neither would concede, just as these two were going at it now—albeit
with a literalism that Remington of old would have considered crass.

The rest of the club was cheering and hooting, and the other
three men lined up to be next. When Bambi lowered Remington's
arm, she didn't bang it, but arced it gracefully to the wood with a hint
of sorrow. You'd think that a husband would be glad of being well
matched, for rhetorically their marriage was a draw. But maybe he
was one of those curious men who found it more erotic to be beaten.

Hank was up next, and didn't have a prayer. "I let you win," he
said, slackening in the hot seat. "More—sivulrish."

"I'd be more *chivalrous*," Bambi said, "not to mention more professional, if I kept you from taking on any athletic challenge when
you're slammed."

"One to talk," Hank said darkly.

"My veins run with red wine," she said. "And I can hold my li-
quor."

Although appearing to find it harder than he expected, after a
brief grapple Chet flattened his coach's arm. Bambi's eyes flashed
before she covered the fury with bluster: "Well, if you couldn't drop a
girl after all those curls, I'd say you need a new personal trainer!" She
curved even defeat into her own success. She really didn't like losing.

When Sloan took his turn, the antagonists were a matched set.
They both had the naturally well-formed limbs of born athletes, and
the elongated figures of avatars in video games. Meeting each other's
gaze, each seemed to apply gradually more force, but nothing moved;
the sides of their palms grew whiter. Only after a full minute did it
become apparent that Sloan was merely holding her there.

"So how long do you want to do this?" His voice was relaxed.

"You're a condescending son of a bitch, aren't you?"

"I'm a man," he said.

"Same thing."

Wham. Bambi's forearm hit the table.

"Pretty impressive force, considering," Sloan allowed.

Bambi massaged her wrestling hand. "Yeah, right. That felt a little like arm wrestling with, like, the *wall.*"

Sloan laughed. "From you, I guess being compared to a mindless slab of Sheetrock is a compliment."

Bambi raised a forefinger. "Planks! More of a gender-level playing field."

Then they were off to the living room, audience trailing. Serenata watched limply from the doorway. Side by side, the two paragons extended over the Oriental carpet, propped on their toes and elbows, forearms forward and flat on the floor. Chet started his stopwatch. Obviously this parlor game was tacky. So their hostess wasn't about to mention that she could maintain that plank herself for a solid five minutes. Besides, among the super race, a mere five minutes was sure to draw derision.

A contest over who could hold a stationary pose the longer was dull. Restless, Chet and Hank began to perform feats of strength with the furniture. Serenata tried to catch Remington's eye to get him to discourage them, but her husband was lifting an armchair overhead. Finally, Sloan sank to the carpet and rolled onto his back.

"Nine minutes, twenty-four seconds!" Chet declared.

"Uncle, bitch," Sloan said. "Happy now?"

But Bambi maintained the position. "Tell me when it's ten!" Her voice was strangled. Only once Chet announced the ten-minute mark did she also collapse, flopping onto her back and gasping.

"Should have known better, Wallace." Still catching her breath, Bambi rose to a stand. "Sheetrock abs."

"How long did it take you to work up to *ten minutes?*" Remington asked.

"Oh, these puppies are a life's work, pal," Bambi said. "You know how pregnant women always have folks wanting to touch their stomach? Well, that's what happens to me in gyms, only without the kid."

"Seriously?" Remington said. "And you let them?"

"Sometimes," Bambi said coyly. Lifting the baby-blue vest, she tensed her abdominal muscles. "Have a feel."

Tentatively, Remington laid a hand on his trainer's midsection.

"Stop."

They all turned to the doorway. Remington took his hand back.

"I think that's quite enough," Serenata said soberly, and turned to the kitchen to help the two other women finish cleaning up. The humorless admonishment put the kibosh on the evening's antics, and within a few minutes their guests had left. She was sorry to see Tommy go. Being left alone with her husband was less of a relief than usual.

Serenata sat on the edge of the bed, facing away. Spouses don't feel close all the time. She and Remington plunged separately into other aspects of their lives, and then reported back. The very obliviousness of these periods of engrossment in other matters, their very ability to put their spouse's entire existence out of mind for hours or even days, sprang from a sensation of safety—a happy complacency. This felt different.

Remington was toweling his hair after his midnight shower. He allowed his terrycloth robe to drape open. He'd become more at ease with nakedness in the last year. Serenata had grown less so. Having undressed, she was aware that the knots of the chenille bedspread would be dimpling her ass, just as the sock-lines scored her ankles and marred what remained of the tibias' once-beguiling slope. The peach-tinted polish on her toenails had partially chipped off, perhaps a point of inattentive grooming that was an early sign of letting herself go. Where the polish was missing, the ugly vertical striations of aging keratin showed through. Crushed in bedraggled running shoes for decades, the toes had contorted, mashing together and overlapping, as if made of wet clay and someone had stepped on them. From a seated vantage point, that inside bulge of a right knee bone was at its most apparent. The distortion was subtle enough—schoolboys weren't likely to point and laugh on the street—but call it what it was: a deformity. Her breasts had long ago dropped; when she experimented with clenching her pectorals, they effectively mounded a second set of mini-mammaries above the first, as if she were a freak, or had tumors. Because her shoulders were drooping as badly as her breasts—precisely this evening, a lifetime commitment to good posture seemed to have run its course—a slight sag of flesh creped over her abdomen, destroying any impression that their muscles were made of Sheetrock. She watched what she ate, but she'd had babies, for which women were reliably punished twice.

Commonly, they had no problem with silence. It only meant they had nothing to say. This silence called for filling, for if it went on much longer something would get worse, or perhaps something awful would happen. Perhaps something awful would happen anyway.

"You didn't seem to have a very good time tonight," he said.

"I wonder why that would be."

"They're not bad people."

"I never said they were bad people."

"You can be very judgmental."

"I exercise judgment. Unlike some people."

"We were horsing around. It was harmless."

"It was embarrassing."

"You're the only one who was embarrassed."

Serenata forced herself to sit more upright. "My dear, I'm sorry to say this, but your obsession with endurance sport has made your conversation a little trying. You used to talk about politics, or urban planning, or even about the television programs we watched as kids—and I'm highly entertained remembering those insufferable child actors in *Flipper*. I've enjoyed analyzing why we both watched so many programs we hated, and why children so often despise other children on TV. But now it's all techniques for getting your wet suit off fast enough during 'T1.' If I didn't have a good time tonight, that was mostly because I was bored."

"The subject of physical fitness has never bored you when it was your fitness."

"You're quite wrong. It bores me to death. Which is why I rarely talk about it, in case you haven't noticed."

"You talk about it more than you realize."

"Well, then, I'm sorry for boring you, too. You know, you say I didn't have a good time tonight like an accusation. As if I refused to have a good time."

"You didn't exactly dive into the spirit of the occasion."

"What spirit would that be?"

"Letting our hair down after a hard ride. Good-natured rivalry. Comparing notes on a challenging long-term project."

"It's not my project."

"You put yourself outside the project and pronounce upon it."

"You hardly spoke to me all night."

"We had guests."

"Yes. And I made a considerable effort to engage with your trainer."

"Everything you said was critical."

"What about what she said?"

"You put her on the defensive."

"Do you find it interesting that the whole club is white?"

"Not really. Hudson is a majority white town."

"It's barely over half white, actually," she said. "A quarter black, coming up on ten percent Latino. I looked it up."

"It wouldn't be surprising to form a small all-white club, even if the town were majority nonwhite." His delivery steady and uninflected, Remington had returned to the punishing neutrality he preferred when subjects of this sensitivity arose. "It might be politically awkward, but most people are more comfortable around people like themselves. They self-sort, often unconsciously. Blacks, Hispanics, and Asians do the same thing. It isn't precisely racism. More a natural desire to recognize one another, and to be able to relax. Those perfectly 'diverse' cliques of friends, like a Coca-Cola ad teaching the world to sing—they're a television fiction."

"But I've glanced at your triathlon videos. The people drawn to this pastime are overwhelmingly white. I think that means something."

"Are you insinuating that endurance sport is only for the well-off?"

"Not at all. Ethan may make a passable living as an ophthalmologist, but he wouldn't get wealthy off a town this size. Sloan had money once, but restoring cars is time intensive, and I bet he barely breaks even. The others are struggling, even Bambi if it weren't for you, and Hank bounces between drug addict and career criminal."

"So what are you getting at?"

Serenata hadn't formulated what she was getting at before she went down this road. As her destination came into focus, she wanted to turn around. "There's a . . . regression, a . . . narrowing, a . . . retreat. A withdrawal. A lowering of horizons. A gross reduction of expectations. A new materialism, which doesn't even extend to patio furniture. The material is the body. It's a shrinking down to the very least you can be without being dead. A battening down of the hatches, a crawling into a hole."

"It doesn't feel like any of that. Getting physically stronger translates directly into strength of other kinds."

"It's a particular brand of flourishing, at the sacrifice of other flourishings. For all that mental resilience your trainer touts, it's anti-intellectual. Which is weird, for you. Have you noticed you've stopped reading? Sports magazines, training manuals, yes. But I can't remember the last time you tackled one of those state-of-the-nation tomes you used to furiously underline in red felt-tip."

"Apparently you're spending your time keeping track of how I spend mine, and I don't see how that's any better."

"Also—have you noticed that we hardly ever have sex anymore?"

"I'm sixty-five. And after training, I'm often tired. Are you proposing we do something about it—like, tonight?"

Serenata's laugh was involuntary. Getting from where they were now to sexual intercourse would have entailed running an emotional marathon before lights-out. "I was wondering whether you miss it."

"Of course. But my powers—we may have to accept that they're on the wane."

"At present, you're focused exclusively on your physical *powers*, which I'm led to believe are only on the increase."

"Listen." He walked around the corner of the bed and touched her shoulder. "I'm not having an affair with my personal trainer."

A year ago, she'd never have imagined this B-movie cliché arising in their bedroom. "Since I didn't think you were, I'm a little perplexed why you feel the need to clarify that."

"You focus on Bambi Buffer to give your jealousy a face. But the jealousy is bigger than one woman. You're jealous of the whole package—the club, the training schedule, my gains, my goals, the project. On that score, I can't help you."

"This 'project' is unworthy of you, and I can't pretend to think something nicer."

"Why do you always have to diminish it?"

"I don't need to diminish it. It's already small."

"The experience of pushing past a mental barrier, and still completing another ten laps when you're at the end of your rope—it isn't small."

"The achievement is small. Ordinary and not an achievement at all."

"Most things are ordinary and not major achievements. I've been fired. I'm retired. Just how do you want me to be spending my time instead?"

"I don't even know," she said honestly. "Just not like this."

"Your taking against this from the start has been a terrible mistake."

"That's the question, then. Who's making the mistake."

"You're trying to come between me and the fulfillment of my potential—"

"Please. The language of vainglorious positivism is worse than *intersectionality* and *micro-aggressions*."

"If anything, our household has suffered from an excess of irony. It's a common disease of the over-educated. All that superior drollery is a cover for effeteness and passivity. It's a fear of putting ourselves on the line."

"You've put yourself on the line plenty. That's why you were fired."

"Ask any other American who's in the wrong in this situation, and they'd say you."

"I'm aware of that. But we're not asking them. I'm asking you. Which would win out if you had to choose? Triathlon"—none of them said *a* triathlon, or *the* triathlon, just *triathlon*, which made it sound more majestic, like an awesome force of nature that simply is, gravity or magnetism, not a series of separate sporting events but something big and indivisible, just as faithful adherents to other religions didn't reference *a* God or *the* God, but simply *God*—"or your marriage?"

"That's a false choice and beneath you. It seems to me that not putting our marriage on the table is one of the rules. An unwritten rule, which makes it only more sacrosanct. Besides which, it's been thirty-three years, and we're old."

"Old enough to stay together out of laziness. From lack of imagination."

"Are you threatening me?"

He was shouting. That made her quiet. "I'm trying to talk to you."

"Because if anyone should threaten anyone here, shouldn't it be the other way around? Aren't you the one who, implicitly or explicitly, has been pissing on my entire purpose for the last year? Aren't I the one who should be reaching my limit?"

"There's no such thing as a limit, according to your guru."

"I'd prefer not to think of our marriage as an endurance sport."

"Maybe you should," she said. "Maybe then you'd take an interest in it."

EIGHT

"I'm not saying we're about to split up," she blurted to her father-in-law in March, after yet another painful pause. When at a total loss for conversation, she ended up unburdening what she probably shouldn't, because the only unexhausted material she could lay hands on was her inmost thoughts. "But we've always enjoyed each other's company. And now I—don't. Enjoy his company. Or not as much."

"It's this triathlaton business," Griff said warily. At ninety, he'd not want to hear that his son was in danger of divorce. Leaving aside his practical and emotional dependence on Serenata, a divorce would mean change, and to Griff even a rearrangement of his late wife's porcelain figurines was anathema.

"Even when he's not training, he reads sports autobiographies, or listens to inspirational podcasts by 'tri' record-setters. I can't tell you how sick I am of the soundtrack to *Chariots of Fire*. He used to read bios of Robert Moses, or the latest Thomas Friedman. I miss the blues, and films with tragic endings. But he won't subject himself to anything sad or dark."

"Remy's always been single-minded. Time was, he was single-minded about *you*. From that first tryout for those subway announcements, I could tell he'd fixed on roping this lady in—the one with the sultry voice. He never confided in his parents much, so when he couldn't stop mentioning you, I knew you were it." Griff's strategy was hardly subtle. Recollection of their courtship was meant to revive romantic coals.

"I'm sorry that he's also been making so little time to come see you—"

Griff snorted. "Try *no* time. That boy hasn't been by here in months."

"He thinks you're hostile to his endeavor. You contaminate his pure heart."

"He's making a damned fool of himself. Tell him to take up cribbage. He can have my board. It's a respectable hobby for a man in his sixties."

"I'm afraid we had a fight," Serenata said, twisting her hands. "Or rather, I got so angry, we *didn't* have a fight. I didn't think we could afford one."

"Not that *woman*, was it?"

"Not this time. But you're right, that trainer he's hired . . . She's younger and physically perfect. She makes me feel haggard, flabby, and hideous."

"Now, sugar, that's one terrible waste. You're the prettiest filly in Hudson."

"I'm a mare, not a filly, and of an age no one rides anymore." Serenata blushed; the off-color insinuation had been inadvertent.

"Remy showed up with that hussy sometime last fall—"

"You never told me you met *Bambi Buffer*!"

"Didn't want to cause trouble. Wasn't sure how aware you were that he was swelling around town with that gal."

"I'm painfully aware. She drops by our house at all hours."

"I wasn't impressed," Griff said. "Mannish."

"To most people, she's a feminine icon. Strong is in."

"Flat-chested," he said. "And *bossy*."

"Don't tell me," Serenata said. "She went straight to the kitchen and helped herself to a six-pack of your best stout."

"Worse. Barely in the door, the lady starts hectoring me about how 'seniors' shouldn't give into being 'sedentary.' Messes with the furniture, to demonstrate how I'm to practice popping up and down in a chair—like I'm getting up and can't remember what I wanted and sit down again. Practice for senility is what I call it. And then she helicoptors her arms in the air to get me to whirlybird along with her, and shows me how to stand on one leg for an eternity, like a goddamned stork. Impertinent. Didn't put the chair back. No appreciation for how much effort it takes at ninety just to fix a sandwich. They weren't here five minutes, and that pushy pain in the backside still wore me out."

"She's paid to be pushy."

"I'd pay that tyrant just to stay out of my house."

"Well, while you're at it, pay her to stay out of mine."

"This *arrangement*, with Remy. Which I can't say I understand, and I'm not sure I want to. Ever ask yourself what she gets out of it?"

Citing a retainer the size of Griff's monthly Social Security check seemed impolitic. "She collects people. She has an insatiable appetite for admiration, so she surrounds herself with acolytes who depend on her to shore up their own self-esteem. She convinces her disciples that they're superior to all the peons who are fat and lazy and sleep late. It's not that different from Scientology."

But Griff wanted nitty-gritty. "Is my son carrying on with that woman? When those two showed up here, I didn't care for it. Like they were a couple. If he's cheating on you, say the word, and I'll read him the riot act. I raised him better than that."

"He's going through a weird period, but he still has too much class to visit his father with a mistress in tow. Still, he is besotted with her. Not in love exactly, but bewitched. I'm the naysayer; she tells him what he wants to hear. You've heard of horse whisperers? Well, she's a sports whisperer. Maybe she's good at it. Remington has sure run, swum, and biked farther and faster than ever before with Bambi egging him on."

"You say that like I'm supposed to care."

"No, but Remington cares. Either *he* believes she can summon a whole new self out of him—a man who's fierce and indestructible and glass-half-full—or she really can. I guess I'm afraid she can. I don't want a brand-new husband who's idiotically self-important. I liked Remington the way he was. Modest, for example."

"Don't know about that. Always thought of that kid as right full of himself. Couldn't wait to get out of Hudson, and earned all those degrees."

"He was a good student, and a confident professional. But he never used to be an inconsiderate cretin. Right, he won't visit his father when it's only a ten-minute walk, and he no longer prunes your hedges—but you think it's only you? I have to do everything now. Shopping, picking up, cooking, finding an electrician to replace the broken shaving socket in the bathroom. Remembering our grand-children's birthdays, wrapping the presents, and posting them on time—not that I give a shit about birthdays, but we can't provide Valeria any excuse to disappear off the face of the earth for another four years. I know Margaret would have done most of that in your day, but I work, too, and my carrying the whole household isn't part of the contract. He's the one who's retired, for Pete's sake, and he did more domestic heavy lifting with a full-time job."

"You said you had a fight, or near to. You fell out over the house-work?"

"It was even more hackneyed than that. We fell out over money. But money in three dimensions. Money that would have taken up space in the garage, except that it's too *damp* in there, so he keeps his precious ward propped beside the dining table, like a newly adopted child we're plying with chocolate pudding."

"Lost me there, pumpkin."

"Sorry, I'm being opaque. He bought a bicycle."

"I thought he had a bicycle."

"He did. But this one . . . is pricier."

"When he was a boy, I got Remy a bike for forty bucks—and he hardly rode the thing. Eventually I got it: bicycles were for sissies. The tough kids all rode mopeds."

"This titanium marvel was more than forty bucks," she said, with dizzying understatement. "But for years Remington brought in the bigger income. Strictly speaking, it's his money. So I'm not supposed to say anything. These days, I'm never supposed to say anything about anything. Like, I can't say that trying to buy athletic excellence is pathetic."

Regarding the probing of deep emotion, Griffith Alabaster had always been awkward at best. Yet he may finally have registered that you'd never address what really mattered in life if you were still giving the crux wide berth at ninety. "You do still—care for my son, don't you, sugar?"

In return for her father-in-law's courage, she answered as honestly as she could. "I love the man I married. But I'm not sure he is the man I married. Here's the thing." Elbows on her knees, she faced the old man—who'd not be here much longer, and she didn't want to kick herself once it was too late for never having spoken to him plainly.

"My parents were Methodists," she said, "but I think their faith was skin-deep. It was mostly social, and because we moved so often, churches were a useful shortcut, especially for my mother. But once I hit my teens, I told them that to me the whole Christ story seemed far-fetched. I didn't want to keep claiming to believe something I didn't. They acted disappointed, but didn't force me to keep going. It wasn't that I lost my faith; I never had it. I'm sorry, because I know Margaret was a devout Catholic, but I've always found religious belief not only foreign, but mindless and—well, a little repellent. The stories you're meant to buy into are absurd. To me, religion is a form of mass hypnosis, or collective psychosis."

"Something to be said for churches," Griff said. "They get folks to gather round each other in times of need. I'm not sure you lapsed youngsters have come up with anything better."

"No, we haven't—which is sort of my point. See, Remington has always been a rationalist. We've enjoyed sparring over a host of issues, but neither of us has ever subscribed to a dogma. On the electoral rolls, Remington is registered as an independent. That's always been important to me about your son: he's a freethinker. His refusal to ape the version of virtue imposed by the political fashions of the time is one of the reasons he lost his job. If he'd abased himself, he might have kept it."

"Remy's got backbone."

"He used to. But I'm not sure loyalty to somebody else's principles qualifies as backbone. Because if you'd asked me years ago what was the one thing that might cripple my marriage, I'd have said the one thing that could never happen: religious conversion. That's why Valeria's having gone born-again has been so alienating. Technically, we've restored relations, but in truth I have no idea who she is anymore. All her Jesus guff has an element of spitefulness about it, and that much I understand. But willingly giving over to a crowd, and signing up wholesale to some kooky creed of other people's contrivance—I don't understand that at all.

"Griff, MettleMan isn't just an exercise regime. MettleMan is a cult. That's why I can't give you a one-word answer to whether I still love your son." She sat back in the chair. "The man I fell in love with has been kidnapped."

"And what about Remy's promises as a husband? *You* haven't been 'kidnapped.' And you're the best thing ever happened to that boy."

She threw up her hands. "I am—irrelevant! For Remington, anything or anyone that doesn't have to do with *triathlon* isn't in the picture. Unless I'm stocking up for another binge with his tri club, I'm just a nuisance. After all, according to the Book of MettleMan, the height of spiritual achievement is perfect self-absorption."

Serenata couldn't sit still, and returned to pacing. "So in Syracuse next month? He and his club are doing a 'half Mettle'—meaning not completely insane, but only sort-of-but-still-basically-insane—and I'm expected to go and wave pom-poms. But I don't want to! It's not only that I hate all this *tri* shit, but I especially hate the idea of reinforcing my role in his life as the one on the sidelines! Besides which, because he *is* getting older, and he's *not* a natural athlete, and his body *isn't* used to this degree of strain, I'm really worried he's going to hurt himself. But to Remington, that's just me being 'dark,' and trying to stop him from achieving nirvana, so any concern I express he interprets as raging antagonism. On the other hand, it's more than possible that I did this to myself, and I did this to our marriage, because I'm rigid, and insensitive, and territorial, and bitter about my knees, and maybe if I'd done nothing but hooray and Hail Mary and holler hallelujah from the start, we'd still be happy as clams."

She'd been ranging the living room with her hands flailing. The outburst was intemperate. But she couldn't confide to Tommy anymore, now that the girl had drunk the Kool-Aid, too; she'd left her few plausible friends back in Albany; least of all could she pour out her heart to Remington.

Her father-in-law frowned. "Not thinking of doing anything rash, are you?"

"Oh, I'm not the first person to be stymied by what's worse: no marriage, or a bad one." She bombed back to the wing chair. "So should

I go to this 'half Mettle,' or not? Staying home seems traitorous, and I leave him at the mercy of *Bambi*."

"You trust a man, or you don't. If you don't, following him around won't do a lick of good. Once this 'Mister Metal' folderol is over—not the littler thing next month, but the big hoo-ha in June—you reckon Remy'll have had enough?"

"I'd like to think so, but that's what I assumed about the marathon last year. Boy, was I wrong. For all I know, he's decided to enter triathlons for the rest of his life. He's not making plans to do anything else."

"Won't that boy get *tired*?"

"The real danger is that I get tired first, Griff."

"Please don't leave me." His voice was shaking.

"Never," she said. Rising to take his face in her hands and kiss his forehead, she whispered in his ear, "But that's what I could stand to hear from Remington."

She put her mac and cheese in the oven, and set the timer so he wouldn't forget. She fished the melting zucchini and crusting cauliflower from the fridge; she always threw a few into the weekly order from AmazonFresh, but Griff didn't have much time for vegetables. Her Swiffer of the kitchen floor was hasty, since Tommy would be in on Friday. In the bathroom, she stacked some extra toilet paper within easy reach, and swabbed the area in front of the bowl, where old men tended to dribble. She laid out his pills, and freshened a glass of water with a slice of lemon.

"Thanks for letting me complain," she said, gathering her things. "And don't lose any sleep over this, because it's out of both our hands. Remington will escape from the clutches of his sect. Or he won't."

When she got home, Remington was still at the gym. The redundant free weights and bells-and-whistles treadmill upstairs were gathering dust. He preferred to worship with his congregation.

She shot a glare at the tri bike propped against the wall. It was constructed of elliptical tubing at peculiar angles, and the handlebars were built so you laid your forearms flat and held on to upturned grips. For the inanimate, it had an aggressively snobbish ambiance. In contrast to the gaudy colors of Remington's running gear, the contraption was ostentatiously sophisticated: a slick slate-gray with a sandy matte finish and slim, tasteful accents of branding in bloodred. A bicycle should appear storied, well traveled; this mechanism was immaculate. It didn't look like something that you'd ride in a park, but more like an art object you'd display in a design museum, where you'd slap the hands of little boys who tried to touch it. Before this haughty intruder slid into their house, she'd never have believed that a bicycle could cost ten grand.

"Gosh, I take it all back," she said aloud over her phone. "Maybe there is a God." For the email that had just pinged in was an offer of work: an extensive recording session in lower Manhattan for a new video game, and the terms were generous. If Remington was going to drop ten big ones on a bike, she had to accept the job. Better yet, the dates would perfectly preclude tagging along to watch the half Mettle in Syracuse. Brilliant.

The phone stirred again: Valeria.

"Thanks a lot, *Mama*," the young woman exploded once her mother had barely said hello. "You'll be glad to hear that Nancee's in the hospital."

"What's happened? And why on earth would I be glad?"

"She's been admitted for exhaustion. And they seem to think she's anorexic."

"Well, you know, back in April I did try to call your attention—"

"She's a picky eater, but she doesn't starve herself," Valeria snapped. "I'm her mother, and I should know."

Valeria was in a vengeful mood, and contributing Tommy's

diagnosis that Nancee was an "exercise bulimic" might not be perceived as helpful. "Did something happen, or is she just rundown?"

"Better believe something *happened*. There's a water tower near our house, and somehow those kids managed to pull down the ladder to the stairway on the outside. The silly girl started running up and down it. Thankfully Logan was keeping watch, not to mention Our Lord and Savior—"

Serenata gasped. "She didn't fall, did she?"

"No, but she could have. Because at some point, she collapsed. Logan was a good boy, and called 911. And me, of course. I had to find someone from the church to watch the other kids, so by the time I got there the medics had already climbed up three flights to carry her down. She may have fainted from dehydration."

"Has she done this sort of thing before?"

"Logan isn't saying. Deacon did nothing but torture me—not that you ever noticed—but Logan is very loyal."

"How is she doing now?"

"Nice of you to get around to asking," Valeria said. "She's on a drip to restore fluids, and they're feeding her intravenously. She's alert, and I'm afraid she's not what you'd call an ideal patient. The nurses are convinced she's freaking out because of the nutrition. I guess they've seen skinny girls ripping out the needles before. But that's not it. I know my girl. She just doesn't like lying in bed. She's promised to keep the IV in, so long as they'll let her march up and down the halls with the thing on wheels. But the doctor is insisting on complete rest, and it's turned into something of a battle."

"I'd hate to go up against Nancee over anything. She's wiry but ferocious."

"You can't imagine how awful it is to see your own child in restraints, like a crazy person. But I got her to admit what she was up to. Apparently in running up and down all those stairs, she was try-ing to beat some sort of record. And guess *whose*?"

Serenata allowed the question to dangle.

"Did you or did you not," Valeria went on, "tell my daughter that you run *two hundred flights* at a time?"

"I may have mentioned that I did that in my twenties—"

"What kind of grandmother are you? Throwing down a gauntlet like that to a little girl?"

"I wasn't throwing down a gauntlet. I noticed she was running up and down the stairs here, and I was only trying to establish a sense of camaraderie."

"You were indoctrinating my daughter into the same lunacy I grew up with!"

"Sweetie, you're one to talk about indoctrination."

"Children are very suggestible!" Valeria shouted. "You can't go planting ideas in their heads without taking responsibility for the consequences!"

"I'd remind you that thanks to your impromptu pause for station identification, your father and I missed out on four highly formative years of your two oldest children. By the time you deigned to get in touch with your parents again, Nancee was already, as you put it yourself, an 'Energizer Bunny.' I didn't invent this thrall to exertion, either. It's in the ether. It's on TV and in the movies and in advertis-ing and all over the internet. For pity's sake, look at what's happened to your father! You flatter me, my dear, but Nancee didn't get the idea of distinguishing herself through sheer fatigue from *me*."

But Valeria had already hung up.

Nancee was just the beginning.

Something was off about Tommy from the moment she arrived. True, her eagerness to busy-bee about the house had lessened somewhat, now that she'd discarded her Fitbit knockoff. (Failing to track a single mile of cycling and insufficiently waterproof for the pool, the mechanism no longer performed its prime function of giving its user *credit*.) But it was still not her habit to begin a stint of cleaning with an immediate plop in a chair.

"Sure you're up for this?" Serenata scrutinized her neighbor while preparing the girl tea. "You look beat. We could always reschedule."

"I'm still trying to get out of paying for a full membership at BruteBody . . . So the other guys in the tri club trade off having me as a . . . as a . . . guest. I don't like to ask too often. Have to take advantage . . . when I'm in." Tommy slumped. It was not entirely clear how she would scrub the upstairs porcelain when she could barely talk.

"Meaning?" Serenata put out shortbread. Maybe the girl had low blood sugar.

"Yesterday. Stationary bike. Really . . . shoulder to the wheel. Sloan got me into the gym this time, and he never . . . never notices me at all."

"Mm-hmm." Serenata had harbored some suspicions along these lines. "Why do you care whether Sloan notices you?"

Tommy glared up through the wisps of her fine honey hair. "Duh. He's, like, the hottest guy in the club—if not in Hudson . . ."

"Or in the world," she finished for the girl with a smile. Goodness, having recently turned sixty-two had many a downside, but thank heavens she was no longer twenty.

"He's like a . . . like a fucking god."

"Take it from me, friend, you never want to have a relationship with a god. They always turn out to be mere mortals in Groucho glasses."

"You're old," Tommy slurred. "You don't remember anything."

"There's plenty from my early twenties I wish I *didn't* remember.

Sorry to be such a downer, but he's twice your age. He's a divorcé whose kids are almost as old as you are. But I know, I know: the heart wants what the heart wants."

"Yesterday—I guess I was trying to impress him," Tommy confessed. Her consonants had thickened. "Full hour, cranked . . . up. Sweat like a . . ." A metaphor seemed beyond her. "Got totally soaked. Wiped me . . . out."

Delivering the tea, Serenata pushed the plate forward. "Energy."

"No cookies," Tommy said. "Feel fat. Pants . . . don't fit."

Serenata drew the hair from her neighbor's face and tucked it behind an ear. "You don't look fat. You look puffy. That's different." Tommy's color was peculiar, too, but remark on its yellowish cast would only make the girl feel more self-conscious.

"Thighs are killing me. Tight. Might just . . . take the day off."

Serenata peered. "Cleaning, or working out?"

". . . Both."

In the lead-up to this half-Mettle malarkey, Tommy's proposing to take a day off from exercise was unheard of. Had Tommy been out in the woods? Serenata asked. Picked off any ticks? No. Had she eaten anything unusual? No. Had she eaten anything at all, since yesterday? No. "You're not well. I think you should see a doctor."

"Uh-uh. No big deal. Just need . . . rest." In Tri World, "rest" was commonly consigned to the same trash heap as "limits" and "overdoing it." Tommy struggled to a stand. Her thighs had bulged overnight from adolescent to menopausal.

Serenata let the girl go—she wasn't Tommy's mother—but the encounter was disturbing. Later that evening, she tried Tommy's cell, but the call went to voice-mail, and a text went unanswered.

Sleep that night was not improved by Remington's being up and down more than once, pacing and stretching at the bedpost, trying to get the clenched skein of fine muscles on the tops of his feet to relax. The seizures had grown chronic since he'd upped his laps in the pool. The spasms spread to the toes, which straightened and separated unnaturally with raised tendons. It was her helplessness in the face of his agony that kept her up. He was clearly trying to be quiet but couldn't keep his breath from rasping. The moonlight through the curtains chiaroscuroed his face into a Kabuki mask of anguish: forehead curdled, eyes squeezed shut, as if not being able to see his feet would make them go away. She loved his feet—his long, dry, shapely feet—and hated to see them convert to instruments of torture. In this light, too, his ever-stringier frame looked less muscular than withered.

Over the tablet at breakfast, she recounted the news from India. "So a teenage girl was gang-raped, and her parents objected—as one might. The village elders levied a punishment on the men of a small monetary fine and one hundred sit-ups. The rapists were enraged, beat the shit out of the parents, doused the girl with kerosene, and burned her alive."

"The lengths to which some people will go to get out of sit-ups," Remington said.

"Gosh, I wonder what penalty that village levies for first-degree murder. Jumping jacks?"

"Only diagonal toe-touches," Remington said. "You don't want them to get too tuckered out for their next rampage."

The interchange was of a sort that once routinely characterized their breakfast-table banter, and she was grateful for it—too grateful.

With still no word from Tommy, she nosed around the web in accelerating agitation, and finally walked around to the Marchs' front door. She had to marshal courage to knock. The few pleasantries she'd lobbed in the mother's direction had been received with suspicion. What did that hoity-toity older lady next-door get out of a relationship with a twenty-year-old kid aside from a clean sink?

"Yeah?" the mother said, opening the door partway. Heavy, bad complexion, prematurely haggard—no wonder her daughter was an exercise nut. "Tommy's not feeling too good."

"I know. That's why I stopped by. I need to ask her a question."

"All right. I can ask her for you."

"Fine, then—ask her about her urine. What color is it?"

"Seems kind of personal, don't it? Why's that matter to you?"

"Please. This is important."

With a glare, the neighbor turned without asking Serenata inside. At length, Tommy shuffled to the door, keeping upright by hanging on the jamb. So advanced had the puffiness grown that for the first time her resemblance to her mother was apparent.

"What's this about wee? It's the least of my problems. I'm turning into a whale, and everything hurts."

"The color. In the toilet bowl, when you pee."

Tommy frowned. "Well, come to think of it, sort of brown. But I thought it was rust in the pipes again."

"Your session at BruteBody, with the stationary bike. Up to a point, you want muscle to break down, so it builds back stronger. But if you take it too far, the fibers get into your bloodstream, and your kidneys shut down. If I'm right, this is nothing to mess with, Tommy. It could kill you. I'm taking you to Columbia Memorial *right now.*"

Tommy didn't have the energy to put up a fight. While Serenata offered to take her mother as well, the woman mumbled something about hospital bills, and begged off. But Tommy was covered by Medicaid. Her mother was a shut-in. Besides, to Mrs. March, Serenata's having arrived at a diagnosis made Tommy's ailment her fault.

"Aren't you being alarmist?" Remington asked when she rushed in for the key fob. "That condition is very rare."

"Not as rare as it used to be."

"And convenient. For your side."

"My *side*?"

"You heard me. And you're kidnapping one of my club members."

It was the same verb she'd used about him. "Not to sound grand, but I prefer to think I'm rescuing her."

"This isn't good timing, for the half Mettle. She should be hitting the road."

"You haven't seen her. She's more like hitting the floor. And medical calamity is notoriously difficult to schedule at one's athletic convenience."

The wait at the ER was extensive, and neither the nurse at reception nor the doctor they saw at last had heard of the diagnosis, either.

"Oh, man, rhabdo!" Bambi exclaimed familiarly, after Serenata updated the club on Tommy's condition around the dining table two days later.

"She'll be hospitalized for about a week," Serenata said. "I'm sure she'd appreciate you guys going by to say hello. Just don't mention how bloated she looks. She feels unattractive enough already."

"Bet she didn't hydrate enough," Bambi said confidently.

"Maybe," Serenata said. "But she also pushed herself too far, and that's why she went into full-blown kidney failure. Her creatinine count was off the charts. They're pumping her with fluids and may do dialysis. There's no way she can enter the half Mettle."

"That's according to you."

"That's according to Columbia Memorial. Recuperation from rhabdomyolysis can take weeks or even months. Frankly, though I haven't pressed the matter with her yet, a full MettleMan is off the table, too."

"Ever notice how happy you sound when delivering bad news?" Bambi said.

"Tommy's my friend, and her circumstances certainly don't make me happy."

"But she's right, my dear," Remington said. "You do sound satisfied. You've won the girl back to your team."

"In this club, the two 'teams' are the supermen and the slobs," Serenata said. "That makes me the queen of the slobs. Is that what you think?"

"That's your formulation, not mine," Remington said.

"It's just, this whole thing is a lot easier when your spouse believes in you," Cherry said. "Take it from me. And that's all Rem means, honey. We all know you're not big on tri. But nobody here thinks you're glad poor Tommy's in the hospital."

Meanwhile, Ethan Crick was diffidently sliding off a running shoe. He peeled off the sock, and then hobbled to their hostess to ask quietly for a Band-Aid. Ethan must have been set on living down his reputation as a whiner, since he was trying valiantly to be nonchalant about the massive blister on his big toe. It appeared to have ripped open and healed over more than once, only to be abraded again on the club's fourteen-mile run that afternoon. The surface was gluey, and its edges were bleeding.

She led him to the bathroom and scrounged the medicine cabinet for a large enough bandage. With an air of benevolence and an innocent moon face, the ophthalmologist wasn't at all pudgy, but his body had blunted contours that no amount of running or weight lifting would sharpen. He'd never attain the sleek build and rippling definition of a Sloan Wallace. She prayed he didn't care. Fat chance.

"Let the sweat dry off, or this won't stick," she said. "And we have to trim the rumpled skin. It hardens when it's dead, and then it tears." Having located the nail scissors, she had him prop the foot on the tub, recoiling slightly from the smell. The wound was the gooey yellow of frothed egg yolks. Worse, the foot had taken his body's blunted quality to an extreme. "This blister's badly infected, Ethan. Doesn't it hurt?"

"Well, sure, some, I guess."

"How in God's name did you run fourteen miles on this? And why?"

They both knew why. "It was a little tricky."

"I thought you were the sensible one."

"Being sensible doesn't get you much respect, in this crowd."

"I'm applying some Bacitracin. But for your whole foot to swell up like this, the infection could be getting into your bloodstream."

He shrugged. "I have a healthy immune system."

"Please. You're a doctor."

"Eye doctor."

"You need antibiotics. Did you know that Calvin Coolidge's son *died* from an infected blister on his foot?"

"Here we go, more *catastrophizing*!" Proprietary about her seven dwarfs, Bambi had stuck her head in.

Nevertheless, Serenata wouldn't let up until Ethan agreed to go directly to the walk-in clinic downtown; he just had time to make it before the doors closed.

"Did you check out how he played up that limp?" Chet said the moment Ethan left. "Like Quasimodo or something."

"His foot is a mess." Serenata wasn't having a reprise of Crick bashing so that they could all feel invincible in comparison. "And sepsis is not a character failing."

Hank Timmerman's offer to refresh everyone's unfinished drinks covered for getting another G&T for himself. He was always at a loss for words around Serenata, whose chronic aloofness made their un-relationship worse. Having gathered that she sometimes read books aloud for a living, he asked as she handed him the tonic, "So—have you ever read Lorrie Moore's *Birds of America*? I thought it was really good."

A perfectly passable effort at small talk, were it not for the fact that Hank had asked her this exact same question five times now. Heaven knew in what rehab joint a copy of those short stories was kicking around, but she was obliged to infer that *Birds of America* was the only book he'd ever read. The first time he'd asked about Lorrie Moore, she'd been touched by his effort to connect, and responded with enthusiasm. But binge drinking obliterated all memory of having already used this icebreaker more than once, and her replies had grown terse.

"*Yesss*," she hissed icily.

He looked stung. Being a little nicer wouldn't have cost her much, but Tommy's situation was preying on her mind and made her cross. It was all so unnecessary.

"That kid's gonna be crushed if she has to quit," Chet said as Hank delivered more beers. "She's into tri super heavy."

"Well, maybe she could get into something else 'super heavy,' then," Serenata said. "She's only got a high school education, and aside from a vague aspiration to become a voice-over artist, she has no plan for her life. So maybe I am glad she's in the hospital, Cherry. As long as she fully recovers, rhabdomyolysis could be a blessing in disguise. For Tommy, MettleMan is a distraction."

"Distraction from *what*?" Bambi said. "Rising to a challenge is what we're put on earth to do."

"I read about an event somewhere in England," Serenata said, "where dozens of people run around a four-hundred-meter track for twenty-four hours straight. The last winner ran a hundred and sixty miles. That's six hundred and forty times around the track. The contestants start to hallucinate. They literally make themselves demented. One runner said the object of the exercise was 'to feel dead.' This kind of event is proliferating all over the Western world. We invented the computer and put a man on the moon. Now we're running in manic circles, like tigers churning ourselves to butter. A once-great civilization, disappearing up its ass."

"It's *hard* to run an ellipse over six hundred times," Bambi said. "You try it."

"It's hard to thread six hundred and forty tiny beads on a limp string."

"Look, we all know about your knees, Sera," Sloan said. "Isn't this sour grapes?"

"I think you can survive one skeptic," Serenata said. "The whole of American culture is cheering you guys on."

"That's not totally true," Bambi said. "There's an element—a pretty fucking big element—that hates our guts. They can be pretty vocal about it, too."

"No joke," Sloan said. "You should hear my ex. 'Oh, you're just into this big ego trip, and you only want to ogle yourself in the mirror.' Before we split, every time I left to train, I'd get it in the neck about how I should be taking the kids to the park. But for Mettles, you have to throw your family under the bus. Otherwise they'll drag you down with them, slumming around on Sunday mornings in bathrobes, with croissants, and travel supplements, and plastic toys."

"I got into it pretty deep with a customer at the café last week," Chet said. "I'd been talking about tri with a regular, and this guy at the next table gets all on his high horse about what a waste of time it is. Like, if we're going to expend all that energy, we should really be working at a homeless shelter—"

"That old saw!" Bambi said. "The why-don't-you-volunteer-for-a-food-bank thing—"

"Or dig wells for starving Africans," Chet said.

"No, no, I always get told I should be visiting the elderly," Cherry said. "Calling bingo in nursing homes."

"But why is the logical alternative to strenuous exercise a posturing altruism?" Remington said. "Really, who stands at the door and decides, 'Well, I could go for a run, or I could go teach immigrants English at my local community center'?"

"I don't know, but I hear this stuff every time I grab a stool at a bar," Bambi said. "What kills me? These same cunts whose dainty ethical sensibilities are so offended by your spending your life the way you fucking well want to—you can bet your last dollar *they* don't volunteer at any damned homeless shelter."

"And MettleMan events raise tons of money for charity!" Cherry said.

"Ever notice how all the guys who take a poke at tri are fat? I mean"—Hank shot a nervous glance at Cherry—"not hard fat, but, you know, blobby fat."

"That's what really bugged my ex," Sloan said. "She started to look her age, and I didn't."

"The slugs just feel inferior—" Bambi said.

Hank punched the air. "'Cause they *are* inferior!"

"—And they're jealous."

As ever, Serenata had retreated behind the butcher-block slab of the kitchen island, like their bartender. This conversation was stock. Any questioning of their purpose read as your own personal inadequacy. Presumably the only way to acquire the standing to cast convincing doubt on the merits of MettleMan was to complete one first. So she could only prove to these people that she didn't want to do what they were doing by doing what they were doing.

"I've never understood what it is about *envy*," Remington speculated, "that makes people disguise it to themselves as a different emotion altogether—sometimes as plain dislike, but more often as *moral disapproval*."

So, Serenata would have rejoined gamely, had it been just the two of them at dinner. *I can never deny feeling envious, because the sensation would appear to me in another guise. It's what you've always said about being called a racist, isn't it? That your very refutation makes it true? And now the same goes for anyone who says a discouraging word about MettleMan: you're just gutless, indolent, and weak. Voilà, your dubious enterprise is forever above reproach.* But she and Remington were anything but alone.

"*I* don't envy anybody." Bambi looked straight at Serenata. "Not a fucking soul."

She glared right back. "According to Remington, if you did, you'd *disapprove* of them instead. Maybe you secretly envy us benchwarmers, then—sleeping in, popping Pringles, and enjoying our lives while you suffer." Her punctuating smile was mirthless.

"So, Rem," Hank said, "seems like you recovered pretty good from last weekend. Any problems since? You must've took in a shitload of water."

"Yeah, and dirty water," Cherry said. "I meant to ask, did it make you sick?"

Remington's rigid shake of the head was perhaps misinterpreted.

"The main thing is," Chet said, "did you make sure to hit the pool this week? You know, jump back on the horse. You don't want to get all phobic or anything."

"What's this about?" Serenata asked.

The club went quiet. Sloan mumbled to Remington, "You didn't tell her?"

"Didn't tell me what?"

"Comes with the territory," Sloan said. "It wasn't a big deal."

"Remington. What wasn't a big deal?"

"He's here, ain't he?" Bambi said. "He ran fourteen miles today, and he's fine."

"Until a minute ago, I took it for granted that my husband was fine. So what happened that should make me grateful that he's even 'here'?"

"I didn't want you to worry about it," Remington said. "Because, obviously, there's nothing to worry about."

"You're talking about last Saturday, aren't you? When you got home weirdly late and you couldn't get warm. It was seventy-four degrees in here, and you wanted me to build a fire. You were shaking. You barely ate a thing, and went straight to bed. Why?"

"We did a swim in open water, in the Hudson," Remington said. "I told you that. I just didn't mention that I—got into difficulties. I may have gotten a chill—"

"My bad," Bambi said. "The water temperature was borderline, so it was a judgment call. Had it to do over again, I'd have gone with wet suits."

"How long a swim was this?" Serenata asked.

"About a mile and a half, give or take," Remington said.

"Have you ever swum that far before?"

"Yes, but in a pool. Open water's a little different."

"Quite," she said. "Your 'difficulties.' Are you trying to tell me that last weekend you nearly drowned?"

"I'm not trying to tell you that. I am telling you that."

"And why didn't you drown?"

"I pulled him out, Sera, of course I did," Bambi said. "I always loop back to check on stragglers, and I hit the pedal to the metal the moment I noticed Rem was in trouble. It's part of my job. My lifeguard skills are top-notch. Got Rem onshore in no time. Called the rest of the club in, too. I don't often cut a training session short, but I do make exceptions when necessary, since whatever you think I'm not totally out of my fucking mind."

"And were you obliged to give mouth-to-mouth?"

"Well, yeah. But don't worry, it was hardly what you'd call romantic."

"I think it is what I'd call romantic. I guess I owe you thanks. For saving my husband's life."

"Well, no, like I said, I was just doing my job. All in a day's work."

"Except you also put him in the circumstances where he required saving."

"I put myself in those circumstances," Remington said. "If I over-estimated my present abilities, that's my fault."

"According to your trainer, these 'difficulties'—that is, I assume, coming within a whisker of floundering to the bottom of the river until you become another trashy castoff along with the spare tires and shopping carts . . . If she says the incident was so pro forma, 'all in a day's work,' why didn't you tell me about it?"

"You know exactly why I didn't tell you about it."

When she was about eight and still learning to swim, Serenata had paddled accidentally into the deep end of a public pool, tried to stand up, and panicked. A lifeguard noticed right away, so she couldn't have been thrashing and taking in chlorinated water salted with gallons of primary-school pee for more than about thirty seconds before a young man threw an arm around her from behind and pulled her to the shallows. But it was a long thirty seconds—a small lifetime of blind animal terror, burned so vividly into her memory that these many years later she could replay those "difficulties" as if they'd occurred yesterday. She refused to believe that the experience of drowning was any less profound at the age of sixty-five than it was at eight. Particularly since by sixty-five you're better equipped to understand just what you may be in the process of losing. Yet her husband came back and failed to mention having inhaled death itself, all because he didn't want to give her ammunition in a dif-ference of opinion over his participation in a sporting event. If the reason for his reticence was absurd, it was also sad. He had all these new friends, but when they went home, she wasn't the only one who felt lonely.

NINE

"You didn't tell me that Remington almost drowned." Serenata said this gently, lest it seem an accusation of betrayal. Already punished beyond reason, Tommy hardly needed to be dumped on for the deficiencies of a marriage older by half than she was.

"So he told you." Tommy flopped her cheek phlegmatically on the flat hospital pillow. "I didn't want to rat him out."

If the girl had converted overnight from superwoman to slug, it was the kind someone had poured salt on. She looked as if she were melting. Even constrained by compression stockings, all four limbs had expanded, and her fingers were sausages—so tight and plump that they'd split in a frying pan. In losing its angles, her newly broad, bland face had lost its intelligence, too.

"You're very loyal," Serenata said. "It's okay to be loyal to someone besides me."

"For a while, we thought he was actually going to snuff it. Even when he started breathing again, seemed like he'd cough, and cough, till his lungs came out." Her mouth might have been full of pudding. The sloppy enunciation wasn't from a physical inability to form the words. Her whole person was bathed in apathy, reflected in the colorlessness of the hospital room. She didn't speak clearly because she didn't care—about what she was saying, or anything else.

"I've watched him swim. He's a sinker. I didn't want to mention this when I was teaching you the crawl, but there are such people. It's body density more than technique. But don't worry. You're not a sinker." She hoped the designation carried metaphorically to Tommy's larger life, which the young woman seemed to believe was over.

"Not now!" Tommy said, with no gaiety. "I'd float like a beach ball now."

"The fluid's started to drain, hasn't it?"

"Not so's you'd notice," she said glumly. "Feels like it's only gotten worse. This IV keeps pumping me full of more water—"

"They have to flush out the myoglobin. They did warn you that getting back to normal size could take a while."

"They said it could take *weeks*. And my whole body hurts. I just lie here all day while every muscle turns to mush. I can practically hear it."

"What does it sound like?"

"Like when there's an air pocket in our kitchen drain. The dirty water backs up, and then a big, fat, greasy bubble burps up through the scum: *blu-blub*."

"I've read that you can go two whole weeks without exercise before the muscles weaken."

"That's bullshit."

Serenata didn't believe it, either. "All that matters is you get well. Your kidneys are finally kicking in. You can always get fit again when this is over."

"Uh-huh." Tommy's eyes were squeezed from the edema, and her glare was slitty. "Would that 'just get well' crap make *you* feel any better?"

"Of course not. Hey, what's that?" Serenata asked. "I never noticed it before."

Tommy flipped her wrist over, but her friend had already spotted the bumblebee. Its workmanship wasn't quite up to the same standard—

Serenata's had been inked by a master—but the newer image was more vivid.

"I was gonna show you," Tommy said, "but then I worried you'd think I was copying you."

"Let's not think of it as imitation, but as *homage*. I take it as a compliment."

"Really? You're not mad?"

"Really. I'm touched."

Tommy pulled herself up on the pillow. "So the half Mettle is in three weeks, and if I can only get back on the road—"

"Forget it," Serenata said. "In three weeks, you'll count yourself lucky if you can walk to the bathroom by yourself. Forget MettleMan, and that includes June, too. Because in your shoes, here's what *would* make me feel better: MettleMan is a franchise. It can trademark the name, but it can't trademark running, swimming, and cycling—any more than I can, which is why you're always ridiculing me, and rightly so. You don't need the organization, or its imprimatur—"

"Imprimatur?" Tommy said with disdain.

"Its seal of approval."

"I want the tattoo."

"You don't need the tattoo. You have our bumblebee."

"I'm gonna lose all my friends."

"Not me," Serenata said. "And if the other members of the tri club care about you, too, they're not going to drop you because you got sick."

"Don't pretend to be an idiot. If you're not doing tri, you don't count. You've been around those guys enough to know the drill. You're in or you're out. Now I'll be one more slacker they make fun of."

"But that's creepy, isn't it? If it's true? And that includes me, too. In their terms, I'm a slacker."

"I know."

Confirmation of what she knew already still smarted. "Have any other club members been to visit?"

"Only Cherry," Tommy said. "And even she couldn't wait to leave. It's like they're afraid they're gonna catch something."

"They're afraid of what they've got already: the capacity to join the rest of us jerk offs with one trip on a curb."

"I feel disgusting. I can't stand looking in the mirror—"

"Then don't."

"I've got nothing to live for," Tommy slurred. "I wish I was dead."

"Oh, you do not."

"This rhabdo-whatever is all my fault. I've never been good enough, and I'm still not. If my thighs had been stronger to begin with, this would never have happened. It's all because I wasn't in good enough shape. That's what they'll say behind my back, too. They'll say the problem was I was never in their league."

"If your thighs had been any stronger, then you'd have pushed yourself to cycle even faster and longer, all to impress Sloan Wallace—and you'd still have nuked your quadriceps into toxic waste. Your only weakness was for a pretty face. Though that's a big weakness, in my experience. Fatal."

"But Remington was hot-looking. You said."

"Yes. Not especially to his credit of course, but he's nicely formed. Also, from the start, I was drawn to how contained he was—how steady he was, how focused. Concentrated, held within himself. Though this same distilled quality seems to have morphed slightly. There's something in his face right now that I don't like."

"What's that?"

"Fanaticism." The word lingered.

"Well, you have to be a little crackers to go for a full Mettle, right?" Tommy said. "It's like going on, you know, *jihad*. But unless you slob out, the only other choice is to be all medium and plain. To say grandma things like 'Everything in moderation.' To not go for a real run, but go *jogging*. To have a personality like the temperature of a baby's bottle."

"No, the alternative is to get a grip, my dear," Serenata said briskly. "You got caught up in a fad, and you may not be through with the fad, but the fad is through with you. We can go back to reading scripts together. You've got a strong voice, and you only need to learn how to use it. You don't need a degree for my kind of work; you just need to be good at it. MettleMan was costing you time and money. Let's learn to make money, and at something more satisfying than swabbing floors. Then if you happen to have the spare time to do a few push-ups, fine. You think completing a MettleMan would make you special, but lots of people have completed one by now, and it's not special. Let's work on making you something special for real."

Alas, it was too early for a pep talk, and it fell on deaf ears.

After Tommy had been home for a week, she was able to join her next-door neighbor in slow, shuffling walks that gradually lengthened to reach downtown. Getting her out of the house at least meant she put on real clothes, even if much of her wardrobe still wouldn't fit; frumping around in shapeless nightgowns made her only more depressed. She'd managed to progress from truly desolate, to dejected, to merely forlorn. Now the resilient young woman was well on her way to a healthy disgruntlement. Preparing for the five-day video-game gig in Manhattan, Serenata felt more regretful about abandoning Tommy to potential emotional backsliding than she did about leaving Remington to fend for himself in Syracuse—which he detected.

"Did you go shopping for a job that would give you a schedule conflict for just the right day?" he inquired, packing.

"You know I didn't, and we've been through this. We need the money."

"Still—you're glad that now you don't have to go."

She discounted a range of more equivocal responses before answering, "Yes."

Putting a load of laundry away, Serenata stored three boxer shorts in his top drawer. Remington removed the three boxer shorts and placed them in his luggage.

"On the swimming segment," she said. "Will there be lifeguards?"

His glance was flinty. "Onondaga Lake will be buoyed, with fully crewed boats at regular intervals."

"I was expressing concern, not condescension."

"Naturally." Ah, the Remington dryness.

"Tommy said you almost died."

"At many points in our lives we almost die, and pull back from the brink. I had a close call yesterday crossing the street. I wouldn't expect you to hold that against me."

"I would if you got run over by tempting fate."

"Can I infer that you'll skip the full Mettle in June as well?" His tone was pleasant.

"I told you, I'll be there. I promised."

"But what if something comes up? And we still 'need the money'?"

"I *said* I'd be there. But as for Syracuse, Valeria is coming, so you'll have your cheering section. I might remind you that over the years I have run, cycled, and swum many thousands of miles. Not once can I remember insisting that you go out and watch."

Tomorrow, planning on an extra day to prepare for his penultimate feat of stamina, Remington would drive to Syracuse for three nights at the Courtyard. The hotel's room charges would ravage the earnings of her first day's recording, which so tragically coincided with the half Mettle. They'd sacrifice the proceeds of her second day's work to cover the hefty entry fee for the race. Were she ever on the lookout for an investment opportunity, MettleMan would be a growth stock.

But she didn't want to waste the evening before they were parted stewing in fiscal resentment, so when Remington raised a theoretical scenario over dinner, out of the blue, she was eager to seem game.

"Thought experiment," he proposed. "Let's say you're walking alone at night in a largely deserted urban area that's a little sketchy. A figure following behind you is making you anxious. You glance over your shoulder. It's a man, all right, but it turns out he's white. How do you feel?"

"Relieved."

"Why is that?"

"I could be unlucky, but my default assumption is that he's harmless."

"Is that because you feel a sense of solidarity with 'your people'? Because white folks will stick together, and would never hurt one another?"

"Hardly. I feel no sense of solidarity with white people. But blacks have higher rates of incarceration . . . Which is partly because of a rigged justice system, but still . . . I've heard blacks admit their fellow *brothers* on the street can make them edgy, too."

"What else do you assume about our nameless white guy, absent any additional information?"

"How old is he?"

"Say, twenties."

"And we're talking middle class or above?"

"Sure. You're not in South Boston. Say he's wearing a Yale sweatshirt."

"Which doesn't mean he went there."

"Which means he at least wants you to think he did. Not a big ghetto pretension."

"Unless he's conspicuously buff, I'd assume he's weak." Serenata surprised herself, but it was true. "In every sense, come to think of it."

"And if you were to imaginatively project yourself into the mind of a *person of color*—another young man who regards this street as his turf—what does a representative of a *marginalized community* think when he spots our white guy?"

Serenata was starting to get the feel of the exercise. "That the interloper is naive. That he shouldn't be here, and doesn't know where he's going. That he's credulous and doesn't watch his back. He might be capable of braggadocio if flanked by flunkies—"

"All men are more daunting when running in packs."

"But on his own? He's probably a coward. I don't like to stereotype, but in the *hypothetical* instance that this *POC* is inclined to be the tiniest bit predatory? Open season. A white guy won't stick up for himself. He's easy to steal from, and easy to push around."

"Good. Anything else?"

"White guy is risk averse. Any trouble, and all he'll care about is scraping through it in one piece. He won't make a stand to preserve his pride; he'll accept any humiliation to save his skin. He may really have gone to Yale, but he's under-confident in a street sense. He's extremely frightened of other men who are black or Latino—though maybe not of Asians, but that just makes him ignorant. So, yeah, he might be technically well educated, but as for being up to speed in a self-preservational sense, he's illiterate. He's timid and desperate to avoid conflict. Careless of his valuables—which he regards as replaceable. Gullible. Probably lives with his parents."

"I submit," Remington said, raising his fork, "that men in their teens and twenties are the most dangerous creatures on earth. They're competing for mates, and trying to establish dominance in the male pecking order. The world over, these are the terrorists, the gang members, the perpetrators of most nonstate murders. But the backstop presumption runs that young white men of any means have effectively been taking testosterone blockers. They may be brilliant at coding or semiotics; as animals, they've been disabled. They can't take care of themselves in unfamiliar situations. They can't think on their feet. They've been raised around their own kind, and by women, and by men who are controlled by women. As a group, they're perceived as incompetent even as social animals. They're bad at badinage; they suck at quick comebacks; they aren't witty. They're helpless without money."

Serenata drummed the table. "I've met a few exceptions. I like to think I married one. But broadly—your witness statement sounds about right."

"But here's another question," Remington said. "If we were in company, and you and I repeated all these slanderous generalizations about young 'privileged' white men, would our set piece be considered inflammatory, or provocative? Even if the gathering were *diverse,* would anyone call us racists? At a dinner party, would anyone of any color or persuasion flounce from the table in consternation?"

"If anything, we'd get a round of applause." She sat back. "What does all this mean to you?"

"I'm not sure."

The peculiar conversation was strangely bonding.

As they lay reading in bed—Remington a book called *Endure: Mind, Body, and the Curiously Elastic Limits of Human Performance,* she a recent *New Yorker*—Serenata took advantage of the genial mood. "You know, the concept of this short story might interest you."

"Okay." Perhaps also grateful for the rare softening of the domestic atmosphere, he laid his book politely on the spread right away.

"In the future, you can hook yourself up to a machine called the Morphatron. It works out every muscle in your body while you sleep—like plugging in an electric car and letting it charge. So everyone's in perfect condition. You can set it to burn any extra calories, so nobody is fat, either. In fact, after going through a phase of gorging, people get bored with eating and have to force themselves to finish meals. This Morphatron has custom settings: some guys go for the Schwarzenegger look or prefer a swimmer build; women will choose to look like ballerinas, or Michelle Obama. It has an aerobic program, so heart disease has gone way down, and so has cancer. There are still heritable diseases, but otherwise the whole global population is in impeccable health. Except—you saw this coming—there's one guy who insists on working out the old-fashioned way. There aren't any gyms anymore, and they don't manufacture weights or Nautiluses, so he jury-rigs his gear with cans of food and backpacks. He runs until he's shattered, and he has the paths to himself, because all the other pre-fit people have more interesting things to do. Everyone thinks he's crazy. If he'd only plug his body in, he'd be in way better shape than he can ever get grunting and 'feeling the burn.'"

"*Brave New World*, with one noble savage."

"Agreed, the premise is straight-up *Twilight Zone*. But here's my question: If you could skip all the torment, and all the expenditure of time, and still get the same or even better results, would you plug in?"

"Of course not. I assume that's the moral of the story. Fitness without effort would be empty. Tri is all mind over matter, force of will. It's about reaching—but, ironically, never quite attaining—total self-domination . . . Excuse me, am I boring you?"

Serenata had grabbed her phone and was punching figures into its calculator app. "No, no—sorry. It's just, I've wanted to add this up for ages. Say I've exercised for an hour and a half, every day, since I was about eight . . . That's just over 29,000 hours . . . Divided by 24 is . . . 1,209 days, or . . . Three and a third years. Since when you subtract eating, sleeping, cooking, shopping, and shitting, at *most* you have maybe twelve hours out of any twenty-four that's discretionary, *exercise* has occupied six or seven years of my life. And that's not including biking, which in my book counts only as transport."

"I've always gotten the impression you consider that time well spent."

"I'm sick up to my eyeballs of doing burpees. I'd hit the Morphatron in a heartbeat."

To catch the 6:17 a.m. train to Penn Station, Serenata arose about the same time as Remington in Syracuse, where the race started at the typically barbaric hour of seven sharp. Taking her bicycle to Manhattan was more trouble than it was worth, but having commuted by bike for years in the city before they moved to Albany, she couldn't bear the prospect of squeezing onto the subway like all the other suckers.

Trusty steed stashed in the baggage car, she assumed her window seat with a view of the Hudson. Nagging awareness that Remington was at this moment climbing into his wet suit interfered with her ability to read. Staring out the window as the sun rose, she gave over to an underrated entertainment: thinking.

She'd characterized MettleMan to Griff as a cult, so maybe it was worth considering what about this vogue for extreme endurance sport slaked a religious thirst, even for secular types like her husband. Repudiation of the flesh was a near constant across the faiths, whose fundamentalist strains encouraged fasting, flagellation, celibacy, and self-denial; during Lent, you renounced something you especially liked. Religion had always been hostile to pleasure. Like many more formal theologies, MettleMan elevated suffering, sacrifice, and the conquest of the spirit over the petty, demeaning desires and complaints of the mortal coil. It was replete with saints (the pros) and ecclesiastical raiments (finisher T-shirts). It offered rites of initiation—today's half Mettle was one—and christenings, like the baptismal inking of mountainous orange double-*M* tattoos on Sloan Wallace's arm. MettleMan invited the faithful into a fellowship of like-minded souls, and so fostered a sense of belonging. More importantly, it also offered un-belonging—the exclusion on which religions often relied even more than on community. So just as traditional creeds shunned the unbeliever, the heretic, the *kaffir*, the cult of tri elevated a select elite over the flabby, the flaccid, the inactive. It dangled the prospect of redemption, resurrection, and rebirth, even to serial sinners like Hank Timmerman—since Bambi may have cast her disciples as uniquely sanctified, her chosen people, but she also hocked the commercially convenient notion that any sluggard could gestate into a champion within nine months.

MettleMan erected a ladder of ascending enlightenment—from layman to penitent to aspirant to the full beatification that Remington had his eye on in June—though the ladder foreshortened skyward and vanished into the firmament. For throughout this infinite process of purification, you could always go on another pilgrimage, and always better your time. As Remington noted, you forever approached yet never attained the athletic ideal, so there was always something to do. Better still, unlike most sacred journeys, these increments of greater sanctity were quantifiable: four minutes and eleven seconds, say, off the 2.6-mile swim.

For the church of exercise delivered clarity. That is, it laid out an unambiguous set of virtues—exertion, exhaustion, the neglect of pain, the defiance of perceived limits, any distance that was longer than the one before, any speed that was swifter—which cleared up all confusion about what qualified as a productive use of your day. Likewise, it defined evil: sloth. Most of all, apropos of Remington's testimonial about the ameliorative powers of a raised heart rate on Parkinson's, insomnia, diabetes, dementia, and depression: only through exercise could you forestall disease, degeneration, and mental decline. Taken to the nth, then, the church of exercise promised not only the end if not reversal of all aging and infirmity, but eternal life.

It was the oldest scam in the world.

At eight fifteen, she retrieved the bike (whose name, unbeknownst to anyone but his master, was Carlisle), hooked on her pannier, wheeled through the concourse, and hoisted the crossbar onto her shoulder to climb the station stairs—a practiced maneuver to which an ominous twang in her right knee was an unwelcome addition. Outside, the sun was shockingly hot, after air-conditioning on the train had driven her to a sweatshirt. This was shaping up to be another of those weird springs in the Northeast, with sudden heat waves worthy of August; weather.com predicted a high in Central Park of 91°F. Damn. She should also have checked the weather in Syracuse.

After walking Carlisle north on Seventh Avenue, she saddled up and sailed down West Thirty-Fourth Street toward the West Side bikeway, only to be immediately engulfed by two dozen other cyclists. It was rush hour, and they were rude, of course, churning feverishly past the older woman and her antiquated men's road bike. But the crazed pedal pushers were also foolhardy, cutting it much too close on the light at the bottom of the hill and streaking across the West Side Highway on a dead red. Serenata had a job to do, whose execution being flattened by a quick-off-the-mark Uber driver wasn't likely to improve, and she alone stopped to wait for the next green.

Running the length of the island alongside the Hudson was the busiest bike lane in the United States. Once a sumptuously capacious two-lane cycling superhighway, the Manhattan Waterfront Greenway now suffered from an invasion of electric scooters, Segways, in-line skates, illegal mopeds, battery-powered skateboards, runners with an infernal affection for the meridian, and baby strollers the size of a double-decker tour bus. And that was in addition to the explosion of actual bicycles, whose number, by Serenata's seat-of-the-pants calculation, had multiplied in the last two decades by ten to twenty times.

Swarmed by converts to a form of transportation for most of her life widely derided as geeky, as ever she resolved to rise above. She would remain calm. She would cultivate a Zen obliviousness to passing slights such as being brazenly cut off or overtaken dangerously on the inside. She would employ the maturity of her advancing years to serenely accommodate the rising popularity of pedal power— which was, after all, in the larger public interest, leading to improved air quality, lower carbon emissions, less obesity, reduced health-care costs, and a happier, more energetic population.

As ever? She failed.

She despised them. Every single one. Hot-shit skinnies in Lycra covered in loud branding on fixed-gear track bikes with no brakes that were conspicuously infelicitous for urban stop-and-start. Wall Streeters with laptop panniers and prissy Velcro straps around the ankles of their suit pants. Whole tourist families on matching rentals riding five abreast and weaving mindlessly out of lane. Underpaid Central American food app deliverymen doing thirty-five whose English was at least good enough to understand NO E-BIKES in foot-high illuminated red letters on park service notice boards. Teenagers texting on smart phones juddering blindly onto adjacent bark cover. Haughty twenty-somethings in designer gymwear who never registered that they didn't need to pass you because you were going the same pace they were, if not a little faster. Gangs of kids on BMXs popping wheelies in the wrong direction. She hated them all. They had invaded her turf, and they were in her way.

Worst of all were the Citibikes, heavy, municipally provided dray horses that could be rented for a pittance. Half the traffic on this path comprised these navy-blue clunkers. Negotiating the free-for-all entailed ceaselessly overtaking this semistationary flotsam—in addition to squeezing around the hulking cement barriers plunked every fifty yards squarely in the middle of the path, the would-be preventive fruits of a vehicular terrorist attack whose obstruction amounted to yet more terrorism.

Perhaps a particular vanity was to be found in making wicked tracks on a piece of junk. In that case, before overtaking a particular Citibiker along the straightaway approach to Canal Street, she should have noted the cyclist's frantic RPM—the signature of the sort who regards being overtaken by anyone at all as a personal affront, and being overtaken by a woman as tantamount to open-air castration. Within seconds of her slipping past the young man—a nondescript white guy in his twenties—he had poured it on furiously, knees jutting at cockamamie angles, and pulled back out in front.

She should let it go. She was a grown-up. She'd cycled the equivalent of the circumference of the Earth multiple times, and had nothing to prove. If anything, she'd arrive at the studio before the building was open, and would have to get coffee. She could ease up, and savor the glint of the sun in the skyscrapers across the river in New Jersey. Yet like most people's, her inner twelve-year-old was forever battling to get out. It got out.

When she geared down and then back up, Carlisle responded like the stallion she had always privately imagined him to be. Nearly clipping an oncoming commuter in the opposite lane—this encounter was turning her into an idiot—she surged past the impertinent Citibiker, with every intention of maxing out all the way to Vesey Street, since a lunatic like this loser wasn't likely to give up.

Pop.

The blaze of agony in her right knee immediately installed the sense of perspective that she was always pushing on Remington.

Barely able to breathe or even see, she coasted to the side. The milquetoast shot past.

People who felt fine were rarely mindful of the fact that their whole state of being—their ostensible personality, what mattered to them, what they thought about, and especially what they didn't think about—was predicated on this feeling-fineness. In an instant, Serenata became a different person. She didn't care about the Citibiker, she didn't care about which point Remington had reached in his stupid half Mettle, and horribly, at this very moment, she didn't care about the fate of her marriage. Least of all did she mind about the accelerating popularity of cycling, as the other bikes whizzed by like meteors in a shower. She was no longer a fit, well-kept woman powering to a lucrative job at a Gold Street studio, but an object of pity—although the piteous in big cities often failed to extract the emotion specified and simply vanished. Professionalism died hard, so she couldn't put altogether from her mind the necessity of arriving at the studio on time, but the means by which she would achieve this punctuality was profoundly in doubt. The faithful Carlisle had converted from steed to yoke; he complicated hailing a taxi.

The pain was disconcertingly private. It seemed inconceivable that she was experiencing something so enormous yet invisible to the hundreds of recreationists coursing this artery. Pain put you in a lonely place, for if you weren't feeling it you didn't believe in it, and if you were feeling it you couldn't really believe in anything else. The state was so separating that it amounted to a form of solitary confinement. No one else cared what she was going through, and she was sympathetic with this obliviousness, too, because she had become a useless person, an even greater burden than Carlisle.

She slipped off the seat enough to verify that the putting of any appreciable weight on her right leg was simply not going to happen. That was the other interesting thing, or it would have been interesting had it been possible to become interested in anything, which it wasn't: Remington and his tri friends were always talking up "pushing through the pain," but in that case the pain was of a penultimate sort that perhaps deserved a different word. This pain-pain, if you will, was not a barrier through which one pushed. One could as well "push through" the Grand Coulee Dam.

Whiffling as Remington did when his foot muscles seized in the middle of the night—had she been compassionate enough? Oh, probably not—Serenata mounted the seat again while tilted to the left. Treating Carlisle like a Razor scooter, she could feebly propel the machine—which no longer felt like a horse—by pushing off with her left foot. Keeping humbly to the very edge of the bike path to stay out of the way of all that hectic feeling-fineness, she eked her way down to Vesey Street.

By the time she propelled herself in this shuffling manner across Vesey and then Ann Street to Gold, preferring the sidewalk and suffering glares, coffee was out of the question. She was late. Locking up was the usual nightmare; these days it was as hard to park a bike in New York as a car. The full-on blast of agony seemed to have subsided somewhat, so that it was just possible to limp, if still at great cost, to the buzzer. Serenata Terpsichore Totally Different Person didn't take the stairs.

Greeting Jon and Coca, a director and engineer she'd worked with before, she worried that her grimace made her appear averse to the workday ahead. She negotiated the outer studio by leaning on the top of a soft chair and then on the desk of the digital soundboard as inconspicuously as possible.

Jon was stringy and undernourished, with the complexion of a man who hadn't been out of doors for ten years. "You okay?" he asked.

Her lurching between furniture had been conspicuous, all right. "Oh, sure," she said. "I mean, I had a little *incident* on the West Side bike path on the way here is all." Even the director was half her age. The word *arthritis* would not pass her lips.

"Ever since they dumped all those concrete girders everywhere," Coca said, "I won't take it. It's not just the pinch points. It's the reminder—that some douchebag plowed his truck through all those people just trying to have a nice time on a nice day. I'd rather take Tenth Avenue and think about something else."

Maybe twenty-five, Coca was distractingly attractive. He appeared mixed race, like Brazilian but with a hint of Filipino or Thai and possibly some Italian. The combination had worked out stunningly, like those casual recipes you invented on the fly, and by accident or instinct the unmeasured ingredients struck a perfect balance that you'd never replicate no matter how many times you tried.

The morning's recording was straight dubbing in the sound booth, which Serenata would traditionally perform standing up. Suddenly preferring to sit would call only more attention to her infirmity, so she kept her weight on her left leg and steadied herself with a hand on the desk. *Kill Joy* had the rather perverse premise that the player was aiming to murder the very character whom the script built up as sympathetically intrepid. Though the graphic of her character looked about sixteen, she'd been cast to read Joy because the protagonist was a fashionably "strong woman" who'd seem more formidable with an older voice. Besides, Serenata could dial up any age they liked.

"Fierce, but vulnerable," Jon instructed in her earphones, after his young female assistant arrived to read the opposing character's dialogue on the other side of the glass.

Her computer screen displayed the dialogue spreadsheet. It never helped to allow into her head that most of the lines were dumb. The assistant's lifeless delivery of the yet-to-be-recorded male lead made them sound even dumber.

"More frightened," Jon said after the read-through. "How long was that, Coca?"

"Forty-two seconds."

"Tighten it up. A little faster." To keep the video modifications to a minimum, the timings of the audio and animation had to roughly match up.

She gave them what they wanted: "more sparkle of life," "a few years younger," "horrified—a little improv, just sounds, maybe a little, you know, 'Wha . . . ?' or 'What the . . . !'" She repeated the same line three or four times with different modulations, so that the producer, who was listening on Skype from Chicago, could choose his preferred coloration. Still, the morning's output lacked her distinctive flair. They did unusually numerous retakes for an old pro. The knee pain was sullen, glowering, like a disruptive activist who'd been asked to leave a lecture and had instead retreated resentfully to a back row. When she tried too hard to move around the booth as if nothing were the matter, the knee rebuked her with flashes of the original anguish on the bike path. She couldn't seem to rest in the pocket of the lines, but was forever focused a trace ahead of the words in her mouth.

Assuming a nonchalant slump in the exterior studio on a break, Serenata lengthened both legs and crossed her ankles, covering for the fact that she couldn't bend the right knee. "I was glad this gig came in," she said, after the assistant left to fetch coffees. "For some reason, the audiobook work has dried up."

"Well, that's hardly surprising," Jon said.

"How's that? I thought audio was a growth market. Going up more than print."

"You have something of a reputation."

"After thirty-five years of this stuff, I'd think so. And this morning may have been a little pro forma, but I hope my reputation is for doing pretty good work."

"Yeah," the director said. "Kind of too good."

"You'll have to explain to me how one can ever be 'too good.'"

"The accents," he announced, as if no more needed to be said.

"What about them?"

"You're known for them, aren't you? And that whole thing's gone toxic."

Serenata frowned, scrounging for what Tommy had told her a year or two ago. "Is it this 'mimicry' issue?"

"That's the buzzword," Coca said. "Touché."

The director said, "The audio companies have gotten so much grief on social media for using white performers to read, you know, black, Chinese, whatever dialogue that it's not worth the hassle. A few producers have brought in special, you know, people of color to read those lines, but that makes the project way more expensive. So if there's racial or ethnic stuff in the book, it's easier to hire a POC to read the whole thing."

"Hold it," Serenata said. "Including the white parts."

"May be hard on veterans like you," Coca said. "Still, the reasoning goes that the privileged have had their day."

"It's not my day?" Who was she kidding. Today was definitely not her day.

"Anybody's ever had a day," Jon said airily, "I guess that makes them lucky."

"These minority readers," Serenata said. "Do they do white accents? Like, some drawling cracker from the Deep South? Or the flat nasality of Nebraska?"

"Mm . . ." Jon hummed. "Some do, some don't."

"So why isn't that 'mimicry'?"

"Turn about," Coca said. "Guess you find out what it feels like, on the other foot."

The right leg stiffening, Serenata slipped her own other foot atop the opposite ankle. "Is that the way we're going to fix things?" she wondered aloud. "By swapping who treats whom like shit?"

"Got a better idea?" Coca said.

This whole area was Remington's bailiwick, and she felt at sea. She'd no desire to offend the engineer. "Maybe. Like, we all quit bruising for a fight. An authentically rendered accent pays tribute to the fact that there are lots of ways to speak English, right? And some vernaculars are especially affecting or expressive."

"Yeah, but those 'vernaculars' don't belong to you," Coca said.

"Does my own vernacular belong to me?"

"Far as I can tell, you don't have one."

"Of course I do. There's no such thing as neutral English."

"If that's what you call an accent, then yeah, you can have it." The two seemed to find the whole idea of Serenata speaking in an "accent" hilarious.

"All these new rules . . ." Serenata said wistfully.

"There's always been rules," Coca said. "Now there's just different ones."

Fortunately, Jon ordered sandwiches, so she didn't have to be seen lurching off to lunch.

The afternoon's recording was motion capture. High-powered pure action scenes would be recorded using gaming stuntmen, who could do rolls, down-and-dirty fights, and leaps from a height. But the less demanding physical stuff integrated with dialogue used the actor playing the part, and today's ructions would have been easily within her gift—on most days. Yet even getting into the mo-cap suit in the changing room was painful. Working the form-fitting black neoprene over her right leg entailed bending it, and even the suit failed to disguise that the joint had blown up. As Jon's assistant affixed some sixty shiny round sensors on Velcro pads across her limbs, over her torso, down her back, and on the cap on the top of her head, simply standing squarely with her arms out required the gritty resolve on which she commonly drew for interval training.

The mo-cap studio was large, open-air, and dotted along its perimeter with cameras to record the motions of her figure, later translated to Joy, her avatar. The set was typically primitive: two lashed-together straight-back chairs and a round wooden disk mounted on a pole, meant to approximate the front seat of a car and a steering wheel. Mo-cap sets recalled the minimalist modernism often employed to stage Samuel Beckett; all the lushness and detail would be left to the animators. In this scene, Joy was to have a ferocious argument with the male lead on her cell phone. As the difference of opinion heated up, she'd grow inattentive, and lose control of the car. Serenata would be obliged to roll violently around the two chairs and end up on the floor, as the car tumbled down a ravine and she was thrown out the door. All in a day's work—ordinarily.

Her first version was destined to be her best—and it was a pity they weren't using facial capture as well, since her expressions of fear, alarm, and agony were oh, so very true to life. The problem came when she had to get up and do it again.

"Serenata," Jon said in her earphones after calling a halt to the second take. "You're not supposed to sound like you're dying *before* the car runs off the road." Frustrated, he cut the session short at four.

Back out on the baking sidewalk, she requested a large capacity Uber, whose driver loaded Carlisle into his minivan for the ride to Penn Station. The disgrace of resorting to a car dovetailed with disappointment in herself over the day's performance. She was always persnickety about her work, critical, convinced particular lines had come out dead, or she'd curse herself for letting a subtle fluff on a consonant go by when she should have insisted on reading the line again, but this more encompassing shame was new. It was a brown feeling.

Unfamiliar with whatever route the *disabled* were meant to take, she wheeled Carlisle to the top of the station stairs and leaned on the frame, looking helpless, until a strapping young man volunteered to hoist the bike to the concourse. Unaccustomed to the kindness of strangers, she wasn't 100 percent sure that Carlisle hadn't been stolen until the boy waited for her to hop the stairs one at a time while groping the railing. "I'm not meaning any insult or anything," he said, "but it seems like you might do better with a cane than a bike."

"It's a cane on wheels," she said (Carlisle would be offended). Though she'd have been mistaken for younger than sixty-two not long ago—like, early this morning—her rescuer clearly regarded her as an old lady. A glance in the studio's restroom mirror that afternoon had confirmed that her pain-makeover personality came replete with a new face: gray, drawn, lined, and asymmetric.

Scootering along as she had down Vesey Street would still qualify as riding in the station, which was banned, so she supported her right side by clutching the handlebars with her left hand while leaning the right one heavily on the crossbar.

Now feeling responsible for her, the Samaritan seemed reluctant to walk off. "You going to be okay?"

Since a truthful answer was *probably not*, she volunteered instead, "My husband is doing a half triathlon today, while I can barely walk."

"You mean, one of the Mettles?" When she nodded, he lifted his T-shirt sleeve. A jag of orange tattoos disappeared around his bicep. The smile glinted with a gold front tooth as he punched the air in farewell. "Hell, yeah, good for him! I done five."

Good grief, was this what it was like in Berlin in the 1930s? First you'd see one, and then a bit later you'd see two, until before you knew it these men in dun shirts were everywhere.

After handing off Carlisle at the baggage car, she accepted an engineer's offer of a helping hand into the carriage and lunged to her seat by holding onto headrests. Once the train got underway, she checked her messages again. Even at his slowest, Remington had to have completed the course by now. His nose was out of joint about her absence in Syracuse, but his not even sending a text seemed churlish. She shouldn't expect him to telepathically intuit while larking about Onondaga Lake that something dreadful had happened to his wife. Yet they both dwelled in bodies, notoriously hazardous housing that couldn't possibly have met modern health-and-safety standards. An occasional solicitation of how *she* was doing didn't seem too much to ask.

DID YOU FINISH? she texted. ARE YOU OKAY? BUY YOURSELF A NEW YORK STRIP AT DELMONICO'S! I BET YOU'VE EARNED IT. PLEASE CALL WHEN YOU'VE SETTLED. No reply. Maybe, as after the marathon, he was sleeping at his hotel. Finally by six o'clock, she texted Valeria, HOW'S DAD? Immediately, the phone rang.

"I'll tell you *how's Dad*," Valeria said in a shouty voice. "He's in Saint Joseph's Hospital."

"*What?*" Whatever had gone down, Valeria had a remarkable ability to imply in few words that it was all her mother's fault.

"You might have noticed that it's hot!" Perhaps the temperature was Serenata's fault as well. "Way too hot, and Papa's not used to it."

"No, he doesn't do well when it's warm." He didn't do well when it was not warm, either. "Did he stop, then? Bow out?"

"No, he was totally amazing! Like, he finally found the God in himself, the way Bambi said—"

"Valeria, would you please can all that praise-the-Lord guff for now and tell me what happened to your father."

"I'm *trying* if you'd be a little *patient.* I managed to be right there at the finish line, because, you know, there were sort of hardly any runners left—"

"You mean he was last."

"I guess so. Maybe. Yeah. But there's a heroism in that, isn't there?" Valeria said defiantly. "I mean, sure, he was going slow. I could probably have walked faster, if you want to know the truth. But it was hot! When the people still watching saw him coming around the final bend, they all went crazy! Cheering, and clapping, and banging these inflatable bat things against the barriers! As he trudged closer I noticed his face was a funny color, and his gait was unsteady, like he was having trouble keeping his balance. His eyes were all glassy, like he wasn't actually seeing anything. Still, he didn't stop. I've never seen anything so brave in all my life. I've never been so proud. I've never felt so strongly that the Lord was on Papa's side—"

"Enough," her mother said. "Why is your father in the hospital?" (A better question might have been, Why is *everyone* in the hospital?)

"When *you* tell a story, you expect everyone to be riveted by every detail. When anyone else tells a story, you're all, shut up and get to the point."

This was utter torture. "Go on. *Detail* away."

"At the end—if you care, and I have to wonder, since you weren't there—he was all, like, floppy, and staggering, and not running quite in a straight line. So the staff and medical people were all, like, hovering, but I guess they're not supposed to help you or you might not get your medal or whatever . . . So he's weaving, and we're all rooting for him, but also starting to get nervous that he's so close but even now he might not make it . . . And you wouldn't believe this, because, you know, right over the finish line there's this bar overhead, and I guess if you don't do that last chin-up then technically you don't finish. And you know what a stickler Papa is, like, you did it or you didn't do it. So he slaps at the air, and has trouble even finding the bar, but then he grabs it, and man oh man, he was so shaky, and we're all like, oh Lordy, is this astonishing man going to get this far and still stumble at the very last hurdle . . . And then he barely,

barely, like, both arms trembling, gets his chin *just* on top of the bar, and the little crowd of us went completely bananas and I burst into tears. I've never been so moved . . . so touched . . . so overwhelmed in all my born days."

"That's nice," Serenata said tightly. *"And?"*

"Well. Then he collapsed. Down in the dirt, passed clean out. The medical team went *whoosh*, and draped him with cold wet towels, and someone got ice and someone else brought orange juice while they took his pulse—I was trying to get over to him, so I heard a medic say his heart rate was uneven and way too fast. And I know you've got some weird problem with her, but Bambi was right in there, and you should be glad she was. She laid Papa out with his feet elevated, and fanned him with newspapers, and sprayed him with mist, while one of the medics on call stuck a thermometer under his arm. Before the ambulance got there, he started coming to, but it was sort of creepy because, though he seemed to recognize Bambi, he didn't seem to know who I was, or even where he was, or that he'd just finished a whole half MettleMan."

"Valeria, do I need to get up there tonight? I'm on the train to Hudson, but I could stay on to Albany, where I could pick up a train to Syracuse—"

"There's no need for all the dramatics," Valeria said. "He's going to be okay. His temperature's already come way down. They're keeping him in overnight just to be extra careful, but they seem to think he'll be totally fine to drive home tomorrow."

"This sounds like heatstroke."

"Heat-something. Yeah."

"If you're absolutely certain he doesn't want me to meet him there . . ."

"Depending on the train schedule, you'd get here at eleven, maybe even after midnight. Papa would be asleep; you'd see him in the morning, only to drive back to Hudson. It would be a big Florence Nightingale song and dance serving no earthly purpose but to make you look good."

Valeria was right for once. Given that Syracuse was hardly en route to her second day of recording tomorrow, the fact that Serenata was still drawn toward the empty gesture was a bad sign. In times past, neither she nor her husband would have entertained grand flights to one another's side of no practical utility, and "looking good" in the other's eyes would have been a foreign consideration for two people who looked good to each other already.

"Fair enough," she said. "But—I'm sorry if this sounds trivial— could you make sure to pick up his finisher coffee mug? You know he's going to want it. Also"—it was embarrassing to have to ask her daughter this—"would you ask him to call me? If he's feeling up to it."

"Oh, sure, I guess. But at the moment to be on the safe side they're running some tests. Besides, you're not exactly Papa's favorite person in the world right now."

Serenata neglected to point out that your "favorite person in the world" should have been the very definition of the person you were married to.

"No, technically it was heat *exhaustion*. It's only heatstroke when your temperature rises above a hundred and four."

Remington was just a few minutes in the door, but beyond a ritual embrace she didn't see the point of pussyfooting. "And yours rose to . . . ?"

"Only a hundred and three." Aside from a pinkening from strong sun the previous afternoon, his color looked normal, though she detected a new precariousness. He wouldn't ordinarily have sunk into a chair at the dining table immediately after a three-hour drive.

"*Only a hundred and three*," she repeated. "If I recall correctly, a hundred and four is right around the point you're in danger of brain damage."

"With ice packs and rehydration, my core temperature came right back down."

"Have you ever considered that you might not be cut out for this stuff?"

"Triathlon isn't something you are or aren't 'cut out for.' It's a challenge you decide to rise to."

Fetching him seltzer from the fridge, she managed the short distance by leaning on the kitchen island. He didn't notice.

"Yesterday hit a historic high for New York State on that date," Remington said at her back. "I don't see hyperthermia as something to be ashamed of."

"Did I say it was?"

"You have a *chiding* quality."

She couldn't imagine marshaling the wherewithal to chide. When she'd awoken early that morning, inflammation in the right knee had spread, and was at this moment traveling wildly up and down the leg—the length of her shin, through the ankle to the top of her foot, up the back of her thigh, and deep into the muscles of the buttock. Over-the-counter anti-inflammatories hadn't touched it. When the fluctuations of fire hit peaks like the one right now, she could feel the pain in her eyes, where the pupils were constricting to pinpricks.

"You're projecting," she said, pouring the water while storking on her left leg. "You imagine I'm *chiding*, when really you're chiding yourself."

"Excuse me, I inferred from your remarks that you think my getting overheated should teach me a lesson: I'm 'not cut out for this stuff.' But this nay-saying of yours is all in my head? You're not trying to get me to quit. No, you're bolstering my confidence: 'Go, team! So you got a little flushed, now hit the trail!'"

"You already have a cheerleader who's utterly oblivious to the risks you're taking, and who's now saved your life twice that I know of. Isn't that supposed to create some special lifelong bond?"

"As my beloved wife and helpmate, you might easily have been the one to fan and mist me, feed me sips of orange juice, and cover me in cold wet towels. But you'd have had to be present. You can't object to my intimacy with someone else and at the same time boycott any opportunities to boost ours."

Sliding on her right hand around the island, she delivered the seltzer.

"For example, don't you think you're forgetting something?" he asked.

"Lemon?"

"Congratulations. If with some difficulty, I finished the course."

"You mean, 'Congratulations for almost killing yourself again.' I didn't realize that was standard social etiquette."

"It's certainly standard etiquette after your husband has completed a feat as demanding as even a half Mettle, or anything close. Lots of people get hugs, flowers, and slaps on the back for finishing a five-K fun run."

"Congratulations," she said stonily.

"Well, that was quite the empty exercise."

"You asked for it."

"No, I asked for something else."

"All these years when I've gone out for a run, or a swim, or a long bike ride, have I ever come back demanding that you *congratulate* me?"

"I'm sorry if I sound insulting, but the scale of your sporting achievements has never been in a realm that would deserve exceptional recognition."

"Got it right there: you do sound insulting." It wasn't in the interest of putting her case forcefully, but she'd soon have to sit down. One of the many unsolicited revelations of the last day and a half: pain was tiring. It even seemed to entail a form of athleticism.

"You're doing your very best to deprive me of any sense of accomplishment, after I've exerted myself to the very limits of my ability—in fact, beyond those limits—"

"If you get this fucked-up finishing a *half* Mettle, what makes you think you can get through a whole one? In only two months' time? In June, when it could be even hotter."

"It's true, I did face—*and overcame*—a medical crisis. I get home, and my only reward is seltzer. Try as I might, I can't remember ever having snidely dismissed something you set your sights on, strived for, and finally succeeded at. I can't remember ever having pissed all over anything that was so important to you."

"What you want from me is patently unavailable," she said, finally plopping into a chair. "It's never been available, from the start of this thing, and you knew it wouldn't be. So if you wanted my admiration, you should have set about achieving something else. It's not fair to say, 'I'm doing this dumb thing. But you're never, ever allowed to observe how dumb it is. I won't accept your merely pretending it's not dumb, either. You have to *believe* it's not dumb, in your very soul.' In demanding some passionate, prostrate *congratulations*, you're asking me to completely relinquish my independent judgment—to relinquish *myself*. Suddenly just because you're my husband, I'm expected to wholeheartedly get on board whatever goofball notion takes your fancy."

"You're expected," he said quietly, "to be a little less selfish."

"Check this out for being selfless," she said. "How's your hamstring?"

It was dreadful to watch his face and actually see in it the indecision about whether to lie to her. "It aches." He'd settled on farcical understatement.

"It's been, what, nine months?"

"Something like that."

"And it's never healed."

She should have been asking about that damned hamstring nonstop, but only her short course in the astonishing existence of agony the day before had brought out the suffering of others in relief. She might have been looking at the world through infrared glasses—and when she turned the viewfinder on her husband, his entire figure lit up crimson.

"That means," she went on, "each time you go for a run, every second step hurts. So you're not leaping hill and dale in a state of transcendent bliss. You're gritting your teeth through an ordeal you can't wait to be over. This whole venture—it's so joyless! What's the point?"

"The point is obviously not *joy*." He pronounced the word with the disdain that Tommy had lent to *imprimatur*.

"Then I repeat: What *is* the point?"

"If you don't understand by now—and I think you do; I think your incomprehension is disingenuous—then we're not going to improve your grasp of my purpose with more talk. So let's wrap this conversation up, shall we?"

As a gesture of conclusion, he took his bag upstairs.

"Hey, I'm surprised to find you home," he said on return. "I'd have thought you'd still be recording in Manhattan."

Old Remington would have remarked on her unanticipated presence first thing. It took some nerve to ride her for being selfish, because New Remington's world stopped at his skin, and the exigencies of other people's lives dawned dimly if at all, and on delay. The note-in-a-bottle message "Your wife isn't supposed to be here" might have just dropped in their backyard from an Amazon drone.

"I was fired," she said.

"Whose desk did *you* slam?"

"For once, I was sent packing for good reason. I did take the train down, but my concentration was poor, and my delivery was subpar. And there's a physical aspect to gaming VO that I don't appear to be up to. They're recasting my character. They'll have to rerecord the work I did yesterday, but the director didn't have any choice. I agreed with him, actually. So I took the train right back up."

Remington's eyes narrowed. "What's wrong?" He seemed to be seeing her for the first time this afternoon, though from far away.

"My right knee exploded. There's a hard knot at the back the size of an egg, and now the whole leg is inflamed, ass to toe. I am no longer functional. And yes, of course I've made an appointment, though I know what he'll say. Churchwell told me that at the outside I had a year and a half. That was a year and a half ago."

"Knee replacement."

"I can't put it off anymore. I can't exercise."

"I'm sorry."

"I am, too."

TEN

Knee replacements had become ordinary—even if a certain ordinary orthopedist had breezily informed a certain ordinary patient that the generation behind her was sure to get injections of stem cells to regenerate connective tissues instead. Thus right around the corner, though not in time for her to benefit, sheering off the ends of the leg bones with a hacksaw and pounding big foreign chunks of metal into their amputated stumps with a polo mallet—that is, attacking the dysfunctions of the human body as a crude carpentry project, as one might repair a garden shed or porch railing—would be regarded the height of barbarism. *Thanks, doc. That makes me feel so much better.*

Thus there was no call for alarm or complaint. Scads of other people had submitted to this same brutal surgery, gone through the same excruciating recovery (or failure to recover), and rolled the same medical dice that, should they come up snake eyes, would preclude not only completing one hour and fifty-eight minutes of high-intensity interval training, but also walking to the mailbox. For that matter, the yawn-inducing nonchalance now expected of candidates for joint replacement surely pertained to the likes of aging and death: They happened to everybody, so what was the big deal?

The big deal was that personally Serenata Terpsichore had never before inhabited a body tenderly preserved for decades—*curated* for decades, since the fashionable verb was now applied to everything from thrift stores to salad—that, despite best efforts, was falling apart. However predictable the monotonous cycle of renewal and decay in the big picture, on a granular level the tragic structure of the human life was forever startling. As she'd understood from childhood that the body wasn't built to last, she should hardly have been surprised when her own body didn't last, either. Nevertheless, she *was* surprised. Even the surprise was surprising.

To her further chagrin, the steady corruptions of the flesh were especially astonishing for her *type*. Much as she'd questioned Bambi's claim that the more extreme the demands placed on a body, the more it thrives—and much as she'd paid lip service to the sensible notion that biological moving parts wear out—she herself had bought wholesale into her generation's popular myth that the body solely flourishes with use. Throughout her life, she had exercised, hard, for a duration, virtually every day. According to legend, she had therefore earned reprieve from the tawdry ailments of sedentary mortals—many of whom were in fact physically better prepared to go the distance into old age than Serenata was now. The cult of MettleMan got up her nose to the degree it did because as a larger umbrella faith it was her church, too. The spouses simply differed on fine points of catechism, like a Methodist and a Pentecostal.

Whether the self was apiece with the body or rode around in a body like a passenger in an open-topped jalopy was one of those irresolvable questions, but it did seem to Serenata that you couldn't have it both ways. You couldn't walk around in a beautiful body and feel, yourself, beautiful when you were seventeen in hot pants, and then conveniently draw a sharp distinction between the *it* of you and the *you* of you when your vacuum cleaner was snarled by fistfuls of fallen-out hair from postmenopausal alopecia. You couldn't identify with the body's powers without also identifying with its deficiencies and even ugliness when those powers failed.

She was under no illusion about other people; that is, lazily, she saw man and manifestation as roughly one and the same, which meant that others also conflated Serenata the remote, obstinate, spitefully private character with a five-seven brunette whose nose was a touch Roman and on the sharp side. After all, it took mental effort to separate body and soul; it took affection, and attention, and the long view. Even with Remington, she had to concentrate in order to see him as an enduring presence—who hadn't changed much and who if anything, the last two years notwithstanding, had improved—rather than as, increasingly, an older man, if not an old man, who by dint of equal parts sweat and lunacy had grown emaciated, with mean little muscles that wouldn't last a month when his own arthritis struck. But with herself, of course, and this was surely universal, body and self were distinct; they would have to be, in order to be *in relationship.*

Plenty of people hated their bodies, and sadly, this antagonism could grow into the central battle of their lives, like bad marriages in a country that forbade divorce. In this respect, Serenata had been fortunate. Until recently, she and the body had for the most part been a team. The relationship was congenial, though there was an eternal tussle over which party was really in control. By conceit, the self was boss, and this was a myth; only at the body's behest was Serenata here at all. Still, she felt responsible for an organism that was at once robust and fragile. Despite its high mileage, it was readily undone by a moment of clumsiness on the stairs or a bad oyster. The dumb ward had to be serviced, fueled but not too much, rested, and, in the absence of the miraculous Morphatron, manually put through its paces; sometimes these animal-husbandry routines wore thin. But overwhelmingly the relationship on the overlord's side had been one of tenderness.

Somehow, the sorrow of watching a sturdy, long-serving charge falter and degrade was not the same sorrow of knowing that she herself, too, would soon perish. Though it would seem so, the claim that she dwelt in a well-crafted creature was not a boast. This body had come to her. The creature was not of her making. She had been *entrusted* with it. If she had broadly done right by it, you would not call that a boast, either. Yes, there was a small pride involved, in having made the body do things it didn't want to that were for its own good, in having fed it something a little better than a steady diet of Velveeta nachos, but this was the pride of a caretaker, not so different from the satisfaction that a faithful janitor takes in the shine of swabbed floors.

Some parts of the body stirred her tenderness more than others. Small bits, in fact, came in for the same hostility that she sensed Valeria, for example, felt toward her whole package. Serenata hated her cuticles. She did not understand the purpose of a transitional scum that did nothing but split, dry, and tear. Left to their own devices, these epidermal predators would clearly have spread to the very tips of her nails, smothering the keratin the way malign algae blooms suffocated whole Great Lakes. In her disgust, she had been wont to strip the things in ragged shreds from fingers and toes, whereupon the bloody remains would stain the pillowcase and ruin her socks. The wounds hurt and took weeks to heal, but she thought of the amateur surgery as reprisal. While she might have felt sheepish about the miniature "self-harm," she felt nothing of the kind. The cuticles had been disciplined into submission, and the conquest was gratifying.

Her legs were another matter. The primary drivers of Remington's *motion of the body through space*, they were the strongest aspect of the organism, and qualified as shapely in the terms that her culture prescribed. Proportionately, they were long. The thighs at tension were solid. In profile, the tibias swooped gently from the knees like ski slopes. The calf muscles cut shadowed commas when she wore heels. The ankles were suitably slender. Wolf whistles when she wore short skirts had never offended her. The stems on which she perched were the lines where self and flesh converged. If in any sense soul was synonymous with body, Serenata was at one with her legs. And now she was offering them up in a grotesque act of human sacrifice.

Naturally her accelerating dysfunctions didn't stop at the knees. A recurrent pang in her right wrist put her on notice that her push-ups were numbered. Or an ankle would freakishly sprain from stepping off a low curb at the wrong angle. Muscle spasms in her back were frequent, arbitrary, paralyzing, and occasioned by nothing she did or refrained from doing. For the last six months, her spine went *pong* every time she rose during her usual five hundred sit-ups—a creepy out-of-kilter slippage that doubtless portended traction. The creaks, the pops, the straining of guy ropes, the groaning of her hull together fostered the suspense of *Titanic* right before the ship sinks.

Worse, abruptly, it was as Tommy March foretold: the right knee had pretty much stopped working altogether. While still characterizing its implosion as an arthritic "flare-up," Dr. Churchwell conceded that at a certain point a flare-up failed to subside and installed unremitting torment as the new normal. Athletically, she was grounded.

Regarding double replacements as tantamount to putting his patients through a six-car pileup, this orthopedist recommended getting the second knee done in three to six months' time—which presented the happy prospect of barely recuperating from one ordeal only to go through the whole horror show all over again. With the right knee in such critical condition, the surgeon fit her into his schedule at Columbia Memorial at the end of May, claiming to have moved heaven and earth on her account. Yet from Serenata's perspective, that meant six long weeks of melting like a bar of soap in a flooded dish.

Meanwhile, Remington had hit the home stretch of training for his full Mettle. He now hewed to a regime of running, cycling, and swimming, all three sports, every other day, with strength training at BruteBody on the odd ones. Rarely laying eyes on each other during daylight hours, she and her husband shared a postal address. In every other respect, their parallel universes barely intersected. Until this cliff-edge ejection from the world of expending energy, she hadn't realized how heavily their marriage of late had depended on the slender Venn diagram of overlapping habits. The excess of the convert might have dwarfed her daily ministrations upstairs into the merely gestural, but heretofore continuing to clear what she'd once considered a fairly high athletic bar had kept her seething sense of inferiority in check. But now the bar was on the floor. She had joined the loamy, misshapen tubers on the living-room sofa.

This impression of total physiological collapse was ridiculous. Even a waterlogged bar of soap didn't dissolve into a gelatinous puddle overnight, and a relatively slim female figure nicely toned for its age would progress toward liquefaction still more gradually. Yet her emotional disintegration was instantaneous.

Disrobing at bedtime, she kept her back to her husband, stripping off her jeans in haste and pulling her shirt overhead in a single desperate motion that snagged the care label on her hair clip. Though she'd formerly have draped the shirt on a hanger for wear a second day, now she didn't even tug it right-side-out before flinging it atop her jeans on the rug, the better to wrench off her running bra and dive into the bedding. Though late spring was warm enough that she'd have commonly sprawled the mattress uncovered, legs extended, arms outstretched, basking in the breeze of the fan on low, now she kept the sheet tucked to her chin. Previously, it wasn't that she'd been conceited about her figure, or put it on parade, but she'd never felt impelled to cover it up. Now she hid from both her husband and herself, averting her gaze from the full-length mirror if she needed to scuttle from the room, limping, to pee. She hadn't realized how comfortable she'd been with her naked body until she was ashamed of it.

By contrast, if also with a limp that he tried to disguise, Remington strolled naked from bedroom to bath with unself-conscious ease. Indeed, before sliding into bed he could happily roam the house bare-assed for an hour or more. He'd already acquired a dark tan, which stopped so starkly a few inches above the knee that he appeared still to be wearing cycling shorts. The endearing swell at his midsection having long ago melted, he sported not an ounce of fat, so that when he walked, sinews rippled in his legs and buttocks in a continuous light show, like the old pixilated billboards in Times Square. Yet he'd just turned sixty-six. Though she'd never tell him so, he looked every year and then some. His figure had grown cadaverous. Creased the more from all that sun, his face looked hunted, wide-eyed, almost crazed.

Often wondering if she'd any real appetite for the rest of her life (and did that mean, in the absence of natural causes, she was threatening suicide?), Serenata was acutely aware that all her melodrama was uncalled for, even if the rending of garments took place mostly in her mind. Equating the end of squats with the end of the world was humiliating; hovering overhead, a more adult intelligence looked down on herself in every sense. Through no fault of her own—or she didn't think it was her fault—her functionality had been compromised. Yet no levelheadedness she summoned could change the fact that imposed idleness had thrown her into a tailspin. What had been offended was deeper than vanity. As mechanically as she portrayed her daily fidelities to Remington, exercise, of all things, had grown nonsensically bound up with who she was, and without it she felt reduced and not a little lost. After the surgery, which would turn her into an invalid proper, the disassociation would only get worse.

She criticized Remington for his disordered priorities, but she was just as neurotic as he was. As May advanced, the signs became unmistakable: excessive sleep; trouble completing even minor voice-over jobs of a few lines; tendency to sit for bizarrely long periods doing nothing; avoidance of mundane chores like laundry, now insurmountable; reluctance to see Tommy or Griff—reluctance, really, to leave the house at all. Clearly, she had sunk into a profound depression. All because she couldn't commence the five hundred burpees that most sane people would do almost anything to avoid.

Deacon couldn't have picked a worse time to visit, which must have pleased him.

When he phoned, their son claimed to be between digs and in need of a bed to bridge the gap, though he was typically vague about the date his apocryphal new apartment would become available. When she asked about his things, he said he "didn't have much stuff." Perhaps it was materialistic to regard someone with negligible possessions as untrustworthy, but if you couldn't take care of a few dishes and a desk lamp by twenty-nine, what else could you not take care of?

With grave misgivings, she and Remington agreed to take him in for a *very short while*. Despite Valeria's suspicions about the nature of her brother's livelihood, they hadn't any proof, and he was still their son.

Deacon's evasiveness about when he'd show up had apparently been code for "tomorrow." That night, Remington had barely worked up his resentful declaration that the boy was not going to interfere with his training regime by *five minutes* or *five feet,* with an air of just getting started. Yet the very next afternoon, Deacon was at the door. Or through the door, since during the young man's last extended period of freeloading their first summer in Hudson they'd provided him a key, which he hadn't returned.

"You could have knocked," Serenata said, tailing lines of green beans for what would *not,* it seemed, be a candlelit tête-à-tête with her husband. Chopping anything in a chair at the dining table still felt awkward. Her knife skills were tailored to standing up.

"Family," Deacon said with a shrug. Kinship was a concept of which he availed himself when it suited him. "You never knocked when barging into my room."

"I did at first. But that only gave you fair warning to hide all the swag you'd stolen."

"Nice to see you, too." He unshouldered a bag that would have fit in a budget airline's overhead bin. As ever, the young man was a measure underweight, so the oversize rayon T-shirt and smartly cut slacks draped his frame with the chic flutter of garments on a mani-kin. He'd doubtless worn the same outfit for days. Preferring the subtle spectrum of laurel, teal, artichoke, and sage in which the af-fluent now painted their houses, he always bought expensive clothes, but he was lazy.

"That's all you own in the world?"

"Easy come, easy go." The expression might have been coined specifically for Deacon Alabaster. He picked up jobs readily enough but just as readily quit. With slim low-slung hips and a gaze both challenging and opaque, he had the effortless good looks and distant bearing that made him a magnet for the pretty but insecure girls he went through like Kleenex. She'd not have been surprised if he'd also sired more than one *easy come* child along the way, whom he'd have unthinkingly left behind in the careless spirit of genetic littering.

"So where's Dad?"

"Where do you think? Trooping the trails with his floozy."

"What? Like, *jogging*?" Since they only heard from Deacon when he wanted something, he wasn't up to speed. One of them must have mentioned the enterprise, since *tri* was all Remington talked about, but if so their son hadn't listened. He'd never seemed interested in either parent, especially not in his father. Deacon had the style of Remington as a young man, but none of the substance. As a consequence, Deacon had only to walk into the room for his father to feel mocked.

"He's entering a triathlon in two weeks."

"Why?"

The simple question left Serenata stymied. "I've asked him before. His answer has never been satisfactory. He seems to think his motivation is self-evident."

"Yeah, those masochists are all over Windham." Never having suffered from the ambition that might have driven him to the city, throughout his twenties Deacon had drifted from one struggling upper New York State town to another—Dormansville, Medusa, Preston-Potter Hollow—where the rents were low and life was neither hard nor pleasant. He seemed to relish the arbitrariness of living just anywhere.

Fetching a beer, Deacon elucidated. "Always in the way, traipsing in the road, since there's no sidewalks. Fists clenched, faces purple and blotchy, like spoiled eggplants. Any day now they'll be dead, and what did the motherfuckers do when they had the chance but make themselves as miserable as possible."

Their son was chronically contemptuous. Yet he'd accomplished little enough—nothing, in most people's terms, aside from hand-to-mouth survival—so it was a puzzle where this superiority was sourced. It was, his mother had concluded, the scorn of the nonparticipant. He hadn't sullied himself with wanting something and trying to get it, which protected him from any sense of failure or disappointment. Remaining apart from the silly toiling, the overcoming of petty obstacles, the fruitless striving, and the sad little comings-up-short that punctuated the pointless churn of all the other suckers in his surround gave him an above-it-all quality that his peers found mesmeric.

"Also, I should warn you that tomorrow I'm getting my right knee replaced."

"Why would you bother to do that?"

"Thanks for your concern," Serenata said. "I'm in pain, and I can barely walk."

"Then don't walk."

"Doc, it hurts when I do this?"

Deacon looked blank.

"It's an old Henny Youngman joke. The doc says, 'Then don't do that.'"

"Pretty lame."

"I am lame. That's the point."

It passed for enjoying each other's company. Why, so far she *was* enjoying her son's company. In some curious fashion she couldn't put her finger on, at this precise moment of dread and desolation, Mr. Who Gives a Shit was the ideal houseguest.

"So both your parents are, as they say, *stressed*," she continued. "I should put you on notice before he gets here, too, that your father doesn't have a sense of humor about this triathlon business. I don't recommend even gentle ribbing. He's very nervous about his ability to complete the course. As he should be. A two-and-a-half-mile swim; well over a hundred miles on a bike; a marathon; and a final chin-up, just in case you improbably get through the rest of that crap without keeling over. I don't think I'd have been able to do it, even in my heyday." She paused; she may never before have said that aloud. "*And* if anything does go wrong in Lake Placid, don't ever say anything. Just promise me. Say absolutely nothing."

"You mean, 'Hey, Dad, I heard you entered this dopy race and fell flat on your face!' Like that?"

She laughed. "Like that. He's got way too much riding on this thing. If the gamble doesn't pay off, he'll be busted."

Rolling a cigarette, Deacon eyed her theatrically, swaying back and forth to examine her face. "You think it's retarded."

Another short laugh escaped, despite herself. Mother and son had always enjoyed a collusion, which she tried to resist. He had no moral compass. Yet she appreciated his anarchic streak. (Well—it was more than a streak.) He treated other people atrociously, but he went his own way. He wasn't a joiner. "You can't smoke that in here. And what I happen to think of your father's endeavor doesn't matter."

Again, the keen appraisal, his head askance. It was fortunate that Deacon was so indolent. When he troubled himself, he was too canny. "I bet it does matter. I bet what you think of all his huffing and puffing is all that matters."

A touch flustered, she nodded at the unlit rollup. "While we're on house rules, I have to ask you something."

"*House rules?* Honest, Mom, I don't remember your being such a downer."

"I want you to tell me how you make a living."

It was always difficult to ask Deacon direct questions. He had a sidling nature; he was good at dodging bullets. To pin him straight on was to invite him to lie. Deacon lied breezily enough, but she found being lied to sufficiently disagreeable that to avoid the falsified answers she usually avoided the questions, too.

"I'm an entrepreneur," he said with a smile.

"Who sells or makes what?"

"People need things, I get them."

"Like what?"

"Whatever. Depends on the market."

"Your sister thinks you're dealing drugs."

"Valeria thinks a lot of things. She thinks Jesus cares personally about her and her drooling, farting, Wal-Marty family. She thinks she's a 'survivor' of child abuse. Valeria's the last person I'd go to for intel about anything."

"So you're not dealing drugs? I don't mind weed. I mean opioids, or heroin."

"I'm sort of curious why you care. Theoretically. Like, I do know plenty of addicts. Supply and demand: they're going to get their fix from somewhere. Plenty of scaggy losers right here in Hudson. Does it make you feel all pure, just so long as they don't get their buzz from me?"

"If we catch you dealing from this house, you're out on your ear."

He chuckled. "Look. If I was into contraband, I wouldn't be lugging around a suitcase of twist-tied baggies. I'd be higher up the food chain than that."

"Because you're such a self-starter. Such a go-getter."

"No, because I aim to get by, and not put myself in the way of any grief. Turns out that doesn't require much. You don't call attention to yourself. You only take advantage of opportunities that land in your lap. You keep your head just high enough above a sea of shit so you can breathe, like dog-paddling in the toilet."

She wasn't going to get past Deacon's stonewalling. At least, as she'd promised Remington, she had delivered their ultimatum. "Also," she added. "No drug taking on the premises, either."

"Do I have to clean my room and set the table?"

"Come to think of it, that would be nice." She wasn't sure about her sudden impulse. Honesty was an experiment. "Deacon, I'm very frightened of this surgery. The physical therapy afterward is horrendous. Surgeons talk an optimistic game, but the people I've met who've had it done are still limping a year later. They can hardly do any exercise, and they gain weight."

"So? Haven't you done enough? Christ, all through my childhood, for hours on end—pounding around Albany, or retiring to your secret torture chamber with its special instruments for waterboarding yourself or something. Put your feet up!" Deacon propped his own heels on a chair. "I'd think you'd be relieved to have an excuse to throw it all over."

"I am, a little," she admitted. He could be her confessor. "The day is so much longer. And there's not this punishment sitting at the end of it. Maybe in declining to sample the pleasures of lethargy, I've been missing out. You don't do anything, do you? I mean, exercise."

"Get out of bed. Slog to the john. Roll a ciggie to recuperate from my terrible exertions. Speaking of which?" He dangled his handiwork.

"Oh, go ahead. Get a saucer. I don't really care." She wasn't sure what impishness had gotten into her, but Deacon was a bad influence, and she was in the mood for a bad influence. She felt feckless, and fuck-it, and flippant.

"Honest." Deacon lit up with a savor that made her envious. "Why not *give up*? You're in your sixties, right? That whole physical plant of yours is going to hell in a handbasket—or a casket—whatever you do. Stop trying to compete with twenty-year-old nymphets who can beat you hands down just by walking down the street in a potato sack. Relax, and throw yourself into the arms of the inevitable. Got to be some advantage to becoming a doddering old bag."

"Thanks."

"Look, you've rated, right? My friends always thought you were smokin'. So hang it up while you're ahead! You're still not a bad-looking broad for a grandmother of . . . Sorry, I've lost count. Is it four or five kids now? In any case, add another notch to your belt. Valeria says she's preggers again."

"Good God, tell me you're pulling my leg."

"When I tell jokes, I don't use the same punch line over and over."

"Would you fetch the chenin blanc in the fridge? You're driving me to drink."

Deacon glugged half the bottle into a balloon glass. "Now seriously," he said, bringing himself another beer. "I don't understand women like you. I see it all the time, too, these rung-out dishrags gasping on treadmills. They're ruining a perfectly decent afternoon, they still look like shit, and they also look pathetic. They're kidding themselves in this totally public and embarrassing way, when plenty of these bitches are rich as fuck, and could be whooping it up and ordering the prime rib. Mom, you've done your bit. You were hot stuff for what, forty-five years? So stop starving yourself. Stop counting alcoholic *units*. Let go. And fuck the knee replacements. Get a walker that has wheels and a little basket for your shopping. Or don't go anywhere. Catch up on *The Simpsons*."

"You are a serpent," she said with a toast. "But this woman—with whom your father now spends most of his time—do you have any idea what his trainer looks like?"

A key rattled in the side door. Given the clamor of voices, to her incredulity on this of all evenings, her husband had invited the tri club. It being still nominally his house, Remington was first in the door, at which point he froze. "Put that out right now."

Deacon would have stirred a milder reaction by meeting his father with a shotgun. "I'm fine, thanks so much for asking." He took another deep drag before reluctantly crushing his rollup in a dish. "And how are *you*, sir?"

Remington turned to his wife. "Since when? What's wrong with you?"

"Where do you want me to start?"

"And please put your feet on the floor," Remington told their son. "We're going to need all these chairs."

"Gosh." Again, Deacon complied in slow motion. "Another lovey-dovey family reunion."

"We may not be gushy, but we can at least keep it civil." With effort, Remington stuck out his hand, which Deacon shook with a limp clasp. "Welcome home."

The club filtered in. They'd done another swim/bike/run day, which the members with jobs could only manage on weekends. As the full Mettle approached, the group had grown jittery and prone to conflict. Cherry DeVries was sometimes weepy. Hank Timmerman had more than once absconded. Chet Mason gave long, uninvited lowdowns on gear, when they'd already bought their gear. Ethan Crick had lost what little sense of humor he'd ever had about his reputation as a hypochondriac. Even Remington had shed his easy self-deprecation, and this evening reacted testily to Chet's grousing that the rest of the club had to wait repeatedly, hours even, for him to finish each leg of the course—"Well, I got there in the end, didn't I?"—whereas in times past he'd have made a joke at his own expense. Having completed Mettles before, only Bambi and Sloan retained their insouciance, though they were watchful of their brood. Earlier in the year, the group had returned tired and cocky; now they returned tired and cross.

Remington introduced the club members to Deacon, whose placid expression conveyed that he was not trying to remember their names. With one exception: "*Bambi*? Seriously? I guess you can call me Thumper then."

"All right, *Thumper*." Unlacing a running shoe on the chair

Deacon's feet had vacated, Bambi put on a pedestal for display what Remington called her artwork.

"You're one of those lumpy chicks," Deacon said.

"You could say that." Unlacing the other shoe, Bambi shot him a once-over glance. "But you're not one of those lumpy dicks."

"Nah," Deacon said with a smile. "I'm just a dick."

The teasing spirit in which the club had once vied over who was faster had given way to a more acrimonious rivalry with higher stakes. "I only struggled on that hill because the derailleur was jumping gears, so sit on this," Chet told Hank blackly with a raised middle finger. As Bambi ramped up to exceed her own personal best in Lake Placid, it seemed that she no longer looped back to check on stragglers, but churned neck and neck with Sloan, who eventually pulled well ahead in all three sports. For Bambi, their competition was now tainted with a drop of acid. She played her sex to her advantage off-road. But at the end of the day, Bambi didn't really like being a girl.

This evening, it was the presence of Deacon Alabaster that really rattled them. The stranger in their midst evinced not the slightest interest in their times. When they cited extraordinary distances with the feigned casualness of name-dropping at parties, he didn't bat an eye. On reflection, when Serenata spelled out the exploits that his dad would tackle in two weeks, Deacon had acted perfectly unfazed. She might as well have said his father was entering a limerick-writing contest. The club was smugly inured to the raging, transparently insecure "why aren't you working in a homeless shelter?" type. But the company of the dismissive and blithely unimpressed was kryptonite.

Worse, here was a guy who hadn't done a calf raise, a deltoid dip, or a bicep curl in his life—a guy whose idea of exercise was carrying a six-pack and bag of corn chips from the 7-Eleven to his car.

Yet owing to the aesthetic multiplier effect of two attractive parents, he was handsome—meaning, rivetingly handsome, *who-the-fuck-is-that?* handsome. In times past, his mother had found this disjunction perplexing or even a touch maddening. Right now, she thought it was great.

Worse still for this crowd, Deacon was hip, a mysterious attribute that her son had embodied since he was eleven or twelve, when he was as popular in the schoolyard as his sister was ignored. During his juvenile delinquent days (assuming they were over) his smooth, aloof, unruffled affect had been infuriating. What exactly hipness comprised was difficult to identify. Suffice it to say that if you needed the texture explained to you then you didn't have it. If you didn't have it, you couldn't go get it, either. Cool was not available for purchase, and it could not be learned.

Thus Deacon drove the tri club to distraction. They were all self-actualizers, and here was this slick customer who epitomized the one characteristic that they could not earn. The only one of their number who evidenced an iota of hipness was Deacon's father—though Remington's was an old-fashioned William Powell version, well spoken and well mannered. Sloan passed for hip in Hudson, but he needed the props of those classic cars. Even Bambi was too needy to be hip—and she'd never win the esteem she craved from Deacon, whose unadulterated indifference to everything she valued was not, to all appearances, a pose. Moreover, Bambi reviled defeat, and no gambit better assured victory in any game than refusing to play it in the first place.

For his parents, Deacon's visits were mostly expensive headaches; by custom, they paid him to leave. But tonight he lent his mother's skeptics' corner a welcome clout. To capitalize on this rare plurality of apostates, she texted Tommy to join them. That first summer, Tommy had mooned day after day at their son as he dozed in the backyard hammock. After learning that Deacon was here, she showed up in five minutes flat. Together, the three of them occupied one end of the table, the rowdies at the back of the class.

"Hey, Bambi." Serenata raised the hardback that Remington was halfway through. "Have you read the new bio of this renowned ultra-runner? Though he's dead, you know."

"Donald Ritchie? Yeah, somebody at BruteBody mentioned he left the building last year."

"I thought it was interesting that he kicked it at only seventy-three."

"Why interesting?" Bambi said warily. "That's old enough."

"Not these days. And he was in pretty bad shape. Diabetes. Lung problems. Actually, he had to stop running altogether at sixty-six. Remington's age." Serenata had only scanned the end of the book: the good part.

"So? Is this another Jim Fixx sneer? Ha-ha, the author of *The Complete Book of Running* keeled over while jogging at fifty-two? So getting off your ass can't possibly be good for you. *Running kills.*"

"To establish any correlation between endurance sports and pre-mature morbidity," Remington instructed his cynical spouse, "one *somewhat* early death is about as statistically significant as, 'There was this guy I knew.'" He turned to his trainer. "It's like my wife here claiming that 'all the people she's met' who've had knee replace-ments can barely walk and get fat. She'd tell you herself that she's an antisocial misanthrope. So how many strangers are we talking? Two maybe. Three max. I don't call that scientific."

"Lots of distance runners die early," Serenata said. "Heart attacks, mostly."

"Not at a higher incidence than the general population," Rem-ington said. "Besides, who says the purpose of elite athletics is to increase longevity? Even if a less taxing existence did mean living longer—to *do what?* Really, what good is living to a hundred and ten? I'm not that keen getting past seventy."

"That's in four years," she said softly.

"I can add," he snapped.

Were she to be generous, Serenata could attribute her husband's irritability to the likelihood that, if she was distraught about the next day's operation, he was also anxious on her account. But she wasn't feeling generous.

"Hey, check this out." Tommy had grabbed the biography and was reading the summary on the back. "This Scotch guy ran a hundred miles at a time, in under twelve hours! That's like . . ."

"A steady eight-minute mile," Bambi said. "Mediocre for a marathon, but not bad for four of the fuckers back-to-back."

"That's nothing," Remington said. "Ritchie ran the entire length of Great Britain—eight hundred and forty miles—in eleven days."

"What was the problem?" Deacon said. "There was a rail strike?"

"You have no respect," his father said.

Deacon licked the paper of another rollup. "Got that right."

"During that long UK run," Serenata read over Tommy's arm, "he developed 'a feverish cold' and then faced 'vicious head winds and sleet.' The cold turned into bronchitis . . . He had 'stomach pains, intestinal blood loss, a sore mouth, regular nose bleeds, chest pains, and torrential rains.' Some people really know how to vacation."

"You can't tell me that you don't admire that," Remington charged her.

"So"—Deacon raised the knife with which his mother had tailed the beans—"if I flay myself alive, I'll finally earn Daddy's approval."

"And why would *that* be admirable?" his father said.

"Suffering for suffering's sake—what's the difference?" Deacon said.

"Donald Ritchie set records!" Historically, only restraint borne of his own beatings in childhood had kept Remington from coming to blows with the boy.

"But records for what?" Deacon's tone remained detached, his slouch languid, but he wasn't backing down. Twiddling the unlit rollup in one hand, he was still holding the knife in the other. "I could set a record for how long I took to bleed to death."

Serenata rose as briskly as her knee allowed. "Deacon simply raised the legitimate question of what running the length of any large island in bad weather and poor health actually accomplishes." She held out her hand for the knife. "Discussion closed."

Her phone rang: Valeria. She took the call to the back porch. "Mama, I made sure to put it in my diary that you're getting that operation tomorrow."

"That's very nice of you to remember."

"I asked around at the church, and everybody says it's terrible! Like, you're in awful pain for months and months, or even years! Online it says that up to one in five patients will be in pain kind of like, all the time, for the rest of their lives!"

"Thanks, Valeria. That's very helpful."

"Well, I think it is helpful! An older gentleman in our congregation said the one thing he wishes somebody had told him ahead of time is what a torment it was going to be. He said it actually tested his faith. He didn't know why Jesus would put him through such a thing. He still uses a cane, and he got his knee ten years ago."

"Well, then. It's kind of you to prepare me."

"And that's not all," Valeria went on.

"Oh, great," her mother said.

"All that running in place and jumping around you do—that's well and truly over. I guess you can do an itty-bitty bit of biking. And go on short walks. That's about it."

"Actually, with the newer joints, you can play tennis, golf, and even ski."

"That's what doctors say up front to get the money, Mama. Then there's all these exceptions—like, just about everybody—along with the blood clots and faulty hardware they also don't tell you about. Did you know if you get a 'deep infection' they'll yank the whole thing out again, and they may even cut off your leg?"

"I'm touched that you've been googling so vigorously on my account."

"I'll be praying for you, Mama."

"That's sure to make all the difference, isn't it? And Deacon tells me you're due congratulations again."

"That's right," Valeria said, her voice tightening. "Due right around Christmas, like Jesus himself. We're real happy about it." But for once she didn't *sound* happy. Why, for a moment it seemed she might cry.

"And how's Nancee doing?"

"*I* think she's in the pink. But those pesky therapists have her on what they call an 'exercise diet.' It's the silliest thing! I'm supposed to keep an eye on her, and if she heads upstairs, I have to follow her and make sure she only goes up once."

After Serenata wrapped up her reassuring family call, Ethan said when she came back inside, "Hey, Sera! Rem just told us your surgery's tomorrow. We all wanted to wish you good luck."

"Yeah," Chet said. "But I heard if you're in half-okay shape to start with, you get through it a ton easier." It was the closest anyone in the club had come to acknowledging that Remington's wife was not, altogether, a slug.

"I was gonna say break a leg," Bambi said. "But I guess they're doing that for you, huh?" Cherry chimed in with the compulsive false confidence of the well-meaning. "You'll be right as rain before you know it!" After Sloan and Hank also expressed greeting-card-grade support, the group moved on to other subjects with palpable relief. The simple scaled-up meal Serenata had halfheartedly entertained suddenly seemed insuperable, and she put the beans in the fridge. Girding for mutilation, she had nothing to spare for these people.

Fielding one more phone call briefly cheered her up. It was Griff, whose very awkwardness about what to say was strangely moving. He promised that when she was up and about he'd teach her to play cribbage. She said it's a deal. Getting him off the phone was excruciating—neither was a master of social graces—since when you'd already said goodbye and then remained on the phone (he'd add "I'll be thinking of you, sugar!" and she'd rejoin, "Thanks, I'm so glad you called!"), you'd already used up your arsenal of conclusion. At her wit's end, she finally cried, "Well, bye, Griff!" and hit the red button as fast as humanly possible.

"Have you gotten back to training, honey?" Cherry was asking Tommy. "Because you look so much better!"

Tommy glowered. "I still look like a jellyfish. I've done a little running, but it's slow and doesn't feel good. The weird thing is, the dinky distances are harder. They don't wow anybody, including me. I'm supposed to 'take it easy,' but I hate taking it easy. So half the time I really do take it easy, and watch TV instead. Turns out the sky doesn't fall. While she's been laid up, too, Serenata and I have been reading her commercial scripts aloud. I'm getting better at sight-reading. I used to need to rehearse, but with VO, especially in the gaming scene, you got to be able to read cold."

Cherry's attention wandered as soon as Tommy stopped talking about running. "I'm ashamed to say this, sweetie, but a couple of times now, Sarge has—he's hit me. He's never done that before. Last time, he knocked me down. I've even wondered if he's hoping he'll hurt me bad enough that I can't compete in Lake Placid."

"God, that sucks, Cherry," Tommy said. "But is it really worth it?"

"Of course it's 'worth it.' What do you mean?"

"Well, Sarge is obviously being a jerk, and I guess you could always walk out. Maybe you should. But if you don't want to do that . . . Is a Mettle worth risking your marriage? I mean, you've got those three kids."

Cherry drew herself up. "I know you're disappointed, Tommy, but I didn't think you'd gotten bitter. I can't believe you're trying to talk me out of my MettleMan."

"I was only thinking, you know, in the long run . . ." Tommy said, beating a feeble retreat. "Like, afterward, what have you got, if you don't have your family?"

"I have my finisher coffee mug, my finisher T-shirt, and my finisher self-respect." She huffed back to the A-students.

Meanwhile, Hank had discovered the remains of the chenin blanc. Bambi put a hand over his glass. "I thought we all agreed: no booze from now till it's over."

"Whatever happened to 'work hard, play hard'?" Hank said.

"In the home stretch," she said, "it's all 'work hard.' Now you get high on tri."

Serenata uncorked a cabernet. Deacon switched to whiskey, and Tommy joined him. Drawn to open bottles, Hank shuffled closer to the punks at the table's far end.

"I'm thinking about hitting the ultras next year," Sloan said. "I'm up for Lake Placid, but doing one Mettle and then putting your feet up starts to feel too easy."

"You mean, the two or three Mettles in a row, or the five?" Chet asked.

"The question," Sloan posed philosophically, "is whether to do a double or triple first, or go straight to the quintuple. You want to really challenge yourself, right?"

"I can't hardly imagine getting through one whole triathlon," Cherry said. "I'm flabbergasted anybody can get up the next morning and do a full Mettle all over again."

"Hell, Cherry," Chet said, "I'm not sure what the record is now, but last I checked there's been at least one guy who's done thirty—thirty Mettles in thirty days."

"Seems like an awful lot of bother and expense," Deacon said. "With one bullet, you can accomplish the same thing in three seconds for fifty cents."

The go-getters ignored him. "We should aim for thirty-one, then!" Hank declared, flushed from the cabernet he'd chugged from a camouflaging coffee mug.

"Sloan, isn't talking up the 'ultras' demoralizing for your friends?" Serenata asked. "It makes doing only one MettleMan seem like no big deal." It didn't occur to anyone that waxing eloquent about outermost feats of strength and stamina in front of a woman on the eve of incapacitating surgery might also be in poor taste.

"Always good to keep your eye on the next mountain," Sloan said. "Otherwise, you've got this flatness problem. You get a huge rush after you cross the finish line, and even the next day—after sleeping fifteen hours—you're still fired up. But then it's like, what's next? You need a longer-term game plan. Without a new goal, you can get kind of low, you know? Like, everything is over, and the best part of your life is behind you."

"Unbelievable," Deacon said, pouring another shot. "This shit for you guys is the 'best part of your life.' I gotta feel sorry for you fuckers."

"And what passes for the best part of your life, *Thumper*?" Bambi asked.

"Banging a sweet kid just past the age of consent, and topping up her tight little box in the morning. Grabbing a pastrami on rye with extra mustard. Boosting my mood with a cost-effective shortcut that doesn't involve gasping around a reservoir fifty times. Hitting the road to Hudson, and basking in a mother's love." Throwing a credibly appreciative glance at Serenata, Deacon just pulled the remark back from sarcasm.

"Sounds great to me!" Tommy clinked her shot glass against Deacon's and downed it. "But I want some melted Swiss on that pastrami."

"To each his own, losers," Bambi said.

"I'm starting to think you're right," Chet told Sloan. "The ultras have to be where the money's at. Like, your routine Mettle is already seeming almost sad, right? To pull in the big-league sponsors, I bet you've got to do at least the quintuple. And in good time, too. Not cranking that final chin-up just before the stroke of midnight—"

"Chet, could you put a lid on the big talk?" Ethan interrupted. Seated equidistant between the troublemakers and the teacher's pets, the ophthalmologist had barely said a word all evening. "You haven't finished one MettleMan yet."

"I *know*," Chet said. "But Sloan's right. You gotta keep expecting more of yourself. Like he said, find the next mountain—"

Deacon started crooning "Climb Every Mountain" from *The Sound of Music*.

"I don't need another *mountain*," Ethan said, once Deacon had forded every stream but before he could follow any rainbows. "Christ, we're not even through with this Lake Placid nightmare, and you're already talking about doing three in a row after that, or five, or *thirty*. Why not sixty, or a hundred? Why not swim, and run, and bike all day, every day, until . . . until what? As for the obvious end point, I hate to say it, but Deacon's right."

"Fuck me," Deacon said. "I've never heard that in this house before."

"I got into tri to begin with to get into better shape," Ethan said. "To feel better, and to feel better about myself. But I'm not feeling better. I get sick, I'm supposed to keep training through it, so I just get sicker. Basically, all the time, I feel sort of terrible. It's always something: a strain, a sprain, an inflamed tendon—"

"Wait till your sixties," Serenata said. "It's like that without getting out of bed."

"Well, yeah—half the time, I do, I feel *old*. Creaky. Achy. Sore. Technically, I guess I'm stronger, but most of the time I feel wiped out. You guys are always ragging on me for being a pussy, but I have a full-time practice. To keep to Bambi's training schedule, I've had to get up at five, and lately four-thirty, or even four. So I'm chronically under-slept. And I'm starting to wonder if this Mettle thing is safe. The distances are unreasonable—"

"They're supposed to be unreasonable," Bambi said.

"Yes, Ethan," Remington said. "The whole idea is intentionally a little crazy."

"There's *crazy* as in *wild and crazy*, and then there's *crazy* as in dangerously fucked-up," Ethan said, backing his chair out and standing up. "Because I admit it, I'm losing the plot. I thought I did, but lately I don't understand why we're doing this anymore. Chet's right on one point: we're none of us setting any records. And Deacon's right, too: even if we were, so what? This thing has ended up taking up a lot of time, and a huge amount of psychic energy, and meanwhile, with all these injuries, I'm actually in worse health. And now I listen to you guys get jacked about the idea of going up yet another level even if we do get through a full Mettle. So I just realized tonight— this stuff is too out for me. I like the idea of that pastrami and Swiss. I like the idea of going for a five-mile run, at a moderate pace, to work up an appetite for dinner. I like the idea of taking a shower, and talking to my wife about something else. In sum, guys: I quit."

No one said anything as Ethan gathered his things and left.

"Wow," Cherry said.

"Wow," Tommy said.

"Face it, he never had the stuff for tri," Bambi said. "With all those doubts, he had DNF written all over him. Let this be a lesson to all of you. It's like I've warned you before: the one thing you *never* allow yourself to question is why you're doing this in the first place. It's total death. You disappear up your own ass in two minutes. You open the floodgates to the laziness of the body, and you drown in the body's complaints. It's like listening to that little dude with horns and a fork on your shoulder. So we're better off without that softie. All along, he's just been a drag on our resolve. Ethan Crick is weak."

Curiously, however, the morale of the remaining stalwarts seemed unaccountably shaken, and they all drifted home.

"They'll never be the same again," Serenata said while still abed early the next morning. She'd been wide-eyed for hours. "They won't look the same, they won't feel the same—even if the operations go technically well. I'll always set off metal detectors. I'll have become part machine. I'm en route to becoming inanimate."

"You'll still be a ways from Robocop," Remington said. "Besides, you don't want your knees to be the same. They hurt like hell."

"On the other side of these two carve-ups, they'll hurt far worse."

"Why are you so apocalyptic? The whole point is to *improve* your mobility. Which is why lots of people approach joint replacement with optimism and good cheer."

"So I have an *attitude problem*." She got up and jerked on a robe, but there was no purpose to heading downstairs; she wasn't allowed to eat or drink as of the previous midnight. Not even being able to make coffee deprived the morning of structure. She wouldn't be able to concentrate on the paper. There was nothing to do but wait.

"You've actually said this means your life is over," he said, "and you might rather be dead. How do you think that makes me feel?"

"The way I did when you told your club that you don't want to live past seventy."

He raised a hand in concession. "Fair enough. Let's make that seventy-two."

"Ever since your marathon jag, you've focused *entirely* on physical competence. So for you to act mystified why I might regard becoming a hopeless cripple as something of the end of the party is hypocritical beyond belief."

"Might your *attitude problem* negatively affect your surgery's outcome?"

"That's New Age hooey." She tied the belt of her robe into a furious knot. "Do you think you can talk me into 'optimism and good cheer'? Why does the fact that this surgery cuts me to the quick, and undermines who I am to myself, and threatens me with having to become someone I don't want to be—why is that such an affront to you? Why do I have to feel the way you tell me to? Because all I'm hearing here is that this isn't happening to *you*."

"We're in different places right now."

"You knew this surgery was on my docket. You *chose* to put yourself in a different place. You've removed yourself from me, and run off to Tri World, like Peter Pan to the Island of Lost Boys. I think you were afraid of really staying with me through this. As if I might suck you into my creepy old-age problems. Just like last night—you dragged that whole club back here with you, so you wouldn't have to be alone with your wife, who'd be crawling the walls. If you picture our marriage as a room, you've marched to a far corner. You've left me all by myself. This tri thing, I thought at first it was your angry overreaction to Lucinda Okonkwo, but now I cotton: it's marital desertion, pure and simple. Except you don't need to find your own apartment."

"I appreciate that you're anxious, but you're being irrational—"

"Deacon saw it in a heartbeat. This perverse pursuit of yours is all about me. About becoming me, or replacing me, or besting me—"

"It's only 'about you' insofar as I'd have thought, at the outset, that I'd earn your regard!"

"I already held you in high regard!"

"But I need to hold *myself* in high regard. And at my age, I have only so much time left. If I'm going to do triathlon, it's now or never."

"So what's wrong with never?"

To her astonishment, he had literally walked to a far corner of the bedroom, where he stood naked, hands on hips. "I've sometimes fantasized about what it would be like to have a wife through my own valley of the shadow of death who would make me fear no evil, because *thou art with me.* Who wished me the best and would be waiting on the finish line with a kiss and champagne."

"True, I was thinking more like cava."

"The close proximity of your knee replacement and my Mettle-Man isn't ideal."

"Huh. Yuh think?"

"But the date for Lake Placid has been set for over a year."

"So this near-synchronicity is my fault."

"No one's fault. It's merely unfortunate."

"For whom?"

"For us both. I won't be as helpful during your recovery as I'd have liked to be."

"I think that pretty much makes it unfortunate for *me.* As for the coincidence, it isn't one, is it? It was foreseeable, more or less. You practically planned it."

"I did no such thing. And the last thing I planned is Deacon's showing up now of all times, too. I'm sorry. It's an extra logistical burden, and he's no ocean of sympathy."

"I've found him a surprising comfort. And if I have trouble with pain management, at least I know where to get opioids."

"That's not funny."

"Not long ago, you would have thought so. You've fallen fatally under the spell of the over-earnest . . . What are you doing?"

"Getting into my cycling clothes, obviously."

"I thought you were going to take me to the hospital."

"I'm planning on it. But I'm meeting Bambi in half an hour. We're working on my gearing technique, going for lower resistance and a higher RPM. Since you don't have to go to Columbia Memorial until noon, I can fit in a thirty miler."

They had always been a talky couple, but the danger of all those words was talking around feelings, or over feelings, or about feelings by way of avoiding actually feeling feelings, and the real moments between them took place in the interstices between the words. This interstice was more than a crack; it was widening to a maw.

"Look," he said, noticing the absence of a sprightly reply. "We're hardly in the Garden of Gethsemane, are we?"

ELEVEN

"Where *is* he? It's ten to twelve!"

Deacon picked toast crumbs from his plate with a forefinger and tsked. "I always remember Dr. DOT as on the *dot*."

"He's not answering his phone, and I refuse to leave another humiliating voice-mail. I cannot believe that this of all mornings he decided to spend with that woman."

Deacon was clearly enjoying this visit's reconfigured family architecture. However divided they'd been in his adolescence over how to contend with a hooligan, his parents' differences back then were merely methodological. In the main, they'd presented a united front—worse, formed a glib, self-reinforcing if not self-congratulatory unit of two, who corroborated that they were right, about everything, by agreeing with each other. As Serenata had only recently appreciated, the couple's show-off Noël-Coward banter had been infuriating. The children saw their parents as sealed in an unassailable bubble, though she thought of the problem otherwise: she and Remington were too happily married. They didn't need other people enough—not friends, not relatives, and not, alas, their own kids. They'd been too satisfied with each other's company, which read to outsiders as self-satisfaction, and their contentment came across as exclusionary. At last the bubble had burst. If she were honest with herself, she was more at ease with Deacon now, because she'd hitherto held back from her son out of loyalty to her husband. The boy made Remington so angry.

"That Bambi chick is a piece of work," Deacon said. "You shouldn't let her get to you. She's yanking your chain on purpose."

"I don't mean to be insulting, but I still don't understand what she sees in your father. I think I've put it together, and then I look at the two of them, so incongruous, and my theories fall apart."

"You said she has a thing about winning," he said. "People like that, doesn't matter what the prize is. She'd compete to her last dying breath for a plastic whistle."

"I know they rarely start surgeries on time, but they're very strict about showing up at admissions by your appointment. If I'm late, I risk losing the slot."

"Isn't that what you'd secretly like anyway?"

"All my life I've prided myself on making myself do things I didn't want to. But I did, sort of, want to do my push-ups. I don't want to do this. It turns out I'm as terrible at making myself do what I really don't want to do as anybody else. We have to go."

Chivalrously, Deacon carried her overnight bag—a small gesture he'd never have made when the bubble was intact—and held open the door of his dented Mercedes.

"Not bothering to get back on time . . ." Ducking in, she supported her right leg by holding on to the door. "I don't know, maybe it's a good sign that he can still hurt my feelings."

"Your honeybunch may not be able to make you feel all warm and gooey inside anymore," Deacon said. "But the ability to fuck you up, well—it's the last magic power to go."

"I'm not sure how consoling that is. Still, thank you for being here."

"De nada," he said at the wheel, reversing.

"If this morning's absenteeism is anything to go by, I'm going to need your help. Obviously, I won't be able to bike. But according to the pre-op seminar they made me take—and it was full of fat people; I wasn't flattered by the company—I also won't be able to drive. You can't move your leg fast enough to shift from the accelerator to the brake. As for incapacities, that's only for starters."

"You can still back out of this if you want to."

"I'm loath to give your father's trainer any credit, but last night she was right on one point: you can't allow yourself to question the premise. Never ask why."

"Seems like that's the first thing you'd do."

"I know it sounds counterintuitive. And it's especially disconcerting for someone like your father, who's so contemplative by nature. But once you make a commitment, it's a big mistake to force yourself to keep remaking it. My knee is killing me. It's going to keep killing me unless I let them saw me to pieces like a bookshelf."

It was a short drive, during which she kept looking out for Remington—pedaling feverishly toward their house, admonishing himself for allowing his trainer to goad him into ten extra miles. When they turned into the Columbia Memorial parking lot, she pictured him skidding into their drive, throwing his precious tri bike carelessly on the lawn, and banging through the side door, praying that they hadn't left without him. All through the admissions paperwork, too, she kept shooting glances at the entrance, through which at any moment her husband might burst at a run. When she returned the clipboard, the receptionist directed her to the surgical waiting room, where, she was advised, she'd be welcome to bring a friend or family member.

"I could be waiting a few minutes, or a few hours," Serenata told her son. "You've done your bit. It's okay if you want to go."

In times past, Deacon would have left. He was anything but an altruist. "Nah," he said. "I brought your portable Scrabble."

She asked the receptionist to direct her husband to the waiting room should he deign to make an appearance, changed into a formless gown and sock slippers with nonskid feet, and stored her clothing and valuables in a locker. Every medical functionary she dealt with, even the one who provided a blanket for her assigned gurney, asked for name, birth date, and body part. She kept her monotonous responses pleasant; they were simply being careful. She and Deacon were given a flimsy privacy with a wraparound curtain. When Dr. Churchwell showed up with a Magic Marker and wrote TKR on the joint soon to be tossed into a medical waste bin, she was a little nonplussed that after all their dealings with one another he was still afraid he'd forget and take out her spleen instead.

The travel Scrabble set turned out to be a godsend. It gave her something to concentrate on. It reprieved them from making conversation. Most of all, it distracted her from supposing that while she'd accused Remington of "marital desertion," she'd never really believed that he didn't want to see her through this tribulation, never really believed that he spent more time with Bambi Buffer than with his own wife because he was infatuated with his trainer, and never really believed what she'd told her father-in-law: that her marriage was in any sense in peril, or diminished, or unhappy like everyone else's. Maybe she told other people things as a substitute for telling herself. She'd made all these dire assertions, and then when nothing dire came of airing them, that seemed to prove they weren't dire after all, or even true. As time ticked on, she played *E-X-U-D-E* with a triple-letter score on the *X*, not bad under the circumstances, until finally the anesthetist appeared, wanting to know if she ever took drugs.

"I think you're asking the wrong party," she said, with a dry glance at Deacon—not bad under the circumstances, either.

After the blood pressure, heart rate, and O2 sat readings, she and Deacon managed three more turns. When they brought the syringe for setting the IV, she objected that she couldn't go under now, because the game wasn't over and she was winning. Neither the anesthetist nor his assistant smiled, for she could feel herself transitioning in their eyes from a *who* to a *what*. It wasn't that they were callous, but that for their professional purposes the fact that someone lived in this artifact had become incidental, or downright inconvenient.

According to Deacon's watch, it had been over two hours. Remington was still a no-show. The tiles restored to their bag, Serenata could no longer obsess over how to squeeze any appreciable points from a rack with six vowels, four of which were *A*'s. Instead she was pelted with all the thoughts she'd been batting away, and not only today but for months, perhaps the whole last year.

For the first time, she wondered who would get the house. For the first time, she weighed up whether either of them would want the place once it became a repository of such jarring late-life desolation, or whether limited resources alone would demand that they sell the property and split the proceeds. For the first time, she questioned whether she'd stay in Hudson, and worried about how devastated Griff would be if she left town. And for the first time, she recognized how much she lied to herself about cherishing solitude, which was only sumptuous when contrasting with something else; solitude without respite went by another name. It was an unwelcome reverie that might have seemed poor preparation for major surgery, but the surgery itself made the reflections apt. If you could offer up your own leg to be cut into pieces, any severance was possible.

As a nurse was about to slip a mask for gas over her face, Serenata started to cry. The wave caught her unawares, as if she were facing the shore and a swell had smacked her crown. It wasn't altogether clear what overwhelmed her, Remington's astonishing abandonment, or the fact that she didn't want to do this and she wanted to go home. When the nurse asked, "Is there something wrong?" the question was, again, not cold exactly, but mechanical. They didn't care what she felt, but only what the body felt.

"I'm sorry," she said in a lull when she could get words out. "I don't think I was this childish when I was a child." Deacon held her hand, and while it might have been better had her husband held her hand, her son was acting more decent than at any time since she could remember, and she had a rare inkling on the waft into oblivion that maybe she hadn't always been an atrocious mother.

Emerging from general anesthesia wasn't so much an awakening as a resurrection. The distinction revealed just how rich and eventful the experience of sleeping was, and how aware one was, throughout a night's slumber, of the passage of time. Sleep was in no way an absence, so it was foolish to imagine dying as in any sense like drifting off in bed. Coming to, Serenata could groggily infer that after holding Deacon's hand something had happened. But the time was missing. It had been hacked from her life, sawed out.

When a nurse arrived to administer an anti-emetic, she wondered if sloshing to nonexistence and back again induced a spiritual seasickness. The nurse's face was ravishing, shades of purple mixing with burnt sienna, and her expression radiated warmth and acumen; so deep was the brown of her eyes that the pupils seemed to drill to the back of her head. Serenata was overwhelmed that a total stranger would worry about whether her stomach was unsettled. She was filled with the same burgeoning gratitude when her vital signs were taken by a second nurse, whom she kept thanking, and reassuring that, yes, she felt comfortable, that's good of you to ask. They all seemed to care so about how she was, though they'd no reason to, and it was all so touching and human and true.

The walls sectioned into soft, gradated grays, like a painting—a subtle painting, at which you could gaze for hours and always find something new. From a far window shafted a single luminous bar, its supersaturated yellow distinct to the midyear's early evening sun; it was the light that photographers lived for, in which every subject appeared golden and chosen by God. As Serenata lay being, so recently returned from not-being, she was newly alert to the luxuriousness of breathing—how marvelous, that you could draw in the very atmosphere, extract from it what you needed, and give most of it gratefully back. How amazing it was to be present. She reproached herself— gently, tenderly—for ever questioning the toil and trouble of remaining in this astounding and unfathomable place, with its colors and shapes, its smells and tastes, for many more years. Simply bearing witness to the physical world was worth the price of admission.

She thought of Remington, claiming that he didn't want to live beyond seventy or was it seventy-two, and of course that made her think of Remington more broadly. She had a trace memory of his disappointing her, but that was swallowed by a larger impression that she had disappointed him, too. She'd been unkind to him, repeatedly unkind, and she had withheld herself. He wanted something, it wasn't entirely clear what, any more than it was clear to Remington either, and he was probably not going to get it, or at least not the way he was going about the quest. But she had to allow him to make his own mistakes and then come back to her, because if she did not he would not. He was doing something that was not a part of their lives together but it didn't hurt her. He was doing something that lots of people were also doing, and just then it did seem curious that she'd ever had a problem with activities in which lots of people took part. Like all those other people on bicycles. She'd loved her long life on a bicycle, so there was no reason she shouldn't want everyone else to enjoy the liberation, the rush of air, the giddy lean into a curve of a bicycle, too.

And that was when she realized she was on drugs.

Dr. Churchwell swung by, airy and brisk as usual. Around sixty-five, he kept his dyed-blond hair in a boyish tousle. It was immediately clear from his closer proximity to the door than to her bed, and from the bland, offhand quality of his pronouncement upon her surgery's success, that by the time she formulated any questions that she badly needed answered, he'd be long gone. In truth, she'd never especially liked Dr. Churchwell, although he was reputedly the best knee surgeon at Columbia Memorial, a moderately sized institution in a small town, so she couldn't be too choosy. Chronically supercilious, he'd spent a goodly portion of their appointments extolling his achievements as a squash champion. With the hucksterism of a television evangelist, he likewise bragged about the NFL players and Olympic team members on whom he'd operated who still sent thankful Christmas cards—and he left Serenata under no illusion that a sorry amateur's piddling ten-mile runs would ever qualify her own cards for his living-room mantel.

Yet under the influence, Serenata could discern behind the arch expression and battered complexion the dashing med student so many mothers would have hoped their daughters would marry. The physician's preening was cover for a garden-variety anxiety about getting old. The more closely he skirted the infirmity of his patients, the more fiercely he worked to maintain a distinction between them, and to carve out a place for himself as an exception—an exception to laws that doctors knew better than anyone allowed for no exceptions. Inexorably, in another five years or so, he'd have to retire, and no one would care about his squash trophies. He'd just be some old guy, like the rest of us, but with more money. As for the boasting, his work was respected but mechanical. He needed to christen certain patients as special to make himself seem special, and maybe it was a good sign that some of them were people to him and not just hunks of furniture. Besides, everyone treated surgeons with such exaggerated deference that in a way their clichéd narcissism was not their fault.

"The operation was perfectly routine," he said, after she'd tried to solicit a little more detail.

"I'm sorry I bored you."

"I do five of these in a day," the surgeon said. "Though I must say, your patella and the articular surface of your lateral condyle looked like someone had taken a pile driver to them. You really should have had this done earlier—*as I advised*. You came to me at the very outside of the window I gave you. I'm skeptical we'll achieve anything close to full extension when you recover."

"In case something went wrong, I've wanted to take advantage of my real knees as long as I could."

"Yes, yes, I hear that all the time. You're all fraidy cats, terrified that you won't be able to play a full round of croquet. Fair enough, but if this aversive delay of yours translates into a limp, you've only yourself to blame. Now, I'm keeping you on Oxycontin for another three days, but then we're moving to NSAIDs. Just don't slacken on the PT, or you don't have a prayer of attaining that extension."

She was a little injured that her orthopedist displayed so little understanding of his patient after seeing her for two years. "I'm not a slacker. I'm more the type to overdo it."

"Well, don't overdo it, either," he said with annoyance. "You could damage the scar tissue and invite inflammation the size of last year's wildfire in California. Worse, you might even loosen the cement, and we'd have to do the whole thing all over again. Now, *that* would be boring." With no goodbye, he was gone.

"You have a visitor, Mrs. Terpsichore," a nurse said a few minutes later, poking his head in the door. He'd mangled her surname, and Serenata didn't care. Absent pharmaceutical intervention, she'd have been crushed that the visitor was not her husband. Instead, when Tommy filtered shyly to the side of the bed, she was enchanted.

"Hey," Tommy said. "How are you feeling?"

"High as a kite," Serenata said. "I suspect I feel dreadful and I have no idea."

"It went okay?"

"Yes, though I'm afraid Dr. Churchwell found my case a little dreary."

"With this medicine stuff?" Tommy said. "I don't think you ever want to be interesting. Have you looked at it?"

"No."

Together, they peered under the blanket. "Oh, wow."

Covered in a thick white rectangle, the bulbous tubular object attached to Serenata's torso did not appear to belong to her body. "It reminds me," Serenata said, "of those big pork roasts in the supermarket, covered with a giant slab of scored fell, tied up with butcher's twine, and bulging in cellophane on an oozy Styrofoam platter. Even the bandage—it's like that little diaper they put under the meat, just upside down."

"Baby, I've been there," Tommy said. "You're like, 'I don't recognize this humongo blob! How'd I get inside a Macy's parade float?'"

"You were so upset. You kept saying, 'I didn't even get to eat any pizza!'"

"You were the only one who was nice to me."

"I'm relieved to hear I've been nice to someone. I don't think I've been very nice to Remington." Her throat was dry. "For the life of me, I don't remember why, either."

"It'll come back to you," Tommy said. "You just have to get off the opioids."

"In that case, I'm not sure I want to get off them."

"Pretty standard reaction. Why do you think they're so addictive?"

"I had no idea . . ." Serenata struggled to formulate what she was thinking. "I'm surprised what this feels like. I'm comforted to discover that these drugs make you so warmly disposed toward people. I mean, I'm glad it turns out that so many young people like you are mostly desperate to feel *benevolent.* Apparently this country is full of people who crave the experience of generosity and optimism. It's strangely moving—that they'll put themselves and their health at risk—they'll go broke or even steal—just to keep thinking of other people as wonderful, and as on their side. That's not a bad thing to find addictive. Maybe Deacon's not as depraved as I've worried he is."

Tommy laughed. "It's almost creepy, but for a change of pace, I kind of like you this way. All philosophical and sappy. So I hate to break it to you: I think you only get that 'Joy to the World' buzz at the beginning. Later you keep taking the stuff just to keep from killing yourself."

"I like my version of opioid addiction better."

"Listen . . ." Tommy paused. "We talked about it. That is, Bambi— sorry—well, she called me. We decided it'd be better to tell you afterward. We didn't think you should get all worked up right before surgery."

"Tell me what?" Pain meds didn't preclude a capacity for alarm.

Tommy raised her hands. "Now, don't freak out! He didn't die or anything. But Remington had a bike accident."

"How bad was it, then?"

"Actually, for your purposes?" Tommy cocked her head. "Probably not quite bad enough."

The assertion didn't register. "Where is he?"

"Here. So he officially gets credit for coming to the hospital when you had your knee done. Except for the first four hours he was in the ER waiting room. He's finally been able to see somebody, and I think they're checking him for concussion. And they must be doing X-rays. He was hurting pretty bad while we hung out with him in the waiting room, and he was super shaken up. But I doubt they're going to admit him overnight. He's cut up, and bruised, and he has these long bloody scrapes on an arm and a leg from sliding along the ground. Still, Bambi doesn't think he broke any bones."

"Did she save his life again? That would make three times. My, a charm." From behind the cotton candy of narcotic goodwill, a glint of sardonicism.

"Now, that's the old Serenata! There wasn't any mouth-to-mouth this time, though I guess she did call the ambulance."

"Not that this matters, really, but . . . It's what I'd worry about: Carlisle."

"Who's that?"

"I'm just asking, what happened to his bike? That Little Lord Fauntleroy may be pretty full of itself, but it's Remington's beloved."

"Totaled. He bent the frame. Kiss of death."

Serenata sighed. It wouldn't do to find the death of this rival too satisfying. "What's ten grand down the drain—so long as I keep taking these meds."

"He does still have the old bike," Tommy reminded her.

After a rap on the door, a female PT came in with a wheeled walker. "Gab fest's over, girls! Time to get to work."

Getting out of bed was slow, confusing, and awkward. Therapist at the ready, Serenata leaned heavily on the frame. The right knee wouldn't bend, but she was cheered when the mandatory shuffle around the room didn't hurt at all, and she wondered whether everyone made far too much of this wretched recovery business, until she clocked: the elephantine leg was still numb. *Oh*. Thereafter, Deacon stopped by, complaining that now both his parents were train wrecks, and they hadn't warned him that a stint living at their house in Hudson would entail "turning into some full-time nursing-home orderly." The objection couldn't have been called good-humored.

At last, the door yawned open to reveal Himself. He was wearing a mismatched shorts and T-shirt combo that one of the women must have grabbed from home—clothes from a few years ago that drooped off him now. Presumably the Lycra cycling gear had been totaled, too. A square of gauze was affixed to his forehead; one cheek was grazed and pointillated with bloody pits. His limbs were covered in so many bandages that he looked like a cartoon.

"So," she said, "we're both back from the wars."

"It's not as bad as it looks," Remington said. "But I'm hugely sorry about this morning—"

"Don't. I understand now. But it was important to me that you went with me. It's important that it was still important."

"That should go without saying."

"Nothing goes without saying. Not right now." She flipped the blanket back to expose the pork roast and nodded at the bandage on his thigh. "Look at you. You're copying me."

"Isn't that what you think I've been doing this whole time? Copying you?"

"I've never been quite sure which proposition is more distressing, that your late-life athletic renaissance has everything to do with me, or nothing to do with me. Would you please sit down? Just looking at you standing there makes me tired."

When he sat, he winced. "Tommy assured me the surgery went fine?"

"As far as I know. And you?" she asked. "Nothing broken?"

"Bruising, swelling, some laceration. Mild concussion—those helmets . . ."

"They're TinkerToy," Serenata said. "And no one tightens the straps enough, because if you do you get a headache. When a helmet is even halfway comfortable, it rides back on your forehead. Then, pitch over the handlebars, you might as well be wearing a Mets cap. With the explosion of cycling in this country, I don't understand why bike helmets are still so hard to adjust, still look so geeky, and still don't work." Powered by the garrulousness taking over now that the general anesthesia had lifted, such convivial commiseration had been signally lacking in their dealings with one another from "I've decided to run a marathon" onward.

"I was told I was lucky," Remington said.

"You sure don't look lucky. What happened?"

"It was a new route, to mix things up. If she, you know—"

"If we couldn't avoid her stupid name for over a year, we can't avoid it now."

"All right, *Bambi* would have warned me, but she hadn't been on this stretch of B-road before, either. She was well behind me, because she wanted me to work on pacing myself, or she might have wiped out, too. We were headed down a hill, and the tarmac was that washed-out gray, with imbedded gravel. So it was impossible to tell that at the very bottom of the descent the surface suddenly turned to gravel-gravel. Loose gravel. In a car, the change of surface wouldn't have mattered much. On a bike . . . No traction. I skidded, then got thrown clear of the bike, which hurtled into a tree."

"People our age should never take down-hills at speed," Serenata said. "People Tommy's age shouldn't, either, but only we ancients know the stakes."

"If you considered the stakes, you'd never do anything."

"Then maybe we should never do anything."

Just then, something gave way in him. His head dropped; he slumped. Serenata had had bike accidents herself, and like any other trauma there was a delayed reaction. She edged carefully to the far side of the single mattress and folded back the bedding. He could just fit alongside her, nestling his temple into the hollow of her shoulder as she wrapped an arm around his back. He slipped a hand under her hospital gown and cupped a breast, always a neat fit in his palm.

If the end of the day had once been steeped in dread, now it was the whole day. When she returned home after two nights in Columbia Memorial, recovery became her full-time job, since any economically productive activity was inconceivable. Demotion from Oxycontin to Tylenol was like a CEO's plummet to the mailroom. Every time the PT showed up for an hour of home therapy, every time she repeated the exercises with a gun to her head later in the day, and every time she lurched from a living-room recliner to the kitchen (only after contemplating for fifteen minutes whether a cup of tea was worth the trip), it was *whoosh* up the same giddy learning curve that she'd climbed on the West Side bikeway—the same fast-forward short course in pain, the same *surprise!-this-is-what-agony-feels-like-and-this-is-why-no-one-likes-it*. She soon grew to regard going upstairs as on the same scale of commitment as moving to Cleveland.

From the start, too, Serenata was obliged to relinquish her precious conceit about having a "high pain threshold," because it turned out her threshold was as low as anyone's, as low as low could be; it was on the floor. All that vaunted "discipline" of hers turned out to be of no use in executing exercises that before her bones were sawed off wouldn't have counted as exercise at all. Besides, reasonably fit people experienced little appreciable pain when they worked out; it was out-of-shape people who really suffered. Thus the presumption that had helped propel her to schedule the surgery in the first place—that she was accustomed to "pushing herself," so she'd "bounce back" in no time—was revealed over the course of three minutes on Day One to be a self-serving, bald-faced lie. As for her image of herself as stoic, that was out the window, too. Wrapping an elastic band around the ankle and forcing the right leg to bend from a 110-degree angle to a 109-degree one, she wept. In front of the therapist, in front of Remington, and the tears didn't even fill her with shame, because shame, like the tears themselves, didn't help.

The whole business was so humbling that she rapidly lost every last shred of self-respect. She was a tired, beaten-down, aging woman whose utility to humanity was zero, whose idea of bliss was sitting still, and whose few ruminations on her circumstances she had thought before: how lonely pain was, and how unreal to people who weren't feeling it, too; how quickly people got bored with other people's pain after an initial display of cheap pity; how the peculiar inability to quite remember the sensation must have served as a primitive survival mechanism, since if you could truly remember agony you'd never forgo the security of the lair even to forage for food. In their repetitiveness, the recurrent reflections were one more torture.

The fact that Remington was also beaten up was a complication. The long scrapes on his arms, in which imbedded chunks of gravel had left deep pits, needed the dressings changed regularly and had to be slicked painfully with antibiotic ointment. On the side of his body that had taken the hit, his shoulder was puffy and sore. Given its restricted range of motion, he might have damaged his rotary cuff. He had a sizable hematoma on his elbow, and the interior bleeding had spread in branching violet all the way down and around his forearm. He also had swelling, bruising, and pitting from the gravel along the one whole leg, and once the thigh scrape barely started to heal, the scab cracked and bled when he walked. The ankle having been yanked in a direction Nature never intended, his Achilles was pulled, paining him with every step. Hard falls occasioned not only a delayed emotional reaction, but also a delayed physical one. After a day or two, a bodywide ache set in, as if you were a house after an earthquake, and now your framing was askew, your two-by-fours were straining at their nails, and your windows and doors were out of plumb.

They found some camaraderie. Yet they inevitably suffered from a low-key competition over which spouse deserved more sympathy, even if the contest made no sense. Sympathy was not zero-sum. Deacon didn't feel especially sorry for either parent, so the only sympathy to fight over was each other's, and they could have agreed simply to swap. Besides, like a cut-rate cologne whose flowery scent instantly evaporated, sympathy didn't do either of them any good.

One irksome problem was getting blood and various paler discharges on the sheets. Neither had the energy to scrub the percale every morning, and if Deacon was ill-tempered about runs to the supermarket, he wasn't going to toil over a sink with his parents' gory bedclothes as if trying to destroy evidence. So the stains would set. They went through fresh sheets nightly, until Serenata resolved that until they both stopped oozing they'd have to sleep on sheets they'd already ruined. The bed soon resembled a Red Cross cot during World War One.

Perhaps oddly, they didn't discuss it. Remington's mute, downcast lumber around the house read, yes, as an understandably sober demeanor after a close call with mortality, but also as the inevitable funk into which anyone would sink after training over a year for an event he could no longer enter. (Unfortunately, it was too late to get back his whacking MettleMan deposit.) He'd take a while to resign himself to the disappointment, so it seemed strategic to give the sensitive subject wide berth. Presumably he would address the letdown when he was good and ready. Maybe in time he'd take a positive view of the experience, even if it hadn't culminated in the expected triumph. He must have gotten something out of all those training sessions in and of themselves. Underneath the bandages, he was in better shape. More adept than his wife at getting along with people from different walks of life, he'd flourished in the company of the tri club. In due course, he might look back on this period as introspectively informative and socially rich. If he had also escaped the potential ignominy of failing to complete the course, she was hardly going to mention *that*. Any intimation that withdrawal was reprieve would sound like an accusation of cowardice. He was pulling out because he'd had a terrible accident. In Tri World, that was a far more respectable excuse than Ethan Crick's sudden attack of sanity.

With the benefit of hindsight, Serenata might even come to soften on his infuriating weakness for that trollop (the archaic pejorative was perfect). He was sixty-six. Younger attentions had been flattering. Once the wounds healed and he regained his energy, maybe they could go back to having sex again, and with a renewed enthusiasm to which residual fantasies about his erstwhile trainer might contribute—just so long as Remington didn't propose a three-way with the detestable woman in real life.

Most of all for Serenata, now that a full Mettle was summarily off the table, the challenge was to disguise her relief.

"What are you doing?" It was the one-week anniversary of her surgery and Remington's crash. She was at the dining table, doing extension and flexion exercises to the eye so farcical that they might have been mistaken for restless leg syndrome.

"What does it look like?" Remington tugged his laces. "I'm going for a run."

Serenata's heart fell. Apparently she'd been hoping he'd throw in the towel on exercise altogether. But keeping active would be good for him, and this sour reaction to Remington's finally getting out of the house was mean-spirited. It was the knee replacement talking. Her own current version of a marathon was hunching down the four steps from the side door and hobbling to the end of the block with a walker. And even there, she had to ask Deacon to lift the walker to the drive; she couldn't carry it and hold on to her cane and the rail as well. She'd have to be mindful of this if-I-can't-then-you-can't-either spitefulness. Recovery was awful enough without also becoming a shrew.

"Isn't it a little soon?"

"It's a little late. The Mettle is in six days."

The screen door banged behind him. "Hey, champ!" a familiar female voice shouted from the end of the drive. "Ready to roll?"

Serenata continued to sit in the chair. Deacon came back from whatever mysterious activities occupied him for most of the day. With unusual alertness to mother-as-domestic-statuary, he asked, "What's up? Your face—you look like someone just hacked the other leg in half."

"Your father is still planning to do that triathlon." Her voice was flat.

"No big surprise. You don't want him to. QED."

"Spouses in their sixties aren't supposed to make decisions like teenagers."

"Take it from me. Let it go. What's the worst that could happen?"

"Funny, that's exactly what I've been thinking about."

"If you're right and he can't do it, then he won't do it," Deacon said. "Simple."

"Deacon, I hate to ask this, since you just got home. But would you mind going out again for a while? I have to talk to your father when he gets back, and in private."

"Okay—but you know you're not going to talk him out of it."

"All right, I'll take that as a dare."

By the time Remington returned, she was ready for them.

"Well, that tumble you took has slowed you down a mite," Bambi was saying behind him when the duo came back in. Though it was in the eighties, her pink running bra was pristine; she hadn't broken a sweat. "Hey, Sera! Haven't seen you since the big carve-up. How's the prosthesis?"

"The *prosthesis* is thriving. It's the rest of me it's attached to that's having a hard time." Serenata tried to keep her tone matter-of-fact when she observed, "Sweetheart, you're bleeding."

Perspiration had loosened the tape on Remington's bandages, which had blossomed in red speckle. The wounds were to be kept dry, so in lieu of a shower he was moistening a dish towel at the sink. "The abrasions crack," he said, rubbing his face and neck. "That's inevitable. Can you excuse me, ladies? I'm going upstairs to change."

The two women were rarely alone with one another. It was awkward.

"Give it a year or two, and you'll be tooling the aisles of Price Chopper without a cane," Bambi said. "I could give you some exercises that would help."

"Thanks," Serenata said. "But I'm in the care of a PT, and more exercises are the last thing I need. Listen, do you mind my asking— is it your idea that Remington still enter the full Mettle, even after that bike accident? Have you in any way enticed him—I mean, challenged him, or flung down a gauntlet? Made him feel embarrassed about the idea of bowing out?"

"Honey, you just don't get tri. For Rem to do it at all, it has to be his idea. Do tri to make somebody else happy, you won't make it ten feet."

Serenata regrouped. "I just wonder if, in your professional opinion, Remington is sufficiently recovered from his injuries to participate. He'd take your assessment seriously, much more than he would mine."

Bambi shrugged. "He's still in one piece. But whether he's up for it is a judgment only Rem can make."

Then what good are you. "Don't you feel responsible? Not for the accident, of course, but for any further damage he might do to himself if he enters the race?"

"I never encourage my clients to hold me responsible, for their decisions or for their performance. That's against everything I teach. 'Sides. It's in the contract."

"I wonder if you wouldn't consider—appealing to him. Suggesting that, at the very least, maybe he should delay, and not enter until next year."

"You been underfoot, so you must have some idea of how much time and sweat goes into training for a Mettle. And Rem's been at it longer than most—not nine months, but fourteen. I can't in good conscience push any client to throw that away, not unless it's a dead cert they can't finish. And that husband of yours has massive heart. That's the secret sauce no trainer can give to a client, since it got to be there from the start. I guess you guys get on, since you two been married a good while. Still, I sometimes can't help but wonder if you know your husband at all."

"It's not a surprise to me that he's pigheaded."

Bambi shook her head. "See, that language . . . How about *steely*, or *brave?* Far as his being kinda beat up right now, that just makes a Mettle more heroic."

"Doesn't heroism entail doing something perilous for the sake of someone *else?*"

The trainer frowned. "Nah," she pronounced after her moment of deep thought. "Tri's about being a hero to yourself, and for the sake of yourself."

"Let me get this straight, then. You have no interest in pushing Remington to reconsider? You won't press him to remember what he'd be asking his body to do when it's just been hurtled at twenty miles an hour across two lanes of scree. You won't console him that under the circumstances his withdrawal wouldn't amount to weakness. I couldn't interest you in persuading him that there's actually a bravery—a *heroism*, to use your word—in accepting a short-term disappointment for long-term perseverance."

"I'm a medium for my clients' aspirations," Bambi said. "Nobody hires me to tell 'em what they *can't* do. There's plenty other folks out there happy to piss on parades for free—not mentioning any names—so that's not my job. And you know, I'm not married; maybe that means I shouldn't do couples counseling. But I'll give it a go anyway. If I did have a husband, I'd try and bring out the best in the guy. I'd have even higher expectations than he has of himself—"

"You're right, you shouldn't do couples counseling." Serenata kept her voice down, lest it carry upstairs. "I'm sorry, but I'm putting you on notice. I believe that by remaining in thrall to that lobotomized rah-rah thinking of yours, you're shirking your duty as a professional. Any idiot can take one look at Remington right now and tell that he belongs in bed. If you had a moral brain cell in your head, you'd order him to put his feet up and to forget doing a MettleMan, or training of any kind, until he's recuperated. I don't know if you belong to any professional body, or whether you have some kind of accreditation to maintain. But if so, and you don't make a convincing effort to stop him, given the compromised condition he's in, I'm reporting you. In writing, in detail, with pictures of his injuries attached. And I'll have you disbarred, or whatever you'd call never again being able to parlay your hack trade in New York State. I'll go on your website and leave a scathing one-star review. I'll also go on every other pertinent website I can find—every sports magazine, every workout blog, every commercial gym within hundreds of miles, including BruteBody—and I'll trash your reputation in the comments. To make sure you don't endanger the well-being of anyone else, I might even overcome my loathing for social media."

Bambi stood up. "I don't take kindly to threats. And you're hardly in the shape to make any. So how's this for a threat: I can tell Rem what you just said. He won't take kindly to that, either."

"'Take kindly' to what?" came from the hallway.

"Blackmail," Bambi said as Remington entered the kitchen. "Rem, I'll see you at the pool tomorrow at three, after I've had a chance to find those waterproof dressings. Just now, thanks for the offer, but I think I'm gonna skip that iced tea."

"What was that about?" Remington asked once she'd slammed the screen door.

"A difference of opinion."

"Over?"

"Take a guess."

Remington fixed himself a sandwich; he may have been hungry, or simply eager to busy himself. He couldn't imagine he was getting out of this conversation.

"Your swelling is still not down," she began as he separated slices of smoked turkey. "You can't raise your arm above your shoulder. Just like your hamstring, your Achilles is strained or inflamed, and on the same leg. Your bruises do nothing but darken as the blood rises to the surface, which means the injuries are deep. Every time the scabs crack you open a new route to infection. Didn't that run you just went on hurt?"

"That's irrelevant." He liked it. He liked that it hurt.

Hectoring would be deadly. Likewise ridicule, and trying to win. She'd gone at this all wrong from the beginning.

"Darling. My beloved." Modulating the voice by occupation should be good for something. Better still, to speak tenderly was to feel tender. "Sit down?"

Reluctantly, he brought his plate over. He didn't touch the sandwich.

"I can see why you can't trust me," she said. "I know I've seemed competitive. Defensive of what always used to be my territory. Resentful that you've exceeded my own feats of stamina. Angry about suddenly becoming such a shipwreck—though if I take some small comfort from your being in the same boat, there's nothing wrong with wanting to feel close to you, is there?"

"Not unless the closeness is smothering."

"And I'm sorry I called this enterprise of yours 'dumb.' It's true I can't help what I think. But the merits of a triathlon are beside the point now. Even according to Bambi, you almost drowned. You were a hair away from heatstroke—"

"Not this again."

"I'm not bringing up your trio of near-death experiences as a bludgeon. But of the three, it's Syracuse that bothers me the most. You can die from heatstroke. Your internal organs shut down. And you didn't stop. You wanted me to be impressed that you still finished that race, and I was, but not the way you hoped. Your continuing to run when you were delirious means *I* can't trust *you*. It's official: you don't know when to quit. Are you trying to kill yourself?"

"Of course not. Though there would be worse ways to make an exit."

She leaned forward. "I am your wife. You made promises when you married me. I am supposed to be able to have and to hold you. I'm only sixty-two. I may not look the part right now, but it's not impossible that I live to ninety. I know neither of us is especially thrilled by old age. Nobody is. But there's only one thing worse than our getting decrepit together. You've been given fair warning—three times. Entering that race would be dubious enough if you were in peak condition, but look at you! Covered in bandages, and bruises, and contusions! I can tell by the way you move around the house that your whole body aches—every muscle, every joint, down to the bones. That was a horrible accident. I realize you weren't to blame. Without any road signs about the change of surface, anyone could have wiped out in that gravel. But being oblivious to what that accident has done to you seems ungrateful for the miracle that you survived at all."

"What would be ungrateful is not taking full advantage of coming out relatively unscathed. Using a few scrapes and bruises as an excuse to give up would be gutless, and would make me feel gutless. I can't understand why you'd want to live with me in a state of emasculation."

"I want to live with you, period, and in what state is secondary! So please. *Please* don't do that triathlon. I'll tell everyone that it was my fault you quit, that I forced you. I know you're suspicious, and I've given you reason to be, but this time I'm not trying to stop you because I'm jealous, or because we've been in some stupid contest over this for months on end and I want to have my way, or even to get you away from Bambi Buffer. It's because I love you, and this race is dangerous. Please, I'm begging you." And now she did the worst possible thing that she could do at this time: she got down on her knees.

"Get up!" he cried, springing to a stand. "Get off that fucking knee!"

"I'm begging you." If she was being manipulative, she couldn't have come up with a better guarantee of generating real tears than her current posture. "Don't do this MettleMan. I know it's a sacrifice, but I don't ask you for that much. So make the sacrifice for me. I despair of getting old anyway; I can't bear the idea of doing it alone."

Remington dragged her upright by the armpits and dumped her back into the chair. "You're always separate, so unto yourself, so needless. You disdain the comforts of other people's company. You're contemptuous of their support. You scorn shared enthusiasms as mindless conformity. I suppose that means I'm special, that it matters to you that I'm here, an actual other person you can stand. All right. I'm glad of that. And it's true. I agree. You don't ask me for much. So it is *wicked, wicked,* that when you finally do, it's for the only thing in the whole wide world that you *know* I can't agree to."

TWELVE

"If you slander my trainer on the internet," Remington said at the wheel, sounding ominously calm, "I will track down every site on which you've mentioned her name with a Google search. I'll append the comment that my aging, sedentary wife is stuck at home and physically fearful after a recent knee replacement. I'll say she's resentful of my discovery of new goals and new associates, and intimidated by my trainer's physique. I'll portray my wife as having tried to keep me from fulfilling my athletic destiny for years. I'll quote you, accurately, as having derogated the whole tri movement as 'goofball,' 'small,' 'unworthy of me,' and oh, my favorite: 'all-white.' I know that community better than you do, since you've no idea what *community* means. So I can assure you whose story will sound more convincing. If anything, you'll raise Bambi's profile, rally allies to her side, and generate more clients for her business."

That was all he said on the whole three-hour drive to Lake Placid on Friday morning. For months Serenata had struggled against her attendance at this preposterous exercise in mass hysteria. For the last few days, she'd pleaded to be allowed to go.

By the outskirts of their destination, the streets were bunted with banners: LAKE PLACID WELCOMES METTLEMAN CHAMPIONS! The four-peaked orange logo fluttered in jagged flags on every lamppost. Big red digital advisories warned motorists to expect delays on Sunday, when cyclists enjoyed the right of way on the fifty-eight-mile double loop. As their car crawled bumper to bumper through the tourist town's main drag, adjacent vehicles sported multiple bicycles on roof racks. Bumper stickers read SOLID METTLE and SUCCEED OR DIE TRI-ING. Special offers on passing sandwich boards offered discounts to diners with official orange entrant badges. The quaint, comely municipality's local businesses—shops for popcorn, flavored olive oils, unguents—were sure to benefit from an uptick in trade.

Their motel proved more of a motor lodge than the palatial quarters befitting a brave-heart. But between health insurance deductibles, reduced household income owing to the new "mimicry" taboo, Bambi's ridiculous retainer, and two whopping entry fees for this franchise, economizing was no longer a choice. Besides, all Serenata really cared about was that accessing their room on the forecourt didn't involve any stairs.

At check-in, the genial proprietor asked Remington if he was entering Sunday's race. In contrast to Saratoga Springs, no one else in line at reception mistook Serenata—leaning on her aluminum cane, the knee bandaged below baggy shorts, the right calf fat, tight, and discolored—for a fellow contestant.

Her presence was an inconvenience. For his wife to come along to the athletes' briefing that afternoon, Remington had to battle traffic back into town to drop her off at the MettleMan site, a large square covered in white tents. Without an invalid in tow, he might have wended to the briefing on his bike. But she'd lobbied to attend even the event's ancillary froufrou because ostensibly she yearned to participate in "the whole experience."

Propped on a bleacher for forty-five minutes while Remington found a place to park, Serenata considered: she did want to keep an eye on him. She was loath to conduct the weekend in a spirit of unrelenting antagonism. And if he insisted on going through with this farce, she was under some obligation to provide moral support.

All those other cars had been bursting with friends and family. But while she'd gone through the motions of inviting Griff, his opposition to his son's display of geriatric vanity was implacable. When she asked Deacon to come, he *laughed*. Tommy couldn't stand the prospect of applauding behind a barrier at an event she'd been slated to enter. Valeria's dour husband, Brian, had come to interpret Nancee's ceaseless physical agitation as demonic possession. Because worship of athletic perfection was a form of "idolatry," he'd even made Valeria drop her spinning class at the Y. As for triathlons, they were an "arrogant confusion of man with the divine." His pregnant wife was flat out forbidden from repeating her frenzy at the finish line in Syracuse. Hank Timmerman had intrigued a small local production company into filming a documentary of his inspiring journey from ruin to rebirth, and was hopping a ride with the crew. The other remaining members of the tri club were driving up separately with their own carloads of supporters.

Thus Remington had arrived in Lake Placid with a cheering section of one, and a dismal excuse for a well-wisher at that. As the stands filled with "lumpy chicks" and "lumpy dicks," as their son would say, his only backer's aversion bordered on nausea.

Remington located her on a bottom bleacher right before the instructional talk for first-timers was to get underway. The temperature was in the mid-eighties, so he'd changed from his slacks and button-down into running shorts and a muscle T. One of the biggest transformations of aging was the way that healing grew horribly slow, as if your cells were reluctant to waste the energy of replacement on an organism en route to the scrap heap; Serenata's tiniest cooking burn now took three weeks to peel to pink skin, and it would scar. Consequently, Remington still looked like an escapee from Intensive Care. Heads turned.

The twenty-something kid on his other side raised an eyebrow at the bandages and bruises just beginning to jaundice. Remington muttered, "Bike wipeout—at speed."

"Wow," the boy said. "And you're doing the race anyway. That's fantastic!" Had she indeed tried to vilify Bambi Buffer online for not forcing a client to concede his infirmity, Serenata never would have gotten anywhere with these people.

"My coach says the main thing in a Mettle is to 'stay within yourself,'" the boy went on, staring straight ahead. Oddly pale and puny, he seemed to be talking mostly to himself. "The biggest mistake he says first-timers make is getting swept up in other people's pace. Then later you blow out. 'Never race faster than you train,' Jason says." The compulsive jittering of his leg was shaking the whole bleacher. The event still two days off, the poor kid was already petrified.

All the information a buoyant young instructor proceeded to provide was clearly explained in his handout. But just as Serenata's joint replacement class merely replicated its handbook, no one trusted you to read anything anymore. Online, text was ceding to the podcast. Civilizationally, we were regressing to oral history around a campfire.

Most of the instructions regarded a plethora of bags—for transitions or one's private "special needs," like peanut butter cups or dry socks. The instructor emphasized the importance of attaching your race number to each and delivering the right-colored bag to the right deposit point. It was vital to arrive here at this time, there at another time, and to report for getting body markings (age, race number) within a set window. During the race, littering earned a "red card," and so did pissing in a residential front yard instead of using a Porta-John; two red cards and you'd "DQ." Water stations with nutritional gels, Gatorade, and bananas would be located every ten miles on the cycle route and every mile on the run—though chicken broth would only be served after dark. Bikes could be collected until one a.m. on Sunday night, and starting at six a.m. on Monday. Getting thousands of people to exhaust themselves all at the same time seemed a considerable organizational undertaking.

"Now, unlike our competitors," the young man said, wrapping up, "Mettles don't have time cutoffs for the first two segments, so you're not going to DNF if you cramp up and take longer than usual on the swim. Some folks are, you know, shit-hot runners but a little slower on the bike, and we don't think you should be penalized for mixed levels of proficiency. *However.* There is an overall event cutoff, and it's *very strict.* If your chin doesn't hit the bar on the finish line by the stroke of midnight, *poof,* your carriage turns into a pumpkin. Got that? Furthermore, midnight is when the Mettle is *over.* So if you're still out on the trail, our people are gonna pick you up. Our volunteers will have put in a lot of hard work on your behalf. It'll be late, they have families, and they deserve to go home. If you didn't make it by the gong, you can always try again next year. Besides, think of it this way: we need that strict cutoff to make sure your becoming a MettleMan means something. If we let you take three weeks to complete the course, that orange-and-gold finisher mug wouldn't be good for anything but coffee. Now, go out there, and show 'em what you're made of!"

With time to kill before the opening ceremony, Remington and Serenata dawdled through the commercial booths, which sold not only high-end sports clothing, but also veino-muscular compression socks; shots of cayenne, ginger, and honey to ward off muscle cramps; protein supplements of beef gelatin or bone broth; muscle rollers; and exotically contorted tri bikes, with inbuilt hydration systems connected to vinyl feeding tubes.

Close relatives of the high-strung steed he'd hurled into a tree, the bikes made Remington doleful, so they hit the franchise tent. Under the sign BOAST OF A LIFETIME! were piles of T-shirts: TRI NOW. WINE LATER; METTLE DETECTOR; I'M BETTER THAN YOU ARE (AND I CAN PROVE IT); SELF IS THE FINAL FRONTIER; LIMITS ARE FOR LOSERS; YOU ARE YOUR TIME. There were MettleMan logoed tea towels, shot glasses, bath plugs, beer mugs, handbags, knapsacks, lunch boxes, ankle bracelets, aprons, watches, wastebaskets, sports diaries, vape pens, paperweights, picture frames, pencil boxes, flip-flops, smart-phone cases, and toothbrushes, as well as MettleBaby teddy bears and bibs. On a popular rack, orange windbreakers were emblazoned in gold across the back, FULL METTLE JACKET.

"What did I tell you?" Serenata quoted *Goodfellas*. "*Don't buy anything.*"

Impatient with his wife's pace on the way back up the hill, Remington remarked, "We should have brought the walker." It was a line she'd never have expected her husband to mutter when she was still in her early sixties.

In the lakeside public park, a stage sat beside an outsize video screen playing advertisements for more gear, as hip-hop pounded from the sound system. Children were showing off toward the front, doing handstands and cartwheels. On the hillside, groups were gathered on blankets, sipping electrolyte drinks and nibbling whole wheat burritos. The scene would have been bucolic, save for an edginess that was palpable. Snippets of discernable conversation were largely about the weather, and it wasn't small talk. The chances of rain on Sunday had risen to 50 percent, and a portion of this gathering wouldn't have the option of staying indoors with the crossword.

Serenata waved, glad to see that Cherry DeVries had brought her whole family—not only the three kids, but also a burly man overdressed for the heat, seated at the edge of their bedspread, and vengefully gnawing a hero.

"Sera, I don't think you've met my husband, Sarge," Cherry said. So at odds with the lithe, gangly stunners strewn on every side, her plus-size figure made her conspicuously more likable.

"It's so nice of you to come and support your wife," Serenata said.

"Cherry's a weaver on interstates," he said. "I wasn't about to entrust my kids to three hours on I-87 with my wife at the wheel."

"So how's the knee?" Cherry asked.

It was never clear what this frequent solicitation was meant to elicit. "Just standing here is making me suicidal"?

"Fine," Serenata said instead. That's what the solicitation was meant to elicit.

Remington located Chet, Sloan, and Hank with much backslapping and high-fiving. After all the attrition and accelerating rivalry, the tiny club seemed to have knit back together with a sense of all-for-one. Flitting among her chicks, their mother hen leaned down to each member in turn to impart last-minute advice: "Now, I know you're pumped, Hank, but remember this isn't a party. And don't let that film crew get in the way of the staff." "Hey, don't get casual, Sloan. It's never easy, I don't care if we've done them before." "Chet, early to bed tonight, too. Ten p.m. max. And tomorrow, I want you guys *asleep*, not just brushing your teeth, by eight thirty." As for whatever she told Remington, she was too down into his ear for Serenata to hear it.

Bambi was in her element. Even in this company, her physique stood out. Ranging palsy-walsy among former clients, she took her time, bestowing blessings ("Lookin' tight, Rex!") or teasing admonishments ("How many times I tell you, Paul? Lay off that calzone!"). The cameraman with the documentary crew couldn't get enough of her. "Hey, I thought this show was about me," Hank carped. "You were gonna interview me about my *bad decisions*—"

"Filler footage," the cameraman said, still panning.

The *filler footage* had chosen her opening ceremony outfit with care: a soft salmon leotard with spaghetti straps and a nap to the fabric that made you want to pet it, filmy cream-colored shorts that fluttered in the breeze to expose the cut of her hip flexors, and killer heels that for some reason didn't sink into the lawn. That body must have saved her business a bundle on advertising.

To spare herself tottering onto the grass with a knee that wouldn't bend beyond ninety degrees, Serenata perched on a rock by the lake. Onstage, testimonials got underway: by charities raising funds for obscure diseases; by the eldest of this year's intake, who at eighty-five was on his sixth full Mettle; and by the previous year's winner, a pro with a guileless, generically handsome face who praised his patient "tri widow" and "tri orphans" for never complaining that he wasn't around for waffles on weekends, and who looked about eight feet tall. Indeed, as she gave the hillside a once-over, the pros were easy to spot. The men were all so towering that they might have been a different species. Their shoulders were broad, but everything else was narrow: the tiny dropped waists, the slight hips, the taut little buns. They tended to have long feet and big hands. But the most mysterious aspect of this breed apart was that they weren't sexy. One simply didn't hanker to fuck a man who desired himself.

Although the MC extolled the multiple nationalities, the range of ages, and the numerous first responders and ex-military among this year's entrants, Serenata's private canvas of the crowd didn't produce big surprises. She located two black athletes, whose insouciant bearing conveyed a prosperous upbringing. One Chinese, check; one Indian, check. Although women were reputably represented, the vast preponderance of the participants were white men.

As for the ages, once you discounted supporters (heavier, more sunburned, more covered up), the cohorts seemed to clump. Like Tommy March, the legion of under-thirties hailed from a generation whose concept of "self-improvement" was integrally bound up with diet and exercise, whereas for Griff's contemporaries the term had meant broadening your vocabulary and learning French. Then there were the second-lifers over fifty—tan, spare, and gray, with close-cropped hair to disguise the balding. They had the same look in their eyes that she'd come to recognize in Remington: enflamed, the focus a gauzy middle-distance. Perhaps they'd built companies or fortunes, but the results had been unsatisfying. The youngsters wanted status. The oldsters wanted meaning.

At last, MettleMan's founder took the mic—a bear of a man named Doug Rausing whose potbelly suggested a latter-day preference for administration. He thanked sponsors and invited the top one hundred finishers to apply for the twentieth anniversary Mettle-of-Mettles in Alaska.

"Believe it or not," Rausing boomed, "when this organization started out eighteen years ago, our first race had only seventy-seven scrappy, never-say-die athletes. Since then, we've grown to a world-wide movement. If you've never been through this test of your very essence before, you may find nearly fifteen hundred contestants a little overwhelming. So I want to say a special word to all you first-timers. It may seem like you're in a crowd, and you can sure count on your brothers and sisters in this fellowship of torment to watch your back. But in the end, you're on your own, because that's what Mettle-Man is all about: facing down what you're made of, facing down if you've got the goods. No matter how many other athletes you see around you when you plunge into that cold lake early on Sunday morning, you are profoundly and, we all have to admit, sometimes disturbingly—*by yourself*.

"I'm betting that more than a few of you are anxious. Hell, maybe even scared to death. But one of the reasons you're battling inner demons is all the *outer* demons you've been combating ever since you first got up the nerve to go public with a commitment that's on the face of it pretty far-fetched. At every step of the way, you've been undermined. Maybe they even laughed at you. Didn't they? Didn't they laugh at you?"

The crowd chuckled in recognition.

"Because *they* say it's impossible," Rausing continued. "*They* say it's insane. *They* say that humans aren't meant to conquer such distances, in the water, on a bike, on foot, one after the other, without rest. *They* say you'll collapse. *They* say you'll do irreversible damage to your body, and end your life beaten down and ailing and drowning in regrets. But whatever happens on Sunday, there's only one regret you want to avoid: never tri-ing—that's *T-R-I*—in the first place. You'd regret listening to the spoilsports, the scaredy-cats, and the sissies. You'd regret listening to the whimpering, sniveling little voice that your tormentors—the naysayers, the excuse-makers, the nervous Nellies, the armchair cynics, the gloomy Guses—have actually *succeeded* in installing *inside your very head*!

"So you tell that little voice to scram. That voice is the sound of failure, inadequacy, and resignation. It's the voice of the Little Engine That Couldn't. It's the voice of the third-grade teacher who gave you a C-minus, the parent who sent you to your room, the counselor who said you'd never get into Princeton. The therapist who wanted to put you on Prozac, the professor who said you'd never graduate, the employer who deleted your job application, the editor who rejected your Great American Novel without reading past page three. It's the same voice that tells you that your country is in decline, your compatriots are all drug addicts, and the future belongs—with apologies to Bao Feng over there, who's a fine citizen of these United States—to the Chinese. It's the voice of the devil, friends. It's the voice of the devil.

"Listen only to your deep self. Concentrate only on getting to that next buoy, and then to the buoy after that. On getting to the top of that next hill, and then to the top of the hill after that. On getting to that next mile marker, and then to the mile marker after that. Pain? Pain is the fire in which we are smelted, and out the other side of that furnace we are tempered like steel. We are the human race, Mach Two. We are the stronger, leaner, meaner, fiercer, more powerful members of mankind who will prove there are *no* limits, and there is *nothing* we can't achieve, because WE—ARE—METTLEMEN!"

The crowd erupted with cheers loud enough to cover Serenata's murmur, "Leni Riefenstahl, where are you?"

"Tell me one more time that I don't have to do this," Remington said, peering through their motel room curtains at the wet parking lot, "and I worry I'm going to hit you."

It was three thirty a.m. The night before, allergic to observing the bedtime of an eight-year-old, Serenata had holed up in the bathroom with a towel under the door to block the light and read on the toilet with the cover down. As she'd only drifted off beside him an hour and a half ago, Remington wasn't the only one who wanted to hit someone. But outwardly, she resolved to seem chipper. Ever since Bambi had ratted her out, she never complained, never criticized, never made snarky remarks. This was her husband's show. She had put up a brave fight, and she had lost.

She ventured out the door. It was pitch-dark. The air was cool and dank. "Right now it's just a mizzle," she reported.

"Now it's sixty percent at seven," he said, poking his phone, "and it goes up from there."

"Well, there's rain and there's rain, right? Sometimes a light mist is refreshing."

Fortunately, she'd brought along a camp stove and espresso pot. Screw the power bars and gels; she'd also brought a box of miniature powdered-sugar doughnuts.

"You didn't have to get up with me, you know." Somehow it was a relief that he couldn't resist a doughnut. "I have to check in by five. You won't have anything to do. And how will you get down there to watch?"

"Uber. Or you could drive me down with you. I could help you get into your wet suit. It's tricky, with the bandages, and your shoulder."

"The volunteers assist in transitions, and they're good at it." He seemed to feel badly about rebuffing her. "But I'll need dry clothes when it's all over. Taking this bag to the finish line would be a big help. Also . . . Sorry, never mind."

"Never mind what?"

"I was going to suggest you could pick up the bike for me while I'm on the marathon segment, from that big sea of racks, which would give us a jump on the traffic Monday morning. But with your knee—"

"A bike makes a nifty walker. I could get it back here in another Uber. I'm supposed to use the knee anyway, and I missed a PT session on Friday."

He gave her the bike pickup slip. "But if it's too challenging, we'll retrieve it on Monday morning; we'll just have to wait in a long line. Don't hurt yourself."

As he shouldered the tote with his sharkskin-style wet suit, she tried to formulate a parting thought—but all she could think to say was that he didn't have to do this. Judiciously, she hugged him hard on the forecourt and kept her mouth shut.

With nothing to do at the motel but eat more doughnuts, Serenata arrived at the spectators' knoll early enough to get a front-row view of the swimmers' entry-point beach around the bend. The sky dim and grainy, she needed the light on her phone to pitch her folding stool on stable ground. She used to stand twelve hours a day. But she was getting a feel for how effortlessly you could switch camps. Once you immigrated to the land of lassitude, all those whirling dervishes leaping and spinning and flailing around grew incomprehensible.

Thus when a staffer onshore pounded the franchise's signature brass gong with a fluffy orange mallet and the first tranche of swimmers, all pros, tumbled into the water, Serenata didn't wish she could have joined them. Especially not when the morning's drizzle gave way to a deluge. Slanted sheets swept the surface of the lake, which bounded upward in reply, as if it were raining upside-down. Droplets drummed the plastic orange buoys like tympanis. She'd borrowed an umbrella from the motel reception, and even the splashes spanking off the nylon onto her legs were irksome. Much was to be said for physical comfort—for rest, for ease; for being dry, sheltered, neither too cold nor too hot, and well fed. Fine, many of her compatriots were overdosing on their own well-being. Nevertheless, for most of human existence the driving aim of the species was not to toil, but to stop toiling; not to suffer, but to stop suffering. It would seem unappreciative of all the forebears instrumental in the evolution of sturdy umbrellas and convenient little folding chairs not to relish the fact that rather than swim a ferocious 2.6 miles in driving rain she could simply sit here.

Doing the crawl in heavy rain could induce a sensation of drowning; the distinction between air and water blurred. Thus the pros' knifing from buoy to buoy was frankly astonishing. Pretty much anyone could ride a bike, and anyone could run. But swimming was a skill, and those strokes were a marvel.

Which didn't prevent her fellow spectators from being blithe and inattentive. The pros didn't seem to arrive with entourages; however oddly, this was a job, and leaving the family at home would keep expenses down. No one on the knoll was rooting for these athletes. To the contrary, a woman nearby complained to her companion,

"George says the pros are ruining this sport for everybody. Not only do they show everyone else up, but when they retire, they enter the age groups as amateurs. Then they win—like, *duh*. It's not exactly cheating, but it's close."

Self-classified by their time, groups of swimmers were staggered every five minutes. Expecting to take over two hours to complete the swim, the final cohort hit the water at 6:35, just after the pros began their second lap—presumably to keep the slowpokes from being run over.

There: Remington was last. His stroke was unmistakable. Each forward arm hit the water with a hard plop. A heaviness had always characterized his crawl, and the shoulder injury would make the right-hand reaches only more labored. His having failed to mention the pain all week was a bad sign. The rain settled into an unrelenting steadiness. This wasn't a passing shower, but a rainy *day*.

Serenata was vigilant. Boats were stationed at regular intervals, but entrant #1,083 was nothing to those lifeguards but a number, and she didn't trust them.

Around seven a.m., the male pros slogged to shore and hit the sand at a run. All the female pros were out of the water ten minutes after the lead. Serenata focused her portable binoculars. Remington still hadn't cleared the far bend that marked his first half-lap.

By the time her husband did reach that bend, a clump of amateurs was overtaking him on their second lap. It was already seven fifteen. One difficulty he'd have to contend with would be all these other swimmers, who weren't necessarily in a considerate frame of mind, who had their own problems with cramps or freak-outs, and whose goggles may have clouded or been knocked sideways, so that even if they were polite, in this torrent they could barely see. Collisions looked common. Splashes from adjacent competitors would add to the rain; being jostled on every side would be discombobulating;

being constantly overtaken by swimmers who'd already completed three-quarters of the course would be demoralizing.

When at last Remington curved around the raft by the shore and began his second lap, it was 7:55. He'd taken an hour and twenty minutes to complete 1.3 miles, a time that most people could beat with a breaststroke. The majority of contestants had left the water, though about three dozen racers were still going at it, all ahead of him. As time went on, the distance between Remington and the next-to-last swimmer lengthened. By 8:50, that penultimate contestant—a woman—sloshed to shore and stumbled through the orange-carnation archway. With nearly half a lap to go, Remington was alone in the lake.

He'd slowed down. That previous half-lap had taken him not forty but fifty minutes, the pace of a dog paddle. The rhythm of his plopping arms had decelerated. One of the motorized dinghies plowed to his side. A lifeguard leaned down, doubtless to ensure he was not in distress, but maybe also to ask if he'd like to climb into the boat and call it a day. She prayed he'd take them up on the offer. *Just tell them, "Sorry, but I had a serious accident right before this race, and I didn't realize the toll it took on me." That's the truth, and it confers no dishonor. Just please get out of the water and out of the rain. We can go back to the motel, where you can take a long, scalding shower. I'll fix you hot cocoa from the in-room amenities, adding coffee creamer and sugar to make it more fortifying. When you're feeling warmer and stronger and get back in dry clothes, we'll find a cozy place for a big breakfast, with sausage and pancakes. You won't even have to talk. And I'll never, ever say I told you so.*

The inflatable retreated—though it followed him watchfully from a few yards back.

All the other bystanders on the knoll had cleared off. Inattentive to the positioning of her umbrella, Serenata was getting soaked, but

she was beside herself. She tried waving, and semaphoring by opening and closing the umbrella, but Remington didn't appear to notice,
and the distraction might have been less than helpful anyway.

At long last, he reached the shallows and Lazarethed to shore. It
was 9:41 a.m.: three hours and six minutes, which must have set a
record, if not the kind he would covet. She should have felt proud of
him, and maybe she did. But this pride felt more like dread.

She folded up the stool, slipped it in her tote, and looped the bag
around her shoulder. As she ventured carefully with the cane in
one hand and the umbrella in the other, her purchase in the mud
was precarious. She shuffled over to the chute through which all
the other contestants had already run toward "T1," while behind the
barrier onlookers had cheered and waved placards for friends and
relatives. Now Serenata was the only spectator. Staff in matching
orange T-shirts and cheap translucent ponchos loitered impatiently
in the wings, eager to start rolling up the sopping carpet of artificial
grass and wrap this wretched segment up. Heading to the tent where
a volunteer would peel off the wet suit and help him into his cycling
gear, Remington loped leadenly toward his wife, bare feet splashing
the AstroTurf.

When they locked eyes as he passed, his expression was hollow.
He didn't seem to recognize her. Aside from a distant growl of thun-
der and the splat of his feet, the silence was sepulchral. Cheering
this spectacle of self-destruction would have been perverse. She
made a feeble effort at an encouraging smile, and looked away.

Having hobbled to a road that overlooked the MettleMan site, she'd
a view of the ocean of bike racks. There must have been slots for
1,500, though Remington's would be easy to find; it was the only one
left. When her husband emerged from the T1 tent and a volunteer
in a poncho delivered the handlebars, Serenata waved, but he had

more on his mind than looking for his wife. From this distance, she couldn't be sure if the wobble as he mounted and pedaled off was all in her head.

Maybe it was the rain, or maybe after eighteen years of hosting this event the locals had grown blasé, but the supporters on the sidelines were sparse. Grim conditions endowed the occasion with an air of can-we-just-get-this-over-with. Yet suddenly cheers, whistles, and clackers created a simulacrum of excitement. Sweeping down the hill and banking on the turn with spray sheeting off their tires, the pros were completing their first fifty-eight-mile cycling lap.

Serenata didn't care. She'd never understood cycling as a spectator sport, which made paint drying seem like a nail-biter. However unseemly self-pity under the circumstances, she was still wet and cold, and the knee was yowling. She shambled up the hill on the commercial side of the cycle route and found a restaurant with outdoor tables and big umbrellas. There she was surprised to find the documentary film crew, surrounded by eggs and hash browns.

"Why aren't you guys out collecting footage of miraculous rebirth?" she asked.

"Contrary to what they told you in science class," the hipster cameraman said, "butterflies sometimes revert to caterpillars."

"Did Hank punk out?"

"We were out kind of late last night, considering," the lantern-jawed producer said. "But he assured us that he'd trained to do this shit on not much sleep."

"If you were all 'out' last night," she said, "do you mean he got plastered?"

"I didn't keep track," the director in an old OBAMA 'o8 cap said diplomatically.

"Did he by any chance start asking you about Lorrie Moore's short stories?"

"Now that you mention it," the director said, "yeah."

"He was plastered," Serenata said.

"When we pounded on his motel room this morning," the cameraman said, "he wouldn't open the door. Fucking hell. Up at four thirty for nothing. Once he missed the swim check-in, we all went back to bed."

"It's not only getting up in pitch-dark that was for nothing," the producer said. "The doc's kaput, and what are we doing in fucking Lake Placid in a downpour? Motel, meals, gas—we're seriously out of pocket."

"I doubt it's any comfort, but however bad you feel," Serenata said, "Hank's going to feel worse. He's been training for this race for months."

"Maybe the Hankster couldn't face the weather forecast," the director supposed. "I mean, look at these guys." He gestured to the flooded cycling course, of which the eatery enjoyed an excellent view, as the last of the pros came through. "They're mental."

"At least, for reasons I don't entirely understand," Serenata said, "the pros make money off this stuff. But for everyone else"—she leaned confidentially across the cameraman's eggs—"*there's absolutely no reason to do this.*"

"But isn't your husband in this race?" the director asked.

"Uh-huh. I'm afraid so."

"Ha!" the director said. "That's the first discouraging word I've heard since we got here. Pull up a chair."

Serenata ordered pancakes and sausage.

The cameraman nodded approvingly. "Not sure why, but ever since we landed in this throng of demigods, all I want to do is eat, sleep, drink, and watch TV. Anything that doesn't involve making an effort or getting wet."

"While my husband ran the Saratoga Springs marathon last year," she said, "I spent loads of money on clothes I didn't need, ate an enormous lunch, and hit the hotel pool, where I refused to do anything more tiring than float."

"I can't wait for the pendulum to swing back to hedonism and hell-raising," the cameraman said. "I think I was born into the wrong generation. This one, it's all about *redemption*, have you noticed? Earning, and striving, and getting holy. All the guys I went to film school with at NYU are in love with purification—forswearing meat, dairy, carbs, out-of-season produce, and plastic. They don't have an indulgent or mutinous bone in their bodies. Oh, and they're not just into redemption, either. Add *rectitude*. They all want to be hallway monitors."

"When I was young, we broke the rules. Far as I can tell, your peers love nothing more than making up more of them." She flicked her hand. "And enforcing them with a whip."

He touched her wrist. "Nice work. Though I'm surprised. Everyone gets tats."

Outliers recognized each other. "Cincinnati, 1973. *They're* copying *me*."

They were flirting, a little. It was nice. The pancakes arrived. The stack was enormous.

"Couldn't you salvage what you've shot," she supposed, "by doing a more general documentary on the rising popularity of the triathlon?"

"Yesterday's news," the cameraman said. "These gonzo endurance races are all over the country. And now the heavies are into ultra-hyper-maxed-out-shitting-yourself stuff, on the tundra in January, or in Death Valley in July. Which makes this one seem pissant in comparison. So we needed the addict-finds-enlightenment angle. About all I've got worth saving is a few clips of that Bambi broad to provide inspiration in moments of, ah, *self-reflection*."

"Speak of the devil." Serenata was gratified to note as the woman streaked past that Bambi's favorite baby-blue and canary-yellow cy-cling outfit was so spattered with black mud that the ensemble was probably ruined.

"That Rausing shyster," the director said, looking up from his phone, "says they've already had three wipeouts on the bikes, in-cluding one multiple-cyclist pileup. Crap traction. One accident was pretty serious. Busted the guy's head open."

Worried, Serenata broke out her own phone. For the cycling and running segments, contestants wore the same electronically tagged ankle bracelets Remington had worn in Saratoga Springs, so she could track his progress with the MettleMan app she'd downloaded at the motel. In the whole field, #1,083 remained last, but the blue dot was still moving faster than a man with a busted head.

When they finished eating, the camera crew decided to check out and head back to Hudson—punitively, without Hank. They gave Ser-enata a lift back to her motel, where she took what should have been her husband's scalding shower and changed into the dry clothes he needed so much more than she did. By noon, #1,083 had crossed the halfway point in the first lap. Restless, she Ubered back to town and bought a heavy sweatshirt; it was chillier than she'd been prepared for. She sampled wild-mushroom olive oil and strawberry balsamic vinegar with scraps of French bread. She dropped into the popcorn store and picked up a novelty seasoning that was supposed to taste like beer-can chicken.

As the blue dot approached the end of its first lap, she returned to the same restaurant with its superlative view of the course, ordering a basket of fried calamari to justify her occupancy of the table. She missed the camera crew. It had been a relief to share solidarity with her fellow "spoilsports, scaredy-cats, and sissies."

Immediately below Serenata's table, an agonizingly thin woman in athletic gear too summery for the chill had stationed herself behind the spectator barrier with a gratingly loud cowbell clacker. The faster amateurs were already finishing their second lap. *Every— single—fucking* time another cyclist passed, the self-appointed cheer- leader went into a frenzy of hooting and clacking, as well as shouting the usual inanities: "Go, baby! You show 'em! Never say die, baby! Keep it up! We're all behind you! Kill—it! Kill that lap!" The constant clacking was a torture.

At last the app showed the blue dot curving around the bend. Ser- enata abandoned her calamari and leaned over the wooden rail around the restaurant's deck. There he was, head down, in the timelessly dopy helmet, and like the rest of the riders, covered in mud. His bandages were diarrheal. In a rare two seconds during which the emaciated fan let up on her ceaseless clacking, Serenata projected with the deep purr that had captivated the man returning his tie to Lord & Taylor, "REM- ING-TON." He turned his head and treated her to a private nod.

Which would have to keep her going for another how many hours? She checked her watch. He'd done that lap in 4:09. He was therefore averaging . . . 14 mph, which considering how shattered he'd looked after the swim was downright okay. So: he hadn't drowned. He hadn't had another bike accident. And if he kept this up, he'd begin the marathon+.2m at about six p.m., which actually gave him half a chance of finishing before midnight. Taking her own temperature, she appeared to be impressed and disgusted in equal measure. Only one sentiment was unambivalent: she'd no desire to spend what remained of their lives in passable health going to events like this one. How she felt about his finishing the full Mettle before the gong was entirely predicated on whether its completion satisfied him, or gave him a taste for more.

That cameraman was onto something about the heathen's natural reaction to all this repudiation of the flesh. She finished the calamari.

According to the app, the winner would come in around 3:40 p.m. Though hardly on the edge of her chair about which total stranger took first place, she wasn't up for another round-trip to the motel. So she lurched back down the hill toward the finish line, where the last few hundred feet of the running track curved around the rows of bike racks, now filling back up. A fair crowd had accumulated behind the spectator barrier. Making shameless use of her disability to receive special treatment, she managed to establish her portable canvas stool as a front-row seat. She arranged the right leg at partial extension while enjoying a good view of the finish line's archway, its orange carnations grown bedraggled in the steady downpour. Between the vertical supports stretched a horizontal pole: the chin-up bar.

For diversion, she looked up the race numbers of the Hudson Tri Club. Hank Timmerman had been disappeared. Right now, ambitious amateurs were already throwing their bikes to volunteers and rushing into the T2 tent, but Cherry DeVries had many miles to go. Serenata found herself rooting for the woman; should she come up short, Sarge would never let her live it down. Sloan Wallace wasn't in the same league as the pros, but he was already three-quarters through the run; he occupied the level of excellence that might have given him a crack at placing if it weren't for the current and recently retired professionals about whom the woman on the knoll had complained. It took resolve to look up *Bam Bam*, whose blue dot, she was gratified to note, was significantly behind Sloan's. That would bug the trainer no end.

"Good Lord!" Serenata exclaimed aloud. Chet Mason was listed "DNF." Her heart was strangely broken on the young man's account.

Volunteers passed around long orange strips, one of which Serenata accepted with perplexity. It looked like a condom for a horse. Around her, more experienced spectators blew them up into batons, as if to make balloon animals. Only when a roar went up on the other side of the bend did she get the drill: spectators leaned over to pound these inflated orange sausages on the hollow plexiglass barrier in rhythmic unison, the while shouting "Go! Go! Go! Go!" as the leading pro hove into view. It was a primitive tribal drumming session in plastic.

Although having flagellated himself for nine hours and forty minutes, the paragon in front, streaming with rain and spatter, was running all out. He leaped at the bar, rose in the same single fluid motion to bring his chin above it, then lifted his long legs overhead and arced back to ground with a gymnast's dismount. A practiced maneuver, and flashy.

"YOU . . . ARE . . . METTLEMAN!" boomed over the loudspeaker.

Volunteers rushed to the winner with towels and a space blanket, as another looped a garish medal around his neck. He was ushered to photographers on the sidelines.

Thirty seconds later, the number two finisher came in—impressively, a woman, lanky, gristled, flat-chested, and so insanely light that the cherry-on-top chin-up looked effortless. Yet once her feet hit the track accompanied by another "YOU . . . ARE . . . METTLEMAN!"—the coronations were unisex—her legs gave way, and she crumpled into the mud. This time the volunteers gathered her into a wheelchair, and hurried the racer through the flaps of a tent marked with a white cross.

Medical attention before the photo op was more the form than not. After the triumphant pounding of the home stretch, most pros were shaking and could barely stand, if at all. One was rarely witness to the expenditure of every last iota of energy, strength, and will, and to what it looked like the moment those quantities were perfectly spent.

But the *poom-pooming* of the batons was giving Serenata a headache. Being incapacitated, and feeling a little threatened by the press of the crowd, she relinquished her prime position, using the cane to part the waters. She pulled herself up on the bleachers where the athletes' briefing had been held, the more distanced view of the finish line wholly adequate, given how little she cared. Each time another contestant came in, the announcer bestowed the same booming baptism of "YOU . . . ARE" etc. with improbably fresh enthusiasm. Checking the app again, she was perturbed that Remington hadn't made more headway on his second bike lap.

She ripped off the price tags and drew on her new sweatshirt, over which she donned the hooded rain poncho from the same shop; the arm holding the umbrella was getting tired. Tugging the nylon tightly around her as drips pattered off the visor, she huddled down for the long haul: the loyal helpmate, the faithful wife, the poor excuse for a fan. They said time passed more quickly when you got older. Well, not always.

By about five p.m., a familiar face penetrated her catatonia: Sloan Wallace had just come in. Assuming he'd entered the water at about 6:10 a.m., he'd finished the course in under eleven hours. Since these people talked ceaselessly about their times, she was painfully aware that "cracking eleven" was not only Sloan's driving ambition, but Bambi's, too. Serenata checked the trainer's blue dot with an evil smile: the bitch would never make it.

But she had nothing against Sloan, so she limped down toward the shelter marked FINISHERS' TENT. Inside, the pros sat by themselves at separate folding tables, not talking to one another, with dull, vacant expressions, like robots that had been switched off. They left nearby baskets of Pop-Tarts and granola bars untouched. The dozen amateurs who'd come in were distinguishable by their clusters of excited friends and family. Yet when she waved to Sloan, just finishing off a liter of Gatorade, he was surrounded by no such retinue, and looked glad to see her.

"I came to congratulate you," she said. "I'm so sorry about the weather. It must have been grueling."

"Yeah, and to think we were mostly worried about the heat!"

"So—where's your family?"

"My ex wouldn't let the kids come," he said. "I have custody every other weekend. This is her weekend."

"Pretty mean-spirited, not being willing to switch."

"Tell me about it."

After they chatted about the course's travails and Serenata affirmed that Remington was still going doggedly at it, she asked, "Any idea what happened to Chet? The app says he's DNF."

Sloan's face clouded. Chet was more or less his protégé. "Damn, that's a shame. I can't believe he'd just quit. Hey, Patti!" he shouted to a volunteer. "Any idea what happened to Chet Mason? Short, compact, about thirty, and had to pull out?"

"Oh, him," Patti said. Gossip about contestant misfortune must have spread quickly. "Muscle spasm in his calf. That's spasm, not cramp, and I guess there's a big difference. They say he tried to keep running, too, and it was totally awful to watch. You know . . ." The girl illustrated with a humping galumph. "I saw him when they brought him to the med tent. Some guys fake injury when really they just can't hack it. But that calf muscle, well, you could *see* it in this gross bunchy knot. He could hardly put any weight on the leg. Not the kind of problem you go to a hospital for—it just has to work itself out—but they wouldn't let him back on the course. Man, I've never seen a grown man cry like that. I mean, he was bawling like a baby."

"From the pain?" Serenata asked.

"I don't think so," Patti said.

"Look what the cat dragged in!" Sloan exclaimed. "What took you so long?"

"What do you think, I stopped for *muffins*," Bambi snarled, approaching their table as she toweled off the mud. "Didn't even beat my PB, much less crack eleven. Though I assume from that smarmy expression that you did?"

"Ten fifty-six fourteen," Sloan said with a smile. "Not bad for a sloppy course."

"I don't appreciate going through this much shit only to feel like a fucking jackass," Bambi groused. Misery had eaten a layer off her character like paint stripper. Gone was the sunny veneer. She exuded malice and resentment, like a normal person.

She turned to the volunteer. "Hey, kid, what'd you say about Chet?"

Patti enjoyed some attention for once (question: Why did anyone *volunteer* for this thankless go-fetch? It wasn't for the glory) and repeated her performance.

"Fuck, my first DNF," Bambi said. "And that camera guy told me at the swim check-in that Hank went AWOL. What a bunch of douches. Hey, gimme that." Having never even said hello, she grabbed Serenata's phone, which would obviously be tracking her husband. "Rem's way too far behind. He's one punk runner, you know. Fucker doesn't have a prayer of finishing. Gotta love this year's stats: one quitter, one casualty, two DNFs, and a no-show."

So much for positive thinking.

Serenata returned to the bleachers. As the light faded a shade at six p.m., she granted that Bambi had a point. Had Remington kept up his original pace, he'd have transitioned to the run by now. The cyclists rolling into T2 reduced to a trickle. By seven p.m., #1,083 was the only bike on the course.

The tracking app eliminated any suspense, so when at 7:40 he banked around the curve, she was ready for him. The wait had provided opportunity to brush up her math skills. His average speed had sunk from fourteen miles per hour to ten. Including getting changed, he now had to run a distance in under 4:20 that the winner might have dispatched in 3:14, but which in the previous year's race the whole field ran at an average 4:57. Why, for today's run even the beatified Bambi Buffer had clocked 4:10. What were the chances that Remington could run 26.4 miles in only ten minutes longer than his Amazonian trainer, when in Saratoga Springs he'd taken almost seven and a half hours to run 26.2? ZEEEEEE-RO!

There was nothing like sitting around for hours cold and damp with zip to do for working up an explosive disgust. Balancing on the cane on an upper bleacher—from which, not only could she see him tool down the last hundred yards of the course, but he could see her—she belted at a volume any voice coach would have warned could damage her instrument, "Remington Alabaster, that's enough! Give it up, and let's have dinner! You'll never make the cutoff!"

Three minutes later the fucking idiot was out the other side of the T2 tent in his running togs.

After a third meal in the same restaurant—it was the closest to the site—she limped back down to the finish line. The distances were short, but this was cumulatively way too much mileage for her knee in one day. She'd been popping NSAIDs like Good & Plentys.

Of course, no need to hurry. It was nearly eleven p.m. when she paid the bill, and Remington's blue dot wasn't halfway through the run. He'd been averaging 3.5 mph: a brisk walk. Were he to run the remaining fifteen miles in an hour—while enjoying a festival of abrasions, a pulled Achilles, a strained hamstring, a damaged rotator cuff, and contusions that had probably done muscle damage—he'd have to rival Hicham El Guerrouj's 3:43 record for the mile fifteen times in a row.

Even unimpaired, Remington had a curious running style. His step high, all his energy seemed to plow into the vertical. From any distance, he appeared to be running in place. Though he was slight for his height, his feet hit the trail with the same dead plop with which his arms hit the water on a swim. Indeed, he managed to haul that sinker quality from the pool to dry land.

Physically, he was a wreck when he started. Emotionally, she couldn't predict how exactly he'd take failing to finish—aside from *not well*.

The curve of the home stretch was now lit up with multicolored lights. The rain having finally stopped improved attendance. This crowd was noticeably more feverish than the audience for the pros. The runners coming in during the final hour were likely to be what the rest of the world regarded as "ordinary people" who were attempting the extraordinary, which they'd imported large groups of rabid supporters to witness. Thus Serenata no sooner established her special disability stool than a battle-ax brunette shoved her hard enough that she almost fell off. "I got three people comin' in, honey. Gotta be in front." With the emergence of every subsequent contestant from around the bend—all of whom couldn't have been "her people"—the pushy spectator screamed at a volume that most women would not have been able to muster during natural childbirth.

Admittedly, the racers at the tail end of the field made for a moving spectacle. These were the housewives, the gas station attendants, the schoolteachers, and the cable guys who were unaccustomed to the spotlight. Sometimes on the short side, or maybe a little plump, they weren't the perfectly proportioned paragons who sold $200 running shoes for Madison Avenue. Most of the eleventh-hour participants would have possessed neither the cash nor the pomposity to spring for personal trainers, and would have relied on websites or a book. The determination that powered them to this finish line must have been relentless. Like Ethan Crick, for months on end many would have been arising at four or five in the morning to swim, bike, or run before heading to a full day's work. Some of the women must have risked substantial familial ridicule during the painfully gradual muscle building required to raise their chins above that consummate bar. It wasn't up to Serenata to decide that this crowning moment— "YOU—ARE—METTLEMAN!"—couldn't be the highlight of their lives.

A subset of the folks barely beating the cutoff would probably have expected to finish many hours earlier. Lean, tall, buff, and male, this conspicuously fit contingent must have found the difficulty of the course a shock. Even with the enticing orange archway within sight, some of these guys were having a murderous time forcing one foot in front of the other, while moving about as fast as Serenata post-surgery with a cane. They doubtless felt a little embarrassed to be finishing in the same time as the likes of . . . Cherry DeVries!

Serenata had yet to hoot, whistle, or pound an inflatable orange wiener against the barrier, much less screech like this lunatic to her left. Yet when the familiar mother-of-three hoofed into view, she broke into a grin and yelled, "Good for you, Cherry!"

"CHER-*REE*! CHER-*REE*! That a girl! You did it! Pumpkin, we love you to death! CHER-*REE*! CHER-*REE*!" It was Sarge.

Shoulders back, head high, Cherry marshaled a final surge of speed. Lunging onto the plastic stool provided, she sacrificed three seconds off her time to bask in the roar before grabbing the bar to do one slow, flawless chin-up with her eyes closed. When she dropped to the ground as the MC deputized her an official MettleMan, it was impossible to tell if she was laughing or crying.

Serenata ceded what little space the screamer had allowed her and threaded to the area outside the finisher tent. By the time she found Cherry, Sarge had an arm around his wife and was posing while the kids took photos on their phones. The man was beaming. Go figure. Maybe triathlons weren't entirely evil.

Serenata cut in and gave the muddy woman a hug; that was it for the new sweatshirt. "You're a great example to your daughters," she whispered in Cherry's ear.

"So what's up with Remington?" Cherry asked.

"He's running a little behind."

Cherry checked her watch. "Oh, no! Is he not going to make it?"

"It looks unlikely. But he'll be touched that in the state you must be in you still asked after him."

"Gimme some sugar, champ! Didn't I *tell* ya you could do it?" Now changed into skinny jeans and a clinging pink sweater, Bambi grabbed Cherry around the neck in a possessive clutch. "Realize you're my only first-timer success story this year? Your pic's going on my website, kid. I expect a written testimonial by end of week."

As Sloan embraced the unlikely finisher ("Welcome to the *real* club, Cherry! Drop by the shop, we'll go get that tat together"), Serenata stepped back to check Remington's dot on MMInc. "That's weird," she said aloud.

"What's that, hon?" Cherry asked.

"His dot hasn't moved for twenty minutes."

"Maybe he's stoking up at a water station. Lemme see." Cherry was clearly nonplussed when she saw how many miles the dot had still to go. "Or maybe, you know . . . He's seen the writing on the wall. It's ten to twelve, sweetie."

But Remington would only quit if forced to. He may have left his phone behind, but he had a watch. He'd known perfectly well when he started that run that he didn't have time to complete it before midnight. As the bronze gong crashed at the stroke of twelve, Serenata felt the vibration in her gut.

Multiple runners came in thereafter, and though they all went through the formality of the chin-up, the MC had gone insultingly silent. They were tired, they were wet, they were far fitter than the average bear, but they were not MettleMen. Medical staff and the volunteer issuing space blankets remained, but all the tension of the occasion went slack. Staff began picking up litter.

As several rugged buggies were revving up, Serenata approached a driver. "I'm concerned about my husband, number 1,083?" She pointed at the dot on the app. "He's about thirteen miles back, and he's been in the same place for half an hour."

"Don't you worry, we're off to pick up all the stragglers."

"Could I come with you?"

"Sorry, we have to save the empty seats for the folks we're picking up. They might not have quite made it, but they'll be tired and—understatement—not in the happiest frame of mind."

"Well, could you at least call me when you find him, so I know he's all right?"

"No prob."

She lodged her number on the staffer's phone. Yet when the helpful young man called half an hour later, he said, "Ma'am? We found the number 1,083 ankle bracelet, but not the guy it was attached to. He took it off."

"He's still out there. You have to find him."

"Sorry to get all legalistic on you, but I sorta like, *don't* have to find him. Check out the fine print on the release he signed. This outfit takes no responsibility for mishaps. Now he's removed his tag, which is way against the rules, we really wash our hands."

"But we're talking about an older man, an elderly man, with some serious injuries, who's never done this before, out all by himself—"

"Ma'am, we've all had a long day. Your husband, or at least his bracelet, was our last straggler, and we're heading back to base. Want my advice? If he doesn't show, check the bars. You wouldn't believe how hard some of these guys take not making the cutoff. There's actually a dive out on 86 called 'The DNF.' Popular with the locals."

"The only bar my husband is headed toward is that chin-up bar. He wouldn't want you to pick him up. I bet he hid from the lights of your buggy—"

The call had already terminated.

Dismayed, she wandered the area behind the finish line, where the atmosphere resembled the all-business party's-over of striking a rock concert set. She ducked into the finisher's tent, which had turned into something of a hang. Cherry and her family were gone. The only person she recognized was Bambi, with her back to Serenata, pink-and-black cowboy boots propped on a table. She was knocking back red wine brimming in a large plastic beer cup with another taut, tough-looking young woman.

"You're a trainer, so you know what a bummer it is," Bambi was saying. "And this one, it was like a clinical experiment, right? Your basic silk purse–sow's ear science fair project. Like, he started out, bar none, absolutely the sorriest athlete I ever coached. Know what he clocked in the Saratoga marathon? *Seven twenty-six.*" The other woman hooted. "So you know me: I rise to a challenge. It's fucking compulsive, actually. I spotted this plodder in Saratoga, I couldn't control myself. I figured if I could shove this Clark Kent into a phone booth—well, the bragging rights would have a shelf life longer than Cheez Whiz. A born-again story on that scale could bring in loads more biz. I even had some money riding on it with Sloan—*another* contest the bastard won today. If that guy wasn't such a good fuck, he'd be unbearable."

"As it is . . ." the other woman allowed, wiggling her eyebrows.

"Only thing harder than that boy's deltoids is his dick. Worth buckets of I-told-you-he-couldn't-do-it. Anyway, good thing I made a fair whack of change on the old guy's retainer. Compensation for the wife, wanna know the truth. The geez's biggest handicap. Bitch wrapped around his ankles like a human ball and chain. What a tight, dismal cunt. One of those 'I do ten jumping jacks a day, so I'm one of you!' types. And *whoooo-ee*! Was she jealous."

"I know that drill," the colleague said, taking a swig straight from the bottle. "All you gotta do is walk into the room."

"And they feel all weak and fat and sad."

"'Cause they are." The two toasted.

"And this geez," Bambi said. "He was following me around like a puppy dog. I let him do me once. Just a hand job. No harm done. You know, all this training, you get a little *tense*."

"Those old guys, they're always so grateful. Like you've let them handle a museum piece. That eighty-five-year-old, doing his sixth? He's one of mine. I let him put his hand down my shirt, I swear he almost *cried*."

Serenata had heard enough. "Bambi, Remington is missing. He's taken off his bracelet, and can't be tracked."

Bambi turned, and didn't look in the least caught out. "What am I supposed to do about it?"

"Most of the running course is off-road. I can't take a taxi. Someone has to head back up the trail and find him."

"Lady. First you threaten me, and now you want a favor?"

"Yes," Serenata said.

"Sipping lemonade on the sidelines, maybe you think this event is a walk in the park. It ain't. I'm tired. I'm pretty drunk. I owe you jack. I'm not going anywhere but back to my motel to get laid."

This wasn't the time to mull over what little Bambi had said that was surprising.

In Serenata's PT sessions, the therapist had just started her on the stationary bicycle. Which meant she was barely capable of riding the kind that went somewhere. It was still twenty minutes to one.

Double-checking the race number against the pickup slip, a volunteer handed her Remington's bike with a glance at her cane. "You gonna be all right?"

"That remains to be seen."

Leaning on the handlebar and frame as she had on Carlisle in Manhattan, she wheeled the bike to the finish line. She located an Allen wrench in its onboard tool kit to lower the seat. She found the handout from the athletes' briefing and studied the topographical map of the running course, memorizing the details as best she could. Leaving the collapsible stool, poncho, and umbrella behind, she tucked the hooked end of the cane snugly beside Remington's change of clothes in the tote, looped its long handles diagonally around her shoulder, and arranged the bag on her back. Standing on her left leg, she angled the bike toward the ground, and eased her right leg over the seat. The extension required was excruciating. When she got the bike unsteadily underway, she was reminded that the sole session she'd done on the stationary one at the therapist's had been painful and short.

She began the deserted running course in reverse. After that harridan screeching in her ear loudly enough to trigger temporary hearing loss, the quiet was glorious.

Beyond silence, there was little to savor. At the top and bottom of every orbit of the right pedal—maximum flexion and extension—her pupils flared in dumb shock. Applying torque on the right was a torture, too, so she relied disproportionately on the left leg. Not easy, because the pedals were clip-on, and she didn't have cleated shoes. The frame was too big, and the brakes were touchy. Given the mud alone, she took it slow. At least the course was well lit and well marked, with jagged orange flags flapping in the breeze every ten feet.

She'd be well within her rights to be angry, and somewhere in there she probably was. He was clearly determined to finish unofficially even after missing the cutoff; he'd be picturing himself doing that final chin-up under the moon, with everyone else gone home. He'd unquestionably hidden from the retrieval buggy. But at the rate he was "running" he wouldn't get to that chin-up bar, assuming they left it up, until four a.m. Never mind the fact that he should never have entered today's event in the first place. This whole triathlon debacle had mangled their marriage at the very point in their lives when they most needed to rely on each other. What, she was going to flounce off and find another husband at sixty-two? Not to mention that he should have kept his fucking hands off Bambi's pussy. The trainer was the type to laser away every last hair. Maybe he liked the novelty, all that creepy prepubescent smoothness.

But in times of crisis, anger was usually a phase, and she seemed to have skipped it. Remington was injured, and he was old. He'd never lost the *sound* of a reasonable man, but the presentation of reasonableness was a lifetime habit; lately, his rationality was all tone and no content. He'd grown a little crazy. His still being out in the woods at this time of night when the race was actually over: that was more than a little crazy. Fury would have been beside the point. She was worried, and she was frightened.

One of the distinguishing features of the Mettle was the off-road run. Competing franchises conducted their marathons on tarmac. A narrower dirt trail added challenge. With roots and rocks, footing was trickier. Overtaking was more difficult. If you didn't take advantage of wider sections, you got stuck behind clumps of slower runners, who would—the horror—ruin your time. Yet what Doug Rausing may not have intended was that an off-road running course would also be more challenging for a bicycle. She was glad so many runners had flattened the path and kept the mud down by splattering it all over their clothes, and grateful that the organizers had strung such powerful lights along a route bound to be run by the end of the field in the dark (for once, she was a big fan of the LED). Still, a dirt track was harder to negotiate than a road, and the hills were murder.

At multiple points the trail was intersected by paved roads, where volunteers would have stopped traffic with flags for the runners to cross. The Plan, then: find Remington. Given the awful price she was paying with her knee, convince him—and this was the part of the plan in which she had little faith—to stop. Go together to the nearest intersection and summon an Uber.

Since they were meant to occur every mile, counting deserted water stations gave her a sense of how far she'd advanced; the bike had an odometer, but she couldn't discern the numbers without her reading glasses. Once she'd passed five stations, she shouted, "REM-INGTON!" every minute or two.

The route crossed another two-lane highway. Looking both ways, she coasted to the flags and lights opposite and climbed the small hill through the woods in low gear. "REMINGTON!" Growing impatient after she crested the rise, she allowed herself to gather a little more speed on the descent.

Everything went black. The front tire hit something. The back tire slid sideways and out from under her. As she hit the ground, something rattled and skittered.

She took stock as her eyes adjusted. They'd turned off the lights. Of course. Why keep them blazing when the event was over? Mercifully, she'd landed on her left side. Her shoulder and hip had taken the impact. She hadn't been going fast. Carefully, she sat up. Everything, so far, seemed to work.

The cursed weather system having finally moved on, the sky had cleared. But the moon wasn't much help in a section like this, with trees overhead. The lights being shut off would slow her down, and in woodsy stretches like this one she might have to walk the bike by the light of her phone. She pulled the tote around and grubbed blindly through the bag of Remington's clothes, the cane, restaurant receipts, ibuprofen, the athletes' briefing handout. By feel, she located the granola bar she'd filched from the finishers' tent. Her wallet. Reading glasses. The ubiquitous bottle of water.

No phone.

That distinctive skittering.

Groping in the pitch-dark, she patted the ground all around her, trying to scan systematically in widening concentric circles. Mud. Rocks. Leaves. Bicycle. She needed the light on the phone to find the fucking phone.

It was an obligatory turn in the contemporary thriller, right? To keep the audience from jeering, "Why didn't she just use *Google Maps*?" you had to get rid of the phone.

Serenata spent a good ten minutes groping the vicinity. But the one thing she couldn't do with this knee was crawl. In fact, the joint replacement handbook said that you might never kneel comfortably again for the rest of your life. In the immediate area where she'd fallen off the bike, it was dark enough that the phone could have been glaringly obvious in daylight and not far away after all and she still wouldn't see it.

Resigned, she wiped her muddy hands on the canvas tote before shoving it to her back. Righting the bike—she wasn't used to one that didn't have a name—she used the machine as a rolling walker to eke her way toward the patch of moonlight at the bottom of the hill. "REMINGTON!"

This was turning into an even bigger fiasco than it had started out. In brighter sections she could still ride, but through the forested ones she could only half-walk, or use the bike as a giant skateboard, as she had on the West Side. "REMINGTON!" The flickering orange flags were mockingly jolly.

At last she emerged into a clearing, where the path striking across a meadow was wide, smooth, and flat. She was in the process of awkwardly mounting the bike for the straightaway when a rumple in the vista snagged her eye. A rumple like a person.

In the middle of the path, he was laid out in the cruciform pose he'd assumed on the floor after his first twenty-mile run—a posture she'd then found comic. Scootering like fury, she cast the bike aside and stooped. In the light of the moon, his complexion was blue. He looked dead.

She found a pulse. But it was weak and erratic. When she patted his cheeks and kissed his forehead, he was unresponsive. She lifted his eyelids, but had no idea what she was supposed to look for.

She should never have gone on this fool's errand. She wasn't accustomed to her new great big uselessness, the pure burden of her postsurgical self. She should have called 911 from the MettleMan site and left rescue to professionals. But regrets were no help now.

One of those intersections with a B-road was less than a mile back. She covered him with the fleece from his change of clothing and balled up her sweatshirt to cushion his head. She left him the granola bar and the bottle of water. On the way back to the intersection, in her haste in one of the dark sections, she had another spill. Now the front wheel had bent, and wouldn't spin past the brakes. She grabbed the cane from the tote and hightailed the last few hundred yards in a lurching sprint. Lo, there was such a thing as pushing beyond a barrier of pain that would seem impassable; when the stakes were high enough, you could indeed streak straight through the stony edifice of the Grand Coulee Dam. In retrospect, it was astonishing that the oncoming car stopped, rather than swerving around the wild woman on the meridian—who was waving a hospital-issue cane, of all things—and stepping on the gas. She must have looked demented.

AFTERWORD

The "generation" was a conceptual artifice. The word hammered hard brackets within a flowing, borderless continuum, as if trying to contain discrete sections of river. A cohort as large as Serenata's, too, would encompass such a range of people that any perceived homogeneity would have to be imposed: a further artifice. Nevertheless, boomers, as they were known, had secured the dubious reputation for denial in the face of aging. In their clinging to fugitive youth, they had made themselves the butt of many a younger stand-up—though chances were that Tommy March, or Chet Mason, wouldn't relish decrepitude any more than boomers did. What was to like?

This idea that in historical terms boomers were unusually deluded about the inexorability of their decay now struck Serenata as unfair. For the abundance of human existence, no one got old. They died. Mass aging was a recent phenomenon, and in joining the "old-old" on any scale she and her peers would be pioneers. Besides, Serenata Terpsichore had never herself grown old before, so it made a certain sense that she wouldn't be very good at it.

What would seem to be required was humility. But this brand of humility wasn't the sort you graciously embraced. It was foisted on you. You grew humble because you had *been humbled*. Aging was an experience to which you succumbed, and you adapted to new circumstances not because you were shrewd, but because you hadn't any choice. *So go ahead*, she beamed to her younger brethren. *Make fun. Of our self-deceit, of our vanity that survives anything to be vain about. Your time will come.*

She and her husband had been humbled. Though Remington had recovered from his heart attack, his cardiologist discouraged any jogging whatsoever. Swimming the doctor restricted to the breast- or backstroke. *Mild* biking was okay (although since Lake Placid Remington had developed an odd aversion to his nameless bicycle, which Sloan had kindly retrieved from the trail; its master only repaired that warped front wheel in order to put it on eBay). Yet Remington engaged in none of these muted activities. Tommy was right: once you'd sampled the extremes, the notion of going back to "grandma" moderation was less attractive than quitting.

His wife's recuperation from her knee-replacement replacement was even more arduous than recovery from the original surgery, and rendered less satisfactory results. Extension and flexion were further reduced. Flaming pain on stairs was apparently permanent. But after a couple of years they could go for walks. Sometimes lingering and contemplative walks, though her gait evidenced a slight hitch until the left knee was also replaced, at which point both legs were a tad shorter. Serenata lost the ripple in her arms, and Remington restored the swell at his waist, but worse things happened at sea, and their frailty as it advanced stirred a compensatory spousal compassion. The scenery during these local perambulations was repetitive, but they could talk, and the boats and wildlife along the river still displayed more variety than high-knees interval training ever had.

They lived modestly—again, of necessity. Health insurance co-pays and the expenses of Remington's bygone obsession had eaten up a goodly proportion of the equity left over from the sale of the house in Albany. As the ban on "mimicry" spread, lucrative audio-book jobs grew rare. For a while, before her Social Security kicked in, Serenata was reduced to writing online college admission essays for students to plagiarize. Ignominious work in its way, but in the process she learned a great deal more about bee keeping, *King Lear*, and invasive plants. More fodder for walks.

With time on his hands again, Remington spearheaded the campaign in Hudson to convert the town's streetlamps to LEDs with a low Kelvin rating, heavy shielding, and a housing in keeping with downtown's nineteenth-century architecture. Substituting socially for the tri club, the small committee of refreshingly mixed-race volunteers included the civic-minded Ethan Crick and, more surprisingly, Brandon Abraham, who took early retirement from Albany's DOT and along with his dazzling wife bought a place in Hudson; Brandon and Remington soon became drinking buddies. Learning from his mistakes, Remington urged the committee to approach the town council in a spirit of camaraderie and shared self-interest.

Once the new energy-saving public illumination was installed, it noticeably increased tourism and vitalized Hudson's fledgling nightlife. Other towns sent emissaries to study the comely designs, returning to their municipalities with enthusiasm for the faux gaslights' warm nocturnal ambience. When the Hudson town council subsequently resolved to make artists' studios out of the dilapidated shoreline fishing shacks in which Margaret Alabaster had cleaned sturgeon, they went straight to Remington for the vetting of blueprints. In one meeting about a less historically respectful proposal, he forgot himself and slammed a hand on the table. When he fell about apologizing, the council was befuddled. After he told them his old DOT story, slamming the table to bring the boisterous group to order became a tireless running joke.

Fully recovered from rhabdomyolysis, Tommy developed a cool disdain for contemporaries who took their fitness regimes too seriously, this scornful phase marked by knocking her fake Fitbit behind the bedstead (still plastered with DOUBT NOT—a flexible motto) and not bothering to grub down amid the dust bunnies to retrieve it. For working up a sweat, a tango class proved genuinely enjoyable. Under Serenata's tutelage, the girl became a popular choice for gaming VO; she had an ideally lithe, lanky figure for roles grown ever more physical. Since the knees made this work, too, out of the question, any jobs that came Serenata's way from old contacts she threw to her neighbor. Tommy soon moved to Brooklyn, which was a loss, but she returned to her ailing mother often enough that the two neighbors stayed friends.

When Serenata ran into Cherry DeVries at Price Chopper, the woman's cart was mounded with brownies and chips, as well as diet soda and Weight Watchers chicken pot pies—the American yin and yang. Cherry's proportions had redistributed along the lines of her Before picture. But she waxed so eloquent about the year she'd devoted to triathlon that its transient effect on her figure seemed immaterial. "Honestly," she enthused, after thanking Serenata for being so generous with her hospitality back in the day, "that whole thing—not just the race itself, but all the training—I swear, it was the most wonderful experience of my life. Ever since, my kids treat me different, and even Sarge does. He *respects* me. He's never laid a hand on me again."

"He may be afraid of you," Serenata said. "Ever consider entering another one?"

"Oh, heaven's no." She raised the double-*M* orange tattoo on her left forearm. "I proved what I needed to, to my family, and to myself. I can't tell you how much happier I've been ever since. Now, you take care of yourself, sweetie."

Score one for MettleMan.

Remington resumed visits with his father, who tactfully refrained from rubbing his son's nose in the calamity of Lake Placid. They played a lot of cribbage. The couple's investment of time and tenderness amounted to the purchase of an insurance policy, which when Griff dropped cleanly dead at ninety-four paid off. They would miss him, but they wouldn't berate themselves for having neglected the cantankerous but secretly soft-touch old man while he was alive.

Remington's well-off brother in Seattle was happy for his sibling to inherit their father's house. The property proved a godsend when Valeria finally left her party-pooper husband and needed an affordable bolt-hole in which to raise six kids. Grandparental babysitting came with the territory, something of a trial, though exposure to sane, secular relatives could help keep the children from growing up into brainwashed nut jobs.

Yet after giving up on homeschooling out of sheer exhaustion, Valeria grew disenchanted with the church, whose born-again branch in Hudson was more cliquish than Rhode Island's Shining Path, and thus too reminiscent of the playgrounds of yore where she'd been cold-shouldered. After her brief but diligent period of heavy drinking, the local chapter of Alcoholics Anonymous proved sufficiently evangelical to fill the void, while also providing just the right combination of self-pity, superiority, and chiding parental proselytizing (her mother, so went the theory, drank too much wine). Why, the second cult substituted so neatly for the first that Serenata wondered if her daughter had forced herself to become a drunk for six months purely to get in. At least the tales Valeria brought back from meetings, lurid with the depths to which dipsos can sink, beat all that insipid *joy, joy, joy, joy down in my heart* by a mile.

Alas, her older children had been indoctrinated a bit too well, and routinely threatened their lapsed parent that if she didn't once again embrace Christ the Lord as her Savior she was going to hell. There was rough justice in Valeria herself being eternally Jesused at.

Nancee remained wary, inward, and weird about food, but she did get into SUNY at New Paltz on a track scholarship, even if a remarkable gift for running in circles would lead to something of an occupational dead end. By contrast, her brother Logan got early admission to Rensselaer; as a chemical engineer, he'd have his pick of jobs. Nonetheless, it was a mystery how such a whip-smart-kid could still believe that the human race shared the Earth with dinosaurs.

Having lost too many customers to the ER, Deacon wasn't prone to moral soul-searching, but he did question the viability of an entrepreneurial venture whose consumer base was self-eliminating. When Chet Mason became Sloan's right-hand man for refurbishing classic cars, Deacon assumed Chet's vacated barista position. The work was suitably low-exertion, and allowed Deacon to languidly hold court. But between beginning to lose his hair early and the downshift of metabolism many men experience in their thirties, Deacon put on a little weight and was in danger of losing his looks. Astonishingly, after dating Bambi Buffer for a few months, if only to goad his father, Deacon, of all people, caught the fitness bug.

Deacon and Bambi didn't last, of course. But when the trainer stopped into his café after their listless breakup, he gleaned news that for his mother should have been nastily satisfying. Rather young for skeletal decay, which must have been hastened by the pounding she'd given her body for decades, Bambi had been diagnosed with "degenerative spondy-somethingorother": a vertebra had edged out of alignment, and the consequent impingement of her sciatic nerves put her in a disabling pain that precluded running, swimming, biking, and weights—anything, in fact, other than sitting or lying abed. The condition would only get worse. Were she eventually to submit to back surgery, spinal fusion would still place marathons, triathlons, and probably her business to boot firmly in the past. Behold, a short course in *limits*.

But Serenata didn't find this turn of the wheel satisfying in the slightest. However ephemeral Bambi's living sculpture proved, the trainer had created a thing of beauty, and the passing of any beauty from this world was nothing to celebrate. The woman was bound to be miserable, doubly so, from both the pain and the melting of her artwork. Any increase in the quantity of misery in this world was nothing to celebrate, either.

Having mourned a similar loss, Serenata was inclined to identify rather than crow. To the casual eye she hadn't changed all that drastically now that she no longer devoted ninety tiresome minutes of every evening to keeping in shape. But she knew the difference. She was an increment thicker. When she stood and rested the tips of her fingers on a thigh, it was no longer firm. She missed the rippling play of light across her shoulders, but arthritis in her wrists now ruled out push-ups. Her legs were marred with vertical scars. Her calves failed to form commas at tension. She remembered her body of a few years before with the wistful, faintly puzzled fondness of a good friend with whom, through no fault on either party's part, she'd lost touch.

She sometimes remembered that exchange in the Gold Street studio, when the engineer referred to "in your day," and she'd responded with playful injury, "It's not my day?" No. It was not her day. She had been fortunate to have been strong, energetic, even fetching, and for decades; as the director had observed, she was fortunate to have ever had a day. But that part of her life, which entailed being looked at, if largely looking at herself, was over. It was fair. Now other people got to have their day. For your day to be over might have been disappointing, but it wasn't tragic.

For the key to the "bucket list" wasn't to systematically check off its to-do items, but to bring yourself to throw the list away. There was a thrill to letting go of the whole shebang—reluctantly, then gleefully.

There was a thrill to dying by degrees. She advanced toward apathy with open arms. She wasn't about to advertise the fact—the argument wasn't worth having—but Serenata was not obliged to give a flying fig about climate change, species extinction, or nuclear proliferation. She had her eye on the door, and had every hope of escaping a great human reckoning almost certainly in the offing. It had been too long since the last one, and a correction of sorts was overdue. All civilizations contained the seeds of their own collapse, and dodging the homicidal havoc lurking right around the corner, merely by dint of having been born a bit earlier than the fresh-faced unfortunates, would qualify as sly. She no longer fought a misanthropy that was increasingly blithe, even whimsical, and which as she approached her own oblivion was shedding its hypocrisy. The very best thing about getting old was basking in this great big not-giving-a-shit. Younger folks like Tommy would decry her happy boredom with all the looming threats that exercised them as criminally irresponsible and unforgivably callous. But Serenata had earned her ennui. Marvelously, nothing she did exerted any appreciable influence on the rest of the world. Nothing she'd ever recorded professionally had changed anything or anyone a jot. Her inconsequence made the planet safer for everyone. She didn't like other people much, nor they her. She didn't plan on worrying about the fate of her fellows as she met her own. Aging was proving one long holiday. She was harmless—although she'd be the first to agree that she and her heedless ilk should probably be denied the vote. The future didn't need her, and she didn't need it. Others behind her would discover it soon enough: the bliss of sublime indifference.

Their lives were almost over, and the finality had a sweet side. A burden had been lifted. The decisions still to be made were few. If the main story was over, all that remained was wrap-up—the luxurious and largely gratuitous tying up of loose ends, like looping satin ribbon around a Tiffany box. Wastefully, Remington had grown convinced that he had something to prove at the very age at which he should have been discarding the whole silly idea of proving anything to anyone. Because, really: Who cared? In due course, no one would remember that they'd lived at all, much less would anyone remember whatever they'd accomplished or failed to accomplish. (Owing to plague, an asteroid, or the sun frying into a red giant, the same amnesia would inexorably obliterate Madonna, Abraham Lincoln, Stephen Hawking, Leonardo da Vinci, Aristotle, the most recent winner of *Dancing with the Stars*, and—sorry, Logan—Jesus Christ. So there was no reason to take being forgotten about personally.) Acceptance that their lives had now mostly been lived didn't have to be depressing, either. The recognition could involve a reflective aspect, a wonderment, a cherishing of all that had gone before.

Although Serenata found growing old astonishing, she knew the surprise to be ordinary; what was exceptional were those rare codgers who accepted their disintegration as only to be expected. Besides, having been nonexistent before one's conception was also astonishing; being here, when before one had not been, was astonishing; then to be here no longer: fine, yes, altogether astonishing. But perhaps nothingness was the easiest state to conceive, the most natural state—the state that required no imagination. In which case, not having been here before was *not* astonishing, while being here was; and thereafter, to once again not be here was not astonishing, either. The hard part, then, was the in-between: the long slow exhale from being to void. How much kinder it would have been, to turn off, like an appliance. The gradual, drawn-out corruption of the body while its host was still trapped inside was a torture of a sort they would have contrived at Guantanamo, or Bergen-Belsen. Every old age was an Edgar Allan Poe story.

So she balanced her grief with a rudimentary gratitude. The

organism in which she sheltered continued to serve its primary animal purposes. With the help of new prescription glasses, it could see: the birds taking wing as the Hudson shimmered in the setting sun; the face of her husband, in which she could still discern the young civil engineer who'd extolled feverishly, "Transport is massively emotional!" It could hear: Miles Davis's *Kind of Blue*, or Remington's views on the merits of the traffic circle, which were ever so much more engaging than his opining about *tri*. If not as quickly as before, it got her from place to place: to one more truly atrocious production at the Hudson Playhouse; through a wine-tasting tour; home. It could feel: the breeze tickling the hairs of her arms at that temperature just before you reached for a sweater; her husband's body, which had worn in perfect tandem with hers so that the parts still faultlessly grooved together in bed, like the chain and cluster on a bike, which eroded in such concert that to replace either, you had to replace them both.

Although no one should have taken for granted even such crude functionality beyond the age of fifty, the culture of the time continued to apply far higher performance standards. More than ever, social status was determined by fat-to-muscle ratio, definition, and belt-notching feats of stamina, so that endurance events of every description did nothing but multiply. According to Deacon, triathlons—even the ultras—had grown passé. Obstacle-course races, or OCRs, were "way cooler," he said. "Crawling under live wires. Lugging hundred-pound sandbags up thirty-degree gradients. Rope climbing, spear chucking. Mud up to the eyeballs. Finish one of those courses, you're so wiped you literally can't think. I'm serious. After that Spartan? I tried to log into my bank account, and I couldn't answer the security questions. I spent five minutes trying to remember the name of my high school."

"Sounds great," she said. The irony went right past him.

Meanwhile, the use of artificial intelligence accelerated, just as Silicon Valley had foretold. Robots that could learn, create, and make informed decisions had eliminated the few remaining manufacturing jobs in New England, and had reduced agricultural employment to a handful of supervisors on local farms. The latest wave of AI was duplicating the work of the professional class: medicine, accountancy, law. Any number of paintings, popular songs, and even novels generated by sophisticated algorithms had become commercial hits.

"I was a little embarrassed about it," Serenata said on a ritual riverside stroll one early summer evening, "so I don't think I told you that I ordered a copy of that computer-generated best seller, *Amygdala*. I was just curious."

"Understandably," Remington said. "What did you make of it?"

"I don't know whether to find this exciting or mortifying, but in all honesty I got pretty hooked. I was obviously aware that underneath it all was just a formula, but the formula works. I wanted to know what happened."

"Here's the test: Did the resolution of the plot surprise you?"

She turned to him with a defeated expression. "*Yes.*"

He laughed. With its deepening crags, his face increasingly resembled Samuel Beckett's. "What about the prose?"

"It was fine!" she said in dismay. "I wouldn't call it great poetry, but there weren't any gaffes. No *oh, God, that's such a terrible metaphor*, no dialogue where it's like, *no one would ever say that in real life*. They've taught it to write prose you just don't especially notice. Actually, I gather that they've fed AI the classics, and computers have also learned to generate distinctive styles. Now, that's real 'mimicry.' Pretty soon we'll have new Hemingway, new Graham Greene, new Dickens. We won't be able to tell the difference."

"I have no doubt that AI could design a more efficient system of traffic flow than I ever did. If it hasn't already, AI could competently replace the entire Albany DOT."

"One employee in particular," Serenata said. "Anyway, I was thinking. About Deacon and his OCRs. Not to bring up a touchy subject, but you and MettleMan. All the hard-body advertisements, Main Streets taken over by gyms. Well, it makes a certain dumb sense, doesn't it? It's as if we're swapping places. Machines have become better people. What's left to do? People become better machines."

He squeezed her shoulder. "You may be onto something there. You know, I'm getting hungry, and the light's failing. What say we turn around?" When she agreed, he peered into her face and said apropos of nothing, "You're still a very, very handsome woman."

"To you," she said.

"What else matters?"

They kissed. Two runners rushed around them, looking annoyed; the elderly couple in the way would be ruining their *time*.

"We're grossing them out," Serenata said.

"Young people don't have sex anymore. They're too tired."

"You're one to talk. For two fucking years you barely touched me, you jerk."

"Well, then. I have some catching up to do."

Hand in hand, they made their way back toward the house. There was a heron, and there were turtles. There would be flank steak, already marinating in the fridge, and a pricier than usual Burgundy that she'd been saving: everything to look forward to, and nothing to dread. Dusk was the very time of day that she'd often squandered upstairs, grunting and panting with *The Big Bang Theory* in the background. When Serenata crossed into menopause, she'd been delighted to see the back of periods. What the hell, aging out of burpees had its upside, too.

Read on for an excerpt from
Lionel Shriver's new novel,

Should We Stay or Should We Go

COMING JUNE 2021

1

The Soap-Dish Box

"Was I supposed to cry?" Kay cast off her heavy, serviceable dark wool coat, for this was one of those interminable Aprils that perpetuated the dull chill of January. The only change that spring had sprung was to have stirred her complacent acceptance of wintertime's bite to active umbrage.

"There aren't any rules." Cyril filled the kettle.

"In respect to certain gritty rites of passage, I rather think there are. And please, I know it's a bit early, but I don't want *tea*." Kay went straight for the dry Amontillado in the fridge. She'd had a nip of wine at the reception and didn't fancy going backwards to English Breakfast. A drink at home was an indulgence at five-thirty p.m., and she was using the technicality of occasion to break the household injunction—unwritten, but no less cast-iron for that—against ever cracking open a bottle before eight p.m. Any impression that she was drowning her sorrows was pure conceit. In truth, the sensation that the afternoon's landmark juncture left in her stomach felt nothing like grief. It was more like that vague, indeterminate squirrelling half-way between hunger and indigestion.

To Kay's surprise, Cyril abandoned the kettle and joined her at the table with a second glass, remembering to slice and twist two wedges of lime. Had one spouse been responsible for establishing the eight p.m.

watershed in the first place, it would have been Cyril, though the couple's intertwined habits went far enough back that no one was keeping track.

"I thought I'd at least feel relieved," she said, clunking her cheap wine tumbler from Barcelona dully against the one sitting on the table in a lacklustre toast. Serviceable, like the coat, the tall, narrow glasses achieved a perfect proportion of which much fine crystal fell short. More betrayal of her inadequacy: that she could consider the geometry of glassware at a time like this.

"You don't feel relieved?"

"To be honest, I've looked forward to this turn of the page for at least ten years. Which may be appalling but won't surprise you. Now that what used to be called 'the inevitable' is upon us—"

"Maybe we should call it 'the optional' now," Cyril said. "Or 'the infinitely delayable.' 'The on-second-thought, maybe-we-can-do-that-next-week, love.'"

"Well, I don't feel any lighter, any sense of release. I only feel leaden and flat. My father sucked so much life from everyone around him by the time he passed. Maybe he used up even the miserable amount of energy we'd need to celebrate the fact that he's dead at last."

"What a waste," Cyril said.

"Yes, but it would have been one thing if the waste were restricted to the one life of Godfrey Poskitt and the discrete misfortune that it ended badly. The waste has been so much more ruinous than that. My poor mother, the carers, even our kids, before they stopped visiting. I'm so glad I gave them permission to give up the pretence of being loving grandchildren. Because what was the point? Most of the time he didn't know who they were, and all they got for going out of their way was abuse. He was physically so unpleasant as well. My mother and I tried, but managing the nappies alone was such a trial, because he fought and kicked a great deal, and sometimes, which was mortifying, got a soft little erection—honestly, *my own father.* So we'd put off changing him, and he often smelt."

"In spite of all that, it was decent of two of his grandchildren to make an appearance today."

"Of course Simon came. He's so duty-bound and hyper-responsible that for pity's sake at twenty-six he's almost middle-aged. And whilst I appreciated that she showed up, if only for my mother, naturally Hayley had to be late—allowing for the usual showy entrance and calling attention to herself. Why, I reckon she planned it, watching a bit of telly beforehand, just to ensure she'd not be boringly on time. Roy's absconding in the end was predictable as well. Being a grandson is simply one more undertaking that he can't follow through on."

"As for the waste," Cyril said, looping back, "you omitted a conspicuous casualty. Yourself."

Best that her husband said it. "I hesitate to calculate how many cumulative years of my life that man's infinite dotage managed to destroy."

"At least you miraculously managed to keep working. It was the leisure time your father hoovered up. The evenings and weekends, the early mornings, the emergency trips to Maida Vale in the middle of the night: all time you might have spent with me."

"So you're the injured party?"

"Merely one more."

Restless, Kay got up to sweep some crumbs from the Corian beside the sink, casting a mournful eye at the half-built would-be conservatory off the kitchen: a work in progress for the last two years and another victim sucked into her father's whirlpool of limitless need. These days the children seemed so envious, but she and Cyril had bought this house in 1972, once they'd found out Kay was pregnant with Hayley and needed more room—and in those days, not only was the whole country a wreck, but so was Lambeth, which was why such a grand structure (if south of the river) had been within the means of an NHS nurse and a GP. These three-storeys-and-loft-to-boot had only looked grand from the outside; good gracious, "fixer-upper" didn't begin to describe it. Now that nineteen years of cost overruns and inconvenience were at last rounding on a habitable property, the kids tended to forget having to step over clatters of raw lumber on the way to the loo or shaking crumbles of plasterboard from their hair before school. They put out of mind, too, the warnings in their childhoods about hurrying home from the Tube, because the neighbourhood in those days was beyond dodgy. No, they didn't see a financial stretch for a young couple on the public payroll, who took on a considerable risk that the whole tumbledown interior would collapse ceiling-to-floor like a portable coffee cup. All the children saw now was the imposing, respectable edifice of Mum and Dad's House, a conventional projection of the establishment that they'd never afford for themselves, what with interest rates at fifteen percent; and Roy, if she didn't miss her guess, already saw a kip he might inherit. Roy was always looking for shortcuts.

Now with Dad gone, presumably she'd the spare time to finish the conservatory, yet her appetite for the project had fled. She was already fifty-one. How much longer would they live here? More starkly, how much longer would they live? Kay had imagined that she'd crossed the signal threshold of fifty with aplomb—*Look at me! I'm sophisticated about the passage of time, and this new decade doesn't bother me in the slightest!*—but such morbid thoughts had never entered her head in her forties.

"I wonder if I should have gone back home with my mother, after the reception," Kay said with misgiving. "Percy said he'd go back to keep her company, but I know my brother. He won't stay long."

"Haven't you had enough of all this sacrifice?" Cyril said. "You women! You complain about how you're always the ones taking care of everybody. Then when you get a single moment to yourselves, you hop up and volunteer to take care of someone else."

"We only, as you put it, 'volunteer' because *no one else will do it*!"

Her anger took them both aback. Kay regrouped. "I'm sorry. You know it's not as if I never asked Percy to help. But he lives that bit further out in Tunbridge Wells, and of course he was terribly busy betraying his wife and children."

"That's not entirely fair."

"I'm not saying that he contrived to be gay purely to escape his filial duties. But he's definitely *used* being gay. 'Oh, I can't mind Dad this weekend because he's obviously uncomfortable with my coming out.' Well, of course he's 'uncomfortable,' you git, the man was born in 1897!"

"The problem is much more institutional than sticking the women with bedpan duty," Cyril said, drawing up and sounding more like his regular authoritative self. "Central government needs to take fuller responsibility for social care. It shouldn't fall on you, your mother, or your extended family—"

"Well, it did, and it does, and it will when you and I fall apart as well. Even the slightest helping hand from your local council—like making up your bed, never mind chasing you down the street when you're raving? Qualification for homecare is means-tested, and my father was a solicitor."

"True, the means-testing is pretty brutal—"

"The savings threshold above which the council won't wipe your bum is a measly twenty grand—which is far more cash than Mum has left after all those carers, but she still wouldn't qualify for any benefits because she has the house. If you've stashed nothing away, or next to nothing? The council picks up the whole tab. How do you like that, Mister Socialist? You slave away your whole life like my father, carrying your own financial weight and supporting your family, and then when you collapse the state says you're on your own. Do nothing, earn nothing, and save nothing—make absolutely no provision for yourself—and the state takes care of you for free, soup to nuts. Talk about moral hazard! Obviously, anyone who does anything, earns anything, and saves anything is a berk."

"You're ranting. And you know I think social care should be a universal benefit, just like the NHS."

"Uh-huh. Make it universal, and then the same responsible people who earn anything at all will still pay for their own social care, as well as everyone else's social care, with such sky-high taxes that they can't afford a pot of jam. You're the one who had to go to that big Trafalgar demonstration against the poll tax—which would have raised money for social care and a great deal else."

"Don't start. The poll tax was regressive and you know it. And thanks to protests like Trafalgar, the 'community charge' is well dead and buried. Besides, I doubt on this of all evenings you're in the best frame of mind to design complex government policy."

"All that grooming—clipping those thick, gnarly toenails, pinching the mucus from his hairy nostrils, going through whole boxes of wet wipes cleaning his bum . . ." Kay had started to range the slate floor, for one of the advantages of having opened up the kitchen and dining area was its improved capacity for pacing. "I can't tell you how awkward it is to brush someone else's teeth, and then he'd bite . . . The chasing and corralling and undressing . . . I was halfway between a daughter and a sheepdog. The eternal surveillance, because we had to watch him like a two-year-old, lest he cut himself, or drink Fairy Liquid, or set the house on fire . . . The spoon-feeding, the wiping the muck from his beard . . . The cajoling, for hours on end, to coax him down from the ladder to the loft, of all places . . .

"Well, paying for all that care for my father alone would have cost the state a fortune. Collectively, caring for all the other train wrecks like him would cost the state the earth, and that's why it's *not* a universal benefit. Honestly, in order to control him, it took the three of us, me, Mum, *and* the hired helper—that is, to *barely* control him. The real problem isn't how that kind of walking decomposition is financed, but that it's financed at all. My father suffered a good four years of steady deterioration, followed by a solid ten of nothing but degradation. Whoever pays for it, it's a grotesque waste of money, and also a waste of younger people's time—my time, my mother's time—that is, the centre cut of our lives whilst we're in still good health, still sane, and still capable of joy. Waste, you said? *Nothing* but waste, and for what? He should have died when he was first diagnosed. Then I could have come home from his funeral and cried my eyes out."

Kay plunked back in the kitchen chair, eyes dry. Why, they were so dry they hurt.

Cyril scrutinized his wife. This seeming stoicism of hers was uncharacteristic. Of the two of them, she was the far more impassioned. He was the methodical thinker, which meant that others sometimes mistook him for cold-hearted. Nevertheless, she was not an emotional liar. Eight days ago, when the call from Maida Vale awoke them at four a.m., Kay had also been matter-of-fact. The news hadn't been unexpected. Apparently they'd had difficulty feeding his father-in-law for weeks, because the poor fellow had trouble swallowing. (That's what happened: the brain became so dysfunctional that it forgot how to close the epiglottis. At its most extreme end, the disease delivered its coup de grace: the brain forgot how to breathe.) After Kay finished talking to her mother in the hallway, she lodged the cordless phone in its cradle at their bedside and announced without ceremony, *"Dead."* She'd slid under the duvet and gone straight to sleep.

"You can't stir up any feeling for him at all, then?" Cyril asked. "Sorrow, a moment of nostalgia?" As of her shockingly unsentimental pragmatism last week, it was a little too easy to picture Kay noticing that he himself had just dropped dead beside her and then harrumphing to her side of the mattress with relief: finally, a certain someone would no longer crank the bedclothes systematically to the left, and she'd have the duvet to herself.

"No, I feel absolutely nothing, and I've tried," she said. "This dying by degrees, it cheats everyone. I feel as if he's been dead for years. I've never been allowed a proper bereavement, either. But I shouldn't feel sorry for myself, because for my mum it's been so much worse. My father continually accused her of stealing his things, or of rummaging through his legal papers. More than once he called the police, and he could have periods of lucidity long enough to persuade an officer at the door that the strange woman in the sitting room really was a con artist or a thief. I can't possibly appreciate how painful it's been for her. I'm sure I must have told you that during the last few years he forgot their entire marriage. Instead he fixated on 'Adelaide,' remember? The sweetheart he married after he came back from the Great War. They hadn't been married two years when Adelaide died; maybe it was influenza. Think how it made my mother feel, her marriage of fifty-five years obliterated by an eighteen-month relationship from 1920. It would be as if in my dotage I eternally pined for David Whatshisname—"

"David Castleveter," Cyril filled in sourly.

"See, you remember my old boyfriends better than I do. So my dad kept calling for Adelaide and accusing my mother of having kidnapped his bride. He thought Mum was some jealous harridan who'd trapped him in this strange house. I've seen the portrait, a black-and-white kept high up on his study bookshelf, and Adelaide was a stunner—more of a knockout than my mother ever was, to be honest, and for Mum I'm sure that didn't help."

"Can't you compartmentalize?" Cyril poured her another half glass. He'd heard about Godfrey's demented obsession with Adelaide before, but this rehearsal seemed to be getting something out of his wife's system. "You seemed to have a real soft spot for your father before his decline. Can't you keep your memory of him in his heyday in a separate place?"

"Nice idea, but memory is too fragile. You can't mangle it like that. My memory of what he once was is like a delicate daddy longlegs that the last ten years have stepped on. I think about my father, and I can't control the pictures that pop in my head. Naked below the waist, purple with rage, and covered in faeces: one of my favourites."

"I still have a fair recollection of Godfrey when he was younger. Bit straight-laced, and a Tory, but we forgive our elders their misjudgements out of respect."

"You forgave no such thing. You two got into terrible rows when Thatcher came in—by which point he'd already lost a marble or two, so it wasn't a fair fight."

"There. You do remember something from before all the marbles rolled away."

"My mother is convinced that she brought this calamity on herself."

"How so?"

"Well, maybe my father really was devastated by losing Adelaide, because he didn't remarry until . . . I think it was 1936. He was a fine-looking chap in his day—trim figure, high cheekbones, that flaming head of hair he kept to the very end. My mum's job as a receptionist for his practice wouldn't have paid much, and marrying a solicitor seemed to offer a security she could only dream of. The only reason a single young woman like my mother would have worked back then was that her family hadn't the means to keep her—and her father was a hand-to-mouth shopkeeper."

"Spare us Maggie's humble origins routine, bab. Your upbringing was altogether prosperous, and you know it."

Back in the day, pompous Britons would lay claim to a distant relative with aristocratic credentials—a baroness, a duke—the better to bootstrap themselves up a social tier in the eyes of their fellows. More recently, the broadly middle-class populace laid pompous claim instead to relations who were coal miners or steel workers. But with a father employed first by Longbridge and then by British Leyland, Cyril the Brummie always won the contest over whose background was the more depressing—although he tended to play down the fact that by the time his father retired automotive workers were handsomely paid. Moreover, he'd invented all manner of explanations for why he'd rigorously erased his Brummie accent after shifting to London from Birmingham, but the real reason was simple: shame. Which made any rare regional residue like 'bab,' an endearment Cyril reserved exclusively for his wife, all the more precious.

"May I finish, oh salt of the earth?" Kay said. "In the mid-1930s the economy was still crap. And of course my mother was flattered by an older man's attentions. I think she did truly fall for him, but in that overawed way you get infatuated with an imposing professional who's your boss. He represented a port in the storm. The eighteen-year age difference must have seemed more an advantage than a sacrifice."

"Young people have no imagination," Cyril said.

"Exactly," Kay said. "She might have considered the consequences for their children—since for Percy and me, our father always seemed like an old man; little did we know how young he still was. Our classmates' fathers had all fought in 'the war,' and we tended to conceal the fact that ours had fought in the other one. Still, the last thing my mother would have calculated at her wedding is that when her groom turned eighty, she'd be only sixty-two, looking right smart for a woman getting on, and stuck with a basket case who suddenly can't remember who's prime minister. And since almost no one lived terribly long in the thirties, the very, *very* last thing my mother would have calculated is that when he finally died at ninety-flipping-four, she'd be seventy-six, with bad hips, after having squandered a decade and a half on toilet duty, cursed and vilified for her efforts, mind you—only to be looking at the next tranche of her life and wondering if the same thing is about to happen to her!"

"I'm not accusing you of being self-centred," Cyril said gently, touching her hand. "But are you crying for your mother, or for you and me?"

"Oh, I have no idea," Kay said, wiping her eyes, on this day of all days relieved to be crying over someone, if only herself.

"Are you by any chance also angry at me?" Cyril asked tentatively. "For not covering for you more often, with your father?"

"No, no, we've talked about this. Please stop castigating yourself. One of us had to be here for Hayley whilst she was still in school, and someone had to remember to pick up a loaf of bread. You surely remember that those few times you relieved me my father got dreadfully agitated. Maybe he perceived you as a rival for *Adelaide*'s affections. Besides, you run up to Birmingham to check on your own ageing parents practically every month. And who knows what will happen to my mother . . . I'm utterly wrung-out, and how much of this overseeing of corruption can we take? It's as if our full-time job in future is watching a fruit bowl rot."

Cyril waited a contemplative beat. "Should your mother also prove long-lived, I can see why you're worried about going through this all over again. After all, Percy has only lent a hand by planning the funeral once the truly hard part was dispensed—"

"And what a hash he made of that. He should have talked Mum out of the main sanctuary at St Mark's, which must seat five hundred people. It looked ridiculous. All my father's friends are dead. His siblings are dead. He'd alienated his nieces and nephews by going doolally, and most of them are also too old to attend a service in North

London without walking frames. No one was there. It looked less like a congregation than a tour group."

"I can also see why you're worried about having to take care of my parents," Cyril resumed patiently. "But my sister is bound to help. And I'll pay whatever it takes to keep them from living with us, because obviously you and my mother have never got on. So. If you don't mind. I'm much more worried about what will happen to *us*."

"In our early fifties, aren't you pushing the programme a mite?"

"Not at all. The time to consider one's options in old age is when one is still relatively young and fit. You've been terribly kind and given me a virtual free pass. But the real reason I avoided doing my part in your father's caretaking is that I found my comparatively brief exposure to his decline intolerable. He wasn't my father, so strictly speaking he wasn't my responsibility, a technicality I eagerly took full advantage of: I didn't take care of him because I didn't have to, full stop. I may have a few patients at the clinic who are also elderly and compromised, but the appointments are only ten minutes, they almost always attend with a relative, and I'm not expected to change their nappies or to decide fifty times a day whether to humour or correct their delusions. I've found these encounters discouraging and gloomy, but not incapacitatingly so. By contrast, your father frankly made me suicidal—or homicidal—or both. Half an hour in his presence passed like a mini ice age. He made me feel as if all of life is pointless and horrid. Politically misguided, yes, but Godfrey had always been well-spoken, well-educated, and well-kept, only to become worse than an animal. At least you can take real animals to the vet to be put down well before they reach a state that biologically scandalous. I will do almost anything to keep the two of us from acceding to such a fate."

"That's what everyone says," Kay said morosely, propping her feet on the opposite chair. "Everyone thinks they're the exception. Everyone looks at what happens to old people and vows that it will never happen to them. They won't put up with it. They have their standards. They value *quality of life*. Somehow they'll do something so their ageing will proceed with *dignity*. If they ever do die—not that most people believe in their heart of hearts that they ever will—they'll be wise, warm, funny, and sound of mind until the very end, with doting friends and family gathered round. Everyone thinks they have too much self-respect to allow a stranger to wash their private parts, or to incarcerate themselves in a care home that's either sterile and impersonal, or filthy and impersonal.

"Then it turns out that, lo and behold, they're exactly like everyone else! And they fall apart like everyone else, and finish out the miserable end of their lives like everyone else: either with some Bulgarian in the spare bedroom who despises them and sneaks their whiskey, or in a cynical institution that cuts corners by serving meat-paste sandwiches on stale white bread for every lunch. Yes, my father was once nattily dressed and erudite. If, back then, a Ghost of Christmas Future provided him with a vision of his life in his nineties, fleeing from a wife he imagines is an MI6 agent whilst streaked in his own waste, don't you think he'd tell that ghost that he'd rather be dead?"

"That's what I'm rounding on," Cyril said. "I've seen enough geriatric patients come and go to surmise pretty conclusively that very few people sustain that 'quality of life' we currently take for granted beyond about the age of eighty. The chronic conditions come thick and furious. Even if the mind doesn't go, the body implodes, and daily life almost exclusively concerns pain. Every advancing year entails a whole new set of things that you used to do and now you can't. Worlds shrink, nothing in the newspaper matters, until all you care about is lessening the pain, or at least not letting it get any worse. And possibly food, in the unlikely event that you still have an appetite. It's a good round number. So I fancy that eighty is the limit."

"At which point, what?"

"As a physician, I'm well positioned to obtain an effective medical solution well in advance. The key to not ending up like everyone else is to be proactive."

"Hold on. Let's be clear." Kay swung her feet back to the floor and sat up straight. "You're proposing that we get to eighty and then commit suicide. You didn't use the word. Anyone who concocts a plan like that shouldn't rely on euphemism and evasion."

"Quite right." Cyril recited, "*I am proposing that we get to eighty and then commit suicide.*"

"But assuming you're actually serious—"

"Deadly serious. For that matter, the flesh is heir to a thousand natural shocks at any age. We should really keep the means to a quick exit at the ready on principle. There are things one can experience over the course of ten minutes that would have either of us begging for oblivion well before the ten minutes were up."

"Is that a threat?"

"An observation. I don't have to remind you what we've both seen."

"But how would this pact work? You're over a year older than I am. So I watch you nod off after taking your nefarious hemlock, don't call nine-nine-nine—for which, in this fantasy paradigm of yours, I'm not arrested—and then I loiter about mourning your passing for the following fourteen months? At which point which I'm under a contractual obligation to top myself."

"I'd rather we did it as we've done everything else since 1963: together. We could opt for my birthday, but unless you're ailing, which of course you might be, that would entail a small sacrifice on your part. So I would propose that I hang on, in whatever shape, and we wait for yours."

"Some birthday," Kay muttered.

"Our commitment would need to be fierce. Although it might comfort you to know that life expectancy in England and Wales for men is presently seventy-three, and for women seventy-nine. Your father was an actuarial aberration. A bookmaker would give us better than even odds of never having to make good on such a pact."

Only a few years later, anyone who rattled off the life expectancy for men and women in England and Wales would fail to impress, as eight-year-olds with access to a phone line would retrieve such statistics in seconds—like magic. A few years after that, eight-year-olds would carry in their hip pockets the means of retrieving such statistics from the very air—as well as the acreage of Micronesia and common treatments for corns—thereby rendering broad general knowledge nearly worthless. But at this time, Cyril could summon these up-to-date figures only because he was a general practitioner who kept up.

"What if I say no?" Kay asked. "Would you still do it?"

"Possibly. As a favour. A big favour, if your father is any guide."

"It might not feel like a favour."

"True kindness doesn't require credit."

At this juncture, Kay could have fobbed her husband off with a casual agreement that would get him off her case, and then they could have carried on as before. As the more vivid images of her father's decay began to fade, Cyril might forget all about his absurd pact. But she knew him better than that. He would not forget. She hadn't fostered a condescending relationship to her husband, and was not about to do so now. After twenty-eight years of marriage, Cyril would easily have detected any insincerity on her part. After twenty-eight years of marriage, Kay would have detected any insincerity on his part as well—any element of whimsy or passing rashness that he was bound to take back. He was a serious person, too serious, often, for her tastes, and she had sometimes found his idealism oppressive. Without question he had contemplated this matter for quite some time, perhaps for years. If he'd now gone so far as to put the proposition on the table, his resolve had reached a point of no return. The least she could do was consider his proposal in earnest and commit deeply, or just as deeply refuse.

So she told Cyril that he'd sprung this idea on her all of a sudden, and given the gravity of what was at stake she had to think about it. Rising to stash the sherry in the fridge, she was dismayed to discover that they, or rather she, had finished the bottle. Lord, at only seven-thirty-five p.m. she was already squiffy, with no enthusiasm for making dinner, and in this condition she shouldn't be trusted to operate a hot cooker anyway. No tipple before eight p.m.! Those rules of Cyril's might have seemed rigid and arbitrary, but a few immovable markers in life provided the structure for productivity and purpose.

Within a week of her husband's modest proposal, Kay was rummaging the top shelf of the fridge in the confidence that they still had an open jar of mint sauce up there, when she encountered a small black box of sturdy cardboard nestled in the back left-hand corner. She recognized the container as the housing of a posh but ill-considered stainless-steel soap dish (stainless steel being an attractive material only when not mucked with bar soap), and in truth she'd saved the impractical accessory only for its classy box, whose top descended with a satisfying *pfff*. As Cyril had not yet accused her of being an agent for MI6, he had clearly not refrigerated a metal soap dish. Indeed, the moment she laid eyes on the box she was sure what it contained. It would be too strong to say that she was afraid of the box. She regarded it with a conflicted combination of curiosity and wariness, though the curiosity was not so intense as to move her to lift the top. She left the container undisturbed and resigned herself to opening a fresh jar of mint sauce.